REBEL SISTERS

Bright, beautiful and intelligent, the Gifford sisters Grace, Muriel and Nellie kick against the conventions of their wealthy Anglo-Irish background. As war erupts across Europe, the spirited sisters are caught up in Ireland's struggle for freedom. They become involved in the Suffragettes, the 1913 Dublin Lockout and the growing Nationalist movement. Muriel falls for writer Thomas MacDonagh, artist Grace meets the enigmatic Joe Plunkett – both leaders of 'The Rising' – while Nellie joins the Citizen Army and bravely takes up arms. On Easter Monday 1916, the biggest uprising in Ireland for two centuries begins and the world of the Gifford sisters is torn apart.

REBEL SISTERS

REBEL SISTERS

by

Marita Conlon-McKenna

Magna Large Print Books
Long Preston, North Yorkshire,
BD23 4ND, England.

British Library Cataloguing in Publication Data.

A catalogue record of this book is
available from the British Library

ISBN   978-0-7505-4383-5

First published in Great Britain in 2016 by Transworld Ireland
an imprint of Transworld Publishers

Published in Large Print 2017 by arrangement with
Transworld Publishers Ltd.

Magna Large Print is an imprint of Library Magna Books Ltd.

Printed and bound in Great Britain by
T.J. (International) Ltd., Cornwall, PL28 8RW

For my wonderful daughter Fiona,
who encouraged and helped me
every step of the way with this book.

We are ready to fight for the Ireland we love
Be the chances great or small:
We are willing to die for the flag above
Be the chances nothing at all.

Verse from 'Easter 1916' by
Constance Markievicz,
published in the *Worker's Republic* on
Easter Saturday, 22 April 1916

Prologue

Friday, 28 April 1916

Nellie Gifford looked out over Dublin, a city at war. She could see clouds of thick smoke rising high in the fiery red sky from the buildings still burning across the other side of the river. Many of the shops and buildings on Sackville Street, Dublin's main thoroughfare, were in flames following the heavy bombardment and gun battles of the last few days.

Perched high on the roof of the College of Surgeons, she looked over St Stephen's Green, the city park with its leafy trees clothed in their spring blossom and its well-tended flowerbeds. Now the park was barricaded and empty, the trenches and shelters they had dug clearly visible.

Countess Markievicz said the rebellion had brought the city to its knees. There was pandemonium, with no trams or trains, no bread, milk or food, and many of Dublin's shops and businesses were closed as the mighty British army tried to regain control.

They still held the General Post Office and the Metropole Hotel on Sackville Street, although despatches said that James Connolly, Tom Clarke and their men were now under severe attack from a heavily armed British gunboat anchored on the River Liffey. There were rebel garrisons in

Boland's Mill and the Four Courts. Eamonn Ceannt and his men controlled the huge South Dublin Union with its workhouses and hospitals, while Thomas MacDonagh was the commandant in charge of Jacob's Biscuit Factory.

She heard a barrage of shots... A nearby sniper? Another army attack? Who could tell? On alert, Nellie crouched down on the narrow parapet of the roof, scanning the nearby buildings. In the Shelbourne Hotel at the other side of the park, a machine gun and rifles were directly trained on them.

Four days ago, on Easter Monday, Nellie had proudly taken her place marching with the Citizen Army and the Irish Volunteers through Dublin's streets, ready to rise up against British rule and join the fight for Irish freedom and independence. Their orders were to take 'the Green' and surrounding area. It was hard to believe that they were occupying one of the finest parts of Dublin.

They had set up a garrison there and dug in, fighting hard to hold their position under heavy attack. On Tuesday Commandant Mallin had given the order to evacuate the open expanse of the park. They had been forced to flee here, to the College of Surgeons, where they were now under constant bombardment from enemy snipers and heavy machine-gun fire.

Food and supplies had run out in their garrison two days ago. Nellie had searched the building and kitchens, and she and the other women had eked out rations as far as they could, making soups and porridges, but now there was absolutely nothing left to eat and she did not see how they would survive much longer.

Down below in the distance she could see an overturned milk float and the bloody, rigid corpse of a horse that someone had shot, still lying on the road. A dead dog, caught in the crossfire, lay sprawled in front of the building, blood and flies everywhere. The shooting was getting nearer and heavier as the city was flooded with new regiments sent from England to suppress the Rising.

Nellie took a deep breath, trying to compose and steady herself, refusing to give in to the fear and trepidation she felt as she thought of her family ... her sisters...

A rebel, like the rest of the men and women in her garrison, she was determined to fight and hold firm and steadfast against the attacks of the approaching British army for as long as she possibly could...

1901–1902

Chapter 1

Isabella

Isabella Gifford studied herself in the mirror. She turned slowly around. She was still a good-looking woman and despite having so many children had somehow kept her slender figure and fine features. She fingered her expensive white lace collar, a contrast to the rich black satin of her dress; French and exquisitely made, it gave a lift to her skin. Patting her fair hair into position, she dabbed her wrist with her favourite perfume.

From upstairs she could hear bedlam as Bridget, their nanny, organized the children for church. Every Sunday it was the same, and although it was important to keep the Lord's Day, she had to admit she found it very difficult when the household staff all enjoyed an afternoon off. But Frederick insisted on the staff having the chance to go to church and then later, time to relax. She lifted her hat and pinned it lightly to her head, gathering her lace gloves and purse.

'Bridget, do make the children hurry up!' she called impatiently as she stood on the landing of their large home.

The boys came first, five of her six sons appearing in an orderly fashion. They were educated, polite young men and boys, the type of whom a mother could be proud. She sighed as she heard

21

Bridget arguing and pleading with her six daughters and went downstairs to wait. She glanced at the clock and was about to send Cecil back up to get his sisters when the girls began to run down the stairs. Giggling and laughing, their long red hair tumbling down their shoulders, her daughters fastened on their warm coats. They all wore a black armband of mourning.

'Are we ready to go, my dear?' enquired Frederick, suddenly appearing from the sanctuary of his book-lined study.

'Hats,' she reminded the girls. 'Where are your hats?'

Kate and Muriel ran back upstairs to fetch them, returning with all the hats. Isabella ignored the grumbling and mutterings of Nellie, Ada, Grace and Sidney as they each pulled at the elastic of their headwear. Satisfied that they were now suitably attired for church, she declared them finally ready.

'Remember you are respectable young ladies!' she warned as Sidney, their youngest daughter, swung on the front gate.

Their home, 8 Temple Villas, was situated among the finest enclaves of Dublin's wealthy and privileged society. As they walked out on to the broad tree-lined avenue of Palmerston Road, with its grand, red-brick Georgian houses and large gardens, Isabella smiled to herself – the large Gifford family was something to be proud of. The girls' felt hats she had designed herself; she considered them stylish but still serving to keep her daughters' luxuriant hair somewhat hidden.

At the end of the driveway she and the children

turned right and Frederick doffed his hat as he turned left towards Ranelagh and the local Catholic church where he worshipped.

Holy Trinity Church was filling up as Isabella and her sons and daughters filed into their usual pew only five from the front. She tilted her hat at a slight angle, picked up her hymn book and silently checked the children. The Gifford family were certainly striking, not just because of their number but because of their strong family resemblance. She dearly wished that Frederick would come to church with them, but he stubbornly refused and insisted on following the faith in which he was raised.

'I think an hour or two to pray in my own church on a Sunday is little to ask,' he said firmly every time she broached the subject.

She glanced around and saw that most of the congregation were respectfully dressed in black today, many already wearing black mourning bands on their sleeves. The organist began to play and she joined in the hymn, Gerald's strong, almost-tenor voice clear above all the others.

Coming to service always reminded her of her childhood, of her own father, a country rector who had done so much for the people of his Carlow parish. She had loved to hear him read the Bible and sing – he had a wonderful baritone voice, and had often given sermons that even as a child she could follow. His death had been untimely, leaving her mother an impoverished widow trying to raise the nine of them, all of them distraught at their father's passing. Her uncle, Frederick Burton, the renowned artist, in an act of great kindness had stepped in to fill the void left by his brother and had generously supported the family over the years.

'Today we remember and dedicate our service to our late queen, Victoria,' said Reverend Samuel Harris, coughing for a moment before looking around the watchful congregation. 'Queen Victoria was a monarch who ruled with fairness, strength and great wisdom for many long years. She will be greatly missed by her Church and her people in Great Britain and Ireland, and across all her colonies and dominions. Her visit to Ireland only a few months ago is one that will always be remembered by the people of Dublin, her loyal subjects. We give thanks for her long life and reign.'

The congregation nodded and muttered in agreement.

Isabella bowed her head and tried to control her emotions. The queen had been old, a woman of eighty-one years, but it had always seemed she would reign for ever. The queen had been so much a part of their lives, her life.

Queen Victoria had knighted her uncle, Sir Frederick Burton, for his services as the director of Britain's National Gallery in London. It was a fitting reward for his life's work, something her kind uncle so richly deserved. His death last March had upset her deeply and she still mourned him. Now the nation was in mourning for Queen Victoria, a monarch whom no one could or would ever forget.

As Reverend Harris took up the Bible, Isabella reached for her handkerchief and daintily and discreetly dried her eyes. God bless the queen!

'Father, we prayed for Queen Victoria today at service,' Sidney announced as the family gathered for Sunday lunch. 'Everyone was sad.'

'Her death is tragic,' Isabella sighed.

'Isabella dear, how can you call it tragic?' Frederick chided her as he helped himself to horseradish sauce. 'She was an old woman who perhaps reigned for far too long.'

'She was our queen!' Isabella protested loyally.

'Victoria was a very fine queen, a good monarch and held the empire together for years,' he agreed.

'Many call her the Famine Queen for what she and her government did to Ireland during the Great Famine,' interjected Nellie from the end of the table. 'Those who faced starvation will certainly not mourn her.'

'Nellie, I will not have you speak of the late queen in such a fashion,' Isabella reprimanded her loudly.

'Nellie's observation is valid, for the queen may not have been a perfect ruler, but I fear we will never see her like again,' Frederick replied. 'Without Queen Victoria on the throne I'm not sure what will happen throughout the empire.'

'Father, what do you mean?' pressed their youngest boy, Cecil.

'The empire might fall,' said Frederick, catching their full attention.

'Never!' shouted their eldest sons, Claude and Gerald, fervently. 'The British Empire will never fall.'

'It is a possibility that must be considered.'

Frederick touched his moustache and top lip thoughtfully. 'Queen Victoria's is a large family, much like our own. Her children are wisely married to half the crowned heads of Europe. But brothers and sisters and cousins – even royal ones – often do not agree, and may perhaps squabble and fall out, especially without a strong hand like the late queen's to keep the peace.'

'They are royalty,' Isabella reminded him.

'Families fight and argue. Without the queen to keep the royal families of Europe in line there is a very real worry about what may or may not happen. The nations may fall out.'

'Edward is our new king,' Isabella insisted. 'He will be a good ruler.'

'I am not so sure.' Her husband sounded serious.

Isabella flushed. There had been rumours about the Prince of Wales's drunken and lecherous behaviour over the years, but now that he was king surely things would be different.

Nora, their maid, came in quietly and went to the long mahogany sideboard. She took their plates away, then served the apple sponge pudding before disappearing.

'This pudding is delicious,' Frederick said as he spooned it into his mouth. 'She's added something to the apple. I must compliment Essie.'

'I made it and I put in a little nutmeg,' admitted Nellie. 'I just used a hint.'

When seventeen-year-old Nellie had told them that she had no intention of doing her final school exams and had pleaded with them to be allowed to stay at home and learn how to cook, Isabella had at first objected to such a role for their daughter. However, Nellie, who had never been academic and certainly did not harbour the same ambitions as her sisters, had soon proved her culinary skills. She was learning to become a fine cook under Essie's guidance and displayed a great ability for organizing and helping with the day-to-day running of such a large household.

Isabella watched approvingly as her six daughters politely ate only a few spoons of the delicious apple pudding. Everyone knew that it was only manners for a young lady, no matter how hungry, to leave a good portion of pudding behind her.

'Father, if the British Empire falls, does that mean Ireland will be free?' questioned eleven-year-old Sidney.

'Don't be such a ninny!' retorted Claude, who was sitting across from her. 'We are *part* of the empire.'

'Where do you get such silly ideas?' added Gerald. 'We are part of the union, ruled and governed by a British king or queen and the parliament in Westminster.'

'But someday Ireland will be free again,' Sidney continued doggedly.

'Boys, your little sister may have a point,' interrupted Frederick calmly as one side of the table erupted into a fierce argument. 'Many people believe that in time Ireland should have Home Rule with a proper parliament of its own here in Dublin.'

'Westminster will never agree it,' argued Claude pompously, as if he were in court.

Isabella sighed. She knew well that it was their nanny and maids who had encouraged such liberal thoughts. Bridget, with all her songs and stories of Irish rebellions and heroes! She had warned Frederick about it, but it was only a minor foible given that the children adored her and she was a very valued and essential member of their household.

'Well, I for one am proud to be part of the union and a loyal subject of the crown,' Isabella joined in. 'Like everyone at this table.'

Sidney stuck out her lip as if she were about to say something. 'And there will be no more arguments on the matter,' Isabella added, giving the signal for Nora to come and clear the table.

Chapter 2

Nellie

Nellie enjoyed cooking and learning the daily regimes of the kitchen and household at 8 Temple Villas.

Father liked to eat beef four times a week, fish once a week and other meats or fowl on the other days. He insisted on a good cheeseboard and enjoyed a different pudding every day of the week. A selection of fine clarets, burgundies, ports and bottles of his favourite malt whiskey were always kept in the drinks cabinet. When his old friend the portrait painter John Butler Yeats visited in winter, both men enjoyed hot toddies with plenty of cloves as they discussed affairs of the day and legal matters. Mother preferred a lighter diet –

chicken, fish, lean meat and soufflés. She liked blancmanges and custards, and a special pepper-mint cordial was kept to aid her digestion. Nellie's sisters, with the exception of Ada, abhorred kidneys. Grace refused to eat semolina or tapioca, while Sidney hated peas. The boys ate mostly everything, though young Cecil seemed to get a rash if he ate strawberries. Her brother Gerald of late had been craving thick slices of gingerbread and fresh ginger biscuits, claiming they aided his study; he was doing his final law exams and often worked till the middle of the night.

'Ginger is good for the brain and for concen-tration,' he declared as she cut him big pieces of her homemade cake.

The ginger clearly worked, as he passed his exams and took up a position with Father and Claude in the family law firm.

It was only a few weeks later when Nellie noticed that Gerald had not attended breakfast or Sunday lunch, claiming he was not hungry – a rare occurrence in any of her brothers.

'Will I make you a sandwich?' she offered as he drank a glass of cold water in the kitchen.

'No, I'm not hungry,' Gerald murmured. 'I've got a thundering headache.'

'It's probably after all that studying for your exams,' she consoled him, noticing that her twenty-four-year-old brother was pale, with dark shadows under his eyes.

'I took a knock playing rugger with a few of the fellows yesterday. Maybe I just need to have a bit of a rest,' Gerald said quietly, disappearing off up the stairs.

Returning from helping all afternoon at the church fair with Mother and her sisters, Nellie went to change her shoes and put away her jacket. There was no sign of Gerald at teatime, so later she carried him up some tea and two scones. He seemed drowsy and she made him sit up a bit.

'I'm fine,' he mumbled. 'I just want to sleep.'

She looked in on him again before she went to bed, relieved to see that he was in a deep, heavy sleep.

When Gerald did not appear the next morning, Nellie decided to bring up his breakfast on a tray. Her brother lay curled up on his side in bed and barely looked at her. She pulled open the heavy damask curtains.

'Close them!' he yelled. 'The light hurts my eyes.'

She did what he said but went over to stand beside him. He looked awful, and then she noticed the blotchy rash on his arms – purplish, nearly black, like blackberries.

She went immediately to her parents' room. Father was getting dressed for work, fixing his tie and pulling on his waistcoat.

'It's Gerald! He's much worse,' Nellie interrupted.

She could read the alarm on both their faces once they saw Gerald. Father told her to send Nora or Essie for their neighbour, Dr Mitchell, as quickly as possible. He arrived immediately.

Nellie waited anxiously in her room as he examined her brother. The doctor took an age, then at last she saw him talking, serious-faced, to her parents on the landing.

'It's some kind of brain infection, meningococ-
cal, very vigorous and in the fluid around Gerald's
brain, judging by that rash. I have only seen it a
few times, but I'm afraid his condition is grave.'

'Should we move him to the hospital?' demanded Mother. 'Get the proper treatment
there?'

'Unfortunately I think your son is far too ill to
move,' said James Mitchell calmly. 'He needs
total rest, peace and quiet in a darkened room.
The next few hours, the next day or two, will be
very critical.'

'Critical?' repeated Father.

'Frederick, his condition is grave – very grave. I
will organize for a nurse to come and attend
Gerald. But you must send for me at once if there
is any change.'

Nellie sat with her brother in the darkened
room as Mother went to dress. Father refused to
go to the office.

'I have my briefcase, so I can read files and case
notes here at home,' he insisted.

Nellie listened to her brother's laboured breathing. His eyes were firmly shut and his face had a
strange pallor.

'Gerald is strong, always has been,' Father
assured her, watching him. 'Boys often have falls
and knocks, but they get over them and so will
he, just you wait and see.'

Nellie didn't know what to say.

'I'll be in my study,' he said, shutting the door
gently and going downstairs.

Mother came and sat with Gerald awhile. She
read aloud from her father's Bible, but Nellie

wasn't sure if her brother could hear her.

The nurse arrived two hours later. She checked his pulse and temperature and made them go outside while she examined his skin. The rash had worsened.

Mother rested for a while in the afternoon and Muriel, who had returned from school, sat with Nellie and sang their brother some of his favourite songs softly.

'He loves to sing,' Nellie explained to the nurse. 'He has a fine tenor voice.'

Muriel sat patiently beside Gerald for hours, asking the nurse how she could help. She sponged his face and moistened his lips so they would not dry out, talking quietly to him all the time.

Claude arrived after work to see his brother and they all took turns sitting by his bedside. He was no better but certainly no worse. Dr Mitchell called to visit him after dinner, conferring quietly with the nurse about his condition. She would stay through the night and another nurse would take over in the morning.

The doctor came again after breakfast. He was most concerned about Gerald's breathing and the fact that he could not be roused.

'The brain at times shuts down to protect itself,' he explained, 'but often this can worsen so the patient slips deeper and deeper into unconsciousness.'

'But he will recover,' Mother said firmly.

'I cannot say or promise that,' Dr Mitchell replied quietly. 'Gerald's position is most unstable.'

The new nurse was older and she gently sponged her patient down. 'You poor, poor boy,' she said kindly, turning down his sheet and combing his hair.

By the time Muriel, Grace, Cecil and Sidney had returned from school, Gerald was much worse. They all sat in the kitchen as Essie made endless cups of tea. Nora took up a tray for Mother and Father, who sat with him, pale-faced and exhausted, Mother holding his hand in hers.

Then the nurse urged them all to come upstairs quietly to say goodbye to their brother. Nellie was shocked, unable to take in the fact that Gerald was going to die. They crowded into the room, each taking a turn to kiss his cheek. Sidney and the twins, Grace and Cecil, were so upset that Nellie had to take them outside. Twenty minutes later it was all over.

Nellie sat on her bed looking out on the dark road and the shadowed plane trees in the moonlight, wondering why this had happened. Her brother had never done a bad thing in his life, never hurt anyone. But now Gerald was dead, her strong, healthy brother taken cruelly from them.

Chapter 3

Isabella

Isabella sat by her son's bed. He looked as if he was asleep, his eyes closed, his mouth slightly open. Her boy – Gerald would always be her boy. He was handsome in his own way, strong and

33

muscular, always happy to have a ball in his hand, football, rugby, tennis or cricket. A lock of hair fell across his brow; unconsciously, she pushed it off his face. Frederick had said the undertakers would arrive soon. Until then Gerald was hers.

He would take no wife, have no child, but stay as he was now on the brink of his life and manhood, his hard work, his years of study no more use to him. It was unfair, unjust and inhuman, what the Lord had done, taking her son. She sat listening to the clock on the landing tick as his hand seemed to grow colder and colder.

Frederick came in and stood beside her. He touched her shoulder.

'Nicholls will be here in an hour,' he sighed, drawing up a chair beside her.

'Then we have an hour with him,' she said as Frederick's large hand clutched hers, his eyes red and raw.

The funeral took place on Thursday in their crowded local church. Reverend Harris's sermon reflected on the shortness of life and the need to become closer to God. Friends, family, neighbours and some of Gerald's old friends from High School and fellow law students from university attended the service. Afterwards he was taken to be buried in Mount Jerome Cemetery.

Standing beside his grave, Isabella was overcome with a strange sense of light-headedness and had to clutch on to Frederick's arm for fear of fainting as the earth, the open grave and grass spun giddily about her. Sidney, white-faced and sobbing, was being comforted by Bridget, while Grace, Cecil and Muriel huddled miserably together. Her other sons were trying to stand tall and maintain their composure; only Liebert, away at sea, was missing. Kate's and Nellie's and Ada's lips moved in prayer.

Afterwards they walked slowly back to the horse-drawn carriages with their black plumes as the gravediggers flung the dark-brown earth in on her boy in his wooden coffin.

Essie and Nora served their guests tea and cordial, offering a small sherry to those who sought one, as Isabella forced herself to stand in the drawing room receiving sympathy and expressions of sorrow for her troubles. Frederick was red-faced, standing near the fireplace, a malt whiskey in his glass.

'He passed his law finals with honours and had just taken his place working with Claude and me in the family firm,' he was explaining loudly. 'His was a fine legal mind. Gerald was a great man for detail. His loss is ... enormous to all of us.'

The two Lane boys, Ambrose and Eustace, came over to Isabella. They and Gerald had been great friends; both of them had regularly visited and stayed in the house. Tears welled in Ambrose's eyes and she was tempted to pass him her embroidered handkerchief.

'I'm sorry,' he said over and over again. 'Gerald will be so missed.'

Her eldest daughter, Kate, made Isabella sit down, bringing her sweetened tea.

It was raining outside, rivulets of water running down the windowpane, and she dared not think of her son in his resting place.

A few of the neighbours clustered around, fussing over her like a crowd of bees. She knew they meant well, but she was too fatigued, too drained to say much. Frederick was deep in conversation with John Yeats, who was doing his best to comfort him. He had lost his own wife the previous year. His son Jack had accompanied him and was discussing illustration work with Gabriel and Ada.

Eventually Isabella could tolerate it no more. She made her excuses and went upstairs to her bedroom, stepping out of the confines of her black satin dress. Nora had put a warming pan on her side of the bed and the heat and softness enveloped her. She could feel her heart pounding in her chest as she lay on the pillow. Grief... She had felt grief before, for her father, her uncle, friends; but nothing had prepared her for this – this pain that seemed to rip through her. The loss of a son – this was true loss.

Hours later, Frederick stood before her. He too was exhausted and, opening her arms, Isabella held her husband tightly as he gave in to grief, his body racked with heavy sobs for what was gone from them.

Chapter 4

Isabella

In the weeks following Gerald's death Isabella found herself enveloped in a strange inertia, unable to think clearly or raise any enthusiasm about anything that was happening around her. She knew the children were equally upset about the loss of their brother, but she had not the heart or energy to contemplate any discussion of the matter. She could not put thoughts of Gerald from her mind and felt a deep anger at the way he had been so suddenly taken from them. Everyone kept reminding her that she and Frederick were fortunate to have been blessed with such a large family. She found no consolation in this fact, for it was her boy Gerald whom she missed, for whom she grieved constantly and who filled her mind.

Every summer they went to Greystones in Wicklow for two months' holiday at the seaside, the days filled with picnics, swimming, walks, tennis parties and musical nights. This year she did not know how she would endure such things and suggested to Frederick that they remain at home instead.

'My dear, a few weeks at the sea with fresh air and sunshine, away from this house, are exactly what we all need,' he insisted, refusing to consider changing their holiday arrangements.

Isabella stood on the granite steps of their imposing, red-brick Georgian residence, supervising operations while Bridget, Nora, Essie and her daughters Kate, Nellie and Ada followed her orders as they carried the trunks of clothes and items needed for their annual trip to Greystones out to the waiting carriage. She had written a list and ticked off items as they were placed down on the gravelled driveway ready to be loaded.

It seemed such upheaval and turmoil arranging for their large family and staff to transfer to another home for the summer weeks. Normally Isabella relished the change from day-to-day routines and responsibilities, but this year was different. Perhaps once she saw the familiar curve of the Sugar Loaf Mountain and Greystones harbour with the sea beyond she would somehow feel more at ease. As usual, Frederick would travel to Dublin some days during July, but for the month of August he too was on holiday as the courts and his law firm closed. He was a diligent man and well deserved a break from the busy world of contracts and legalities.

'Grace, there is an easel already in the house,' Isabella warned, noting her daughter's attempt to bring her usual boxes of art paraphernalia with her. 'Your sketchbooks and a few small canvases should suffice. So please put the rest back.'

Grace looked as if she was about to argue.

'Do what your mother says, Miss Grace,' nodded Bridget, who always seemed to be better able to manage the children than she ever could herself. Unfortunately, their long-serving nanny had recently given her notice, announcing that she intended to marry. Bridget planned to return to her native county, where she and her husband hoped to run a simple boarding house.

Muriel, as ever, was organized, looking serene and lovely as she placed her belongings beside the carriages. She always reminded Isabella of a beautiful swan gliding along while everyone else flapped and splashed around her like ducks.

It mystified her that, having given birth to twelve children, they could all be so different. When she had held each of her newborn children she had thought them so alike, cherubic mirror images of each other, but as the months and years followed they changed, slipping away from her. And now dear Gerald was gone, lost to them for ever.

'Mam, do you want the good linen tablecloths and napkins?' interrupted Nora.

Isabella forced herself to think.

'Yes, Nora, please pack them,' she ordered and the maid disappeared quickly back into the house to fetch them as they climbed into their waiting carriages.

The train was busy, packed with holidaymakers and residents returning from the city to Bray and Greystones and Wicklow. As it made its way through Blackrock, Kingstown, Dalkey and Killiney they enjoyed sweeping views of Dublin Bay, the sea and the coastline. They stopped in the seaside resort of Bray with its wide promenade overlooking the beach, an array of hotels, tea-rooms and cafés all along the seafront. Sidney and Cecil gave whoops of excitement as the train shuddered and began to move once more, clinging to the curving railway track along by the cliffs to enter the dark of the railway tunnel.

Isabella tried not to think of the speed and precarious position of the train, and instead began to gather up her bag, gloves and the tickets for their arrival as Greystones, with its fishing harbour, North Beach and South Beach, came into view.

'We're here!' shouted Muriel and Grace as the train stopped.

Isabella took control as they alighted from the train and the porters ferried their luggage from the station to three waiting carriages. As the horse clip-clopped along Marine Road towards the imposing white-gabled house overlooking the sea, she had to admit she could already feel her heart begin to lighten.

Chapter 5

Nellie

Nellie watched as mother sat reading a book under a large garden parasol. Since they had arrived in Greystones she would often sit for hours reading a novel, or dozing, saying that she was not in the humour for going to the beach or joining in their usual excursions and summer concerts.

'Your poor mother needs to rest,' Bridget reminded them gently. 'She has suffered a terrible loss.'

Father had taken her brothers, Claude, Gabriel, Ernest and Cecil, fishing earlier this morning, carrying their fishing lines and a big box of wriggling, smelly worm bait.

'You are on holiday too,' Father had reminded Nellie, telling her that for the next few weeks she was not expected to help in the kitchen or with the house.

'Mam, as it is such a warm day I thought to bring the girls for a walk down by the harbour and maybe have a paddle on the beach and let you have a bit of peace,' suggested Bridget. 'Miss Ada and Miss Kate have gone to play tennis with friends.'

Mother looked relieved – she would have the garden to herself.

'Bridget, the girls must all wear their hats in this weather,' she reminded the nanny, noticing that they were not in their straw boaters. 'With their colouring they will get burned and red in no time.'

'I'll fetch them straight away, mam,' Bridget said, disappearing back into the house.

'I'm not wearing my stupid hat,' brown haired Sidney protested stubbornly.

'Then you may stay in the garden in the shade with me,' Mother insisted.

Bridget reappeared with the hats a few minutes later and Nellie was annoyed as, under Mother's gaze, she had to plomp her hated straw boater on to her head.

Down at Greystones harbour boys sold fish to

41

passing holidaymakers as the fishermen cleaned their nets. They walked up by the imposing new Grand Hotel, where guests played croquet on the front lawn, and past the rocky cove, where the tide was out, revealing tempting, deep, rocky pools and the stony beach below.

'Bridget, please can we go down to the cove and hunt for crabs and shells?' begged Sidney.

Bridget agreed and they carefully climbed down to the beach. For the next hour or so they had the steep, rock-bound cove to themselves as they scrambled around searching in the rockpools for startled crabs and little fish.

'Don't get your dresses wet!' warned Bridget as she found a shady spot to rest for a bit.

Too late, thought Nellie, aware of the heavy wet hem of her dress as she pushed her silly straw boater towards the back of her head. She clambered out on the rocky promontory to see if there was any sign of Father and the boys. It was slightly breezy and her stupid hat was so annoying... Suddenly it lifted off her head and she couldn't resist it – Nellie grabbed the boater and flung it out over the waves. The straw was so light it caught the wind and seemed almost to fly across the water before dipping down and floating into the distance. In a few minutes it was engulfed, disappearing into the deep blue sea.

With a whoop of glee Sidney joined her, sending her hat like a skimming stone as far as she could across the water. The sisters all watched as it bounced lightly for a second or two, before being caught by the waves and floating along. All of them laughed, and immediately Grace defiantly cast her straw hat out over the water too, then Muriel did the same. Grace clapped as she got three – four – bounces along the top of the water from her boater.

'What are you four doing?' demanded Bridget, coming over to see what all the fun was. 'Where are your sun hats?'

'In the water,' they replied in unison, 'and good riddance!'

'Oh dear Lord! What will your mother say?' fretted Bridget, aware of the seriousness of the situation. 'I'll be murdered!'

'No, you won't,' they assured her loyally.

'We'll tell Mother the wind and the sea took them,' added Sidney calmly.

Bridget looked doubtful, for she knew well that their mother had the eyes of an eagle and nothing, but nothing, got by her.

'Hey, there's Father,' called Grace, spotting the boat in the distance.

'You are all creating such a racket your poor father can probably hear you, and I'm sure you are scaring all the fish away!' admonished Bridget as they walked towards the South Beach with promises that they could paddle there.

Two hours later, as they walked back along Marine Road to the house, Nellie's skin felt hot and already she could see a line of freckles on her arms. Bridget had promised a family picnic on the beach and swimming tomorrow for anyone who wanted. They were all good swimmers, as Father had insisted on them having lessons.

'Can we go for a ride on the donkeys too?'

begged Sidney.

'Of course. It wouldn't be summer without a few donkey rides on the beach,' laughed Bridget as they turned in at their gateway.

'Nellie, your face is as red as a turkey cock and I can see freckles everywhere!' chastised Mother as she greeted them. 'Where is your sun hat?'

'I'm sorry, but the wind caught it and it blew out to sea,' Nellie responded nervously with her half-truth as she stood in the tiled hallway.

'And where is yours, Muriel? You have a red patch on your nose. And Grace, your hair looks like a hayrick! You are all a disgrace! Bridget, why aren't the girls wearing their sun hats?'

Poor Bridget – Nellie could see that she looked totally flummoxed, torn between loyalty to her employer and fondness for her charges.

'Mother, it wasn't Bridget's fault,' Nellie said defensively. 'She was sitting on the beach and we were all down on the rocks at the water's edge.'

This was their last summer with Bridget and Nellie would not have Mother blame her for their antics.

'Mother, I'm sorry,' Grace explained, looking innocent. 'The strong sea breeze just caught my straw boater and it floated out over the water and then...'

'The wind took all our hats and blew them away,' added Sidney dramatically. 'It wasn't our fault, Mother.'

'I'm sorry, mam,' apologized Bridget, 'but it was far too dangerous for us to try to retrieve the hats with the rocks and the current and the waves.'

Nellie could see that their mother was not at all

convinced by their description of events and suspected they had all simply defied her.

'Why is it that you girls can never obey or heed me?' she complained angrily.

They all tried to look suitably apologetic as Mother raged on.

'I am most put out and vexed. I do not know where we will find suitable sun hats at this stage of the holiday. In this weather it is paramount that a lady protects her good complexion.'

'Yes, mam,' Bridget nodded meekly.

Nellie was relieved finally to escape upstairs to her bedroom, wondering why Mother, even though they were on holiday, still managed to annoy them so with her stupid etiquette and manners, her rules and regulations.

As the weeks went on, Father gradually persuaded Mother to go for walks or come down to the beach or take a jaunt in the pony and trap to Rathnew or Delgany with him.

Their annual picnic to Sugar Loaf Mountain was one of the summer's special outings. Along with a number of friends' families, the Giffords rented a large wagonette to drive them all up to have a picnic on the grassy lower slopes of the mountain.

I wish Gerald was here with us, thought Nellie as they joined the Garveys, the Duggans, the Hancocks, the Heustons with their twin boys, and the Goodbodys. All the young people raced to climb to the top of the mountain; later they would be rewarded with sandwiches, cheese and pickles, hardboiled eggs and cups of homemade lemonade, buns and sweet cake from the picnic hampers as they played games and chased each other.

'Isabella, I'm so glad that you came today,' said pretty Mrs Heuston, squeezing Mother's hand as she joined the coterie of women sitting on cushions and rugs in the sunshine. Mother's friends and neighbours in Greystones were full of kindness and understanding of her grief, fussing over her as they talked about Gerald and remembered him with great fondness.

As the days of summer ended, Nellie dreaded having to say goodbye to Bridget, the nanny who had helped to raise them all, loving each and every one of them in turn.

On their last evening Mother and Father had gone out to dinner and a summer music concert down at the seafront, so Essie and Nora decided to organize a farewell party for Bridget in the kitchen. Nellie had secretly made her a large chocolate sponge cake and there were coconut macaroons and cherry Bakewells and large jugs of lemonade for everyone, and they also had to sing or dance or do a recitation. Kate, Ada and Muriel performed *'Three Little Maids'* from The Mikado; Gabriel and Ernest did a funny sailor's dance. She, Grace and Muriel sang 'Gypsy Rover', one of Bridget's favourite songs, and everyone joined in, singing verse after verse. Sidney read a beautiful poem she had written about Bridget which had them all in tears.

'My work is done, for you are all growing up to be fine gentlemen and young ladies to be proud of ... too old to have a nanny!' Bridget said, blowing her nose noisily. 'Hopefully you will all remember your old nanny and come to visit Mr Byrne and me in our little home in Wexford, where you will always find a warm welcome.'

Nellie and her sisters and brothers felt immensely sad, wishing that Bridget never had to leave them. Nellie had brought her violin along and Bridget asked her to play a few tunes to get everyone tapping their feet and dancing. When Mother and Father returned from the concert they heard the singing and music, so they joined them in the kitchen and the whole family said a fond farewell to Bridget.

Chapter 6

Isabella

'My dear, it is good to see that you have colour back in your cheeks,' said Frederick encouragingly on their return to Dublin.

Isabella finally sat down to tackle the vast correspondence they had received following their son's death, the letters often making her weep as she drafted a reply. Then she turned to their social engagements. Frederick always relied on her to organize their calendar of social affairs and entertaining. She made notes in her diary of the usual Law Society dinners and balls, and of dinner and lunch invitations from friends for the next few months; but she was still in mourning and not sure she could face them yet, so she sent out polite notes of apology and regret.

'Mother, why don't you invite your friends to tea?' Kate pleaded.

'I will consider it in a few weeks,' she promised, though she had no inclination at present to host her regular afternoons at home.

One morning Isabella realized that months had passed and their garden was now filled with bright spring daffodils and purple lilac blossom.

Claude had announced his engagement to Ethel Parks, a rather serious young woman whose family lived nearby on Temple Road. Claude was devoted to her and their temperaments seemed well suited. While Ethel seemed quiet and rather solitary, Isabella suspected that she was possessed of a much stronger character than appeared and was well cut out to be the wife of a talented young barrister, with all the demands the role would bring.

'Ethel and I plan to marry at the end of the summer,' Claude told her happily, 'and we hope to rent a home near both families.'

'We are very pleased for you,' Isabella smiled, hugging her son but saddened by the fact that Gerald would not be there to see his older brother wed.

Isabella and Frederick had been invited to an important ball at Dublin Castle which Lord and Lady Aberdeen, the lord lieutenant and his wife, were hosting. It was an invitation that Frederick insisted they accept. As she dressed in her expensive black satin gown Isabella caught a glimpse of herself in the mirror. She looked like a small black crow. She ran her hands over the smooth waist and bodice. It was a beautiful dress, exquisitely made, her dress of mourning. Isabella had worn it first for her dear uncle Frederick's funeral service and to the special exhibition of his art and paintings in Dublin's National Gallery. A few months later she had worn it for the queen's death, and then for Gerald.

Her breath caught in her throat as she thought of the great sadness and grief she had endured. She could barely draw breath, for it felt as though the black fabric was constricting her lungs and suffocating her. Suddenly she could bear it no more and began frantically trying to undo the dress. She called for Nora.

Her maid immediately ran upstairs as Isabella beckoned urgently for her to undo all her buttons and help her out of the dress.

'Are you all right, mam?' asked Nora anxiously.

'Yes, but Nora, please pass me out the blue satin gown to wear instead,' she ordered, trying to slow her erratic breathing and calm down.

As Nora helped to fasten up the pearl buttons of the blue satin, Isabella felt that at last she could breathe again.

The maid went to return the black dress to the large mahogany wardrobe.

'No, don't hang it up,' Isabella told her firmly. 'I will not wear the black again.'

'Shall I have it cleaned, mam?' she offered, studying the material and bodice.

'No.' Isabella shook her head vehemently. 'I will never wear that dress again. Do you want to take it, Nora? You can have it. Get it altered, or Essie can have it. Or sell it if you like. But I promise you that I will never wear that black gown again.'

Puzzled by the behaviour of her mistress, Nora left the room with the expensive black satin dress folded over her arm.

The carriage had arrived and, fixing her pearl hairpins, Isabella went to join Frederick, who was waiting patiently for her downstairs.

'You look beautiful, Isabella dear,' he said, smiling gallantly, making no mention of the fact that she was not attired in mourning. She slipped on her velvet evening cloak and they stepped out into the night air together.

1904–1909

Chapter 7

Nellie

Nellie gave a final check to the drawing room before Mother's guests arrived for afternoon tea. Nora had lit the fire and, with great care, Nellie had dusted each little china figurine and carved teak or ivory ornament in her mother's collection. The silver shone, the glass sparkled and everything was ready for Mother's regular 'At Home', which was held twice a month. Mother enjoyed hosting these occasions and, in turn, visited her friends and neighbours at their homes.

The drawing room was Mother's sanctuary and no one was permitted to use it unless invited.

Nellie slipped down to the kitchen to check that all was ready, then at three o'clock precisely the doorbell rang. Nora ran to open it, taking Mrs Fox's coat as she left her card on the silver salver on the hall table before being shown into the drawing room.

Twenty minutes later Mother was busy entertaining her guests. Glancing at the clock in the kitchen, Nellie prepared the special blend of tea her mother preferred for these gatherings, sending Nora to serve it as the ladies chatted. Then a few minutes later Nellie joined them in the drawing room, offering small fresh scones with cream and jam and delicate slices of freshly made cake to each of the guests. She usually baked two cakes on the morning of an At Home, icing one and leaving the other plain. Mother disapproved of guests being offered or eating too much, which she felt was impolite.

'How are you, Nellie?' enquired Mother's friends as she served them.

'Did I tell you Alice is getting married next month to a chap from Sussex?' asked Beatrice Woods, whose daughter Alice had been in school with her.

'Please convey my good wishes to her.'

'Jerome's regiment is being sent to India, so they will move to live there in two months' time.'

Nellie could see Mrs Woods was upset.

'Jerome is a fine young man, but India is so far away,' she continued, trying to control her emotions. 'Alice is our only daughter and we will miss her so. Your mother and father are fortunate to have Claude and his wife married and living so near to them.'

Nellie was filled with great sympathy for her and offered to fetch her more tea.

As she moved around the drawing room, Nellie picked up snippets of conversation. She was returning with the pot of tea when she heard Henrietta Lewis talking loudly.

'Isn't it wonderful for you and Frederick to have Nellie so devoted to helping you here at home? Mark my words, when all the others are gone away and married, Nellie will be the one looking after you both in your old age and running the house and kitchen.'

Nellie held her breath outside the door.

'Yes, I expect so,' responded Mother lightly. 'Nellie was never one for school and has no interest in studying, and in fact has become an excellent cook.'

Nellie swallowed hard as she pushed open the drawing-room door and refilled the tea cups, trying not to meet her mother's eyes and to remain composed as she received compliments about her scones.

'Nellie dear, that walnut cake is delicious. Did you make it yourself?' asked Mrs Fox.

'Yes, it's a new American recipe I followed.'

Back in the kitchen she sat down. She could feel her heart pumping wildly as her mind raced. Was this what she wanted for her future? Baking and cooking, running the household for her parents and family?

Essie and Nora at least got paid their wages, but she only got the same allowance from her parents that her sisters received, despite all her hard work.

Her mind was in turmoil at the thought of living at home in Temple Villas while everyone else went and got on with their lives. This had never been her intention, but now Nellie realized she was caught in a trap of her own making that might prove very difficult to escape from as she did not possess the academic or artistic attributes that so many of her siblings had.

'Why are you so glum?' teased her older sister Kate a few days later.

'I heard one of Mother's friends talking the other day and she was saying how wonderful it was for Mother and Father that I would be the one here looking after them when they are old and everyone else is married and settled,' Nellie confided, unable to hide her upset.

'But I presumed – we all presumed – that you enjoy housekeeping and cookery and running things so well at home.'

'I do,' she admitted. 'I far prefer cooking and helping Essie manage the household than school, but that doesn't mean I want to do it for ever. Everyone just presumes...'

'Good old Nellie will cook a delicious dinner,' said Kate. 'Deal with ordering the provisions from Findlaters. Get the fish in Hanlon's fishmongers. Attend to the household budget, and of course be perfectly happy even if Mother harps on at her.'

'Yes,' she agreed, a lump in her throat. 'And I don't know what to do.'

Nellie wished that she was more like her sisters, all of whom seemed to know what they wanted. Kate, one of the first Irish women to gain a place in university, was set on the world of academia; Grace, like Ada, cared only about art and painting; Muriel talked about nursing; and even little Sidney was obsessed with writing. Nellie was the only one with absolutely no clear idea of what she wanted from life or the future.

'It is a problem that has to be solved,' Kate decreed wisely. 'We must try to find exactly the right opportunity for you.'

A week later Kate came bounding excitedly into the bedroom and passed Nellie part of the newspaper.

'Read it,' she urged.

Nellie glanced at the printed page – details of a concert and a ballet and piano recital.

'The other side,' her sister prompted impatiently.

Nellie read the advertisement over and over again. It was for a course run by the Department of Agriculture and Technical Instruction in the School of Domestic Economy in Kildare Street to train as a rural domestic instructress. The course was for six months and participants would attain a qualification linked to a job travelling the country teaching cooking and domestic skills.

'Do you think I should apply?' she asked.

'Most definitely,' her sister assured her.

A few days later, Nellie slipped on her hat and gloves and went along to the college. She enjoyed a very agreeable interview and was immediately offered a place on the course, which would start in September. Now there was just the question of breaking the news to her mother and father, and paying the tuition fees. She had absolutely no money of her own and relied on her parents to cover the general costs of her clothes and going-out money.

Mother had grave reservations about the course, saying she wasn't at all sure it was suitable for a young lady of her background and means.

'Don't come complaining to us if this course isn't what you expect,' she warned. Nellie suspected she was put out, as she realized her daughter would no longer be at her beck and call to help with cooking and household affairs.

As usual, Father said little, but he agreed to pay.

'I do believe that you will enjoy this, Nellie, and make a success of it,' he said, handing her a cheque for the fees. 'Also, the benefit is that you will have a proper qualification.'

Delighted, Nellie hugged him. This was her opportunity to be independent and perhaps, if she passed the course, to have a career of her own.

Chapter 8

Nellie

For the first time in her life, Nellie enjoyed her classes. She had a huge regard for the lecturers in the School of Domestic Economy, who constantly reminded their students, 'Ladies, you will be professional and are expected to always behave as professionals.'

She relished the practical work and soon learned about hygiene, storage of meat, budgeting, correct and safe use of new household mechanical, electrical and gas stoves and equipment, special invalid diets, sewing and design, catering for large numbers, baking and breadmaking, choosing cuts of meat, and de-boning, gutting and cleaning fish, game, meats and fowl. She had an ability to keep calm and work under pressure that some of her classmates envied. She suspected it had been gained from working with Essie in the kitchens of Temple Villas catering for their large family.

To her delight, after six months she passed not

only her practicals but also her written exams and qualified as a rural domestic instructress.

Kate took her out for lunch to celebrate.

'It's hard to credit that I am now qualified to teach people how to cook, and use new ranges and stoves and equipment, which are safer and far more labour-saving than the way they cooked before,' said Nellie, laughing.

'Well done,' smiled her sister. 'I am so proud of you.'

'I've been offered a position in Meath already,' Nellie confided. 'I will be based in different parts of the county, giving practical lessons in cookery and the use of these new stoves to groups of people.'

'Are you going to accept it?'

'Yes, but I haven't told Mother and Father yet.'

'Miss Independent.'

'You can talk,' Nellie teased. 'When are you going to study in Germany?'

'Next year,' Kate said, blushing modestly. 'I hope to study at the university in Berlin and I plan to give language classes too.'

'What if you meet a handsome German man?'

'Nellie, I doubt that will happen.' Kate laughed. 'I'm sure German men are much the same as Irish or English ones and are not exactly keen on carrot-haired women of a certain age and demeanour.'

Kate was the kindest sister, blessed with an amazing intelligence but overly conscious of her homely face, high colouring and red hair.

Linking arms as they approached Temple Villas, Kate promised to lend her moral support when

Nellie told Mother about the position she had been offered.

As predicted, Mother took the news badly.

'A young woman travelling the countryside without a chaperone, exposed to all kinds of situations? It is certainly not desirable, and not what your father and I would have wanted or expected for you,' she remonstrated. 'What would our neighbours and friends think of us if we should let one of our daughters be involved in such a thing, traversing the countryside and at risk of all kinds of things?'

'They would think what forward-looking parents the Giffords are,' retorted Kate. 'What bright, intelligent young women they have raised, ready to take up careers of their own and be independent.'

Mother coloured.

'Mother, it is very safe, I promise,' Nellie assured her. 'I will be transported to each place where I am to give my demonstrations and lessons, along with my equipment, and I will stay there for a few weeks giving the course to local women.'

'And where will you stay – in some local hotel with rough salesmen and tradesmen?'

'It is arranged that I will lodge and have meals with a respectable local family in their own home, either in the town or on a farm,' she explained. 'There would be no impropriety involved, Mother. It is a very respectable position, I am assured.'

Mother didn't look convinced.

'Nellie is very competent and able,' interjected Kate. 'Otherwise she would not have been offered such a position. What would you have her do –

return to cook here at home for you and Father while the rest of us go on to study and have careers? My sister deserves better and should at least be given the opportunity to prove herself.'

Kate's appeal was like some legal argument and, much to Nellie's surprise, Father and Mother agreed, with the proviso that, if her position proved unsuitable, she would agree to return to Dublin.

'Well done!' chorused her sisters and brothers when she proudly told them the good news of her official appointment.

Three weeks later she nervously stepped off the train in Meath with all her cooking equipment and was met by a man in a pony and trap, already loaded with her stove, ready to bring her to where she was to set up in an old hall in the middle of Enfield town. She was staying with an elderly couple who lived only a few doors away from the hall and made her feel immediately welcome. A woman had been assigned to help her during the six-week course she was teaching in basic cookery and domestic skills.

As Nellie looked out on the sea of eager faces when she stood up to talk in her new apron, she put her nervousness behind her and concentrated on the task in hand, passing on the knowledge and experience she had gained. Young wives eager to learn; women wanting to discover how to feed a large, hungry family on a small budget, or how to feed workhands on a busy farm; single girls with no idea how to manage a kitchen; two older women who planned to set up a boarding house of their own... Nellie gave everyone attention as she tried to demonstrate how to use the new stove correctly to cook and bake a wide variety of meals.

The classes filled up quickly. Sometimes when she saw hungry faces she ensured that at the end of class they got to take home any leftover food and ingredients to their families.

She enjoyed the freedom of the countryside, as well as earning a wage and being self-sufficient. At times her accommodation was rough and not very comfortable, but most of the people she stayed with tried their best to provide her with a fairly clean room of her own and shared their simple meals with her. The countryside may be lush and green, the fields full of crops and animals grazing, but many people she met were poor, barely eking out a living from the soil and land they tended, often living on smallholdings and unable to support their large families, their children forced either to work in the cities or take the boat to Liverpool and London.

She always appreciated returning home to Temple Villas to her family, friends and comforts, but Nellie had to admit she welcomed getting back to the freedom of rural life and her independence.

Chapter 9

Grace

Grace Gifford gazed surreptitiously at her fellow passengers on the tram, trying to gauge if any of them were new students like she was, bound for Dublin's Metropolitan School of Art. She should have been returning to school in September like the rest of the girls in her class at Alexandra College, but she had somehow managed to persuade Mother and Father to let her continue her studies at the famous art school instead. She had no interest in studying maths or Latin or geography but just wanted to spend all her time painting, drawing and sketching, and now she had the opportunity to do just that.

Gabriel and Ada had both studied art at the college and Mother always boasted to them of how she had met Father at the evening art classes there. Now it was Grace's turn.

She tried to hide her nervousness as she entered the art school building on Kildare Street. In an effort to make herself appear older than sixteen, she had pinned up her long, golden-red hair neatly and wore a dark-green skirt, white blouse and her fitted navy jacket, borrowing a brown leather satchel of Ada's to hold her pencils and pads. She joined the crowd of students pushing and shoving in the hall as they checked the large noticeboard with the college's enrolment list, searching for her own name among the Gs.

A girl from the tram was standing beside her, looking down the columns of names.

'Gray,' she said aloud, searching, her long, thin finger running down the sheet. 'There I am!' she added triumphantly.

She blushed suddenly, aware of Grace's gaze.

'I'm Hilda Gray,' she introduced herself.

Falling into step, Grace and Hilda made their way up flight after flight of stairs. On the second floor there was a large lecture hall and they slid into seats beside each other, chatting as the room filled up. A striking girl called Florence flopped down beside them.

Richard Henry Willis, who had only recently been appointed head of the School of Art, stood in front of them. A well-respected artist, with a long beard and kind eyes, he made it clear that his tenure would bring some changes to the school.

'We may be part of the great British tradition of art schools, but to my mind there is no denying the influence of our Gaelic and Celtic heritage, an influence that I hope will now be encouraged and fostered here in the Metropolitan School of Art. We want all our students to develop expertise and knowledge in an area of art which satisfies them creatively and also to gain the technical skills that form the basis of any good working art discipline.'

Grace paid full attention as Mr Willis outlined the curriculum they would study, which included not only all types of painting, sculpture, charcoal, etching, stained glass, enamel work, mosaic and design, but even traditional Irish lacemaking. It all sounded exciting and new to her, and she was determined to learn as much as she could.

'Are there any questions?'

A few brave people put up their hands, but Grace kept her eyes fixed firmly ahead as one young man near them asked question after question about the use of a private studio and then, unabashed, wanted to know when they got to paint nude models.

Grace could see a few of the girls blush at the mention of the word 'nude'. The college principal looked momentarily uncomfortable.

'All life-drawing classes are segregated,' he reassured the young ladies present. 'Now I want to introduce you to Mr Child, who will advise you of your daily and weekly lecture schedule and bring you on a tour of the school of art.'

Grace took out her notepad and wrote furiously as he launched into the day-to-day classes they would attend, then the exam timetables and the broad list of lectures that would be held here in this hall and which they would be expected to attend.

'Non-attendance is frowned on,' he reminded them firmly.

An hour later they were conducted on a tour of the buildings – a real rabbit warren of rooms, studios and offices.

'I don't know how we are expected to remember it all,' groaned Hilda dramatically. Grace had always prided herself on a good sense of direction and made a mental note of the layout as best she could.

The class was split into groups and soon afterwards she found herself in a bright, sunny studio faced with a composition of fruit and a jug laid out on a wooden table. She opened her sketchpad and began to draw exactly what she saw before her.

'Nothing is what it seems,' their tutor reminded her. 'Consider the light on the apple, the shade, the shadow on the jug, the slight decay already evident on a few of the grapes. Use your eyes well before you even begin to draw a line.'

Embarrassed, Grace turned over to a new page and began again.

The weeks passed quickly and Grace was happy to spend hours and hours with sketchpad and pen or pencils. They had fine lecturers and tutors and she considered it a particular privilege to study under William Orpen, the celebrated portrait painter who worked between London and Dublin. She hated antique drawing with a vengeance – she hadn't the patience for it, far preferring to draw and sketch people. She also enjoyed design and lettering and the formal use of black and white. When she attended a few classes on printing, she discovered to her surprise that she enjoyed designing patterns. Stained-glass work was difficult, but she loved the effect of creating simple shapes and patterns in various glass colours under the guidance of Mr Child and Miss Purser.

Grace cycled into Kildare Street most days like many of the students. Soon she made a few friends and was finding the Metropolitan School of Art a far happier environment than her old school. She suddenly felt grown up and, attending a lecture given by her father's friend John Yeats at the Royal Hibernian Academy after Christmas with her parents, brother and sister, she was delighted when he and his family congratulated her on joining the illustrious world of art.

Everyone was full of talk about the opening of the new Abbey Theatre two nights earlier in the old Mechanics' Institute building on Abbey Street, which, thanks to the generosity of benefactor Miss Horniman, had been transformed into a very fine theatre. It had opened with two of John Yeats's son William's plays and one by Lady Gregory, all of which had received a great reception from the packed audience.

'We most definitely will get tickets,' promised Father and Gabriel.

To Grace's annoyance, Mother deemed her too young to attend the Abbey and its programme of what she considered Irish nationalist-type plays.

Grace decided to attend the college's evening classes in sculpture. It was an area she knew little about: she loved sculptures but had no experience with working in clay and plaster and was curious to discover the process from model to mould to bronze or from stone to statue.

The students who attended the evening classes often worked and used the opportunity to study after their day's labours. She was full of admiration for them. The age group was generally older and the students more serious.

'Tonight we all make a horse,' announced their teacher, sculptor Oliver Sheppard. 'Take your clay in your hands and begin to model.'

'Here, better put this on,' advised the student

sitting next to Grace, passing her an apron. 'You don't want to destroy your clothes.'

Grace was about to protest that she was fine, but already she could see the table was spattered with clay, so she pulled on the protective apron and tied it.

She watched enviously as the young man with the floppy dark hair beside her worked easily and soon had a perfect horse standing on the table in front of him. Its ears, head, fetlocks, back were all perfect, she thought, as she clumsily tried to shape her own strange equine creature.

'Too small, and the clay is difficult to work with,' advised her neighbour. She tried to make it bigger. 'And now too big, and those long legs will fall off.'

Aware of his scrutiny, she took a deep breath and concentrated on letting her fingers work as finally a small, stocky horse took shape.

'Your beautiful horse is a racehorse and mine, I suppose, is a carthorse,' she suggested.

They both burst out laughing, and the young man politely introduced himself as Willie Pearse.

'My father is a stonemason so I usually work with marble and stone,' he explained, 'but it's tempting to try bronze and using the foundry. There is much to learn from someone like Mr Sheppard.'

Willie was very involved with the Gaelic League and he taught Gaelic language classes in the art school which were becoming very popular. Grace and her friends immediately signed up to attend them. Grace found it difficult to learn this new language, which they had never studied in school, but over time she managed to learn new words and sentences which she tried to use. Mr Willis himself sometimes joined them.

She far preferred going to the ceili dances that Willie Pearse and his friends helped to organize. They were lively affairs, with everyone joining in and being swung around the room to traditional fiddle music. Mother and Father objected at first, saying she was too young to attend college socials and the famous Nine Arts Ball, but thankfully her brothers and sisters interfered on her behalf and they relented, giving her permission to go along with the other young ladies in her class.

Grace was happier than she had ever been before, studying and drawing during the day and in the evening attending a constant round of concerts, exhibitions, lectures and dances with Hilda and Florence and her friends.

Returning for her second year the following September, Grace felt more confident and assured as she re-entered the milieu where she felt most comfortable and at ease. But like all the other students she was shocked and saddened to discover that the head of the art school, Mr Willis, had died only a few days previously. A born teacher, he had transformed the college and would be sorely missed at their ceilithe and classes. Old Mr Luke, appointed to take over his position, was by all accounts set in the old traditional ways of teaching art. However, both students and lecturers were determined that the new spirit of Gaelic culture that Mr Willis had introduced would never disappear from Dublin's Metropolitan School of Art.

Chapter 10

Grace

Grace carefully considered the old man in his shirt and cloth cap posing before them on a chair in the college's largest first-floor art room, which caught the afternoon light. Today, instead of charcoal, she was using her soft-leaded pencil as she began to sketch him, shading his lined face and careworn eyes carefully, noting his work-worn hands, biting her lips as she tried to concentrate. William Orpen was taking them for life drawing again.

As they drew, Orpen often went around checking their work and giving his opinion. Some of her fellow students found him too direct but she valued his comments, be they good or bad.

Finishing quickly, Grace couldn't resist sketching Orpen himself. A small, dark-haired man with strong features, he had a maturity beyond his years. He always looked very dapper in his expensive suits and shirts, with a cigarette in his hand. His classes were far more relaxed than those of other teachers, as he did not insist on silence and usually, as he smoked himself, he permitted his students to smoke too.

Orpen came over to study her pencil portrait of the old man and nodded approvingly, pointing out how well she had drawn his hands. Grace held her breath as Orpen suddenly turned over the pages of her sketchbook to look at the rest of her work. Embarrassed, she blushed as he studied the caricature of himself, cigarette in hand in front of an easel, that appeared on the next page.

'So, Miss Gifford, that's what I look like!' He laughed.

'I like doing caricatures,' she admitted nervously. 'It's only a bit of fun.'

'That depends on who is the subject,' he teased, 'and how well they respond to your wit!'

Grace had no idea what to say.

He took the pad and went through it, flicking over page after page. Most of their lecturers and tutors were there, faces elongated, noses enlarged, scrawny limbs now like sticks. There were also some of her friends.

Orpen laughed loudly on discovering a sketch she had made of William Butler Yeats.

'You are a very talented young woman, Miss Gifford, with a rare gift for caricature.'

'Thank you.'

She valued Orpen's opinion. She was in her third year now and was like a sponge, absorbing what she could from him and his way of working. While some in the class felt afraid of and slightly intimidated by him, strangely she didn't.

'Ladies, next week we will be drawing a female nude,' he informed them. 'One of my beautiful young models from London is prepared to come over to Dublin to pose for us, so please ensure that you do not miss the classes.'

Everyone clapped and Grace smiled, knowing full well no one would dare miss it.

She had agreed to stay behind after class today,

71

as Orpen wanted to do some sketches of her. He had asked to draw her a few times and, as she posed, she loved watching him work, seeing how a few simple lines built up to become a proper portrait. She couldn't believe how quickly he worked and how well he captured her features. She sat quietly as the others filed out of the studio and he beckoned for her to sit where the model previously had. Grace felt embarrassed as some of her fellow students lingered to watch her.

'Don't mind them,' he urged, concentrating hard as Grace tried to keep still. Her tawny hair fell in front of her face and she gently pushed it back off her shoulder.

'You have wonderful hair, Miss Gifford.'

'My sisters and I hate it,' she confessed. 'We were constantly teased about being carrot-heads when we were young.'

'My wife was the same,' he said, coming over to fix her hair slightly, 'but I have always found this colour most agreeable and attractive. My daughter Kit fortunately has inherited her mother's colouring.'

Grace was pleased with the compliment and held her gaze steady as he worked.

'Now that's enough for today. I have a meeting with an artist friend in Davy Byrne's pub,' he said, closing his large sketchbook. 'But Miss Gifford, I wanted to ask if you would agree to sit for me in my studio, as I would really like to paint you for a special series that I am working on.'

Flattered, Grace didn't quite know how to respond.

'Obviously I will get proper permission from

your parents. I will write to them personally with my request.'

'Yes,' beamed Grace, giving him her home address, 'I would very much like that.'

Mother and Father pored over his letter.

'He is a renowned portrait painter,' sighed Mother. 'To commission him for a portrait apparently costs a fortune. And yet here it is he wants to paint our Grace.'

'Mother, please say yes!' urged Grace excitedly.

'The fellow has a terrible reputation,' objected Father. 'A roving eye for the women, apparently.'

'All artists have an eye for beauty!' exclaimed Mother, exasperated. 'But you are right – Grace has her reputation to think of.'

'Mr Orpen is married and lives in Howth with his family,' she protested. 'His studio is in the college. He is the only lecturer who is let keep a studio there. He goes back and forwards between classes every day as it's only a few yards away from our art room.' Her parents suddenly looked more assured.

'You are very young, but perhaps Ada can chaperone you,' proposed Mother with a smile. 'I will write to Mr Orpen to give our permission and explain to him our condition that your sister must accompany you to these sittings.'

Grace sighed. Her older sister had decided to return to the School of Art this year to further her studies as she was finding it difficult to get work. Ada was forthright and opinionated, and as they cycled or travelled into town together she had made it very clear from the outset that she still considered Grace a child and had absolutely no intention of spending any time with her during college hours. Ada had her own group of friends, which suited Grace perfectly. But now she was suddenly dependent on her big sister acting as a chaperone if she wanted to visit Orpen's studio. It was all so unfair.

'Grace, what a pleasure.' William Orpen was smoking a cigarette, the air heavy with the scent of it, as she introduced her sister. Light from the street flooded into the studio through the tall glass windows, with the street and treetops below.

Grace was dressed in a pretty white dress that he had requested she come in, but she had also brought along a pale-pink one of Muriel's in case this one wasn't suitable.

'Ideal,' he said as he picked out a selection of coloured beads, bangles and rings that he wanted her to wear. Then he turned his attention to her hair. It could be unruly at the best of times and Ada laughed as she helped him to pin it up into the style he wanted, with a bun on either side of Grace's face.

Finally satisfied, Orpen posed her in a chair near the window with a pale curtain behind and a few flowers on her lap. Grace touched the scented pink roses as he sketched her quickly before taking his palette and knife, his oil paints and brushes and beginning to paint.

Ada watched him for about half an hour, then politely excused herself, saying she had a lesson but would return later.

As William Orpen worked, Grace endeavoured

to keep perfectly still, silently taking in his array of drawings, sketches and paintings on easels and canvases littered around the room. Many were portraits of well-known figures – politicians and businessmen and their wives. In the far corner of the room a large canvas depicted a beautiful red-haired woman on a hill overlooking the sea. Grace, curious as to who the woman was, studied it more closely when she had finished posing.

'That's my wife,' said Orpen proudly. 'She's also named Grace.'

'It's a wonderful painting,' said Grace as Ada arrived, and Orpen made an arrangement for her to visit the studio again a few days later.

Over the following three weeks she continued to pose for him. She felt privileged to be able to see how he worked, watching enviously the way he mixed colours on his palette so easily and how, with what seemed like only a few simple touches of his knife and brushes, he managed to capture her in almost a pool of bright light. Orpen put her at her ease by telling her stories of his childhood in Stillorgan and of coming to study art here at the college when he was only thirteen.

Finally he was finished and Grace was able to stand in front of her portrait, which he entitled *The Spirit of Young Ireland.*

'It is full of light,' she said, studying it in detail. On canvas she looked different, mischievous and high-spirited, her dress made of light, attired with jewels and flowers. 'You've made me seem far more attractive than I am.'

'Miss Gifford, you embody the hope of a new generation ready to take on the world,' he said with a smile, and he told her how he intended exhibiting the portrait in London.

Ada said very little when she saw the painting and Grace suspected she was rather jealous.

A photographer called at the studio as they were getting ready to leave and Orpen insisted that he take a photograph of Grace and himself together.

'We are both artists,' he said firmly, insisting that Grace hold his palette and brushes.

Nervous and rather overawed at being photographed with him, she did her best to gaze steadily at the camera and appear calm and poised.

Grace's three years at the School of Art were coming to an end and Orpen, as one of her main tutors, suggested that she should consider applying for a place at the renowned Slade School of Art in London. Her work had changed and developed: she now mostly worked in black and white, creating strong, clear, simple images, designs and illustrations. Her hobby of drawing caricatures had become an art form she wanted to develop and use for print work.

'At the Slade there are some of the finest art teachers in the world. I promise you, Miss Gifford, it's a wonderful place for a young artist of your calibre to learn and to develop your techniques.'

Grace thanked him, but was very unsure about Father and Mother even entertaining a proposal that she study in London.

Attending the Nine Arts Ball in the Metropole Hotel at the end of her final term, Grace and her friends were dressed in Spanish costumes, with painted fans, mantillas, high combs in their hair and swirling red, black and white dresses. Other girls came as witches and demons, and her male classmates, dressed as hairy cavemen, dashing musketeers and Roman centurions, pulled them all up to dance as the band played its heart out. The noise level was high and, dancing with her friends, they all laughed and joked and made promises to keep in touch with each other as the music played on long into the night.

At the School of Art's annual prizegiving Grace was proud to receive the award for 'Drawing on the Blackboard and Model Drawing' from Lady Aberdeen, who enquired about her plans, shook her hand and wished her well in her future art career.

'What did you say to her?' Mother asked.

'I told her of my intention to study at London's Slade School of Art,' replied Grace defiantly.

Mother said nothing, refusing to be drawn into a discussion on the matter.

'The Aberdeens will be kept busy this summer with King Edward VII's visit here in July,' she said, changing the subject. 'He has been invited to visit the Irish International Exhibition which has just opened in Ballsbridge.'

Grace said no more, but was determined that she would somehow persuade her parents to let her attend the Slade. She had the long weeks of summer ahead to convince them.

Taking a final look around the art studios and lecture halls of the Metropolitan School of Art on her last day, and saying goodbye to her lecturers and all the friends she had made there, Grace felt close to tears.

Chapter 11

Nellie

Nellie joined the large crowds streaming from the packed tram towards the domed entrance of the Irish International Exhibition in Ballsbridge, she and her sisters growing more excited as the tall, Italian-style colonnades and pinnacles came into view. Father, generous as ever, paid for their tickets as the Gifford family passed through the entrance with its high arch and made their way towards the enormous concert hall and array of restaurants that could seat thousands.

The exhibition had already been deemed a great success, and King Edward and Queen Alexandra on their visit to Dublin earlier in July had declared it a wondrous place to enjoy.

'How lovely it all is,' declared Mother as she stood to take in the spectacle, looking around approvingly at ladies in their finest style, a cascade of pastel-coloured summer dresses and wide-brimmed hats, gentlemen attired in suits, hats and boaters, children's eyes agog with all the delights and amusements in store. It was all so glorious, and Nellie couldn't wait to explore the exhibitions, halls and the large amusement park, including the highest water chute in the world which she was very determined to try.

First of all Father was keen to visit the Palace of

Mechanical Arts – the area of innovation and industry, which was filled with all kinds of new mechanical inventions. Nellie and Gabriel accompanied him, as they too were attracted to the range of beautiful new automobiles on display. Father climbed into one of them and Nellie sat beside him in the polished black and wine-coloured vehicle. He examined everything carefully, testing the steering wheel and the horn. He then stepped out and, intrigued, peered at the motor's engine and its wheels and tyres.

'What an absolutely fascinating piece of machinery!' he enthused. Nellie could see that he was enthralled and she smiled as he interrogated the eager motor-car salesman about the speed, fuel, stopping and weatherproof abilities of such a vehicle. The two of them were deep in conversation for a long time before he finally returned to her side.

'Father, are you considering buying an automobile?' she asked, admiring the gleaming metal paintwork, the polished silver and beautiful seats. 'It would be wonderful for you to own such a vehicle and you could drive it all over the place.'

'I fear I'm too old to learn to drive,' Father admitted rather sadly.

'Then Gabriel and I could learn,' she offered excitedly. 'We could drive you and Mother to all the places you want to visit or see. Dr Mitchell took delivery of a lovely new black motor car six weeks ago and I heard that Mr Hughes on the far end of Palmerston Road has got one.'

'I'd worry about accidents if half of Dublin were cavorting themselves around in these vehicles.'

Why did Father have to be such an old stick-in-the-mud? If she ever wanted to drive a motor car like this, Nellie suspected that she would have to earn the money to purchase it herself.

She and Gabriel tested out new telephone equipment, wireless radios, typewriters and gramophones. Father read all the pages of detailed information about these new products and designs as earnest young men patiently explained the way they worked and were used. She and her brother tried to persuade him of the advantages of having the telephone service in their house.

'For the office, perhaps, but what use would we have at home for such unnecessary equipment?'

It was clear to Nellie and Gabriel that they were witnessing an exciting era of new machines and inventions of which Father and his generation were not a part.

She joined Grace and Ada in the huge Palace of Industries with its arts and craft section where there was a great array of paintings and sculpture on view, including works by Father's friend John B. Yeats and by Grace's tutor William Orpen. Mother was fascinated by the displays of exquisite lace and embroidery, and the silver-and glasswork.

Down by the lake Nellie, Grace and Sidney decided to hire a small swan boat. It was bliss listening to the open-air concert, given by a fine orchestra, as they rowed around the central lake in the sunshine.

Afterwards Mother insisted that they view the Somali Village, where a group of native Somali men and women, who wore hardly any clothing, went about their daily African village routine, lighting fires with sticks and cow dung as large crowds gathered to watch them.

'They must find it so chilly here compared to their own warm land,' observed Mother.

'Those poor people must feel like monkeys in the zoo with everyone gawping at them!' retorted Sidney angrily as the Somali women began to sing, their strange African music filling the air.

'Lady Aberdeen has a wonderful stand with a display on tuberculosis and its management which we all should visit,' Mother announced. Father and Gabriel beat a hasty retreat in the other direction, but the rest accompanied her to the display.

'It is a scourge, a very scourge!' Mother reminded them as they studied the information and figures on tuberculosis, which was endemic in Dublin and throughout the country. Muriel had a special interest in Lady Aberdeen's display as she had recently applied to train as a probationer nurse in Sir Patrick Dun's Hospital and hoped to be offered a place there.

'What if you have patients with this awful disease?' worried Mother, who had made no secret of her opposition to Muriel studying nursing.

As they were all beginning to tire, Father suggested they take a seat in the open-air tea-rooms, where they enjoyed tall dishes piled high with Italian glacé ice-cream flavoured with almonds, cherries and chocolate while they took their ease and considered their illustrated programmes.

'Now I understand why the king was so impressed,' Father said proudly as they looked around at the vast acres of the exhibits. 'It is no wonder that he wanted to reward Mr William

Martin Murphy with a knighthood for all his good work organizing this spectacle.'

'God bless the king,' interjected Gabriel, laughing, 'but he must have got a bit of a shock when he produced his sword to knight Mr Murphy and he politely declined.'

'The man is an absolute disgrace, not only to insult the king but also to cause such embarrassment during the royal visit,' declared Mother angrily.

Nellie wondered why on earth Mr Murphy, one of Dublin's most powerful citizens, who not only owned the Dublin Tram Company but also Independent Newspapers and was the driving force behind this exhibition of modern industry and innovation, would refuse such a royal honour.

'Perhaps he sets no store by a British or royal title,' she suggested.

'Sir Murphy ... Lord William Murphy...' giggled Sidney. 'Why, it doesn't even sound right!'

'Well, title or not, Mr Murphy and his fellow organizers deserve huge credit for the planning of this magnificent event,' said Father as a waiter cleared their table. 'So let us go and see more of the many amusements on offer.'

Nellie and her sisters joined the enormous queue for the famous Giant Water Chute, which towered above them into the sky. Muriel gripped her hand as their painted boat was raised up and up, climbing an alarming height to the top of the steep chute. The two of them screamed madly as they were suddenly pitched downwards in a terrifying, soaking plunge into the splashing water below. It left them gasping and laughing and wet, but longing to do it all over again.

They went on the helter-skelter, the swing boats, the big carousel, and watched a hilarious Punch and Judy show. Nellie had also noticed a tantalizing hot-air balloon floating high in the sky and persuaded her sisters to come along to see it. The balloon itself was enormous and seemed to wobble and move in the air, a fierce gushing sound emanating from it every now and then as a gas burner heated the air that filled it. There was also a large wicker basket attached to the balloon and the man who owned it would permit a few people to clamber in, and then release the hot-air-filled balloon to fly upwards into the sky.

Nellie watched entranced as it lifted off, climbing higher and higher above their heads, the passengers in their basket seeming almost to disappear. However, the huge balloon was tethered and anchored firmly to the ground to stop it from floating away. It was the most thrilling thing she had ever seen and she just knew she had to try it.

Eventually their turn came. Nellie paid for her sisters to come with her and they all climbed in. She was shaking with nerves as the basket began to wobble and tilt. Suddenly it lifted as the balloon filled and moved upwards, the basket lurching off the ground as they went higher and higher. She held on to her hat as she felt the wind catch it, and looking down below she could see the heads of people, the lake and the carousel all becoming more and more distant.

Afraid, Muriel had clenched her eyes tightly shut.

'Open them,' Nellie urged her sister, feeling

giddy and excited. 'Look around – it is amazing. We are flying, like birds high in the sky, like the aviator Mr Wright and his brother.'

Far below she could see the roads of the city and the churches, Sandymount Strand and Dublin Bay, with a few sailing boats bobbing in the waves. Nellie dearly wished that she could stay up here for ever, that the balloon would slip its anchor ropes so they could fly away across the blue, blue sky...

Ten minutes later the hot-air balloon began to descend. Disappointed, Nellie took a firm grip on the basket as the exhibition and visitors all came gradually back into focus and they landed with a thud where they had started.

Her legs felt weak, but she would have adored to have gone straight back up again.

Father, to their surprise, had booked a large table in the Palace Restaurant so they could dine in fine style before attending that night's concert.

'It is all so beautiful here,' sighed Mother, looking dreamily around her, 'but what will happen when the exhibition ends in November?'

'The Earl of Pembroke gave this land to the council to honour his son Herbert's coming of age, and some say that in the future it may become a public park,' said Father.

As the sky grew dark and night fell, they watched thousands of lights illuminate the Italianate terraces and the palaces and lake, and Nellie vowed to return to visit the wonderful exhibition again.

Chapter 12

Muriel

Muriel sat nervously awaiting her turn to be interviewed by the lady superintendent in charge of Sir Patrick Dun's Nursing School. Miss Haughton had a formidable reputation and was said to be ruthless in weeding out those she considered unsuitable to train as probationers in the hospital.

This interview was hugely important to Muriel – she had her heart set on becoming a nurse. She was growing tired of assisting Mother with her church work, and was bored attending the rounds of teas, lunches, balls and other engagements that filled an unmarried young lady's social calendar. She had always considered nursing a fine profession and now that she was twenty-one she was finally old enough to apply for the nursing school here at Sir Patrick Dun's.

Suddenly the heavy wooden door opened and a tall girl emerged, looking red-faced and flustered. Muriel wished she could ask her about the interview, but suddenly her own name was called.

Miss Haughton sat upright at a big mahogany desk in front of a bookcase lined with an array of medical texts. She was smaller than Muriel had expected. On the far wall was a plaque from Guy's Hospital in London where she had trained.

'So you want to be a nurse?' she began, her bright eyes inquisitive.

'Yes,' stammered Muriel. 'I've wanted to train as a nurse for years. I–'

'Do tell me why,' said the other woman firmly. 'It is the obvious question, given the long hours and punishing work most of my nurses must learn to accept.'

Muriel had planned to say that she would find nursing patients both interesting and rewarding, but instead, strangely, she found herself talking about Gerald.

'My brother died when I was only sixteen,' she said slowly, trying to keep her voice steady. 'The doctor told us that he had a brain infection. It was hopeless, although everyone did everything they could to try to save him. Nothing could be done. He was well one day and dying a day later ... how could that be?'

The other woman leaned forward slightly in her chair, listening.

'I sat with him, cared for him and helped my mother to nurse him, and even right up to the end I talked to him all the time, for I knew he would be scared.'

'Could he hear you?' Miss Haughton asked gently.

'I'm not sure. They said he was unconscious near the end, but I kept talking as I didn't want Gerald to be afraid. He died at home.'

'So, you have seen death.'

'Yes,' she whispered, looking down at the floor, trying to control her voice and emotions.

'No easy thing, no matter how often we see it.'

Nodding in agreement, Muriel took a sharp breath.

'Now, Miss Gifford, please tell me about your schooling and exam results.'

Muriel found herself wishing she had applied herself better during her time at Alexandra College, but the other woman seemed satisfied with her answers.

'I see you have provided references of your character and also the necessary medical and dental certificates fully signed by your own physician and dentist. We must ensure our probationers are healthy enough to work on the wards looking after sick patients, which is demanding to say the least. You haven't had any back problems, have you?'

'No,' she replied, looking Miss Haughton straight in the eye.

'Also, our probationers must pass an English exam, which we will arrange for you to take at the Technical School for Nurses within the next two weeks. Have you any questions, Miss Gifford?'

'I just wondered how soon I would be working on the wards.' Muriel stopped suddenly, realizing that she sounded presumptuous. 'What I mean is, if I am considered at all suitable...'

She saw Miss Haughton stiffen.

'All our probationers are on a three-month trial and must attend the hospital's preliminary training school for six weeks' instruction before they are admitted to the wards. Our probationers also attend lectures at the Dublin Metropolitan Technical School for Nurses. Have you any more questions?'

'No, thank you, Miss Haughton.' Muriel's

mouth felt horribly dry.

Suddenly the older woman closed the paper folder in front of her. The interview was at an end.

'Miss Gifford, once we know the results of your English exam you will receive a letter confirming whether or not you have been accepted as a probationer here at Sir Patrick Dun's. All decisions are final. There is no appeal process.'

'I understand,' Muriel said, pushing back her chair and standing up. 'Thank you, Miss Haughton.'

Walking along Grand Canal Street she felt almost dizzy with relief that the ordeal was over and hoped fervently that she had met Miss Haughton's stringent criteria.

Muriel was overjoyed when the official letter arrived from Sir Patrick Dun's Hospital offering her a place as probationer nurse.

'You will make a wonderful nurse,' Nellie congratulated her warmly. 'They are lucky to get you.'

Mother pursed her lips when Muriel showed her the letter. She and Father both tried to dissuade her from accepting the position, saying that nursing was too onerous a career for a bright, intelligent young woman of means.

'My three sisters were wedded to their nursing careers and where did it get them?' Mother proclaimed disapprovingly. 'Spinsters, with no time for suitors or husbands.'

'Nursing is important work,' Father reminded her gently, 'and Muriel is not like your sisters.'

'You are over twenty-one, Muriel,' Mother finally conceded, 'and if this is what you want there is little your father and I can do to stop you.'

'Mother, can't you be happy for me, please?'

'I am, dear, and naturally very proud that you are accepted by one of Dublin's foremost hospitals, but–'

'Please Mother – no buts!'

Father, despite his reservations, generously agreed to pay the hospital's £25 enrolment fee and also to provide the money necessary for Muriel's indoor and outdoor nurse's uniforms.

'You'll probably meet a handsome doctor and fall madly in love,' Sidney sighed enviously.

'I will be far too busy working on the wards for something like that to happen,' she retorted primly. 'Nursing is very hard work.'

Her youngest sister could be annoying at times. Set on becoming a journalist, Sidney was already secretly submitting articles to a number of papers, some of which Mother and Father would certainly never approve of, including Mr Griffith's *Sinn Fein* paper, which Claude called a Fenian rag.

'Talk about surprising the mater and pater,' joked Gabriel when he heard Muriel's news. 'You're a beauty and they probably both thought they would have you married off to one of Claude's boring rich legal friends by now!'

'Don't be such a tease,' Muriel begged her brother. 'I am doing exactly what I want to do.'

'I know,' he said. 'Poor Mother.'

Chapter 13

Grace

Grace could hardly believe her good fortune. Mother and Father had finally agreed to let her apply to continue her art studies at the Slade School of Art in London and she had succeeded in securing a much-coveted interview there.

As she began to pack and organize for this great adventure, Mother informed her that she had decided that she herself would chaperone and oversee her journey to London and her enrolment at the Slade that September.

Despite Grace's vehement protests that she was well able to cross the Irish Sea unaccompanied, Mother would not change her mind.

'But I will be safe, and Ernest has promised he will meet me at the station,' she pleaded, hoping that the fact that she would be in the care of her older brother, who was working in London as an engineer, would satisfy Mother.

'We will share a cabin, so that will make the crossing easier,' Mother insisted, determined to travel to London with her daughter and ensure that she found accommodation suitable for a young lady attending college.

'Oh how I wish she would stay at home!' Grace whispered to Muriel, who was due shortly to start her training as a nurse.

As they got ready to leave Dublin, Grace grew nervous. The Slade School of Art was known the world over, and William Orpen had no doubt had a hand in helping her be considered for a place.

'Lucky you,' said Sidney enviously as Grace said goodbye. Father hugged her, slipping her some pound notes to hide from her mother.

A cab collected them to take them to Kingstown, from where they would take the boat to Holyhead and then travel on by train directly to London.

The boat was crowded and Grace was relieved that they had a cabin as other people tried to find somewhere to sit on the main passenger deck. She watched as their fellow travellers clung to the rails outside, waving goodbye to sweethearts and family. Some would never return to Ireland – gangs of young Irish men in search of better-paid labouring work and pale-faced girls who would take up jobs as waitresses and maids in big households and hotels.

They had a light supper in the dining room and Grace took a turn around the deck before returning to the confines of their small cabin. Mother was feeling most unwell and lay silently on her bunk with her eyes closed, gripping a cologne-soaked handkerchief. Grace had to admit to feeling rather queasy too as they set off across the Irish Sea.

Arriving in London after the long journey, Grace and Mother both longed for their hotel and the chance to freshen up with a bath and a rest before Ernest arrived to join them for dinner.

Later, when they met in the dining room of the Cumberland Hotel, her brother twirled Grace in his arms and told her she looked very striking and elegant and was already attracting the attention of their fellow diners.

He was well settled into London life and society and promised to introduce Grace to some of his circle of friends.

'I will guard her as a big brother should,' he promised Mother as she interrogated him about his work, friends and the kind of milieu in which he mixed.

She and Mother went shopping on Oxford Street and Regent Street. Grace had her own sense of style, knowing well what suited her tall, slender frame and her colouring. Mother nodded approvingly at the fine wool suit and the classic shirts with pin-tucked details she bought in Dickins & Jones. The next day they visited Harrods, a stunning department store on Brompton Road in Knightsbridge, where Mother bought a fitted oyster-coloured suit which showed off her slender frame, as well as a beautiful, pale-grey evening dress with a fine pattern of silk and pearls around the neckline – ideal for dinner parties and the opera.

'Mother, you have a wonderful figure and it is perfect for you. Father will definitely approve.'

They went for lunch in The Savoy to celebrate buying two beautiful hats from the milliner near their hotel. Mother's keen eye raked over their fellow guests and their style. Grace was already giddy with the heady pace of London life compared to Dublin.

The following day she took a cab from their hotel to Gower Street, to the Slade, part of University College London. Passing through the gates, she was immediately impressed by the large Greek-style building with its columns and ornate dome which overlooked a wide quadrangle flanked on either side by sweeping bow-centred buildings.

A student directed her to the left, where she found the entrance to the Slade School of Fine Art. Inside the door was a large stone staircase which fanned out in both directions at the top. As she walked in, she caught a glimpse through a doorway of an airy, high-ceilinged studio where students were busy sculpting.

A few minutes later she was shown into an office that overlooked the grounds, its walls adorned with the work of previous students and a photograph of some of them. She had brought a portfolio of her work and was nervous about her interview with Miss Morison, the lady superintendent who met all potential women students. Admittance to the Slade was based solely on her recommendation. A tall woman with bright eyes, wearing a crisp white shirt with a navy suit, she studied Grace's exam results from Alexandra College and Dublin's Metropolitan School of Art.

'I see here that you won some prizes there and also that Mr William Orpen considers that you have a talent that should be developed here in our fine art department,' she said, looking over her glasses.

Grace blushed as the other woman lightly turned the pages and studied some of her artwork, enquiring why she had chosen to apply to the Slade.

'I want to come and study here because I need to learn more if I ever hope to become a fine artist,' Grace explained truthfully, trying to hide her nervousness.

Miss Morison said very little and seemed to be far more interested in the samples of her work than in continuing the conversation. 'For those who are accepted, the first term at the Slade begins in October and runs until Christmas week,' she stated.

'When will I hear?' Grace pressed, her voice suddenly quivering.

'I presume you are in London for the present? Where are you staying?'

Grace gave the address of their hotel.

'Then you should hear in the next day or two,' Miss Morison said, reaching to shake her hand.

Walking back out across the quad, Grace lingered in the early-autumn sunshine, hoping fervently that she would be accepted to study here.

Next day they visited London's National Gallery and Mother talked about her uncle, Sir Frederick Burton, the director of the gallery who had enlarged it and purchased so many of the Old Masters that were on display. Grace was suddenly filled with a strange sense of belonging and of destiny, thinking of what her grand-uncle had achieved here in the heart of the British Empire. Outside the gallery, which stood like a Greek colossus overlooking Trafalgar Square, Grace thought about how Sir Frederick had filled his life with painting and art and travel, and she felt immensely proud of all his achievements.

Two days later, much to her relief, she got a letter to say that she had been accepted to study at the Slade. Mother congratulated her warmly.

'Grace, we must find accommodation for you immediately,' she urged. 'Somewhere close to the Slade.'

Grace was delighted when they discovered ladies' accommodation in a building at 113 Gower Street, which was practically across the road from the art school. It passed muster with her mother, and a number of her fellow fine arts students would be living there too. Her room was basic but clean and comfortable, and meals were provided.

Ernest had booked tickets for them to attend *Peter Pan, or the Boy Who Wouldn't Grow Up* at the Duke of York's Theatre – a big success for playwright J. M. Barrie. Mother had baulked when she first heard that the play was about children being spirited away to Neverland by a flying boy.

'Oh what a marvellous play!' she enthused afterwards as both the play and the actress Pauline Chase, who played Peter, got a huge ovation from the stunned audience.

'I have never seen anything quite like it,' Grace commented, her head filled with images and pictures from Mr Barrie's wondrous drama.

A few days later she moved into 113 Gower Street and was looking forward to starting her first term at the Slade.

'Grace, I do envy you,' Mother admitted. 'Studying at the Slade will be good for you. I always enjoyed my painting and art, but I never pursued it the way you have. I suppose marriage and family came first. Use this opportunity wisely, as you clearly have inherited the Burton talent and it is all so new and exciting for a young woman like you.'

'I will, and I promise to write regularly to you and Father.' She smiled as Mother kissed her cheek and got into a waiting cab which would take her to Euston station.

A frisson of excitement ran through Grace as Mother disappeared and she contemplated almost a year of freedom here in London without either a chaperone or her mother's eagle eye watching her.

Chapter 14

Grace

Professor Fred Brown welcomed the large group of students to the Slade, many of whom, like Grace, were from the colonies and overseas.

'Each and every one of you sitting here in front of me has the potential to leave your mark on the world of art,' he said, staring down at them. 'Many of our alumni have attained great success in their chosen field. Perhaps some of you in time will join that august list of Slade artists.'

Grace could see he held everyone rapt, each student determined that they would be the one on that list.

Glancing around at her fellow students, she

couldn't help but notice they were for the most part female, with only a handful of men in the large group of about ninety assembled together.

'Where are all the men?' wondered Alice Evans, the pretty Welsh girl beside her.

'Studying law or medicine,' whispered a dark-haired American girl on the other side, 'but I promise there are plenty of them about.'

Alice introduced her sister, also called Grace, who had fair hair and looked nothing like Alice except for the same colour eyes.

'Can you believe it, there are three of us with the same first name,' she said, concerned. 'I do hope the lecturers don't get us all mixed up.'

'Hopefully not,' Grace reassured her, knowing full well that her red hair, height and colouring meant that people generally tended to recognize and remember her – besides which, she was Irish and there seemed to be only one other Irish student in her year, a thoughtful young woman with an elegant style who introduced herself as Mary Lane.

'Are you any relation to Hugh and Ambrose and Eustace Lane?' Grace enquired.

'We are cousins actually,' Mary confirmed. 'Our families had houses practically beside each other in Cork. Do you know them?'

'Ambrose and Eustace were friends of my late brother, Gerald. They used to come and stay in our house in Dublin.'

Mary was older than Grace and was staying in a hotel in Montague Street, near the British Museum.

'It's very quiet and not very fancy, but it will do

for the present.'

The days were packed with lectures as well as with painting and drawing classes. Professor Brown took them for composition every month, choosing all kinds of subjects. Grace found the classes on perspective with Mr Thomson difficult.

'Try to do exactly what he does,' urged her friends Minnie and Alice. 'Draw exactly what he tells you.'

Grace tried, but once again made a mess of it, crumpling up her work and beginning again.

Mr MacColl took them for art history. With his strong Scottish accent and passion for art, he seemed to have a rare ability to make every painting they studied and every artist of the past interesting.

'I do adore his lectures,' enthused Theodora as they all scribbled notes madly.

There were also lectures on architecture, archaeology and Egyptology, which Grace found fascinating.

Working in the large upstairs studio, she always found it hard to believe that thirty students could all paint, draw or sketch the same object or subject or landscape and yet every piece would be entirely different in its interpretation.

'That's style,' Mr Steer encouraged them. 'I never want to see two pieces the exact same in this studio.'

Grace was enjoying herself so much that the weeks flew by. True to his word, her brother kept in touch with her, treating her to lunch or dinner; he also brought her along to a meeting of some Gaelic League friends, where he introduced her to a pretty young woman named Sylvia Dryhurst, who had also attended the Slade and was a talented poet and writer.

'You and Ernest share such a strong resemblance. I suppose you must get fed up with people mentioning it.'

'It's because most of our family are blessed or cursed with the same red hair!' laughed Grace.

She discovered that Sylvia's mother, Nora, was Irish too and was a well-known journalist. Sylvia was following in her footsteps, and she was engaged to a tall, serious young journalist, Robert Lynd, who hailed from Belfast. Along with Ernest, Sylvia kindly introduced her to many of her artist friends.

Grace's friend Theodora told Grace and the others of a large meeting of 'the Suffragettes' that was to be held near their college. 'Oh, do let's all go and support them,' she urged the group of friends.

Grace, Alice and many of their fellow students listened as the suffragettes passionately outlined their campaign for justice and for the right of women to be allowed to vote in elections. Undeterred by being arrested, they often attracted attention for their cause through what was considered violent and unladylike behaviour, which they believed was justified. Grace and her friends joined in the lively discussion and became determined to support the suffragette movement and their growing campaign.

As they left the building a crowd of men on the steps heckled and jeered at them, which only served to make Grace even more resolved to fight for the rights which men enjoyed but which had been denied to women.

With invitations to art exhibitions, supper parties, the theatre and concerts, there was little occasion for Grace ever to feel bored or homesick. She was relishing every minute of her time at the Slade and week by week she could see her work improving as she developed a style of her own.

Chapter 15

Muriel

In October Muriel joined the other sixteen probationers starting at Sir Patrick Dun's Hospital. Miss Haughton, the lady superintendent, was there to greet them and inspect their uniforms.

'Your uniforms must be always spick and span, starched and clean. No trace of lipstick, face powder or rouge is permitted, and hair must be pinned up neatly under your nurse's veil to avoid risk of infection.'

She spent almost an hour going through rules and regulations.

'This is far worse than school,' whispered a probationer named Hannah Woods loudly under her breath.

For the first six weeks they were not let near the wards and had to learn the basics, from how to make a bed, clean and disinfect a ward or room, to how to prepare good, nutritious invalid food for patients – scrambled eggs, lamb's liver, poached chicken or fish, beef tea, chicken soup, blancmange and a disgusting dish called tripe. Muriel dearly wished she had paid some attention to Essie's cookery over the years and made a secret vow to get Nellie to help her learn to cook. She was pretty useless, and the smell of offal made her feel sick. Many of her fellow probationers were well used to bedmaking and cleaning and Muriel realized just how cosseted and spoilt she was.

'Miss Gifford, surely you know how to turn a neat corner in a bed!'

'Miss Gifford, don't you know how to clean tiles?'

'Miss Gifford, you must learn how to carry and empty a full bedpan properly.'

Hannah grimaced and held her nose, which made Muriel get a fit of the giggles. She was glad that she wasn't the only one as she and a few other trainees struggled to learn the basics and overcome their prejudices.

When it came, the first day on the ward was a shock. In the long, high-ceilinged rooms filled with sick people, the air at times was fetid despite the smell of disinfectant, the beds in neat rows rarely empty unless someone was in theatre or having treatment. A girl named Adele nearly burst into tears when one of the nurses asked her to give a bedbath to Mr Lonergan, an elderly patient recuperating after surgery.

'I've never seen a man down there ... like that...' she cringed.

Muriel thanked heaven for having six brothers, as the basics of male anatomy were something she couldn't avoid as she was growing up.

'I'll help you,' she offered, trying to disguise her own embarrassment.

Alongside basic ward work, lectures on anatomy, physiology, hygiene, and surgical and medical nursing were held in the Dublin Metropolitan Technical School for Nurses. The training was exhausting; Muriel was on her feet for so long every day that her legs and feet ached. But her focus was on her patients, the sick, the invalids, the dying.

Sir Patrick Dun's was a busy hospital with a fine reputation for surgery under professor of surgery Edward Hallaran Bennett and surgeons like Sir Charles Bell and Edward Taylor. Mr Woods was the head of the ear, nose and throat department, while Sir John Banks, Dr Mallet and Dr Smith were in the medical department. There was so much to learn and try to understand, and as a probationer Muriel was always conscious of being on the lowest rung of the medical ladder.

'We are all a team,' Dr Watson would remind them. 'Everyone has to learn.'

Muriel liked being part of a team and developed a close friendship with her fellow probationers, all bound by a sense of camaraderie and duty to help each other no matter how awful things were on the ward. The junior doctors floated around the wards too, regularly flirting with the girls and asking them to attend the medical college and hospital socials with them. Muriel and one of the young doctors, Andrew Richardson, invariably ended up sitting talking or even dancing together and he invited her to accompany him to the hospital's annual ball.

'He likes you!' warned Hannah, who was attending the event with one of his friends.

Muriel blushed – she was beginning to feel the same about him. On the rare occasions they were ever alone, they mostly talked about the hospital and work, but she supposed that was because they were both kept so busy.

She always seemed to be at someone's beck and call. Making beds, dealing with people who were very sick, running fevers and needing total care. Often her work was menial – emptying urine bottles and bedpans, cleaning up, changing sheets and bathing patients. There was little dignity for those who were ill and she often had to mask her own reactions and dismay.

'Nurse, can you get me something for the pain, please?' pleaded an elderly woman, who had a racking cough. 'I can't stick it no more.'

Muriel, unsure of what to do, approached a doctor who was standing in the corridor writing notes on a chart.

'Please, doctor, Mrs Scott is in a lot of pain. Could you give her something to help as she–'

The doctor kept writing and ignored her. Maybe he hadn't heard her. She began again.

'Miss?' He raised his eyebrows. He had a round face with a florid complexion and pale, almost grey, eyes.

'Gifford.'

'I suggest you talk to the nurse on the ward if there is a problem with a patient,' he said pompously. 'I have rounds with Sir Charles and am too busy.'

'Yes, doctor,' she apologized, delighted to

escape from him. She would find Nurse Roberts and ask her to take a look at Margaret Scott.

'Mrs Scott has had her dose of morphine,' sighed the older nurse impatiently. 'She will have to last out until she is due her next dose.'

'Even though she is in so much pain?'

'Yes, Miss Gifford. You must realize that we are nurses and doctors here, not miracle-workers. Mrs Scott is fatally ill and there is nothing any of us can do about it.'

Muriel felt overwhelmed. She was powerless, and worse still she had to tell poor Margaret that she would have to wait hours for her next dose of medicine.

The old woman said nothing, tears running down her face. Pulling up a chair, Muriel sat down beside her bed, holding her hand until her patient, who was struggling to breathe, fell asleep.

'Miss Gifford, might I remind you that there are other patients who are in need of your attention,' interrupted the ward sister crossly. 'Mrs Power is still waiting for a commode.'

'I'll fetch it,' she said, standing up. There was no point arguing with her superior. But she knew in her heart that she had done the right thing in staying with the old lady.

Good nursing, to her mind, should always centre on caring for the needs of the sick and the elderly, her patients.

Chapter 16

Grace

In January their class at the Slade studied anatomy. Grace felt queasy as she contemplated the tall skeleton placed in front of them, with its skull and gaping bare eye sockets, nose and mouth.

'Professor Thane must have borrowed him from the medical school,' whispered Minnie.

'Look at the arms and shoulders, ladies, please. Do you notice the joints of the elbows and the knees and the hips and spine? You must study these well so that, if you ever hope to, you can accurately re-create and paint the human form.'

Grace sketched it all quickly on her pad, taking great care over the sockets and joints and where bones met. The human skeleton was a miracle when you imagined flesh, muscle, tissue and veins covering it. Every Monday and Thursday afternoon Professor Thane also used live models to demonstrate the movement and shape of bones, joints and muscles, often marking muscle in colour on the skin of whoever was modelling for them.

Grace had returned home with Ernest to see her family at Christmas. Nellie, Muriel and Sidney interrogated her about her exploits in London and wanted to know if there were any romances, of which so far there were unfortunately none.

While in Dublin she attended the opening of art dealer Hugh Lane's Municipal Gallery in Harcourt Street, which housed some of his fine collection of French Impressionists, though his intention was to build a much larger gallery in the city to house his growing collection of modern art. Grace was entranced by this new style of painting, which somehow managed to capture the quality of light in a way artists hadn't done before and which gloriously demonstrated a new, unique interpretation of a subject – 'the artist's impression', as Hugh Lane called it.

She experimented back in London, painting in this style briefly, but soon realized that she far preferred to work in a medium that involved strong, broad lines with definition and simple colour, for drawing gave her the greatest pleasure. She once again found herself doing quick sketches of her lecturers and fellow students, and in only a few strokes of black ink seemed to be able to capture their personality and physical traits. Professor Tonks, who taught figure drawing and painting, was very encouraging as he studied an ink portrait that she'd done of Professor Brown and some of their other lecturers.

'Grace, you are talented at line drawing and caricatures. You display great flair for design and illustration rather than ordinary portraiture.'

Alice, Grace and Minnie all enjoyed landscape painting, Mary Lane was a very fine portrait painter, while Theodora's illustration work was full of tiny details, pleats, bows and beads, for she loved to draw and sketch fashion. Grace, on the other hand, hated including these fussy things and wanted just to sweep her black ink pen over the page and capture in almost one go the person she was drawing or a scene from a play or book that she had recently seen or read.

Grace attended lectures and talks held by the Women's Social Political Union. She and her friends were all supporters of the suffragettes and their campaign to get the vote for women.

As her last term at the Slade approached, Grace began to wish that she could stay in London for ever, finding some kind of work that would enable her to be independent and continue to live in the city.

'Maybe we could share a flat together,' suggested Minnie and Theodora.

She responded to various advertisements looking for sketch artists for journals and newspapers, but had no success, and the galleries she visited all seemed to have enough artists without taking on the work of an unknown young Irish woman.

'Grace, don't keep thinking about it,' advised Mary, who was returning to her home at Vernon Mount in Cork. 'Enjoy being here and these last few weeks at the Slade.'

Also, Charlie Taylor, a handsome young law student, had invited her out. She'd been to the college's law ball with him, as well as to the theatre and a dinner party at his best friend's home in Belgravia. They took long walks around the nearby park together and spent hours talking in tea-rooms and cafés near the college. Grace looked forward to seeing Charlie, hearing his voice and spending time with him.

The exams came and she sat up late studying, trying to memorize the various Italian, French and German art schools, the masters and artists and their work. She was also frantically trying to finish her own project and three pieces for her final exhibition at the end of June.

'I have to study for my exams,' she told Charlie, who found it hard to accept that she was serious and had to study, paint and draw instead of joining him for lunch or tea.

'Does it really matter that much?' he argued.

'Yes!' she snapped, fiercely annoyed with him. 'It does matter. Art is what I do, surely you understand that?'

She could tell from his wounded expression that he didn't, but was one of those men who believed that a woman should not aspire to work or have a career, or for that matter to vote.

Disappointed in each other, the very brief relationship petered out and Grace realized that she could never get involved with such a man, no matter how handsome and charming he appeared.

The suffragettes were planning a large rally in Hyde Park in June, and she and her friends were determined to take part. Grace and Minnie were despatched to MacCulloch & Wallis, the large haberdashery store in Poland Street, to buy yards and yards of ribbon in the suffragette colours – purple, white and green – for everyone. If only Grace had Mother's sewing machine, she would have been able to run up a stylish dress in the colours, but, instead, she would have to make do with trimming an outfit.

'Thirty yards of purple ribbon?' queried the pretty young shop attendant. She could not believe her luck as she unrolled and measured yard after yard of ribbons for the female students of the Slade.

'It's for the rally next Sunday,' Grace confided. 'We are all supporters of Mrs Pankhurst.'

'My sister and I are going too, as are most of the girls here,' she said quietly, hoping the shop manager would not overhear her.

'Perhaps we will see you in the park.' Minnie grinned as they gathered up their purchases.

As they set off on Sunday to join the rally, they all wore dresses, skirts and blouses in the suffragette colours. They made the multicoloured ribbons into sashes, belts and bows as well as tying them gaily around their hats.

The sun shone as Grace and her friends marched from Kensington to Hyde Park behind tall banners, shouting loudly 'Votes for Women!' and arrived to form an enormous crowd of hundreds of thousands of supporters of the movement. Even little girls and children sported the coloured ribbons in their plaits, braids and hairbands. Grace had never seen anything like it – so many women united in one cause.

They gave a roaring cheer as Emmeline Pankhurst, flanked by her daughters Christabel and Sylvia, blinking in the sunshine, stood proudly to address them. They could see she was clearly overwhelmed by the massive reception from all the women, young and old, who were present.

'Even I am shocked by this huge crowd before me,' she said, gazing at the crowd of about three hundred thousand women. 'Thank you so much for making the effort to attend today. Deeds, not words, have always been our motto and your presence is absolute proof of the support for our campaign for votes for women.'

Listening to Mrs Pankhurst's conviction and belief in the fight for women's rights, and looking around her at the sea of female faces of all ages, full of hope and desperate for change, Grace knew that it was only a matter of time until all women were considered equal to men and given the vote, and that it was the duty of young women like her to continue to campaign for it.

Ernest came to the final-year show at the Slade, declaring in his brotherly fashion that her work was astounding. She had designed a selection of theatre posters, programmes and illustrations, along with ink portraits, including some of her friends and some of the college's esteemed artists. There was also a fine display of her life drawing and a range of prints based on Greek design.

Grace had written to Mother and Father requesting permission to stay on in London for a few months, but the reply had been very clear. Grace was too young and was expected back home in Dublin immediately.

'My parents want me back on the Isle of Wight,' complained Minnie.

'Grace and I planned to go to Paris,' confided Alice, 'but Father is being difficult about it.'

They may have graduated from the Slade but, disappointingly, it made no difference to what any of them could do; they were single young

110

women with no source of income or support other than their families. As she packed up her clothes and art materials for the journey home to Ireland, Grace wondered if she would ever return to work and exhibit in London.

Chapter 17

Grace

Dublin seemed desperately drab and dreary to Grace when she returned to the almost claustrophobic world of Temple Villas, living under Mother's watchful eyes. It was such a contrast to the freedom she'd enjoyed in Gower Street.

Mother and Father constantly enquired about her situation.

'Why can't they leave me alone?' she complained to her twin brother Cecil, who had also recently returned to Dublin following travels in Canada. 'They know I am trying my best to find work.'

'At least you don't have to go and work in Father's law firm like I have to,' he consoled her.

Poor Cecil! Despite his protestations that he did not have any intention of doing law, he was working as an apprentice in Father's office in Dawson Street, a job he certainly did not enjoy.

'You are silly, Grace – you should have stayed in London!' pronounced Ada, forthright as ever. 'Believe me, there is scarcely any commissioned work here if you are a woman.' She confided to

Grace that she was getting desperate and was considering making her career elsewhere, perhaps in America.

Grace, however, was determined to prove herself.

So, armed with a sample portfolio of her work, she set off to visit every theatre, magazine and newspaper office in the city to try to persuade them about her artistic ability and availability. Her younger sister, Sidney, who was making quite a name for herself as a journalist, had given her introductions to some of her editors, including *Sinn Fein*'s Arthur Griffith.

Grace got used to sitting across cluttered desks in cramped, decrepit offices trying to appear professional and businesslike as managers or editors studied and scrutinized her work. She only needed one or two to commission her and it would be the stepping stone to being considered a proper artist for print, which is what she wanted.

A few considered her work very suited to their requirements, which was pleasing, but they made it clear that unfortunately there would be no possibility of paying a fee if they used it.

'Am I supposed to starve and be grateful?' she complained to Sidney as she tried not to give in to a growing sense of despair.

'I often don't get paid for my writing either,' her sister admitted, 'but it all helps to build my name and reputation. That is part of the reason why I chose to use "John Brennan" as my pen-name. It's strange, but people find it easier to accept a man writing articles for the newspapers and magazines than a young woman, and they believe a young

112

man deserves to be paid. Besides, I far prefer the name to my own,' she added with a grin.

Grace found it strange that even at home her sister now preferred them all to call her John instead of Sidney.

Her youngest sister had changed and grown up so much while Grace had been away in London. She was only eighteen, but she had a mind of her own, together with an unusual confidence and sense of importance about her work. She had joined a group set up by Maud Gonne and Helena Malony, which pledged to fight against English influence in Ireland and to champion the cause of Irish independence and the revival of the Irish language and customs.

'It's called Inghinidhe na hEireann,' John explained.

'You are talking in Irish!' Grace laughed.

'I'm taking classes in the language.'

'Inghi...' Grace had no idea how even to attempt to say it.

'It means "Daughters of Ireland", but some people call us "the Ninnies",' John revealed. 'Grace, you should come to some of the meetings. They hold lectures and ceilithe and debates.'

John was deeply involved with this organization, but for the moment Grace felt she needed to concentrate her efforts on finding work.

Father quietly suggested she set up a meeting with his old friend John Butler Yeats's son, Willie. John Yeats had moved to live in America and Father still missed his old friend and their discussions.

'The Abbey Theatre is popular and they seem

always to be putting on new Irish plays. Most are not really to our taste, but I hear they do well.'

From her visits to the Abbey, Grace knew that they prided themselves on reflecting Irish culture and tradition on the stage. William Butler Yeats had said nothing when she first met him in the theatre. He had always seemed rather lofty and distant, but now she went to see him and he enquired politely about her parents' wellbeing as she handed him her portfolio. She knew he had a very keen, critical eye and her spirits sank as he sat across from her in his office, silently studying her work. She was relieved when, looking at her over his dark-rimmed glasses, he told her he considered her design and artwork striking and that it suited the demands of the theatre.

The Abbey already had a few artists they used, he explained, but he promised to send her the script of a play they planned to stage next year and asked her to submit a sample of her design ideas to them for consideration.

'Thank you,' she smiled, gathering up her portfolio. He had made no commitment to using her work, but Grace felt at least he was giving her the opportunity to demonstrate her ideas. The Abbey Theatre, with its strong nationalist focus, was staging work that differed very much from Dublin's other theatres with their popular London-type productions. She would relish the challenge of working for it.

Two small newspapers also gave her work, asking her to do some caricature sketches for them, which they used. Mother proudly showed her drawings to everyone.

'The Daughters of Ireland' have invited me to attend a committee meeting about the new women's journal we hope to publish,' John told her one day. 'Perhaps they will need some artists and illustrators!'

Grace did not want to get her hopes up, but she waited anxiously for her sister to return home. She was delighted when John told her that their new journal, *Bean na hEireann*, would be published monthly and would reflect both nationalist and feminist sentiment with a broad appeal and a range of articles from various contributors – and it would most definitely need some illustrative artwork.

'Countess Constance Markievicz turned up to the meeting in a ball gown and a tiara, straight from an event in Dublin Castle, to offer her services,' John laughed. 'Can you imagine her with all the committee ladies in their brown and grey tweeds and woollens? She certainly caused a bit of a stir. She offered not only to write or provide some artwork, but also to sell her diamond brooch to raise funds for the journal. Honestly, she is an extraordinary woman, unconventional to say the least. We took the tram home together and I have to say I do like her.'

John encouraged Grace to send samples of her work to the new journal's editor, Nora Dryhurst, a well-respected Irish journalist and suffragette who lived in London but had offered at the meeting to help with editing and setting up *Bean na hEireann* while she was in Dublin. John had become friendly with the older journalist, who was very encouraging about her writing career.

'I met her daughter Sylvia in London,' said Grace. 'She is a friend of Ernest's.'

'Nora Dryhurst is a fine journalist,' enthused John. 'When I told her that Ernest is coming home on holidays she said we must have afternoon tea together. So I have invited her to come here for tea next week.'

Mother was barely able to disguise her surprise at the petite, intelligent, pretty, middle-aged suffragette sitting in their drawing room and telling tales of political intrigue and scandals in London.

'Working as a journalist, one has to always be curious,' Nora Dryhurst declared.

'And what do you do with such knowledge?' Mother asked.

'Why, Isabella, I edit it and then write it in my column. That is what I am paid to do.'

'I wish that I could find such stories, but Dublin is a bit of a backwater,' admitted John enviously.

Grace could not help but smile to see how Mrs Dryhurst was well able to charm and get her way around Mother.

'I'm afraid I have to leave you, Nora,' Mother apologized after a while. 'Sidney should have given me better notice of your visit, but I had already made other arrangements with one of my neighbours and cannot let her down. Perhaps we will meet again.'

'I'm sure that we will, Isabella dear,' replied Nora, smiling as she stood up to say goodbye to her.

'Your mother is nothing like what you told me!'

she teased John and Ernest.

She enquired about Muriel's work as a nurse. 'It is such a wonderful vocation, my dear, but the work is so demanding. I have no doubt that you give great care and comfort to all your patients.'

'The wards are always so busy,' Muriel agreed, 'but it is rewarding.'

'Now, Grace dear, tell me about your artistic endeavours.'

'I have had a few caricature sketches published in two newspapers,' Grace replied ruefully, 'but little else for the past few weeks.'

'Talent often takes time to be discovered,' said Mrs Dryhurst gently. 'But often giving a push in the right direction can prove very helpful. I'm invited to George Russell's home on Sunday. I never miss his salons when I am in Dublin, as he is what I would call a renaissance man, blessed with the type of intellect that is open and interested in everything and everyone. Why don't you all come along with me? It's a wonderful place to meet people – contacts that might prove useful.'

'George Russell knows everyone!' John laughed, delighted at the invitation. 'His salons are famous.'

'Then it is agreed that we will all go.' The older woman clapped her hands in delight. 'And Ernest, will you escort the ladies on Sunday?'

Embarrassed, Ernest flushed slightly, but with a little persuasion agreed that he too would attend.

'But as I said, George's is always rather different, so we must dress up and find the right costumes for such an evening. What do you say?'

'Yes,' agreed Grace excitedly, knowing that an invitation to George Russell's At Home was considered a great entrée to Dublin's literary and arts world.

'Then we will find the costumes we need and ready ourselves for Sunday,' smiled. Nora Dryhurst as she sipped a second cup of tea.

Chapter 18

Grace

Excited by the prospect of Mr Russell's costume party, Grace dressed as an Egyptian, wearing an off-white robe that was patterned with gold and fashioning a golden headband to go with it. She had borrowed a black silk cummerbund of her father's, which she wrapped tightly around her middle, and used heavy black liner to define her eyes in the Egyptian style. Pleased with the rather striking result, she turned to help Muriel, who was wearing a green and pink floral-patterned silk gown which was meant to resemble some kind of Chinese robe. Grace braided her sister's long red hair with a ribbon and showed her how to highlight her eyes. John chose a sweeping length of purple chiffon she had bought only a few weeks ago and wound it around her so that it vaguely resembled an Indian sari. Ernest had hunted through the house and was dressed like a Russian peasant, with boots, purple and green patterned waistcoat and a fur hat. Standing together, they created a rather bizarre-looking theatrical spectacle.

Mother was visiting some friends for the evening but Father stepped out into the hallway on hearing the commotion as they got ready to leave.

'Where are you all off to?' he asked, taking in their attire. 'A fancy-dress party, is it?'

The evening was warm and dry and, as they walked to George Russell's house on Rathgar Avenue, their strange attire attracted much attention from passers-by. When the large, bearded figure of Mr Russell opened the door, Grace could see immediately that their literary host was both amused and surprised at their appearance. Nora Dryhurst appeared and immediately ushered them inside the crowded drawing room to introduce them to the assembled company of artists and writers.

'You all look divine,' she gushed. She herself was attired in a deep-green gown with a billowing skirt and a wrapover tartan scarf. She announced the Giffords as if they were some type of famous heroic figures.

'Ladies and gentlemen, let me introduce the wonderful spirits from a bygone age – Deirdre, Fionnuala, Grania and of course the Great Cuchulainn himself,' she proclaimed with a flourish.

Looking around the book-filled room, Grace could see the other guests staring at them, torn between mirth and bewilderment at their clothing, for no one else was in costume as they had been told, but in conventional dresses and skirts, suits and jackets. Ernest was absolutely horrified at the position they were in. Grace, deeply em-

119

barrassed and humiliated by their appearance, just wanted to escape.

'Don't be so self-conscious and shy,' urged an unrepentant Nora, pleading with them to enjoy the company and party, but the four of them fled to the safety of a smaller front room which was unoccupied except for a man sitting petting a dog.

'Let's go home,' Muriel begged. 'I don't want to stay. I'm so embarrassed.'

'Nor do I,' agreed Grace, disappointed that the salon she had so looked forward to attending was such a disaster. She pulled the golden band from her head.

Curious, the little dog came over to them to sniff at their brother's boots and Russian costume.

'Do you like dogs?' the man interrupted, showing no reaction to the way they were dressed. For some reason he too had obviously sought sanctuary away from Mr Russell's other guests.

'We thought it was a costume party,' explained Ernest apologetically. 'That is why we are dressed up in these ridiculous costumes.'

'I expected tonight that only two or three other writers would attend,' the man confided. 'George asked me to come along to read him some of the poems from my collection, but I certainly did not expect such a large and illustrious gathering.'

'His salon is very famous,' added John, 'but we really did expect that everyone would be dressed up in costume too.'

They introduced themselves and discovered that they were talking to the writer James Stephens.

'Are you intending to rejoin the rest of the guests?' he asked.

Muriel, Ernest and Grace had no interest in any further humiliation, though John was tempted to swan in and join Nora Dryhurst.

'Absolutely not, Mr Stephens, we intend leaving quietly,' Grace said firmly. She had no intention of staying on at the party, no matter what her sister said or did.

'Then let us all make our escape together,' he suggested.

At the hall door George Russell came politely up to say goodbye.

'I'm sorry that we did not get the opportunity to converse properly this evening, but do say that you will all come and visit me again,' he entreated them.

'Yes, we will,' Grace promised. She knew well the importance of being accepted by Mr Russell and his coterie of artist and writer friends if she hoped to become part of the Dublin art scene.

Chapter 19

Muriel

'Muriel, do say you want to come with Grace and me to see St Enda's, the new school Mr Pearse has opened in Ranelagh,' urged John. 'Mrs Dryhurst has invited us to join her.'

'I'm not sure I want to be involved in another escapade with your friend after all the embarrassment she caused us at Mr Russell's house,'

Muriel replied tartly.

'This time will be different,' her sister promised. 'Mr Pearse has some very revolutionary ideas about education, and Nora says that he may even agree to let me write a piece about his new school.'

'Oh very well,' she sighed. She had done a week of night duty at the hospital and was still tired, enjoying her well-earned day off before she was back on duty tomorrow.

Her youngest sister was enthralled by Mrs Dryhurst, who seemed always to get invited to openings and exhibitions and enjoyed bringing along a few female friends for company.

St Enda's, the new school for boys, was in Ranelagh, close to their home in Rathmines. Mother considered it a nest of vipers, a school full of nationalists and Sinn Feiners and Gaelic Leaguers.

'They speak Gaelic and have no business opening such a school in a good area like Ranelagh,' she complained.

When they arrived at the school in Oakley Road, Mr Padraig Pearse, the headmaster, was outside, standing there with his mother to welcome guests. He was a serious young man, dressed in a tweed suit and dark tie, his hair short, and his grey-blue eyes were earnest as he greeted them.

'I'm very much looking forward to seeing your school, Mr Pearse,' said Nora Dryhurst enthusiastically. 'I have heard great reports about St Enda's and the Gaelic-based curriculum you offer the boys instead of the British system.'

Despite her reservations, Muriel had to admit that she was curious.

They were just about to take the steps when a young man with tousled, curly brown hair bounded towards them.

'Mrs Dryhurst, how nice to meet you again,' he said formally.

'I am glad to see you, Mr MacDonagh,' she beamed. 'I have asked some friends to accompany me, as I do believe they too will be fascinated by your new school.'

Muriel studied him. He seemed pleasant and more at ease than Mr Pearse.

'Oh, I am forgetting my manners,' continued Nora. 'This is Mr Thomas MacDonagh, the deputy principal, but also a gifted writer. His new play is being staged at the Abbey. Let me introduce you to my friends. These beautiful young women are the Gifford sisters, Muriel, Grace and John. Aren't they wonderful? My advice to you, Thomas, is to fall in love with one of these girls and marry her!'

Muriel could feel the redness flush her cheeks. John was laughing and Grace had a sphinx-like smile on her face. Was she the only one to feel absolutely embarrassed and put out by Mrs Dryhurst's very forward comments?

Thomas MacDonagh threw his head back and laughed aloud. 'That would be easy, for they are all utterly charming. The difficulty would be to decide which one.'

Muriel prayed that the ground would open up and swallow her. She should never have listened to her sister; she should have stayed safely at home. Mr MacDonagh caught her eye and had the good grace to look at least momentarily contrite.

'I do hope you will enjoy seeing the school and gain an understanding of what we are trying to do here. Our school is bilingual, the boys learning and speaking both Gaelic and English. Padraig's work will not only change minds, I believe, but also I suspect the future of education here in Ireland,' he said proudly.

'Don't let the Castle or Westminster hear you say that!' Nora teased. 'I hear they do not take well to change.'

'Please excuse me, ladies – I have a few things to do. But I'm sure we will talk later. There will be refreshments served.' A few boys were hovering around and Mr MacDonagh beckoned to one of them to come over.

'Sean, please show these ladies around and bring them back to the halla afterwards.'

The classrooms along the corridor were large and bright with tall, long windows, the desks forming a semicircle around the teacher. There was the usual blackboard, but on one wall were pictures of Irish monuments, Celtic crosses, round towers, old castles and the burial mounds at Newgrange.

'These are the important places in our land, our heritage,' said young Sean proudly.

There was a large map of Ireland and its counties, showing its rivers, mountains and roads. As they had had only a map of Britain in her school, Muriel knew its rivers, counties and countryside far better than those of her own country, she was ashamed to say.

Along another wall hung prints and paintings

of famous Irish men – Robert Emmet, Theobald Wolfe Tone, Charles Stewart Parnell, Daniel O'Connell and Irish chieftains of old. The next classroom had the alphabet in Gaelic and simple words written in Irish.

'This is for the younger boys,' explained Sean. 'To help them learn the basics, they practise songs and rhymes and poems. Master Pearse believes that learning our native language is essential but should be made easier.'

He led them to the art room next, where vivid canvases almost covered one wall and a range of clay animal models stood on a long table. A tall young man was talking to two or three other visitors.

'Art is an important part of our curriculum,' he was saying. 'We believe that even the youngest student is able to express his inner self through colour and form.'

A few minutes later, Grace introduced them to Willie Pearse. 'We went to the Metropolitan School of Art together. Willie is a wonderful sculptor.'

'How does a sculptor come to work here?' asked Nora, curious.

'Padraig is my older brother,' he explained, 'so it's hard not to become involved in his endeavours. Besides, I enjoy teaching and it leaves me time for my own work too.'

'That is good to hear,' nodded Grace.

'Some of my pieces are on display in the school if you want to see them, Grace?' he offered.

Muriel could tell her sister was anxious to talk to Willie.

'You run along, Grace dear,' urged Nora. 'We will catch up with you in a while, but for the moment we'll continue our tour with young Sean.'

Grace threw them a glance of gratitude as she and Willie disappeared, talking together.

Muriel was impressed with the music room, noting that the instruments included fiddles, simple tin whistles and a drum that Sean told them was called a bodhran. The young lad picked up an unusual instrument that looked a bit like a small set of Scottish bagpipes and, sitting down, he began to play. The haunting sound of ancient Irish music filled the room.

'These are called the Uilleann pipes,' he explained. 'Master Pearse said if I practise almost every day I will in time become a fine piper.'

As she walked around, Muriel could see that St Enda's bore no resemblance to the schools she and her brothers and sisters had attended. The school emblem, which was displayed widely, was certainly different: it was a Gaelic warrior holding a sword with the words 'Strength in our limbs, truth on our lips and purity in our hearts'. The school's corridors, instead of the usual boring charts and maps, displayed art and sculpture, and each classroom was named after a legendary Irish figure – Cuchulainn, Oisin, Brian Boru. The boys at St Enda's played Gaelic sports, hurling and football, and everyone was expected to train and be physically fit. Sean told them that, unlike in his old school, there was no corporal punishment for misbehaviour.

'I really must find out more about Mr Pearse's philosophy in setting up this school,' Nora

Dryhurst said, equally impressed. 'Maybe I will see if I can find him.'

'I should like to talk to him too,' agreed John. 'I want to write about this place.'

'I can bring you back to the master,' offered the boy.

'You two go. I'll just ramble around a bit more,' said Muriel, not wanting to intrude.

'Very well, my dear, we will see you back in the big hall,' said Nora with a smile as she and John followed the boy.

Muriel was intrigued by a small plot of vegetables planted at the back of the school. Potatoes, cabbage and beans were growing there.

'Padraig believes the boys should be able to learn how to grow food and support themselves if needed,' interrupted a voice.

She turned to find Mr MacDonagh watching her. 'He wants our pupils to not only be academic but practical too.'

'It's all wonderful, truly it is,' she said sincerely. 'If I were a boy it is a school I would love to attend.'

'That is what Padraig is hoping, that this break with years of old-fashioned tradition and methods will encourage students, and of course their parents.'

'I'm sure it will.'

'Where is Mrs Dryhurst?'

'She and my sister have gone to meet Mr Pearse to discuss the school and his principles.'

'They could be a while then,' he grinned. 'Would you like to continue the tour?'

127

As he showed her around the rest of the school she discovered that his mother and father had both been teachers too.

'My mother is a wonderful teacher – she even teaches the piano.'

Muriel could tell that Thomas MacDonagh was equally well regarded by his own students, as boys kept coming up to greet him. He knew all their names and chatted easily with them.

'What about you, Miss Gifford, what are your interests? What does a young lady in your position enjoy?'

She sensed a slight cynicism in his voice and felt annoyed at his presumption of her being idle and wealthy.

'I don't get as much time as I want to pursue the things I like because I always seem to be working.'

'Work?' She could tell that he was surprised.

'I'm training as a nurse in Sir Patrick Dun's,' she explained. 'It's my day off, but my sister insisted on dragging me along here.'

'I'm glad that she did,' he said, his eyes resting on her face.

Muriel felt embarrassed by his attention.

He laughed, sensing her discomfort. 'It must be time for us to go to the Halla Mor. Padraig will be ready to give his address.'

They walked together back towards the large room, where Muriel was relieved to sit down and rejoin her sisters and Nora. They listened for about twenty minutes as Padraig Pearse outlined the ethos of his school and his aim – to teach and educate young Irish men who would be able to make a valid contribution to Irish society and life and their nation. St Enda's education principles were rooted in the Gaelic language, literature, poetry and history, a love of the countryside and traditional Irish games, culture and music.

'Stirring stuff,' agreed Nora as everyone applauded.

Mr Pearse was a born orator and swept everyone along with him. Following his speech, a number of boys got up and sang in the choir, the notes of a traditional song filling the hall. It was so beautiful that Muriel couldn't help being captivated by their voices. For an instant her eyes met those of Mr MacDonagh, who was standing at the side of the stage listening. She glanced away quickly.

Afterwards there was tea, sandwiches and cakes made by Mr Pearse's sister. Muriel stayed in the group, noticing that the curly-haired teacher was busy, engrossed in talking to some prospective parents. Instead, Willie Pearse joined them. Strange, but Muriel felt slightly disappointed.

As they were leaving, Thomas MacDonagh came over to say goodbye to them.

'I do hope that we will see each other again soon,' he said. 'Young ladies are always welcome along to the Gaelic League and our ceili evenings.'

'I'm sure we would all love to go,' replied John, smiling.

Walking home, Muriel had to admit that the thought of meeting up with Mr MacDonagh again was rather appealing.

Chapter 20

Muriel

Music filled the still evening air as Muriel and her sisters joined the crowd gathering outside on Harcourt Street. They had decided to take Mr MacDonagh up on his suggestion and attend a Gaelic League ceili. They couldn't wait to join the dancers inside.

Muriel noticed that Mr MacDonagh was deep in conversation with a few friends on the other side of the big, high-ceilinged room. A few people were up dancing already, girls and young men of all ages hand in hand in a large circle as a group of musicians played their fiddles, whistles and bodhran.

Immediately on seeing them Thomas Mac-Donagh came over to welcome them, just as a lively jig began to play.

'Congratulations on your play, Mr MacDonagh.' Muriel, Grace and John had all attended *When the Dawn Is Come*, his play about a rebellion which had been staged by the Abbey Theatre only a few weeks earlier.

'I'm afraid there were quite a few faults with the production,' he admitted rather humbly. 'Costumes and the set, unfortunately, left a lot to be desired.'

'To have a play staged at the Abbey with Miss

Sara Allgood is surely the thing,' said John enthusiastically, 'and it was very well received by the audience.'

'You are most kind, Miss Gifford.'

'We very much look forward to your next production,' Muriel encouraged him, conscious that he must have been wounded by the poor reviews his play had received.

Mr MacDonagh invited them all up on to the dance floor, gesturing for his friends to join them. Muriel was suddenly aware of his strong, muscular arms holding her as he almost spun her around the floor, grasping her elbow firmly.

'I'll get dizzy!' she laughed.

'Then look at me,' he ordered.

The music was fast and furious and Muriel had never enjoyed anything like it. Grace was dancing with Willie Pearse, while John was swung around the room by one of his friends.

'These are all teachers from St Enda's,' Thomas MacDonagh said formally when the dance was finished, introducing them to his brother Joseph and his friend Con Colbert.

'Is Mr Pearse here this evening?' Muriel enquired.

'Yes, but Padraig is not much of a dancer.' He shrugged. The other men laughed aloud at the suggestion.

Next they danced 'The Walls of Limerick', a rousing jig, followed by a slower set. After that they sat for a time listening to the band as they sipped some lemonade. Muriel listened intently as Eamonn Ceannt, a friend of MacDonagh's, played the Uilleann pipes. The music was so beautiful and

131

haunting – a real contrast to the piano and violins of the usual bands and orchestras that entertained them.

Padraig Pearse appeared then and the room hushed as he stepped up to recite two poems that he had written in Gaelic. Muriel didn't understand them, but those around her clapped loudly.

The ceili band started up again and they danced until they were out of breath, their hearts racing. She couldn't believe it when the fiddles finally ceased and it was time to go home.

'I do hope you all enjoyed the night, Miss Gifford,' Mr MacDonagh said, smiling at her as they prepared to leave. 'Perhaps you and your sisters will return another time?'

'Thank you, Mr MacDonagh, I'm sure we will.'

'MacDonagh,' he corrected her. 'My friends always call me MacDonagh!'

Riding home in the carriage, they were all agreed that the young men and women of the Gaelic League were certainly an interesting crowd. Thomas MacDonagh and his friends were part of the movement to revive not only the Gaelic language but also Gaelic music and culture, which certainly had an attraction.

'Thank heaven for a night with no boring, polite drawing-room conversation or dance cards and dreadful waltzes,' pronounced Grace.

'Mother would hate us being involved with such people,' teased John. 'So I do think we should definitely come again.'

Chapter 21

Muriel

Muriel felt giddy as she climbed the stairs to the ward. It had happened to her a few times over the past two days, but somehow she had steadied herself.

Dr Rutledge passed her and glanced over, mildly curious, as Muriel took a few slow, deep breaths before she continued up the stairs.

By mid-afternoon her head was reeling and her throat was sore. She was on duty in the sluice room washing bedpans and jars, a job she detested. By teatime she was hot and flushed and running a temperature. The ward sister was annoyed at her as she was not fit to continue to work.

Muriel had to stay at home for weeks as she had rheumatic fever and all her bones and joints ached and she felt as weak as a kitten. Her summer exams were only a few weeks away and she urgently needed to study, but even lifting her head off the pillow seemed to leave her sweating and exhausted.

'Are you sure you are fit to return to work?' Mother worried on the day she finally felt able to get up and was preparing to take the tram into town. 'Heaven knows what other disease or illness you may pick up from those people you have to look after.'

'Mother, I am fine,' she lied.

'Nurse Gifford, I see that we are blessed with your presence,' the ward sister commented sarcastically when she went back to the hospital. 'I hope you are returned to full health.'

'Yes,' said Muriel quietly, not wanting to engage in any discussion with her as she returned to the wards.

There was much work to be done, with three patients back from theatre all needing full attention. Blood loss and haemorrhage, shock and sepsis – events for which they must all be on high alert. Muriel watched appalled as the young appendectomy patient in the middle bed began to shake and shiver, his teeth chattering so hard that he could barely breathe. She immediately fetched him a blanket and took his temperature before informing the sister that he needed a doctor.

His parents came that evening, but his breathing was already laboured, his lungs filling with fluid. Two hours later he was dead, and Muriel wiped away her tears as she and her colleague Lucinda were given the task of washing and laying him out.

Most of her day-to-day nursing work was tedious: making beds, emptying and washing bedpans, endlessly scrubbing and cleaning the wards and corridors, and helping to feed and wash patients who needed assistance. She tried to study in the evenings, but often was too tired to read her medical books and notes.

'Are you all right?' asked her friend Hannah. 'You still look peaky.'

'I'm fine,' she lied, sitting on the corner of an

empty bed.

On the day of the exams Muriel followed her fellow probationers into the exam hall and sat down. She tried to concentrate as she read the exam paper over slowly and began to fill in the answers. Walking out of the hall afterwards, she felt a strange sense of calm. She had written as much as she could and believed she had imparted as much nursing and medical knowledge as she was able.

Over the next ten days they all waited in trepidation for their results. Muriel had been assigned to assist in the crowded outpatient clinic, where people came in with every type of wound, injury or illness, from influenza to dysentery, scabies to lice, abscesses in their mouths and on their bodies, to broken bones and jagged cuts that needed stitching.

One poor soul had dropped a kettle of boiling water on her leg and her screams of pain haunted Muriel as the junior doctor attended to her. She squeezed tightly on Muriel's hand as he began to examine her burns.

'Nurse, are you stupid? Run and fetch me more dressings and a bowl with some iodine solution,' he shouted.

'I'm afraid my patient needs me,' she objected, trying not to upset the poor woman.

'You do what I say, Nurse Gifford,' he ordered. 'Let go of her hand.'

The minute she did, the woman began to wail and scream again.

The consultant in charge, Dr Stevenson, heard the commotion and came over, admonishing the young doctor before taking over tending to the patient himself

'Nurse Gifford, are you quite recovered from your own recent illness?' he asked kindly as they worked together, gently dressing the burns. Muriel assured him that she was.

On Tuesday each of the probationers in her group would have an interview with Superintendent Haughton at which they would not only discuss their exam results but also their position and progress. Like everyone else, Muriel was anxious about it.

Lucinda emerged from the superintendent's office crestfallen. She had, as predicted, failed her exams. Miss Haughton had discussed her leaving the hospital, but she'd been given a brief reprieve and would continue her training for another six months and then resit her exams. Failure this time would mean a definite end to her nursing career.

'I have been given one last chance,' she confided to her fellow students.

Hannah had passed with honours and would progress in her training.

Muriel was quaking with nerves by the time she was called into the office.

'Miss Gifford, I am pleased to say that you have passed your exams,' said Miss Haughton.

'Oh, that is such a relief!' she gasped, delighted that despite her fears she had managed to pass her exams.

'You must be pleased, for I know that you were ill, Miss Gifford. You must have worked very hard.'

'Yes,' she nodded, close to tears.

'Now you must decide on the next stage: whether to continue getting more experience on the wards here, or to accept nursing assignments?'

Muriel sat there, unsure.

'You are quite well again?' the woman probed. 'Are you finding the wards too much for you since you returned on duty?'

'No, I'm fine...' She trailed off.

'Physical stamina is very much a requirement of nursing and I worry if you are strong enough. Dr Stevenson said that you looked very drawn the other day and that he was concerned for you.'

Muriel wanted to refute what Miss Haughton was saying, deny it, but she couldn't. She knew in her heart that she wasn't as strong as Lucinda or Hannah, or most of the probationers for that matter.

'You have passed your exams and are a bright, intelligent young woman, Miss Gifford, but there is a doubt in my mind whether you should continue your training as a nurse by getting experience working here at Sir Patrick Dun's with us.'

Muriel sat silent. She should fight and beg, like Lucinda, for another chance to continue, but she knew somewhere deep inside that she didn't fit in. She cared deeply for her patients and for nursing them, but she suspected that she wasn't strong enough or tough enough for the day-to-day routine of nursing. Some of it she hated, no matter how hard she tried.

'We obviously hope that you will progress your nursing career, but there is no shame in not continuing,' said the superintendent gently. 'Once they have passed their exams, many of my nurses or probationers leave to get married or for family reasons, or because they simply just want to do something else. You have passed your exams and I promise that you will have a good reference as far as I am concerned.'

Muriel did not know what to say or do.

'Perhaps you can give the matter some consideration, Muriel, and we can discuss it again on Thursday. I will see you at two o'clock.'

Her friends congratulated her on passing her exams and she longed to confide in them about her situation, but she was on duty all week and had to work. She was an adult and it was her decision, one that only she could make.

By Thursday her mind was made up. The superintendent was right, and with great reluctance and a heavy heart Muriel agreed to resign officially from her probationary nurse training. Miss Haughton made it clear that, given the circumstances, there could be no refund of the fees paid by her father.

'I think that you have made a wise decision, Miss Gifford, and though you may feel rather let down about it all at present, I have no doubt that as an intelligent young woman you will continue to make a worthwhile contribution to society and your fellow man. I wish you luck in the future.' Superintendent Haughton smiled kindly as she walked her out to the corridor. 'We thank you for your service to the hospital and our patients.'

By the time she reached home Muriel was utterly dejected and tearful. She confided in Nellie and Grace about what had happened and how it had been her decision.

'I am just glad that you are home and safe and well.' Grace hugged her.

'Muriel, I've been so worried about you. For the past few months you've looked so drained and exhausted. Some days I wondered if you were even happy with what you were doing,' said Nellie, who had an uncanny knack of seeing things more clearly than most other people. 'I know it is upsetting for you, but there are plenty of other things to do in life, I promise you.'

'What will Mother and Father say? What will I tell them?'

She worried how her parents would take such news. They had been badly upset when Ada had announced out of the blue in February that she was going to live in America and that she and Ernest would sail together on the *Celtic* to New York. Then Grace's twin brother, Cecil, had decided that he no longer wanted to work for Father and left for America too. Now they faced another disappointment with the news of her decision to leave Sir Patrick Dun's.

Muriel made them both sit down as she explained the situation.

'Oh, what a relief!' gushed Mother. 'Thank heaven that you have finally seen good sense and no longer have to work in that awful place. Every time you crossed our door, Muriel, I was waiting for one of us to come down with some terrible contagion or infestation or illness that you had brought from that hospital. My poor father met his death in such a fashion, helping sick parishioners.'

Muriel was surprised by such unexpected support from her mother.

'I did warn you about the demands of such a career,' Mother added knowingly. 'Nursing is not meant for a refined young lady like you.'

Muriel could see Father taking in every word of what she had said. And then he spoke.

'It is good news that you passed your exams, Muriel dear, and have achieved some nursing qualifications and experience, which I'm sure will stand you in good stead for the rest of your life, but I agree with your mother. I too am relieved to have you home here with us where you belong. I was worried that you might be like your sister or brothers and want to work overseas, nursing in some foreign hospital. I couldn't bear it.'

'I am sad about leaving Sir Patrick Dun's,' she said, suddenly tearful. 'I thought that you would both be angry and disappointed in me over what has happened. I feel that I have let everyone down.'

'How can you think such a thing!' exclaimed Father. 'All we want, Muriel, is for you to be happy and well.'

'Muriel dear, I sometimes wonder if you know us at all.' Mother sounded puzzled as she returned to her delicate embroidery stitching. 'Honestly, Frederick, where did we get such daughters?'

Chapter 22

Muriel

Muriel felt as if a great weight had been lifted off her shoulders. She had not realized how much the day-to-day physical demands of nursing had affected her.

'I think you nurses are treated like slaves,' remarked John angrily, announcing that she intended to write an article for *Bean na hEireann* about the terrible situation young trainee hospital nurses in Ireland found themselves in. Muriel tried to persuade her to drop the matter, as people would assume she had inspired the article.

'We talk about equality for women and women's rights,' her sister persisted. 'Someone has to write about this situation. Nursing is a noble profession, but I say it is drudgery. It is not noble for a girl to work such hours, not be paid and be treated so badly, and I intend writing about it.'

Muriel sighed, realizing that John had dug her heels in and would not change her mind.

She kept up her friendship with Hannah, Lucinda and a few of the other girls, but her young doctor friend Andrew barely noticed her absence as he had already turned his attention to some new probationer.

Her eldest sister, Kate, surprised them by announcing her engagement to a Welsh man she had come to know and of whom she had grown very fond – Mr Walter Harris Wilson.

Mother took the news badly.

'How could Kate marry such a man?' she railed angrily, for not only was Mr Wilson a Catholic but, worse still, her daughter had decided to convert to his faith for their marriage in Holyhead in Wales.

'But, my dear, you too married a Catholic, and ours has been a good marriage,' Father reminded her. 'We should be pleased that our Kate has found someone to love and care for her instead of remaining unmarried for the rest of her life.'

Mother reluctantly shook her head.

'Then we will have no more of it. We will write to congratulate them and invite her to bring Mr Wilson over to Ireland to visit us.'

Muriel joined her parents for two weeks in Greystones, swimming every day, going for jaunts in the pony and trap and taking long walks. The sea air and exercise revived her spirits. When they returned to Dublin, leaving their parents behind, she and her sisters made the most of having 8 Temple Villas to themselves by hosting a constant round of lunches, dinners and parties. The house was filled with friends during those summer weeks.

They wrote to Mr MacDonagh inviting him to join them and a few friends for a long late breakfast. Muriel was delighted when he accepted. He was such good company, easy and quick-witted but with a great kindness. He was studying for a degree in Irish, French and English at University

College Dublin and his head seemed always full of ideas. They sat around listening as he regaled them with stories and told them of a new poem he was working on.

At one stage Mother and Father returned from Wicklow for two nights, as they had tickets to go to the Theatre Royal to see the world-renowned Italian tenor Enrico Caruso perform. He took his Dublin audience by storm.

'His voice is like no other,' proclaimed Mother afterwards, admitting to being moved to tears by his singing.

Father, who was a keen fan of opera, had also enjoyed the performance. 'Such a voice feeds the spirit and soothes the soul like nothing else,' he said, slowly sipping a whiskey before retiring for the night.

Muriel missed the hospital but resolved to keep herself busy. She had enrolled in Gaelic-language classes and agreed to assist Mother and Reverend Harris with their church's fundraising campaign to provide beds for a hospital in India. She also joined *Inghinidhe na hEireann,* telling Helena Molony that she was available and would be very honoured to help with anything that they were organizing.

1910–1912

Chapter 23

Muriel

Muriel slipped into her seat in the abbey theatre, nodding across at Thomas MacDonagh who was sitting only a few seats away from her. Grace had persuaded her to come along to see *Deirdre of the Sorrows*. Sadly, its author, John Millington Synge, had not lived to see its staging. He had died last March and it was left to Willie Yeats and Synge's fiancée, the actress Molly Allgood, to complete the play. As in Synge's previous plays, Muriel was glad to see that Molly was taking the lead role.

This time there were no riots or objections to Synge's play as there had been three years ago when his *Playboy of the Western World* was first staged; the audience were moved instead by the story of Deirdre's loss of her beloved and her tragic end. Muriel tried in vain to hide her emotions as they got up to leave the theatre; concerned, both Grace and MacDonagh offered her a handkerchief.

'Synge was steadfast and true, a fine writer, and I will always hold him in high regard,' MacDonagh said, glancing at the empty stage.

Muriel knew Synge had directed MacDonagh's first play in the Abbey and that MacDonagh had strongly defended *The Playboy of the Western World* and after Synge's death had written a fulsome tribute praising his life and work.

As they walked towards the foyer he told them he was engaged in writing a new play as well as a book of poetry. He always seemed to have endless energy and enthusiasm and these days their paths regularly crossed. Muriel valued his friendship and looked forward to their meetings, but she suspected as they took their leave of him that Mac-Donagh already had a romantic involvement.

She herself had begun recently to see a Mr George Murray. He was, she supposed, rather handsome and certainly most attentive. Gabriel had first introduced them, and George had invited her to a concert, then a recital, then to dinner a number of times. She enjoyed his company but found him rather old-fashioned and self-conscious. At thirty-eight years of age, with a successful insurance business, he believed that it was time for him to consider the next stage of his life – marriage, family and the purchase of a large home of his own. Muriel guessed that, even though their relationship was still at an early stage, somehow she was part of this plan.

'George is far too stuffy for you,' warned John as she and Grace joined the crowds in the Round Room of The Rotunda in March for a talk organized by the Irishwomen's Franchise League. British suffragette leader Christabel Pankhurst got a rousing welcome as she stood up to speak to them.

'Votes for women!' chanted the audience loudly. 'We want votes for women!'

Hanna Sheehy-Skeffington, the organization's founder, explained to the packed hall that Irish women must join the fight for women's emanci-

148

pation alongside their suffragette sisters in Britain as John Redmond, the leader of the Irish Parliamentary Party in Westminster, and Herbert Asquith, the British prime minister, were both equally opposed to supporting the Women's Franchise Bill.

'A woman having the right to vote is a threat to such men and their parties!'

'It is appalling that Irish and British MPs have no care for the women they are supposed to represent,' Grace declared angrily. 'That is why we must have the vote, so we can elect better people to represent us.'

John scribbled furiously in her notepad throughout the meeting. Muriel wished that she possessed such a talent. Her sister, now a well-respected journalist, had become a regular contributor to Arthur Griffith's *Sinn Fein,* the nationalist newspaper, and had introduced Muriel to Griffith, who along with his friends took them all out rowing in a boat in Sandycove. Griffith was full of praise for her sister's work.

Grace, too, was getting more regular commissions for her witty sketches and drawings, and of late had been working with Fred and Jack Morrow on some designs for new Theatre of Ireland productions.

Muriel wished that she could find something to engage and interest her in a similar fashion.

She attended a meeting of the Daughters of Ireland at which Maud Gonne MacBride, who had recently returned from France, addressed the gathering.

'I am appalled by what I have seen, the deplorable conditions that the poor children of Dublin must endure, living in such abject poverty in the slums, tenements and lanes of Dublin.' Maud passionately implored the members of her organization to rally together to help them.

'We have to feed and nourish these children. Westminster has brought in free school meals for children in Britain, but has unfortunately refused to implement the same policy in Ireland.'

Everyone was in agreement: the Daughters of Ireland would step in to provide school meals for poor children and Muriel, well used to seeing the poverty of some of her patients in the hospital clinics and wards, immediately volunteered her own services. She also persuaded her sisters to help with the meals in schools in High Street and St John's Lane when they were available.

The schools were surrounded by tall rows of run-down tenement houses. Once the fine Georgian homes of Dublin's wealthy merchants, they now lay in a state of utter decay and neglect and housed hundreds of poor families. Many were forced to live in the overcrowded, dingy squalor and filth of a single room. Broken doors, steps and stairways could be seen everywhere; sewers overflowed and there was little sanitation. Muriel wondered how people survived living in such terrible conditions.

Jim Larkin, a union man from Liverpool, had set up the Irish Transport and General Workers' Union to fight for better pay and conditions for these people – bus, rail and tram workers, factory workers, and thousands of casual workers who barely eked out a living.

The children of these city streets and lanes were dirty and hungry, sores around their mouths, hair unwashed, often dressed in rags and barefoot. Muriel's heart filled with pity for them. School was their only refuge from the filthy, crowded rooms where they lived. Their teachers helped them to learn to read and write to give them the tools of an education which might some day lift them from the hell of poverty into which they had been born.

When Muriel and Grace first came to help in St John's Lane, Grace paled as they were met by the sight of long tables of hungry children, eyes huge and staring, all waiting to be fed.

'Grace, remember they are only children like we were,' Muriel reassured her as the boys and girls noisily nudged and shoved against each other. 'For most of them this small bowl of stew is often the only meal they get.'

The children were each served a nourishing bowl of stew with meat, potatoes and vegetables on most days, and on Fridays they got rice pudding and jam. The food was provided in big containers by the Ladies Committee in Meath Street, but Maud Gonne and Helena Molony demanded that Dublin Corporation should rightfully incur the costs of the meals.

Rolling up her sleeves, Muriel accepted an apron from one of the other women as Maud Gonne helped to ladle the hot stew evenly into bowls. Studying her discreetly, Muriel could understand why men lost their hearts to her, for Maud was a truly beautiful woman, with large,

151

soulful eyes and high cheekbones, poised and elegant, and possessed of a great kindness. It was no wonder that the poet William Butler Yeats was said to adore her. She had a daughter by a French man and had been involved in a very public divorce scandal from her husband Major John MacBride and a battle over their son, but Maud made no mention of such things and instead involved herself energetically with the revolutionary organization she had founded.

Muriel and Grace helped by passing the bowls around the tables of waiting children.

'I'm starving, miss,' murmured one little girl, shoving a spoonful of food into her mouth.

'You can take your time,' Muriel promised. 'No one is let take your bowl.'

The girl looked doubtful.

'The Ladies Committee would never permit it,' Muriel assured her, smiling as she saw the child relax and actually properly taste and enjoy the meal.

She went up and down the tables, serving bowl after bowl to the children. A few of them paid a little for their food, but most could not afford it. One or two asked for second helpings which unfortunately they were not permitted.

'They are good children, but some try to bring their meal back for their families,' cautioned Madeleine ffrench-Mullen, one of the organizers. 'The meal we serve here is a school dinner, which means the parents will make sure the children attend, as these dinners are often the only form of regular nourishment some of these children will get.'

As Muriel gathered up the piles of empty bowls and spoons for washing up, she felt guilty for the life of privilege and wealth she and her brothers and sisters had enjoyed. How could families and children live in such a state less than a mile from the leafy road where she grew up?

Chapter 24

Muriel

The residents of Rathmines and Ranelagh breathed a great sigh of relief when Padraig Pearse announced his decision to move his Gaelic boys' school, St Enda's, from Cullenswood House in Ranelagh to The Hermitage, a much larger property in Rathfarnham on the outskirts of Dublin.

'We will all certainly feel safer without those young rebels in our midst,' declared Mother, who was certainly no fan of Mr Pearse's school and its nationalist educational system. Muriel did not have the heart to tell her that she had heard rumours that the Pearses were now considering opening a Gaelic school for girls in its place.

She and her sisters were delighted to accept an official invitation from Padraig Pearse to the opening of the new St Enda's in September. They were curious about the greatly enlarged school and, turning up the long, tree-lined driveway, they could not help but be impressed. The Hermitage was a rather grand, rambling granite house with a large portico, tall columns and steps, set in acres of land and with a magnificent view of the Dublin Mountains. The fresh air and country setting would be better for the boys, and they certainly would have more space for classrooms and dormitories to fit more pupils, as well as fields for sports and training.

Many of their acquaintances came along to support Padraig Pearse and his family in this new endeavour, and Padraig and Willie were both proud to show off the school's facilities. Countess Markievicz walked around declaring that this was an ideal place for her Irish boy scouts group, Na Fianna. Many of the boys from St Enda's had enrolled in it and here they would have no shortage of fields for outdoor training, drilling and activities.

As Muriel strolled around the grounds, MacDonagh fell into step with her, pointing out a tree carved with the initials of the 1803 Irish Rebellion leader Robert Emmet and his sweetheart Sarah Curran.

'Sarah's family lived nearby and they used to meet here secretly.'

'That's so romantic,' Muriel said, touching the indentations in the bark.

'Unfortunately Emmet was hanged before they could marry.'

'How sad,' she murmured. 'But this is such a beautiful place, no wonder Padraig wanted to move his school here.'

'The boys will be able to enjoy the countryside and fresh air, especially the boarders, but I'm not sure if the day-boys and their families may find the school is too far from the city.'

She was surprised to hear from MacDonagh that he had not rejoined the full-time staff of the school but would perhaps teach there only part-time.

'I am undertaking a Masters degree in English in the university,' he explained, 'so I need time to research my thesis on Thomas Campion, the English poet and composer. I also hope to concentrate on my own writing.'

She congratulated him warmly on the publication of his new collection of poetry, *Songs of Myself* which she considered very personal and suspected were based on his youth.

'You will know me better than myself,' he said quietly and Muriel flushed.

MacDonagh had been away in Paris for most of the summer and had recently moved into a small gate lodge in Rathfarnham which he was renting from Professor David Houston, a lecturer friend.

'The rent is thankfully affordable and I am happy to mostly keep my own company there.'

Muriel was puzzled, as he was usually the most sociable and outgoing of men, surrounded by friends.

'But perhaps some time I will invite you and you will come?' he suggested.

'I would like that,' she answered, meeting his eyes, both of them aware that something had somehow changed between them.

Weeks went by and Muriel had no word of him. Then, in January, MacDonagh wrote to invite her and her sisters to visit him at Grange Lodge

House. She was glad to see that his time of being a recluse was over.

MacDonagh's cottage in Rathfarnham was small and rather isolated, surrounded by frost-covered fields, a fire blazing warmly in the chilly drawing room. The house soon filled with visitors – his good friends Padraic Colum and Mary Maguire, writer James Stephens and poet Francis Ledwidge. Muriel and Grace offered to make pots of tea, while John perched herself on a cushion on the floor and engaged in a lively discussion of poetry.

'I think you are creating a new literary salon here in the cottage,' teased James Stephens.

MacDonagh, Padraic Colum and Stephens were full of setting up a new literary monthly magazine, the *Irish Review*, which they would run from this cottage and which would provide a much-needed journal of political and literary discussion for the intelligent reader. David Houston would help to finance it and Padraic offered to serve as its editor, with MacDonagh as sub-editor.

'You will be inundated with books and poems to review,' warned John, 'and with contributors.'

'And perhaps I will illustrate for you,' laughed Grace.

'All I can do is to buy the *Irish Review* and read it,' Muriel promised.

A few days later Muriel met MacDonagh again, this time at the United Arts Club exhibition of post-impressionist painters. It was the talk of Dublin, and Count and Countess Markievicz, the founders of the club, were proud to have such a fine collection of work by Paul Gauguin, Henri

Matisse, Vincent van Gogh, Henri Manguin, Pablo Picasso, Paul Signac and Paul Cézanne on display in their gallery near St Stephen's Green.

'Muriel! Come and see the Van Goghs!' urged Grace. 'And look how Paul Signac manages to paint with such colour and light.'

Muriel had to admit that she too had never seen such a wonderful collection of paintings. If this was modern art, then she certainly was a fan. She was especially captivated by Van Gogh's painting of an orchard in Provence.

'Good evening, Miss Gifford.'

Muriel smiled as MacDonagh came over to greet her. Grace had disappeared to join Jack Morrow and his group, who had just arrived. As always, MacDonagh was charming and friendly to her, telling her how impressed he was with the paintings, and the two of them chatted as they moved around to view the work together.

He introduced her briefly to his friend, Joseph Plunkett, a tall, thin, bespectacled, rather serious young man who politely shook her hand.

'Joe is learning Gaelic,' said MacDonagh with a grin. 'He is a fine writer and poet and keeps me on my toes.'

'What do you think of the exhibition, Mr Plunkett?' asked Muriel politely. 'Isn't it wonderful?'

'People think so,' he said rather cryptically, before moving away to talk to someone else.

'Some people are such heathens as far as art is concerned,' Grace complained angrily when she joined them later. 'Why would they even bother to come to the exhibition?'

'Art, like literature, should be controversial,'

MacDonagh joked.

'See that stupid fellow there with the glasses? I saw him scribbling on his programme as he was standing near me. He wrote that Picasso is an idiot and Van Gogh should be shot. Honestly, I was tempted to punch him or shoot *him* myself.'

Muriel laughed, conscious suddenly of Joe Plunkett's return clutching the offending exhibition programme in his hand as Grace threw her eyes to heaven and deliberately moved away.

'Muriel, I'm not sure if I told you that Mr Plunkett has a keen interest in theatre,' interjected MacDonagh, diplomatically avoiding any discussion of the art on show. 'He is due to act in the Theatre of Ireland's new Russian play, *The Storm*.'

'I'm sure it will be a success for you,' Muriel told him with an encouraging smile.

As they were driving home in a cab, she told Grace about the play that MacDonagh's friend Joe Plunkett was due to appear in. Grace was always keen to hear of new productions.

'Joe's father is Count Plunkett, the art historian and director of the National Museum.'

'Well, thank heaven that it's the museum he's in charge of, not the National Gallery,' quipped Grace wryly.

Chapter 25

Muriel

The letter came a few days after they had met at the exhibition. Muriel was excited when she read MacDonagh's invitation to join him for afternoon tea.

'You are very welcome to bring your sister or a friend along,' he had added politely. With little persuasion, John agreed to go with her.

That Saturday Muriel changed her dress three times. She couldn't wear the black, as Thomas MacDonagh had seen it already. The pink was too fancy, so in the end she chose her navy blue with its white lace trim, which showed off her neat waist, her complexion and red hair.

'You look divine,' John promised as they walked to the nearby tram stop.

'What will we talk about?' Muriel fretted when they reached their stop. 'What will I say to him?'

'MacDonagh is the type of man who is never short of conversation,' her sister reminded her as they approached the tea-rooms.

MacDonagh was already there, sitting at a table near the window.

'Best seat in the house,' he laughed, pulling out their chairs politely. 'I am so glad that you and your sister could make it.'

As Muriel perused the menu she noticed he was

watching her. A waitress hovered around them and took their order for cucumber and chicken sandwiches.

MacDonagh and John chatted easily while Muriel tried to keep up with their conversation which was about their mutual acquaintances Arthur Griffith and Tom Clarke.

'I used to buy the *Sinn Fein* paper in Tom Clarke's shop and he was the first person to encourage me to submit my work there.'

'Clarke may be an old Fenian, but he has the respect of all of us who know him,' said Mac-Donagh. 'His long years of being imprisoned in England have never dampened his beliefs.'

'I suspect they have made them even stronger,' suggested John. 'More radical.'

'Muriel, do you know Tom Clarke?' he asked, as if suddenly remembering she was sitting at the table too.

'I've never been to Mr Clarke's tobacconist shop,' Muriel admitted, feeling rather left out as her sister and MacDonagh seemed to have many acquaintances in common. It felt peculiar that her younger sister knew far more about the society he mixed in than she did. 'But I have often heard John speak of him and his wife Kathleen.'

MacDonagh, utterly polite, changed the subject and began to talk about the university, telling them stories that made them both laugh aloud. How he managed to juggle his study, his work on the *Irish Review,* his writing and his involvement in many organizations was a mystery.

'I hate to be bored,' he confessed.

Mr MacDonagh certainly did have a way with

160

words and a fine mind, and he was unafraid of speaking his thoughts, which was truly admirable.

John spotted some friends and went over to join them.

Muriel suddenly became conscious that they were alone, but MacDonagh began asking her about her work assisting with the school dinners and suddenly they were both chatting easily about their own childhoods and family.

'Our parents have raised twelve of us, six boys and six girls,' explained Muriel. 'They had high expectations for the education of all their children equally. Kate attended the University of Dublin and was one of its first female graduates.'

'Your parents sound most enlightened – different from many of their generation.'

'Enlightened – Mother and Father are certainly not that!' She laughed. 'They are fierce unionists loyal to the crown and the empire.'

'But they obviously do believe in the education of all their children equally and that young women must use their intelligence and talent,' he said approvingly as John returned to join them.

The teapot was finally empty and the waitress had started to clear the cake stand and their plates.

'I am afraid we must go, Mr MacDonagh, but thank you so much for inviting us,' said Muriel graciously as he paid the bill.

They walked together to the tram stop, where MacDonagh politely waited with them until their tram arrived.

As she rode home, Muriel couldn't help wondering why MacDonagh had invited her to meet him; it was quite clear he had far more in common with John than with her. Watching the houses and rear gardens of Harcourt Street and Ranelagh from the tram window, she felt disappointed, as she suspected that she was unlikely to hear from Mr MacDonagh again.

However, she was wrong...

A second letter! Muriel's heart sang as she opened the note. She could scarcely believe it. This time he was inviting her to join him on a visit to Dublin's Botanic Gardens, where they could stroll and enjoy the formal planting and the magnificent glass Palm House. She searched his letter for a hidden meaning, perusing each word, studying his handwriting. This time there was no mention of bringing her sister or a chaperone. She couldn't help smiling, deliriously happy because MacDonagh wanted to see her again.

After that they met as often as they could, often secretly at the National Gallery, at exhibitions, the museum, the National Library, grabbing every precious minute they could together. Some days MacDonagh would cycle to their road to meet her and they would walk together around the area or in the park, hoping they would not encounter anyone they knew. Muriel was aware that her parents would not approve of her relationship with such a nationalist.

At night, the theatre, concerts and visits to the Gaelic League became the perfect places for them to see each other. Sometimes when they met he wore his kilt, which Muriel found most attractive. In this traditional dress MacDonagh conveyed the type of man he was, proud of his

Gaelic heritage and not afraid to demonstrate his strong beliefs that Ireland was a separate nation from Britain. He was in favour of the Home Rule Bill, believing that an Irish parliament with its own members and ministers would be an important first step towards Irish freedom.

As her relationship with MacDonagh deepened, Muriel saw little of George and made constant excuses as to why she could not meet him, wishing that he would stop writing to invite her out.

MacDonagh was the most wonderful man and he excited her in a way no one else had. He was reckless and brave, funny and charming, and when she was with him he made her feel that she was beautiful. No one had ever told her that she was pretty or beautiful, but he told her all the time. He buried his face in her long, thick red hair, saying how much he adored it. Ever since she was a little girl her mother had made her feel ashamed of her hair, forcing her to wear it up and covered with a hat. MacDonagh laughed as he unpinned it and let it tumble and ripple around her shoulders.

'You are the most beautiful girl in the world, Muriel,' he said, 'and the wonderful thing is that you do not even realize it.'

Sometimes when she saw him in conversation with another woman she worried that he had grown bored with her. She could not help it, but at times she even grew jealous of her sisters and the attention he paid to them.

'But it's you I love,' he teased.

When she visited his cottage it felt as if they were a proper couple, cooking meals together, playing with his dog, curled up together on the couch reading. She would sit and watch him work for hours, noticing his long, dark eyelashes and the funny furrowed wrinkle he got on his brow when he was concentrating, and she loved the way he sang under his breath when he was happy.

Every day she cared more and more for him, but she knew she must keep their growing involvement a secret from Mother, who would not countenance such an arrangement. John, Grace and Nellie all knew about their relationship but she said nothing to her sister Kate, who had moved back to Dublin with her husband, Walter. Kate was the best sister in the world but had never been good at keeping secrets from their mother.

Now Muriel wrote to George to tell him clearly and politely that they could no longer see each other or correspond. In her heart she knew that she loved only Thomas MacDonagh.

Chapter 26

Muriel

In June fireworks and bonfires lit up the skies in Dublin and all across the empire to celebrate the official coronation of the new king, George V, who had succeeded his father, the late King Edward VII, on the British throne. Plans for a visit by King George to Ireland later in the summer to meet his loyal subjects had already been announced.

MacDonagh confided in Muriel as they strolled

along by the canal that he and his friends Padraig, Eamonn Ceannt and Sean Mac Diarmada were set on organizing a nationalist protest against the king's visit and Dublin Corporation's plan to make an official Loyal Address on behalf of his subjects to offer allegiance to him as it would not represent the growing nationalist view of the monarchy.

She and her sisters soon found themselves involved too, as Countess Markievicz and Helena Molony urged members of the Daughters of Ireland to join the massive demonstration to be held in Beresford Place.

'We are not King George's subjects and the Lord Mayor and his councillors do not speak for us or represent the opinion of Irish nationalists,' they declared fiercely to the crowd.

Countess Markievicz had hung a large banner proclaiming 'Dear Land, Thou art not conquered yet' across the bottom of Grafton Street, but the Dublin Metropolitan Police had quickly taken it down.

Thousands crowded on to the street, everyone pushing, shoving and shouting. Muriel was afraid she would be knocked off her feet as the crowds gathered to listen to speakers express their opposition to the visit of the new British king. She, Grace and John handed out leaflets that Helena had printed up.

Countess Markievicz defiantly attempted to set fire to the Union flag, which she had stolen from Leinster House, and Helena was arrested and imprisoned for throwing stones at a giant illuminated picture of the king and queen and for publicly calling the king 'a scoundrel'.

The demonstrations continued over the next few days and, surrounded by police, Muriel and her sisters protested outside City Hall as the city councillors tried to enter the building. Skirmishes and fighting broke out as nationalists demanded that Dublin Corporation cancel any plans for an official Loyal Address to the king.

MacDonagh teased her unmercifully when the newspaper reports mentioned 'the Gifford sisters looking like a musical comedy in their pretty pale linen dresses as they attended the demonstration'.

'What will Mother say if she reads it?' fretted Muriel.

'Mother would never read such a nationalist paper,' John assured her.

In July King George V arrived in Ireland, the sun blazing as the royal party's yacht sailed into Kingstown and anchored. The streets of the seaside town and the roads into Dublin were bedecked with bright-coloured bunting and flags, flowers and Venetian poles to celebrate the royal visit of King George V, Queen Mary and their children, Prince Edward and Princess Mary. A national holiday had been declared for 8 July and thousands of people began to line the route from early morning to welcome the king.

Muriel, Grace and John dressed quickly and carried bundles of freshly printed protest leaflets to distribute among the crowds all along the route that the royal party would take.

'I am pleased to see you girls making the effort to see our new king,' beamed Mother as they prepared to leave. 'I'm not able for such standing, but I look forward to hearing of the royal visit on your return.'

Muriel felt guilty at their subterfuge, but their mother had no idea of the circles they now moved in.

She had never seen such crowds. Thousands of Dubliners lined the coast road all the way from the pretty harbour town of Kingstown towards the city. Men attired in blazers and straw boaters, women in their white summer dresses and hats, children in light pinafores and short trousers – everyone was in holiday mood, cheering and waving flags to welcome the royal visitors. Many had brought picnics and sandwiches as they patiently waited to watch the procession of carriages escorted by the 5th Royal Irish Lancers pass before them on their journey into the city and up to the Phoenix Park.

Muriel was glad of her hat, for the sun beat down on them as they moved along distributing their leaflets. A loud cheer went up as the royal procession approached. King George waved grandly from his carriage and everyone pressed forward, determined to get a glimpse of the monarch and his entourage. As she handed out her leaflets most people did not even bother to read them, but simply tossed them away, presuming that they were suffragettes.

Her feet ached by the time they returned home. Mother and Father were both eager to hear every little detail about the royal party and the welcome the king had received. Muriel could not deny that the visit was an enormous success, for the people of Dublin had certainly taken their new monarch to their hearts.

Their only consolation was that, at the last hour, Dublin Corporation had reconsidered and cancelled the Lord Mayor's Loyal Address to His Majesty.

'A small victory, but a victory none the less.' MacDonagh looked pleased when they met later that summer's evening to stroll by the canal.

Chapter 27

Muriel

She loved MacDonagh so much, perhaps too much at times. As their relationship deepened Muriel could not imagine her life without him. She kept a photograph of him under her pillow, secretly kissing it morning and night. She had given him a studio portrait she'd had taken wearing a cream lace dress, and she cut a lock of her red hair and tied it with a green satin ribbon for him to keep under his pillow.

Her heart sang when he gave or sent her pages of his new plays and poems to read, entrusting his words and thoughts to her. Muriel carefully read every line and word so that she could offer an informed opinion, aware that she was sharing his innermost thoughts and emotions. He had gained his Masters degree and was desperately trying to find a university job.

MacDonagh wrote to her every day; sometimes the letters came twice or even three times a day. Muriel tried to intercept the postman before her parents or someone else in the house noticed. She would write by return, her heart racing as she poured her words and feelings for him on to the page. Father eventually became puzzled by how many times the poor postman came to 8 Temple Villas.

They met as often as they could, for she longed to see and speak to him and found it unbearable to be without him. She wrote and asked him to wear his kilt when they met, for it pleased her so. Was it possible to love someone so much, she wondered as she wrote to him secretly by candlelight or moonlight, then sealing each precious letter to him.

She worried about her mother and father's reaction to her romantic involvement. They would most certainly disapprove. Mother would forbid such a relationship with a man who was not only a Roman Catholic and financially insecure, but also committed to the nationalist cause and an Irish speaker. MacDonagh's family might also be very upset at his involvement with a Protestant, as his sister Mary had become a Catholic nun, taking the name Sister Francesca.

'Your family will all get used to it,' he soothed her. 'You told me your father is Catholic and your sister Kate's husband is Catholic too, so why should they object to us when I love you so much?'

In October MacDonagh proposed to her. First he wrote her a testament declaring his intention to marry her and included a lock of his thick brown hair and a penny with a hole in it. She cried with happiness. This was all she wanted, all she had dreamed of.

Then he took her out for dinner and, as they walked home, his face serious, he stopped under a golden avenue of trees and asked Muriel to marry him. She could barely speak with happiness as he kissed her and promised to love her always. He gave her the most beautiful ring, slipping it on to her finger. He had had it designed for her, along with a silver and blue enamelled cross with a moonstone at its centre and designs of the alpha and omega, a dove and flowers. No other man would conceive of such a piece and she loved him for it. With his ring on her finger, the two of them were now linked for ever.

'Muriel, I will come and talk to your father about my intentions and our plans to marry. Tell him that we will, however, wait to wed until my prospects improve and I am more financially secure and able to provide for you.'

'I don't care a toss about money,' she reassured him.

She knew that MacDonagh considered himself poor and that he worried for the future. He even talked of going to America, lecturing there and trying to find a job in a school, as Padraig couldn't afford to increase his wages.

'But please wait to talk to my father and let me judge the time to break the news to them,' she implored. 'You do not know how old-fashioned and staid and strict they really are.'

He gently kissed the tip of her nose. 'I do not believe such a kind beauty could have such ogres of parents.'

Muriel was happier than she had ever been before. Touching the beautiful ring he had had made, she felt as if he was holding her fingers. Soon she would be married to the man she loved. Mrs Thomas MacDonagh – she liked the sound of it. But what if Mother tried to prevent them marrying? She couldn't bear it. But she loved MacDonagh and she was determined that she would marry him whether they approved or not...

Chapter 28

Muriel

Muriel paced up and down in the hall trying to work up her courage to tell her parents. Mac-Donagh had insisted she tell them, threatening otherwise to arrive at Temple Villas and break the news of their engagement himself.

'You don't know them,' she had pleaded. 'You don't know how difficult my mother can be! Trust me, I need to choose the right time, find the perfect opportunity to tell them about us.'

'You have to tell them, Muriel!' urged Grace. 'Maud Gonne asked me if it was true about the engagement today when we were down serving meals at the school.'

'And Kate keeps snooping around about who is sending you all the letters,' warned John. 'Mother is bound to find out from her.'

'Very well ... but promise me you two will stay with me when I tell them,' she begged.

Muriel knew in her heart that she couldn't delay it any longer. It had been three weeks and word was bound to get out of their engagement. If her parents heard it from someone else they would never forgive her.

Returning from a meeting in Rathmines with her sisters, she decided that she could not put it off any more. Mother and Father were both sitting at the fire relaxing when their three daughters joined them.

'Perhaps I will go to my study,' Father excused himself, beginning to stand up. 'I will take my coffee there.'

'Wait, Father, stay, there is something I want to tell you and Mother.' She thought of MacDonagh as she took a deep, steadying breath.

Mother put down her cup and Father looked up, worried. 'Are you well, my dear?'

'I am well – very well indeed,' she said with forced bravado. 'Very well, for I am in love, and in fact I am going to get married.'

'Get married?' repeated Mother, shocked.

'Yes, it is very good news, for Mr Thomas MacDonagh has asked me to be his wife and I have accepted his proposal.'

'MacDonagh? Who is he? We have no knowledge of this Mr MacDonagh or of your involvement with him!' exploded Mother angrily. 'Why has there been no mention of this Mr MacDonagh before? MacDonagh – the name is Roman Catholic.'

'Mr MacDonagh is a Catholic,' confirmed Muriel resolutely. 'He is a teacher and works part-time in Mr Pearse's school, but he has recently been awarded his Masters degree from the university and is intent on finding a lecturing position.'

'That rebel school! I cannot credit that a daughter of ours would even consider involvement with any of the teachers employed there!' Mother raged. 'This Mr MacDonagh is certainly not a person we would consider fit to be part of this family, let alone marry one of our daughters.'

'Thomas is a good man and I love him,' Muriel countered fiercely. 'He loves me and I love him and I would be honoured to be his wife.'

'Mother, you and Father will grow to love him, I promise that,' interjected Grace.

'Everyone who knows Mr MacDonagh knows his kindness and good spirit, and what a dedicated teacher he is and how hard he works,' Muriel continued, determined to win them over.

'He's one of the best!' declared John loyally. 'He and Muriel are a wonderful couple, perfect for each other. You and Father will like him.'

'When did this subterfuge and secret dealing occur?' demanded Mother. 'Are your sisters involved in it?'

'There is no secret, Mother,' Muriel explained, trying not to lose her temper. 'Thomas MacDonagh asked me to be his wife a few weeks ago and I said yes.'

'It is obvious that your sisters knew but there was no thought to what your father and I may think or say on the matter – is that it?'

'Father and Mother, please! When you meet MacDonagh you will see that he is a good man and will be a good husband. We love each other

173

and want to marry.'

'We do not approve of this underhand engagement and will not countenance such a marriage,' Mother threw back at her. 'Your father and I forbid it.'

'How can you be so harsh?' interrupted John, furious.

'Now I understand Muriel's reluctance to tell you,' added Grace bitterly. 'I don't blame her for hiding it from you. I would do the same.'

'Go upstairs immediately and leave us!' Mother ordered her and John. 'This is between Muriel and your father and me.'

Reluctantly, her sisters stood up. Muriel could tell John was ready to take up the fight but she signalled for them to go.

'Muriel, it is very strange that your Mr Mac-Donagh did not even have the good manners to come and ask your father for your hand as I would expect a gentleman to do,' Mother continued. 'We have had no inkling of these plans you and Mr MacDonagh have made.'

'He wanted to ask Father but I told him not to,' she replied tearfully, 'because I knew what the reaction would be.'

'As a Roman Catholic,' Mother continued, 'he will expect you to convert and give up your own faith.'

'He has not asked me to do that – he never would.'

'Mark my words but he will,' Mother argued bitterly. 'He will expect you to be like him.'

'MacDonagh is not like that about religion.'

'All men are like that.'

'Father wasn't,' she countered, looking across the table. 'When you married, he never forced you to join his church, or any of us for that matter.'

'Your father was an exception,' Mother conceded reluctantly. 'But my family were totally opposed to the marriage and it had repercussions.'

'Then don't oppose our marriage,' Muriel pleaded. 'Please give MacDonagh and me a chance.'

'This Mr MacDonagh is not the right person for you to marry,' her mother insisted, her cheeks hot. 'Muriel, you are beautiful, bright and intelligent. There are endless numbers of young men who would love to marry you – men of position and standing and wealth instead of this teacher from that rebel school. Your Mr MacDonagh, I fear, is opposed to all we hold dear and value. How could you possibly be happy living with such a person?'

'Mother, I love him. Don't you remember how you felt, marrying Father? Despite opposition you went ahead and married him. How then can you try to stop me?'

'I knew that we would overcome such things. Your father was a man of prospects, already building his legal career.'

'Thomas MacDonagh has prospects too. He hopes to obtain a lecturing position in one of the universities and he writes the most wonderful poems and plays.'

'Poems and plays will not put a roof over your head, nor pay for pretty dresses,' responded her mother sarcastically. 'You are not used to struggle, nor have you any idea of financial penury. How could we wish our beautiful daughter to marry

175

into such a situation?'

'This is not about what you want, Mother, it's about Thomas MacDonagh and me building a life together. I want to marry him.'

Father had sat there silent for most of her mother's tirade. For once Muriel secretly begged him to stand up against his wife and not just follow her opinion. 'Father,' she appealed, 'what do you say?'

But as usual Father sat at the table saying nothing.

'Think of what people will say of such a union, Muriel,' said her mother.

'Mother, to be honest I don't care what other people say or think. I only care about Mac-Donagh and being his wife. We love each other.'

'My advice is that you immediately break off this so-called engagement,' ordered Mother.

'No, never!' she shouted. 'Why can't you both understand that I have met the man I love and I intend marrying him and nothing either of you say or do will change that! I am of age and we will get married whether you approve or not.'

With nothing more to say, Muriel left the room and ran upstairs. Only when she sat down at the table was she aware that she was shaking, but it was with a strange sense of relief that she took out her pen and wrote to MacDonagh to tell him that she had dropped the bomb and their engagement was no longer a secret.

Chapter 29

Muriel

Muriel slipped her engagement ring on to her finger where it rightfully belonged, relieved that there was no longer any need to keep it hidden in her pocket.

Mother and Father were already down at breakfast. Father was hiding behind the daily newspaper as usual while Mother slowly added some honey to her morning porridge, her lips pursed as if she wanted to say something; but neither of them said a word to her, the silence oppressive as they ate. How Muriel longed for one of her sisters to appear as she helped herself to bacon and some scrambled egg and sat down.

She was almost finished eating when she saw Father draining his teacup, preparing to leave for work.

'Mother and Father, I have invited Mr Mac-Donagh to join us here at home for tea on Sunday,' she said calmly. 'I want to introduce my fiancé to you. I am very sorry, but it was most remiss of me not to have invited him here sooner.'

Father threw a worried glance at Mother, unsure of how to react. The silence hung between them.

'Very well,' agreed Mother tersely a minute later. 'We will await his visit and the opportunity to form our own impression of this man you tell us you intend to marry.'

Muriel resisted the temptation to get entangled in another war of words with her mother and instead smiled sweetly.

'I know that MacDonagh is anxious to meet you both and will look forward to the visit.'

Father practically fled from the room, and Muriel got up quickly and excused herself. Upstairs she grabbed her things and her letter to MacDonagh, which she would post on her way into town.

On Sunday there were butterflies in her stomach. She couldn't help but be nervous about what Mother would say or do when she met Mac-Donagh. He had reassured her when they met at the theatre the previous night that all would go well – but then he did not know her mother.

Muriel decided to wear her new pale-pink silk shirt and fine wool skirt, and anxiously counted the minutes until his arrival.

MacDonagh refused to be nervous about things and was puzzled by her apprehension. He was genial and affable and got on well with everyone. He also reminded her that he was well used to standing up in front of classrooms of boys and students, giving talks and even performing on stage, so to him meeting her parents was not a worry.

But she *was* worried and had pleaded with her sisters to cancel any arrangements they had made and be home for her sake. Grace, John and Nellie all agreed to be present in case Mother erupted.

The doorbell went and Muriel braced herself for the ordeal ahead as their maid answered the door and came up to the landing to tell her that a man in a skirt was downstairs waiting for her.

Muriel flew down to welcome him. She loved it when MacDonagh wore his kilt, but somehow had not expected him to wear it today of all days. What would Mother and Father think?

'I'm so glad you are here,' she laughed as he hugged her and kissed her hand, his grey eyes sparkling. He was dressed in his green kilt with his brat, the woollen material swept up to his shoulder and held with a large engraved traditional copper brooch.

'Come into the drawing room,' she said, ushering him inside. 'The family will join us in a minute.'

'Don't fret, Muriel dear,' he reassured her, taking her hands in his. 'Everything will be fine.'

She could not disguise her trepidation as Father came in and shook MacDonagh's hand politely.

'So, Mr MacDonagh, we finally get to meet.'

'Yes, sir. I wish it could have been sooner, but at least it is happening now.'

Mother appeared a few minutes later, her eyes widening in incredulity at the sight of a man in a kilt standing in their drawing room in front of the fireplace, nonchalantly discussing his home county of Tipperary with Father.

'Do please sit down, Mr MacDonagh, as tea will be served in a few minutes.' She gestured towards the sofas and chairs.

Muriel's heart sank as he sat down beside Mother, who would without doubt interrogate him – but then she sat and listened awestruck as MacDonagh first commended her mother on her beautiful drawing room and fine taste, then even complimented her on her lace blouse.

'Now I know where Muriel gets her great beauty and sense of style from,' he said approvingly.

'I have been designing and making clothes since I got married,' Mother admitted proudly. 'This skirt I'm wearing is one I made myself.'

'What a talented lady.'

Grace smiled over at her as Nellie took charge of pouring the tea and John passed around plates of dainty sandwiches.

Thomas and Father discussed the new Parnell monument on Sackville Street, which had been unveiled by John Redmond, Parnell's successor as leader of the Irish Parliamentary Party.

'I have to agree with you, Mr MacDonagh, that Parnell's monument does not have the same presence as that of Daniel O'Connell's statue,' said Father. 'I have always felt the man was poorly treated and deserved recognition for all he accomplished.'

Mother bristled, for she always referred to Charles Stewart Parnell as the Adulterer.

'Parnell was a fine leader. Gladstone considered him remarkable,' agreed MacDonagh, 'and Asquith believed he was one of the greatest men of the century.'

Muriel smiled when she saw how he and Father were getting along, the conversation moving on to music. MacDonagh impressed both her parents by telling them about the musical composition he had written for a choir a few years earlier.

'My mother was raised in the Church of Ireland and taught the piano,' he explained, 'so choral music was always very important to her and naturally she made sure we could all play and give a good account of ourselves musically.'

'Do you still play, Mr MacDonagh?' asked Mother, curious.

'Of course. Perhaps some time I will have the opportunity to play for you.'

Mother's mouth tightened.

'I admit I'm a Gilbert and Sullivan man myself,' revealed Father, 'but Isabella and I both enjoy the opera and endeavour to go as often as possible.'

'Do you teach music yourself?' asked Mother.

'Unfortunately I don't. My field is English and French, especially poetry like Keats and Shelley. The thing I find is to create an interest with the students. I have just finished writing about Thomas Campion, one of the renowned Elizabethan poets.'

An hour, two hours passed quickly.

'I have to say, when Muriel and I first visited the National Gallery I had no idea about her family connection with Sir Frederick Burton and his wonderful collection of work.'

Muriel had to stop herself from smiling as Mother took the bait and, leaning forward, began to tell him the complete history of her beloved uncle.

It was getting late when MacDonagh apologized and said that, sadly, it was time for him to leave.

Muriel held her breath, waiting for Mother to say or do something that would wreck the pleasant ambience they had enjoyed.

'I do hope that you will permit me to call again,'

he ventured, his grey eyes deadly serious.

Mother hesitated, taken aback by his forthright request and all too aware of what such an agreement would mean – perhaps even a grudging acceptance of him as part of her daughter's life.

'Mr MacDonagh, I'm sure that can be arranged,' she said coldly, remembering her opposition.

'MacDonagh, please do come to visit again soon,' begged John wickedly.

Muriel accompanied him out to the hallway. She felt as though she was walking on air as he held her.

'This is only the first step, darling girl,' he teased, 'on our long road together.'

Watching him walk along Palmerston Road, she gave silent thanks that the enormous hurdle of meeting her parents had finally been overcome.

Chapter 30

Muriel

Muriel's happiness was complete when, in December, MacDonagh was offered a position as an English lecturer in the National University, a position that he had so craved. He immediately accepted it.

'This means we can get married without delay,' he said excitedly. 'Now my income should be sufficient to support a wife and family. You will be marrying a respected lecturer in the English department instead of a poor teacher. Let's organize our wedding and marry straight away if that is what you want.'

'You know that is what I want,' she replied, hugging him and holding him close.

Father and Mother congratulated him when he told them about his appointment. Mother was an inveterate snob and Muriel knew that having a son-in-law who was a lecturer in the university sounded far better than a teacher!

Theirs would be a small wedding at the start of the new year. Mother was upset that the wedding would be held in the local Catholic Church on Beechwood Avenue.

'Why can't it be in our church where we always worship?' she persisted.

'Because this is what Thomas and I have agreed,' said Muriel firmly, refusing to budge.

'Then promise me that you will not convert,' Mother urged. 'I could not bear it.'

'Mother, I will follow my own beliefs,' Muriel reassured her.

The MacDonagh family were finding the fact that Thomas was marrying a non-Catholic difficult too. His older sister Mary – the nun Sister Francesca – though she was delighted for them, had expressed her concerns and reservations about their religious differences when Muriel went to see her.

'Our wedding will be a small affair,' Muriel told her with a smile, 'but we hope both families will attend.'

MacDonagh talked about continuing to live in

Grange House Lodge in Rathfarnham once they were married, but while Muriel liked visiting the remote countryside lodge, she could not imagine it being their home.

'It is so quiet and peaceful here,' he enthused, 'and the rent is very manageable.'

'But it is too quiet, too peaceful and far too lonely,' she said ruefully. 'I like visiting the lodge when you are here and there are friends calling and visiting, but what about when you are away?'

MacDonagh was the type of man who couldn't sit still and was always busy and active, involved in all sorts of things that took him away from home. She considered the cottage much too isolated a place to live.

'I would be far too nervous to stay here alone, surrounded by woods and fields,' she explained. 'What if we had a child – how would I manage?'

MacDonagh wrapped her in his arms protectively and promised her that they would find somewhere else to live closer to town, the university, their friends and family.

They found a perfect little flat on Upper Baggot Street, one of Dublin's busy areas, above Hayes, Conyngham & Robinson's chemist. They had a large sitting room, a tiny kitchen, a good-sized bedroom and a cold, leaky bathroom on the landing.

Despite her objection to their marriage, Mother was curious to see where they were going to live, so Muriel brought her to see the flat. She was nervous, making sure that everything was clean and tidy as her mother inspected their first home.

'It is charming – better than I expected. You

have good taste, Muriel, and no doubt will soon furnish it and make it your own.'

'Thank you,' she said, delighted with her mother's rare compliment.

'However, I could not help but notice that you are short of silver spoons and forks and servers. There are plenty at home. Also, there are lots of things in the china cupboard that I will not use again. Perhaps they may be of use to you and Thomas when you are entertaining. I will let you have them if you wish.'

'Thank you, that would be lovely, Mother.'

'Some of the plates and dishes are from your grandmother's side of the family,' Mother went on. 'I would like to see someone in the family use them.'

Muriel smiled. Perhaps MacDonagh had been right. In time Mother would come round and learn to accept their marriage.

The night before her wedding, Muriel read and re-read MacDonagh's latest letter. She loved the way he constantly wrote to her, expressing his true feelings in a way most men never would. His words were always heartfelt and romantic.

'Tomorrow begins life for us ... my darling.'

She loved him so much and could hardly believe that in only a few short hours they would make their vows and be husband and wife.

She wore a cream lace dress with a warm, lined matching jacket and a pearl and floral headpiece with a short veil.

'You look wonderful!' exclaimed Grace, passing Muriel her wedding posy, which was tied with a blue ribbon.

'Topping!' grinned her brother Gabriel.

'You look like a film star,' John gushed as she dressed for church.

'You are a beautiful bride, Muriel dear,' Father said as they drove in the carriage to the church. He squeezed her hand when they saw MacDonagh nervously waiting there for her. He was dressed in his kilt, just as they had planned. Padraig was to be his best man, but she could see no sign of him.

Mother, in her grey wool suit and hat, sat ramrod straight in her pew in the church, as if the very devil were about to attack her.

Father walked Muriel slowly up the aisle as the organist played. They could wait no longer for the best man, so Canon Hogan asked a parish workman to stand in his place. When Muriel repeated her marriage vows and gazed into Mac-Donagh's serious grey eyes she knew this was the happiest day of her life and that she was marrying the man she truly loved.

MacDonagh slipped the wedding ring on to her finger as they promised to love each other for the rest of their lives.

They enjoyed a small wedding breakfast in the Russell Hotel then went to Woodenbridge in Wicklow, where they stayed for five days on their honeymoon. The weather was cold and damp but neither of them cared as they walked and talked and sat by a blazing turf fire, and fell even more in love.

Chapter 31

Muriel

Marriage was bliss. She and MacDonagh living together, sharing everything, heart, soul and spirit – Muriel had never known such happiness. The tread of his footstep on the stairs was enough to make her smile. She loved their small flat, with the fire blazing in the grate and their large settee and cushions; it felt as if they were two birds in a cosy nest. MacDonagh had immense energy and, though busy at the university, still found time to edit the *Irish Review* and to write his own plays and poetry. He wrote a poem for her called 'A Song for Muriel'.

She knew that he valued her opinion of his work and was immensely proud of his writing and the fact that often she was his first reader.

Nellie had given her a cookery book and insisted on showing her how to cook some basic tasty dishes, as she had never cooked at home.

'You won't have a cook or a maid,' her practical sister warned, 'so you have to learn to cook, Muriel!' She even gave her a special leather notebook to write recipes down in. 'I always find that helps and before you know it you will have a collection.'

They were near to Findlaters, Grocers and Providers, and over the weeks she tested out cooking on their temperamental stove, managing to destroy an expensive roast of beef and burn a rice pudding, one of MacDonagh's favourite desserts.

'I will learn,' she promised him, determined to be a good wife and hostess.

Grace had given them a set of serving dishes and two of her paintings, while Claude and his wife had given them a set of pretty crystal glasses and Mother had provided a glorious dinner service which Muriel fully intended to use.

MacDonagh gave her a housekeeping allowance and one day, shopping on Grafton Street with Grace, she saw the most divine hat in a shop window and could not resist trying it on.

'You must buy it!' urged her sister, who was purchasing a new lace blouse herself.

Muriel studied herself in the mirror and had to agree the wide-brimmed hat was exquisite. Impulsively, she found herself purchasing it.

Three days later she realized that she had no money in her purse to buy milk or butter or meat, and had instead made scrambled eggs for their dinner. MacDonagh looked puzzled when he saw his plate.

'I'm so sorry, but I have no money left to buy food,' she apologized. 'I spent it all.'

'Spent it all?'

'I bought a beautiful new hat,' she confessed, waiting for him to get angry and shout at her.

Their finances were scanty to say the least, and MacDonagh's own plans to purchase a new bicycle a few weeks ago had been cancelled as he could not afford it.

'Walking will do me no harm,' he'd said with a

smile, even though he had lost his deposit. And now here she was, frittering away his precious income on an unnecessary frivolous item. What kind of wife was she?

'Go and put on your hat,' he urged gently.

She returned nervously, wearing her new millinery creation, and he swept her up in his arms and kissed her, telling her that she was the most beautiful creature he had ever seen and that her hat was magnificent.

'You must have a portrait done wearing your new hat,' he insisted and the next day they went to photographer Roe McMahon's studio in Harcourt Street where he paid for her to have a photograph taken wearing it.

Muriel was overcome by the fact that she had the kindest, most romantic and generous of husbands.

Their small upstairs flat soon became a place filled with friends, many dropping in after the theatre or a concert, a ceili or a lecture. Sundays became their evenings at home. MacDonagh welcomed everyone with open arms and James Stephens, George Russell, Padraic Colum, Mary Maguire, Padraig Pearse and a host of other friends, as well as her sisters and his brothers, all regularly called in.

Discussions and arguments raged, with opinions on everything: plays, poetry, politics. The new Home Rule Bill – would it be passed or not passed; the shortcomings and inadequacy of the Bill and unionist opposition; how the glory days of the Abbey Theatre were gone, its programme now mostly peasant plays... MacDonagh sat in his armchair, in his element in the midst of it all, his friend Joe Plunkett – returned after months away in Algiers – by his side voicing his own strongly held opinions.

Muriel made cakes and scones and stews, and provided cheese and homemade bread for their visitors. As she and MacDonagh looked after their guests there was often music, songs and stories, and she sat and listened as new poems, plays and prose were read and debated in their small literary salon. She was entranced as she listened to their friend James Stephens read from his remarkable new novel *The Crock of Gold*.

The April newspapers were filled with the tragic story of the *Titanic*. The great passenger liner built in Belfast had sunk following a collision with a giant iceberg as she crossed the Atlantic on her maiden voyage. Muriel could not out it from her mind. MacDonagh held her and comforted her in the middle of the night as she dreamed of hundreds of men, women and children drowning in the icy Atlantic seas with no one to hear their cries or to rescue them.

'Hush, my love. You are safe here with me,' he soothed.

MacDonagh was not only busy with lecturing and with his work on the *Irish Review*, but was also excited as he watched rehearsals of his new play, *Metempsychosis*, which was being staged by the Theatre of Ireland. All their friends came to see it and support him, but Muriel knew that he was disappointed when it garnered mixed reviews, with some of the audience unable to understand its complex theme and dialogue.

'You must continue writing for the stage,' she encouraged him. 'You are a wonderful playwright and even the critics say your work shows great promise.'

Their happiness was complete when she discovered that she was going to have a child. Mac-Donagh lifted her off her feet, swinging her around with excitement at the thought of being a father. She knew that he'd be a wonderful father and prayed that she would be a good mother too.

'I want us to have lots of children,' he teased, 'like in your family.'

'Twelve children!' she protested. 'I cannot imagine it. All of us here, cramped together in our little flat.'

'Then five or six – that is a good number.'

'Let us wish for a child that is well and healthy and strong,' she said seriously. 'That is all I ask.'

'Already you are a beautiful mother,' he said, softly reassuring her.

Chapter 32

Isabella

Isabella sat enjoying afternoon tea in the garden with her daughters. This summer their roses were at their best, heavy with scent and in full bloom, while the herbaceous border was filled with towers of tall hollyhocks, pink foxgloves, pretty perfumed stock and blue lobelia.

'I heard the suffragettes attacked Prime Minister Asquith and John Redmond on their way to address a meeting here about Home Rule,' she sighed, sipping her tea. 'It is a miracle that poor Mr Redmond only has a cut to his ear and was not more seriously injured, as apparently two of them flung an axe at their carriage, and others planned to set fire to the Theatre Royal where they were due to speak.'

'It was a small axe thrown by two British suffragettes,' retorted Sidney defensively. 'They were only trying to persuade Mr Asquith and Mr Redmond to agree to amend the Home Rule Bill for Ireland to include votes for women.'

'Committing such an act of violence against the prime minister is certainly no way to get attention,' Isabella countered angrily. 'Only last month that Sheehy-Skeffington woman and her friends smashed the windows of the GPO, Dublin Castle, the Custom House and City Hall for their so-called cause. Those women are a disgrace.'

'Mother, how can you not support the cause of women's suffrage,' Grace chided her, 'when you have the six of us?'

'Do you not think we all deserve to vote?' pressed Sidney.

Isabella had to admit she was rather taken aback. Her daughters had a point, for they were exactly the kind of young women who demanded to vote and, she suspected, would be most unwilling to kowtow to any man and blindly follow his political beliefs.

'Of course you do,' she found herself agreeing. 'Women of intelligence, education and means deserve the right to vote, but I do not approve of using violence to obtain it.'

'Mother, sometimes women must stand up and fight for what they believe in,' expounded Sidney, getting up from her wicker chair to go inside.

Isabella said nothing. She suspected that both Sidney and Grace were involved with the suffragettes. She had seen them regularly talking to Hanna Sheehy-Skeffington and her journalist husband, Frank. The couple lived nearby and by all account were agitators.

'Don't mind Sidney,' said Muriel soothingly, moving slightly into the shade. 'Being a journalist, she's so intense about everything!'

'How are you feeling, my dear?'

She and Frederick had welcomed the news that Muriel and her husband were going to have a child and that they would be grandparents again.

'A little tired, especially when I have to carry the messages up the stairs.'

'Then you must rest,' Isabella advised. She had noticed that Muriel was rather drawn and pale, but her daughter was very much looking forward to motherhood.

'You need to get MacDonagh to help lift the messages,' teased Grace.

The following week Isabella and Frederick left for Greystones and Isabella was glad that Muriel and her husband had agreed to join them for a week. Escaping the city and taking the fresh sea air was most reviving and would do her daughter good.

By September, however, Muriel's legs and feet seemed puffy and there was a slight blue shadow under her eyes and around her mouth. Isabella could not help but be concerned for her daughter; she had noticed while on holiday that even a promenade along the seafront seemed to tire her.

Dr Kathleen Lynn was called to see Muriel and admitted her to the Rotunda Hospital, saying that her condition was of great concern and that she needed complete rest until the birth of her child in November.

Desperately concerned, MacDonagh spoke to Isabella and Frederick, worried about Muriel staying in their Baggot Street flat all day alone while he worked, so Isabella insisted that her daughter return home to Temple Villas to stay with them. Dr Lynn discharged her from hospital on condition that she had bed rest and care, with no walking, lifting or housework. Isabella knew that Thomas was deeply concerned for his wife and unborn child, and the most sensible solution was that Muriel was entrusted to the care of her family.

'She will have complete rest and all her meals served to her and will be totally cosseted,' she persuaded him. 'Muriel's health and wellbeing is paramount to all of us.'

MacDonagh agreed. He would remain in the flat and Muriel would return home.

She was pale and very unwell, both her legs swollen, the pregnancy taking a huge toll on her as she lay resting in her bed in her old bedroom.

'I'm sorry to be a bother to everyone,' she apologized.

'We will have no talk of that,' chided Isabella as

194

she fussed around fetching her cologne and books.

'I'm afraid I do not feel much like reading,' Muriel sighed, 'but I do want my pen and writing set so I can write to MacDonagh.'

'Of course, my dear, though I do believe he will call this evening to visit you.'

Her son-in-law visited every day, and Grace, Sidney, Nellie and Kate did their best to entertain their sister and lift her spirits. Grace and Sidney played card games and amused her with their day-to-day goings-on and gossip. Essie fussed over her as if she were a child, making her hot milky drinks and nourishing broths, while Isabella visited her room a few times a day to check how she was feeling.

'Mother, I am quite well,' Muriel tried to reassure her. 'I am resting and doing all I have been told to do. I just wish my baby would be born soon.'

'The baby will come when it is ready,' Isabella informed her. 'They always do.'

However, as the days went on her concern for her daughter heightened. Despite the rest, Muriel seemed exhausted and drained, often sleepy. The doctor and nurse called regularly to check on her blood pressure and general condition.

Isabella herself had enjoyed a strong constitution during each of her pregnancies, a trait she had inherited from her mother, Emily, who had borne nine children, and her grandmother Emily, who had married her grandfather Captain Claude Hamilton Walsh at sixteen and went on to have twenty-three children, including twins. However, she and Frederick had lost their first child at birth

– a pale little thing that had not breathed. She had collapsed with grief and despair.

It was Frederick who had held her in his arms and, despite her sobs, promised that in time there would be more children. The birth of each of their sons and daughters had been a blessing – though she admitted she was never much taken with the day-to-day care of babies or small children and instead was happy to trust them to the care of their nanny.

She constantly promised Muriel that soon she would deliver a healthy baby and all would be well, but she could not shake off a niggling fear that her daughter might follow Frederick's poor mother, who had not long survived his birth.

There was immense relief throughout the household when Muriel gave birth to a healthy boy in November. The baby was christened Donagh after his father, to whom he bore a strong resemblance. MacDonagh, to Muriel's delight, wrote a beautiful poem for his newly born son.

Muriel and MacDonagh were both overjoyed with their baby and were keen to take him home, but within only a short time, much to everyone's shock, she became very unwell again. Seeing her condition, the doctor ordered her to remain with her parents. Frederick insisted they hire a nurse to help with the care of the new baby and attend to Muriel.

Christmas came and went and Muriel continued to stay with them, far too sick to return home to their flat. Poor MacDonagh was beside himself with worry and felt guilty that he could not help more with his wife and child.

'She and the baby are safer staying here with us,' Isabella had to tell him as the old year passed and a new one began.

Gradually her daughter's health improved and she slowly began to recover. Her baby boy, now known by everyone as Don, was thriving.

'He's going to be a lively young lad,' Frederick laughed as he held him in his arms.

'I cannot wait to bring him home,' said Muriel, who was getting stronger day by day.

Isabella thanked heaven as she watched the little family pack up to leave and return to their own home a few weeks later, Muriel proudly holding their baby in her arms as her devoted husband helped her into the carriage.

1913–1915

Chapter 33

Nellie

Dublin basked in the dog days of late summer and Nellie took an early tram into Sackville Street (now O'Connell Street). She needed to purchase a sturdy pair of walking shoes and a few aprons before returning to work in Meath next week. She would get off at the Nelson's Pillar stop, as it left her closest to Tyler's boot and shoe shop and MacInerney's Drapery on Henry Street.

The tram had barely crossed over the bridge on to Sackville Street when, without warning, the crowded passenger vehicle came to a grinding halt in the middle of the street.

It must be some kind of mechanical failure, for Nellie could see the tram driver and conductor were standing outside on the street, agitated, talking. Then she realized that all the other trams around them on Sackville Street had also come to a halt, some in the middle of busy junctions. No doubt a fault with the electricity system. Was it safe, she wondered anxiously.

There was confusion among the passengers, but suddenly their conductor returned briefly to inform them of the situation.

'We are on strike!' he announced defiantly. 'Mr Murphy and the Dublin United Tramways Company have forbidden us from joining the Irish

Transport and General Workers' Union and threaten us with dismissal if we do join. Mr Murphy has sacked forty men who worked for his newspaper for joining the union and now he wants to sack us too. We are all on strike until the matter is resolved.'

'Young man, what about getting to the horse show in Ballsbridge?' enquired a grey-haired man. 'Will those trams run?'

'There are no trams or transport in the city.' The conductor shrugged. 'If you want to get to the horse show you'se will have to walk or take a carriage.'

As she got off the tram Nellie felt only sympathy for the tram-workers, who were rumoured to be poorly paid and treated. She hoped that the tram company would deal fairly with their employees and resolve the dispute. Later, having completed her purchases, she was fortunate to find a horse-drawn cab to take her home.

By the next day the trams were running on schedule again, manned by new relief workers. The strikers were now protesting against the employment of scab workers by the tram company.

Dublin was in a strange state of unease as the tension between the tram company and other businesses and their workers throughout the city worsened. William Martin Murphy and the city's other large employers were united in their hatred of Jim Larkin, the union leader, and his demands for improved pay and conditions.

'Don't go into town,' warned Father. 'The police are expecting trouble with all this union business. They've been ordered to keep the trams

202

running for the Dublin Horse Show and there may well be fighting and disturbances.'

'Nellie, do say you'll come to the party in Surrey House this evening,' cajoled John. 'Count Markievicz has just returned from Poland today and the countess is having a big party to celebrate. Their parties are always splendid affairs.'

'It will be fun with the three of us together,' agreed Grace.

A party with her sisters would most definitely be fun and Nellie was delighted to show off the new cream silk dress she had just purchased in Arnotts. Grace urged her to wear her beaded headband too. John was in her usual blue satin, while Grace wore a striking layered chiffon dress that she had designed and made herself. She was obsessed with style and creating an individual look, and she pirouetted in front of the bedroom mirror for them.

'You'll turn heads tonight,' Nellie teased.

'Well, that is the intention!'

Satisfied, they set off for Surrey House, which was only a few minutes' walk away on Leinster Road in Rathmines. The three-storey red-brick building was all lit up, its windows flung open on such a warm summer's night, and the music playing inside could be heard from the road.

As they approached they noticed a group of Dublin Metropolitan Police officers standing outside the house, watching it and the comings and goings of guests.

'Why are they here?' Nellie asked.

'The Castle hate Madame – they keep her

under watch at times,' whispered John. 'They know she's a supporter of Larkin and his union.'

Count and Countess Markievicz's housekeeper, Mrs Delaney, opened the door to them. She was like a guard dog, protective of the countess, and for a moment Nellie was aware of her steely gaze raking over her; however, as John had become close friends with her mistress, she welcomed them warmly inside.

The party was in full swing, the house thronged with people, abuzz with noise and laughter. Countess Markievicz, dressed in a purple lace gown with some kind of feathers in her hair, immediately came to welcome them, telling them that Casimir, her husband, had just returned from Poland and the party was in his honour.

The house was full of books. They were everywhere – on tables, shelves and sideboards and stacked on the floor. The walls were covered with paintings, for the countess, like Grace, had studied at the Slade and was a very fine artist. A portrait of Constance Markievicz by her husband hung on one wall, while a human skull sat on a shelf close by it along with bronze busts of Robert Emmet, Wolfe Tone and Henry Grattan. Stage posters, programmes and scripts littered a circular table in the corner.

Grace and John introduced Nellie to lots of artists and theatre people – she was delighted to meet a few of her favourite actors.

Helena Molony was there and Nellie found herself chatting to her as her sisters, along with the countess, lit up their cigarettes and smoked. She had tried cigarettes herself a few times and found it vaguely pleasant but was not a huge fan of tobacco. Con Colbert, a friend of Mac-Donagh's who taught in St Enda's and helped train Countess Markievicz's boys in the Fianna, came to join them and entertained them with a story of their recent camping trip up in the Dublin Mountains in July.

'We camped in tents and the boys had lessons in scouting and orienteering, and even did a bit of fishing. The countess is a powerful shot and told the boys about how she grew up hunting all kinds of birds in her home in Lissadell in Sligo. She showed some of the older boys how to shoot.' He laughed. 'I swear I never saw anything like it, for the young fellas must have shot every poor blackbird, crow and thrush in the place.'

Countess Markievicz chatted easily to her guests, but often moved to the window where she would stand for a few minutes, smoking her cigarette as she watched the policemen grouped outside her home. Nellie also noticed that their hostess seemed rather distracted and kept disappearing off into another room. A burley young man seemed to be standing guard outside it, while drinks and plates of food were brought in and out of it by the housekeeper.

A handsome young man played the piano and there was singing and later some dancing, which everyone joined in. Grace was off talking with her coterie from the United Arts Club, in a heated discussion about Hugh Lane's annoyance at the opposition to the audacious new art gallery, designed by Edwin Lutyens, which he proposed be built straddling both sides of the River Liffey.

William Martin Murphy and many members of Dublin Corporation were objecting to the plans, as the city was expected to foot half the costs while Hugh Lane paid the other half.

'Lady Gregory will support it and has raised some of the funds for the new venture, but a decision must be made,' said the countess.

'The city needs a proper new gallery that will garner attention,' insisted Casimir. 'Yeats says a refusal of Hugh Lane's grand plans will discourage a whole generation of artists and leave Ireland considered a huckster nation.'

Most of the guests at the party agreed with him. Nellie said nothing. She liked the view up the River Liffey and did not think replacing the Halfpenny Bridge with an art gallery that blocked the view was the right thing to do. Surely it would be far better for Dublin Corporation to tear down some of the city's appalling slum dwellings and instead invest in some decent housing for the poor instead of a gallery? But then she was no artist!

It was late when they finally said their goodbyes. As they thanked her for the party, Countess Markievicz expressed relief that only a solitary DMP man could be seen loitering near a tall hedge.

'Perhaps his friends have finally gone home for the night. But I fear that they will be back in full force in the morning. John, promise me that you will all return here to the house to join us for breakfast in the morning,' she urged anxiously as they hopped in a cab for the ride home. 'I will explain the situation to you then, as I have a very special secret guest and may have need of my friends here...'

'Of course we will come,' John assured her as they took their leave, all curious as to what the next morning's visit would bring.

Chapter 34

Nellie

Arriving at Surrey house on Sunday morning for breakfast, Nellie could see the DMP men were already on duty watching the building.

Mrs Delaney quickly ushered them inside to the dining room, where they found Countess Markievicz in a slightly agitated state, smoking as she paced up and down the room. A tall man was sitting in the chair watching her. Nellie immediately recognized Mr Jim Larkin, the union leader. Now the reason for subterfuge was clear, for the DMP were searching the city for Jim Larkin. There was a warrant out for his arrest for sedition and disturbing the public peace by raising discontent among His Majesty's subjects.

'Jim has been staying here secretly,' confided the countess. 'Hiding him here among our crowd of friends, we decided, was the best way to confuse the police, but today we need to move him, for he has promised to talk at a workers' rally on Sackville Street.'

Only two nights ago Larkin had spoken to thousands of people in Beresford Place, tearing up the legal document banning the meeting, telling the crowd that he cared as little for the king as he did for the magistrate who issued it.

'Jim is set on talking to the workers again today and won't think of letting them down,' explained Helena Molony, who was also present, 'though getting him out of here is going to be difficult as the house is under heavy surveillance.'

Countess Markievicz made sure she introduced Jim Larkin to everyone.

'This young lady is Miss Nellie Gifford. She is a sister of John and Grace.'

Nellie felt the union leader's strong fingers grip her hand.

'Are you an artist too, Miss Gifford?'

'No, I teach cookery,' she said, suddenly embarrassed by the practical, mundane nature of her work compared to her sisters. 'I give domestic courses in towns and villages outside Dublin.'

'Then you must get to see all walks of life on your travels around the countryside.'

'Indeed I do,' she said with a smile.

She could see understanding in his long face before he was called away by another guest.

As she drank a cup of rich coffee, Nellie couldn't help but worry how exactly Jim Larkin would avoid arrest once he stepped outside the safety of Surrey House, but he made it very clear to everyone in the room that he fully intended to keep his promise to his union members to speak on Sackville Street at midday. But surely he must know that both the Dublin police and the Royal Irish Constabulary would be there in full force, ready to arrest and imprison him?

Plans were afoot to transport him secretly, with

talk of hiding him inside a funeral casket in a hearse, but unfortunately no undertaker could be found who would agree to provide one.

'We have to somehow get him to Sackville Street without being recognized,' the countess appealed to them.

Nellie took in the striking six-foot-four figure with his strong features, long, distinctive nose and his Liverpool accent. She suspected that unless he *were* hidden in a funeral casket it would be nigh impossible.

'Our only hope is to disguise him, like we do with actors on the stage,' suggested Helena. 'We could use wigs and make-up and a costume to transform him.'

'Do you think it would possibly work, Helena?' the countess asked seriously.

'Yes, maybe. To carry it off Jim must acquire a different persona. Then hopefully he can be safely transported from here to Sackville Street without being recognized by those awful police. An elderly gentleman, perhaps in the care of a relative – a daughter or a niece... Jim cannot talk or utter a word at all in case it gives the game away.'

Larkin listened to their plan. Realizing that there was no alternative, he agreed to wear some kind of disguise. Gussie McGrath was sent to book two rooms in the Imperial Hotel under the name of Donnelly, with a request that the rooms have a balcony overlooking Sackville Street so that Larkin could talk as intended to the crowd below.

The transformation of Jim Larkin into an elderly gentleman would be undertaken by Helena, who, as an actress, was well used to theatrical make-up.

Countess Markievicz fetched the boxes of wigs and theatrical props that she and her husband used for their own stage productions. The count, who was almost as tall as Larkin, searched his own wardrobe for something for the union leader to wear.

'Who will accompany Mr Larkin to the hotel?' worried the countess.

John, excited by the adventure, immediately volunteered.

'I'm afraid, my dear, that you, like Helena and myself and most of us here, are far too well known by those hound dogs that sit outside the house or at Liberty Hall and so are used to seeing you visiting me.'

John then suggested Grace.

'I'm not much of an actress,' admitted Grace, who far preferred painting backdrops and sets or making costumes to being on stage.

'My dear, I'm also afraid you are far too striking and well known to take on this venture,' agreed the countess, who had witnessed Grace's lack of stage ability in her own plays.

'What about my sister Nellie?' suggested John. 'She's certainly not known to the police.'

All eyes turned to Nellie. She blushed. She would have liked to strangle John there and then for volunteering her.

'Nellie, would you be willing to accompany Mr Larkin in this risky endeavour?' asked Countess Markievicz, coming over to her. 'You could be of great help and service to us in this dangerous plan.'

Nellie was conscious of everyone watching her

and awaiting her response. She held the renowned union leader in high regard and very much believed in his cause, but attempting to fool the DMP was a different matter... Then, pushing all caution aside, Nellie decided that despite her misgivings she would at least try to help him.

'Yes,' she found herself saying. 'I'll accompany Mr Larkin.'

'Thank you, young lady,' he said as Helena whisked him upstairs to transform him.

About fifteen minutes later a stooped, elderly gentleman of the church in a silk hat, long black frock-coat, high collar and striped trousers walked slowly down the stairs. His thick, dark hair was now coloured grey, and he had a grey-white beard and moustache, bushy grey eyebrows and wore gold-rimmed glasses. Lines had been painted on his face and brow to age him.

'Perfect!'

'I can't believe it!'

They all gasped as he stood before them, for Jim Larkin had been utterly transformed. He now looked smaller and much frailer. He was now Reverend Donnelly, a country rector, up in Dublin for a medical appointment at the hospital.

It was coming near midday, so a cab was ordered and they were given two pieces of luggage. Just before Nellie got ready to leave, Helena quickly handed her a pair of horn-rimmed spectacles and a floral-patterned shawl.

'Put these on, Nellie,' she advised. 'The glasses, like Jim's, are for the stage and you must try to make sure you hide your hair well up under your hat.'

Nervously slipping on the glasses and shawl, she joined the other guests, who were all filing outside, saying loud goodbyes to the Markieviczs and thanking them for breakfast as the cab arrived.

'Be careful,' whispered the countess as Nellie helped Larkin into the cab and gave instructions for the driver to take them to the Imperial Hotel. Larkin, lost in contemplation, remained silent during the journey.

Nellie's hands began to tremble when she saw that a crowd had already gathered in expectation of his appearance on Sackville Street and prayed that none of his union members or those that frequented Liberty Hall would recognize him. The Dublin Metropolitan Police formed almost a cordon around the Imperial Hotel and her heart froze as she wondered how they could possibly pass them.

The cab driver came to a halt outside the hotel and she immediately paid him, dismounting from the cab as the driver fetched the two suitcases. She could see a DMP man staring at them as Larkin slowly and rather erratically began to climb out, keeping his face down. The cab driver rushed over to give his elderly passenger a hand.

'It's all right, Uncle,' she said soothingly, taking his arm firmly, and Larkin gave her a reassuring squeeze as the cab pulled off.

'Sir, what is your business in this place?' enquired the DMP man and his fellow officer.

Larkin said nothing, his eyes downcast, his features unchanging.

'I'm afraid my uncle cannot hear you, Officer.

212

He is deaf,' Nellie replied on his behalf, 'very deaf.'

'Are you visiting this hotel?'

'My uncle is booked to stay here for the next few nights. He's in Dublin to attend medical appointments at the hospital tomorrow,' she explained slowly, trying not to shake.

'I'm sorry to hold you up,' the officer apologized, stepping out of their way. 'It's just that we are expecting a bit of trouble today with the strikers.'

'My uncle and I wouldn't want to be caught up in that.' Nellie smiled weakly as a hotel porter took their luggage and she helped Larkin slowly to the desk, where she checked him in. Another DMP officer stood observing the desk as she dealt with the clerk.

'We have reserved rooms,' she stated, doing her best to appear confident.

'What is the name, please, madam?'

Nellie stood frozen with sudden panic. She had totally forgotten the name and she knew that Larkin dare not utter a word lest he gave himself away.

'Sorry, madam – what name is your reservation booked under?' the clerk persisted politely, trying to be helpful.

She could see the policeman looking over towards them.

'Reverend Donnelly and Miss Donnelly,' she blurted out, suddenly remembering.

Her heart was hammering as they went slowly up the stairs, Larkin holding her arm. Relief washed over her as a curly-haired porter opened first one door and then another to a room overlooking the street and deposited their luggage inside.

The door firmly shut, Larkin immediately went to the long, tall window to see the street below where the crowds were gathering. He went to open the balcony door to step outside, but the window wouldn't open fully as a large flower planter was positioned outside on the balcony.

'This is no good!' he shouted. 'I need to get into another room.'

Nellie watched as he ran frantically along the corridor to see if he could find an open room. At the far end was a dining room with windows that overlooked the street and a veranda-type balcony. Guests were partaking of Sunday lunch and coffees when Larkin rushed through. Realizing that he was too well disguised to be recognized by the crowd outside, he began to peel off his beard and whiskers and shake the powder from his hair as he went outside on to the balcony. Nellie slipped back into the bedroom in case he returned.

Watching from the window, she heard the crowd give an enormous roar as Jim Larkin stepped outside and began to address them.

'Comrades and friends, the police have forbidden a meeting to take place on Sackville Street today, but I am here to speak and will remain till I am arrested...'

All traces of the elderly Reverend Donnelly were gone and Larkin's voice boomed as he spoke to the workers and poor of Dublin below.

Nellie grew alarmed when, from the window, she saw about a hundred members of the police armed with batons suddenly converging. A few ran directly towards the entrance of the hotel. A few minutes later she heard a huge commotion as Larkin was arrested, with people protesting and some cheering for the union leader.

She heard the sound of broken glass and watched, horrified, as the crowds below swelled with people coming from mass in the Pro-Cathedral. Suddenly they were surrounded by a huge group of policemen, who with raised batons began to charge. Appalled, she realized that many were just women and children out for a Sunday stroll. Panic ensued as they tried to run away to escape the riot and many innocent people were attacked and injured, beaten by the police until they lay down on the ground.

Nellie could not help shaking. She had never witnessed such a terrible thing – young and old screaming in terror, many left lying bleeding and wounded on the street. Fearing for her own safety, she hid the spectacles and shawl and fled from the room just as the police began a search of the hotel corridor for Larkin's accomplice. The stairs were blocked by policemen so she turned instead to join the crowd of guests on the dining-room veranda, hoping not to attract attention.

However, ten minutes later two policemen stopped her, saying they wanted to interview her about Larkin. Nellie tried not to give into the mounting panic she felt, but despite her protests of innocence she was led away for questioning.

There was sheer bedlam at the police station; crowds of people had been arrested. Sitting in a police cell, she was determined to give little away. When she was interviewed she gave her name, her employer's name and told them she was lodging in Meath at present. She suspected that if she gave her home address in Rathmines they might well connect her with John and the countess. She concocted a story that she had simply gone to the hotel to meet a friend for lunch when mayhem broke out below them on the street.

'No wonder she left me high and dry – she must have been terrified, like we all were, by what happened,' she said tearfully.

The officer looked rather sceptical and asked her if she had any involvement with Mr Larkin's union. 'No, I'm not a member of the union or associated with it,' she replied truthfully.

With no proof of her wrongdoing, Nellie was eventually released.

When she returned home hours later she heard from her sisters that Jim Larkin was in jail and that there had been a huge amount of fighting and violence on the streets. Countess Markievicz, who had driven into Sackville Street, had got caught in it too and had been injured by a blow from a policeman and needed medical treatment.

The violence continued throughout the night, while the police raided homes all across the slum areas of the city. Hundreds of innocent people were hurt and two men died from injuries they received from the police. Many were calling it 'Bloody Sunday'.

Nellie could not put the awful scenes she had witnessed from her mind. She feared greatly for Jim Larkin and the strikers, and for their families now caught up in this battle for fairness and justice.

Chapter 35

Nellie

Nellie returned to work in Athboy in County Meath the next week, lodging with a poor family who eked out an existence selling eggs; she felt glad that her rent payment would provide some income to them. She was still haunted by the sight of the charging police using their batons on unarmed civilians. So much blood and terror. The situation in Dublin was worsening, from what she could gather, as more workers decided to join the strike and the employers became even more entrenched in their opposition to the workers' union.

Nellie was called to a meeting with her supervisor. As she dressed in her green tweed suit and white blouse she wondered why she had been summoned. Perhaps he wanted her report on the new stove: it was proving much easier to use for her demonstration lessons than the previous model, which had been more cumbersome to move by cart from place to place and most definitely suffered temperature problems.

'Miss Gifford, please sit down,' gestured her supervisor, Mr Hughes.

'You will be glad to hear that my new stove is working perfectly,' Nellie smiled. 'It is proving an excellent model.'

'That is good to hear,' he said, making a note in his book. 'However, I'm afraid that is not the issue I wanted to discuss with you.'

Of late her employers had complained that she was too familiar with the families with whom she lodged and she had been reprimanded for attending a local wake; it was considered inappropriate, given her position. They constantly reminded her that she must keep a professional distance from those she was instructing.

'I'm afraid, Miss Gifford, the issue of providing free items of food to those that attend your demonstrations and classes must be raised again,' Mr Hughes said peevishly.

'It is only tasting samples and leftovers,' Nellie defended herself stoutly. 'Where am I to store this food, Mr Hughes? No family would thank me for storing it in my room and encouraging rodents. It's far better to distribute food remainders to those who have attended the class demonstration.'

'But you are aware of our concerns over costs in this regard?'

'Of course, and I will endeavour to reduce the ingredients I use.' She hoped the offer would satisfy them. Petty rules and regulations – how she hated them. At least her superiors could not reproach her about her work, for her classes and demonstrations were well organized and attended, and there were certainly no complaints from any of her students.

'Miss Gifford, there is another matter I need to raise with you. A member of the DMP contacted us to verify your employment with us,' Mr Hughes continued ominously, tapping his fingers on the mahogany desk. 'They said that you were considered a person of interest by the police in relation to the recent incident with James Larkin, the union leader in Dublin.'

Nellie's stomach turned over. She certainly had not expected this. Most of the newspapers had carried the story of Larkin's entry into the hotel and his arrest but had been unable to identify the young woman involved, some claiming it was an actress of his acquaintance from Liverpool, others suggesting Helena Molony.

'Were you questioned about the said incident, Miss Gifford?'

'Yes, I was interviewed, as were many other hotel guests,' she admitted, trying to make light of it. 'I happened to be having lunch in the Imperial Hotel at the time and was questioned by the DMP. I assure you that I was released without any charge.'

'Do you know this Mr Larkin and approve of his trade union?'

'I approve of the union's stance,' she said resolutely. 'But I fail to see what this has to do with my work.'

'It is just another concern,' he responded pompously.

Nellie sighed as the meeting finished and she took her leave.

A week later, much to her dismay, she received an official letter to say that her services as a rural domestic instructress were no longer required. Packing her bags, she returned home to Dublin.

Chapter 36

Nellie

Nellie found Dublin a changed place, with poverty-stricken men and women roaming the docks and factories looking for work that would help to feed and keep their families.

William Martin Murphy and most of the city's employers, determined to break the union, had come together to form a Federation of Employers that agreed to 'lock out from working' any of their employees who joined the transport union. Guinness's Brewery, Jacob's Biscuit Factory and Eason's, Dublin's large newsagent and bookseller, closed their doors firmly against their own workers unless they totally renounced membership of Larkin's union. Nellie considered it disgraceful, shameful behaviour by privileged, powerful men and their companies against the weak, vulnerable and poor. They were all using temporary scab labour, protected by the police, to break the strike, as their workforce stood firm and refused to back down.

In only a few short weeks 'the Lockout' had had a profound effect on Dublin as fear, hunger and poverty gripped the strikers and their families. Nellie volunteered immediately to help in the union headquarters, Liberty Hall, working alongside Countess Markievicz in the soup kitchens that had been set up by James Connolly and Larkin's sister Delia to feed those who were destitute and 'locked out' from work.

'Thank you, dear girl, for joining us,' Countess Markievicz welcomed her, attired in a long apron as she helped to mix up a stew of meat, vegetables and potatoes in an enormous cauldron for the strikers and their families. 'I was sorry to hear from John about the loss of your position,' she sympathized. The countess was in charge of the Women and Children's Relief Fund and Nellie had heard rumours that she was covering some of the costs of the soup kitchen from her own allowance from the Gore-Booth family estate in Sligo and by selling some of her valuable collection of jewellery. She was full of her usual energy and enthusiasm, her hair pinned up, smoking one cigarette after another as she organized food for those that needed it.

Nellie set a young woman named Rosie Hackett and the girls locked out of Jacob's and other factories to cutting up ingredients in the union's kitchen. The crowds that attended seemed to grow day by day as people became even more desperate. All their meagre possessions – chairs, tables, blankets, bedding, clothes and what little else they had – they had pawned or sold to raise some cash, but now that too was gone.

Every day in Liberty Hall Nellie saw gaunt, worn-out women trying not to eat in order to pass on their own food to their husbands and children.

'What can we do?' she fretted. 'I saw Annie Lynch almost fainting with hunger, passing her bowl of stew to her three sons.'

221

'We must have a separate area for mothers to sit and eat on their own to ensure that they receive adequate nourishment,' insisted Countess Markievicz.

Jim Larkin was in prison, but James Connolly, a committed socialist born to Irish parents in Scotland, was equally devoted to the cause of workers' rights and had assumed Larkin's mantle, determined to help the twenty-five thousand striking workers and their desperate situation.

'A fair day's wage for a fair day's work is all the workers want,' Connolly complained angrily.

But the employers continued to harden their hearts to their demands, determined to break the men, women and their union.

Following an appeal by the Irish transport union, their comrades in the British trade unions sent much-needed funds; they also generously sent ships over from Liverpool with food parcels to aid the strikers. It was a sight to see, the crowds gathered all along the quays in Dublin, cheering as the ships docked and they were each issued with a docket to receive a food parcel, everyone bolstered by the fact that their fellow workers on the other side of the Irish Sea were demonstrating support for their stance.

As autumn turned to winter, conditions for the strikers and their families worsened. Ragged children ran barefoot in the streets searching for food scraps or lumps of coal for the fire; for in the tenements and slums there was no fuel to warm them, no food to feed them and very little clothing to keep out the chill of winter days.

The union had plans to bring the children of strikers to stay with the families of English union workers for a holiday, but the Catholic Church had come out forcefully against the scheme. The opposition came from bishops and priests fearful of Protestant influence, so the children were prevented from boarding trains to the Dublin docks and the ships that could take them to England.

Thomas MacDonagh offered to do an interview with James Connolly for the *Irish Review*, the editorship of which had been taken over by Joe Plunkett. They wanted Connolly to give the workers' side of the story and his thoughts on how they could break the deadlock.

Tom Kettle, a professor friend of MacDonagh's, set up the Industrial Peace Committee, calling for a truce between the two sides. MacDonagh and Joe Plunkett joined him in his efforts to make peace. But Jim Larkin and William Martin Murphy were two stubborn, strong leaders and despite their best efforts, MacDonagh told Nellie, it was impossible to reach any kind of agreement.

At rallies and protests strikers and police clashed, and James Connolly suggested that the union set up an army of its own made up of the striking workers – a citizen's army, formed to provide self-defence. Captain Jack White, who had served in the British army, offered to train the men in the grounds of Croydon Park, which was used by the union as a recreation centre. Even though they were armed only with hurling sticks and bats, training and drilling kept the men active and gave them something to do.

Liberty Hall was open every day, thronged with

the needy, and Nellie worked tirelessly alongside the countess and Hanna Sheehy-Skeffington, Larkin's sister Delia, Rosie Hackett and the other girls from Jacob's to help as many people as they could. Here she did not have to hide her feelings or pretend to be something she wasn't. Here she could put her training and experience to good use.

Grace frequently came to Liberty Hall to help too, but poor Muriel was unwell again and had been admitted to a nursing home, while John had been laid low with some awful kind of eye infection which left her hardly able to read a book or write.

'Oh do tell me what happened today,' John would beg when Nellie arrived home, exhausted. Her sister was bored and desperate for news, wishing that she was well enough to work alongside them.

'A young woman went into labour today in the queue and we worried that the baby would be born in Liberty Hall,' Nellie told her. 'Fortunately, one of the women is a midwife and they managed to bring her to a nearby flat where she delivered a healthy baby boy – but what terrible times for a baby to be born into.'

'How different your day was to mine,' John sighed enviously. 'My eyes are too sore to even read a few words and Mother had one of her afternoons and insisted that I join them. All they do is gossip and complain about the Lockout. Not the same service in the shops and hotels. Impossible to get proper workmen or seamstresses. Do you know that they actually blame the workers?'

'I'm presuming you tried to enlighten them?' teased Nellie.

'Mother would have killed me. That awful friend of hers that lives in Dartry was saying what a wonderful man William Martin Murphy is; apparently they are neighbours. The worst thing was, they were all agreeing with her, including Mother. Can you believe it, Nellie?'

'Unfortunately Mother and her friends do not take well to change – any change.'

'Then Dorothy actually asked me if I had a beau in front of them all. She said a young woman my age should be giving consideration to marriage.'

Nellie burst out laughing.

'It was terrible. I excused myself and said that it was time to bathe my eyes and put in my eye drops.'

'Mother's friends are always the same when they see either Grace or me.'

'Honestly, sometimes I think of going away to America like Ada and leaving all this nonsense behind.'

'Well, at least wait until your eyes feel better,' Nellie cautioned.

'Why are you always so sensible!' John declared, giving her a hug.

Nellie also visited Muriel as often as she could in the nursing home on Baggot Street, calling in quickly on her way home from Liberty Hall. Her sister hated being unwell and separated from her little boy and her husband. In November she was moved to a convalescent home near the sea in Sandycove. When the weather permitted, Nellie would cycle out to visit her.

'You are looking much better,' she said encouragingly, relieved to see that the pale, gaunt look had given way to a healthier colour now that Muriel had more energy and a better appetite.

The two of them strolled arm in arm along the seafront by the beach and rocks, breathing in the iodine-scented sea air. They stopped to watch two seals.

'They remind me of the stories of the selkies that Bridget used to tell us when we were young,' said Muriel.

'She was always a great woman for the stories.'

'I must show them to MacDonagh when he comes to see me on Sunday. Hopefully the day will be dry and we can take a stroll together.'

'He misses you terribly, you know,' Nellie said gently. 'It must be hard for him managing with the baby and work and everything.'

'Thank heaven he's found a lovely woman, Mrs Kelly, to mind Don while he is at the university. It is just that he is always so busy with the *Review* and his writing, and now he tells me he has joined up with Eoin MacNeill in the Irish Volunteers, a new group committed to Home Rule.'

'Everyone is talking about the huge meeting they held in the Rotunda – apparently thousands of men turned up and enrolled. They could hardly fit them all in the building.'

'MacDonagh had flu so he missed the meeting, but Eoin and his friends were all delighted by the response, with so many men from the Gaelic Athletic Association and all kinds of places and groups joining. The Irish Volunteers intend setting up more branches in different parts of the country. You know MacDonagh – he is already elected on to the committee.'

'He's always a great man for organizing and doing things,' Nellie agreed.

'He's excited, as this new Volunteer force will help protect Home Rule and ensure that it's implemented fairly with a proper Irish parliament here in Dublin, which he believes will be the first step towards Irish freedom. Edward Carson and his mob of Ulster Volunteers may be sworn to do all in their power to prevent it, but now they will have the Irish Volunteers to contend with.'

'Will the Volunteers train and drill like the Citizen Army?'

'I expect so.' Muriel shrugged. 'I just wish that I was able to be of more help to him instead of being such a burden with my illness.'

'Well you are getting better now,' Nellie consoled her, 'and soon you will be home again.'

'I feel my strength and energy returning and hopefully I might be home with MacDonagh and the baby in another week or so. Did I tell you that Mother has invited us for Christmas dinner?'

'Well there is something for us all to look forward to.' Nellie smiled as she said goodbye to her sister and set off to cycle back to Rathmines.

Chapter 37

Nellie

The Gifford family enjoyed a traditional Christmas at Temple Villas, with everyone delighted to have Muriel, MacDonagh and baby Donagh join them for lunch. Don had just started to take his first baby steps and tottered around the house, holding on to couches, chairs, table edges and any available hand that was offered. Muriel, wearing a pretty new lace blouse, clapped with joy as he reached for her. She was still perhaps a little too thin, but to everyone's relief seemed to be almost herself again.

Nellie, unable to resist a wooden ark in the window of Lawrence's Toy Shop, had bought it for Donagh and knelt on the floor showing him all the wooden animals. Claude, Ethel and their son Eric had also joined them and Father was delighted to watch his two grandsons playing together.

The fire blazed and the table was laden with baked ham, a goose and a turkey, plum pudding, brandy butter and custard. Everyone was dressed up in their Christmas finery. As they sat around playing charades and singing their favourite carols, Father and Gabriel, Claude and MacDonagh argued about the passing of the Home Rule Bill in the coming year.

'The British House of Commons and House of

Lords can no longer delay it, and we will see it implemented next year, mark my words,' nodded Father.

'Carson and his Ulster Volunteer Force will never accept it,' insisted Claude. 'They are pledged to stop Home Rule and are armed and ready to fight if it is introduced. They will never accept a Dublin parliament.'

'Well, the thing is that we have our own Irish Volunteers now,' MacDonagh reminded them, 'and they are ready to defend Home Rule if necessary.'

Nellie knew that her brother-in-law was wisely keeping his deep involvement with the Irish Volunteers a secret from her parents and brothers.

'Well, Home Rule or not, let us hope that 1914 will be a better year for everyone,' declared Father as they all raised their glasses in a toast.

The New Year brought heavy snow, the avenue of plane trees along Temple Road white, the paths and roads icy as freezing weather gripped the countryside. Nellie's thoughts turned to all the families that were locked out: how would they endure such terrible weather in the tenement buildings they lived in? She needed to get back to work.

Before leaving early in the morning, she grabbed a basket and began to fill it with jars, packets of tea, sugar and flour from their well-stocked pantry, praying that no one would notice what was missing.

'Ahhemm...' She looked around to discover Father watching her quietly from the door.

She froze – caught in the act... She wondered if she should return the items.

Suddenly Father stepped into the pantry beside her and began to take more jars and cans from the shelf: potted shrimp, Bovril, vegetable broth, corned beef, tinned sardines and herrings. He put them in another basket along with a fruit cake, a small plum pudding, oaten crackers and a freshly baked brown loaf.

'Wait here a minute,' he told her.

He returned with a large block of cheese and two pieces of smoked bacon. 'Take these too.'

Nellie pulled on her boots and heavy, fur-trimmed wool coat and hat, then grasped the baskets tight as she gingerly walked through the snow to the tram stop. She would call at the Lynchs and the Murphys before she went to work at Liberty Hall for the day.

The children were playing on the step outside the run-down tenement building, making snowballs with their hands, chasing each other, their breath hanging in clouds in the cold air. Nellie trudged up flight after flight of the rickety stairs, her nose wrinkling at the awful smells of humanity. She knocked on one door and delivered half the food to Annie Lynch and her family. Behind another door, Lil Murphy lay in bed in the corner of the room with a bad chest infection; her husband thanked Nellie for thinking of them as she handed him a basket.

She shivered with the cold despite her warm coat as she walked back down through the building with its broken windows, peeling plaster and hole in the roof, and she wondered how much longer these people could hold out against the Federation of Employers.

Snow, cold and hunger made for bad bedfellows, and Larkin and Connolly also worried how much longer the strikers could possibly endure such misery. Even the union's ability to continue strike pay was now in jeopardy. The food shipments from Britain's unions were about to end and the British Trades Union Congress had refused to sanction and implement the sympathetic strike policy that the ITGWU had hoped for.

Everyone in Liberty Hall knew that Larkin and Connolly were desperately trying to negotiate better terms with Mr Murphy and the city's other employers, but their efforts were to no avail. A special meeting was held in mid-January in Croydon Park and Nellie's heart broke as Jim Larkin, trying to control his own emotions, addressed the huge crowd of workers and advised them that the time had come for them to accept that they must return to work. After that, he told them, they should try to negotiate a fairer deal with their employers. Shocked, they listened, aware that the fight was over – for they could continue it no longer. They had been beaten by poverty, hunger and cold.

In dribs and drabs they returned to work, many feeling defeated and let down, but with no other option. Nellie watched, relieved, as the numbers attending the soup kitchen in Liberty Hall finally fell and as February passed most had resumed their jobs in Dublin's warehouses, factories, trams and docks. A few employers agreed to some improvements in conditions and pay, but many insisted that on their return the workers give up their union membership.

The union was nearly broken, but James Connolly believed that a new spirit had been born between the workers: they had shown a strength, courage and sense of unity never seen before, something they could build on for the future.

'Hold your heads high,' he told Rosie Hackett and the other girls from Jacob's as they put away their aprons and went back to Dublin's huge biscuit factory.

As the men returned to work, membership of the Citizen Army decreased and by spring it was decided to disband it as it was no longer necessary. But Larkin and Captain White decided that it might yet have a new role, so they reorganized it to become an army for the people of Ireland, open to all who believed in fighting for equal rights.

It seemed strange to see the kitchen nearly empty, the large dining halls no longer in use. Nellie was aware that she too must begin the search for a new job for herself. She was surprised when James Connolly asked her to consider working in Liberty Hall, giving cookery lessons to teach women and young wives how to feed their families with nutritious, low-cost meals. This time it would be a proper job with a rather modest salary, giving two or maybe three classes a week.

Nellie didn't have to give the matter any consideration, for she knew that she would relish the chance to continue working in Liberty Hall. She had come to love the old building on Beresford Place overlooking the River Liffey. She was pleased to accept and thanked James Connolly for this unexpected opportunity.

Chapter 38

Muriel

Muriel finally felt that she was returned to good health, and MacDonagh told her every day that he loved her and cared for her and that she was even more beautiful than ever. He also bought her a present – a wonderful box camera.

'You can learn to use it yourself,' he said and he taught her how to insert the film, adjust the focus and capture an image within the box.

Muriel was entranced, and she took photographs of the baby and of her husband and family, pleased with the results.

Her sisters invited her to join them at the Irish Women's Franchise League's Daffodil Day Fête in Molesworth Hall.

'Everyone will be there. I am helping with the set for the *tableau vivant*,' enthused Grace.

MacDonagh insisted that she join them and offered to mind little Don for the weekend.

Muriel received a warm welcome from Helena and all her friends. Many, like her, had enrolled at the beginning of April in Cumann na mBan, or the Irishwomen's Council, the new women's group that would work alongside the Irish Volunteers and which now included most of the members of Maud Gonne's Daughters of Ireland.

For the 'Tableau of Famous Women in History', John had been chosen to play the brave Anne Devlin, the staunch young nationalist who had supported patriot Robert Emmet and had been tortured and imprisoned for her beliefs.

'At least I don't have to speak on stage,' she grinned, her eyes sparkling dramatically. 'I just have to look suitably broken but sad and strong.'

'I told them that I am much better with a paintbrush,' said Grace, who had refused to play a part.

Nellie had volunteered as usual to help organize refreshments for the large group over the two days.

Muriel soon found herself roped in by organizer Hanna Sheehy-Skeffington to play the part of Queen Maebh in the tableau.

'Do say you will do it, Muriel dear. You are perfect for the role and everyone is giving a hand.'

Hanna could be very persuasive and before long Muriel had agreed.

She studied her costume – a long purple robe and a torc-type crown, with a huge Celtic brooch on her shoulder holding her flowing cloak of green. Countess Markievicz handed her a wooden spear and a cardboard shield to carry on stage. Muriel wasn't at all sure this was what the legendary warrior queen, Maebh of Ulster, would actually look like; she suspected the colour of her hair was the only reason she had been selected to play such a part. She would have far preferred to be Florence Nightingale, but that role had gone to someone else.

Countess Markievicz was playing the warrior

Joan of Arc and she certainly fitted the part in a suit of armour she had fashioned out of linoleum that had been painted silver; it looked very effective with high boots, some kind of fitted legging and a sword. Everyone clapped wildly when she appeared.

'I could imagine her on a battlefield leading an army,' whispered Grace, who had helped her with the costume.

The sight of Joan of Arc – this time played by Kathleen Heuston – being burned at the stake brought gasps from everyone as they watched her silent demise amidst the flames.

The tableau got a generous reception from a large female audience who were pleased to applaud their favourite heroines.

'It makes a difference to see women instead of the usual male heroes,' said Nellie approvingly, watching her sisters trying to remain perfectly still on stage.

Later the group turned their attention to discussing the important issue of women's suffrage and Home Rule for Ireland.

The countess told them that there were three great movements going on at the same time – the national movement, the women's movement and the industrial movement – but she believed that they were in essence the same movement, because they were all fighting the same fight for the extension of human liberty. Everyone agreed wholeheartedly, with Muriel, like her sisters, proud to be part of it all.

The fête ended the next day with a Cinderella Ball, at which the Women's Orchestra provided the music and Muriel got up to dance with her sisters and friends, all laughing and spinning around the hall together.

MacDonagh had minded the baby and she could tell when she returned home that he was distracted.

'We've had news that the Ulster Volunteers have got guns,' he sighed heavily. 'They have landed thousands of guns and rounds of ammunition at Larne and Bangor.'

'Why would they do such a thing?' she asked, alarmed.

'Now Carson and his men are armed, the Ulster Volunteers will not budge on Home Rule. They are openly arming to fight it and us every inch of the way in order to stop it.'

'But parliament and the prime minister have promised us that Home Rule for Ireland will come.'

'Parliament will not be able to stop a force that is heavily armed and trained and prepared to defend the north of Ireland,' he explained. 'Without rifles we cannot expect to stop Carson and his Ulstermen's demands to be governed by Westminster rather than Dublin. The Irish Volunteers may need to arm too if we want to defend Home Rule.'

'But how would you afford such weapons?'

'We would have to fundraise, not only here but in America.' His eyes were serious.

'And what happens if you are both armed?' she asked, worried.

'Then I'm afraid there could be a war between

236

us, as we both want different things. We want an independent Ireland with our own parliament here in Dublin, and the unionists want to be governed by Westminster and to have nothing to do with us.'

Muriel felt suddenly afraid, frightened by her husband's talk of guns and fighting and war. She went to look at their small son sleeping in his cot. MacDonagh was an intelligent, bright man. Surely he and his fellow Volunteers would never let such a thing happen?

Chapter 39

Grace

Grace stood on the busy quayside with her parents, waiting for her sister to board the boat to Liverpool. John's luggage was stacked neatly to one side, ready for a porter to collect it. Grace still could not believe that her youngest sister was moving to New York. Admittedly John had often talked about going away to work, but Grace had always presumed that it was just idle chatter and that she did not really intend leaving Ireland. Then John, with great bravado, had shown them all her ticket for America.

'I want to work in New York,' she announced. 'It's such a big adventure, but I can stay with Ada until I can afford a place of my own.'

'Why are you going away?' Grace asked,

puzzled, for John was a well-known journalist with plenty of work on papers and journals like *Sinn Fein*, the *Irish Citizen* and *Irish Freedom*.

'Grace, I know that I am fortunate to write for popular papers, but do you know how many million people live in New York and the rest of America? How many papers and journals and magazines they have there?'

Grace shook her head.

'I have a hunch about going to America and trying to make my name in journalism over there. Tom Clarke has given me a list with some useful contacts of his from when he and Kathleen were living there, and he has written a letter of introduction for me to John Devoy, the editor of the *Gaelic American.*'

Grace knew that John had always been the ambitious one, craving attention and notice with her mimicry, her sharp tongue and lively wit. Now she was ready to take on New York – a very brave step, one that Grace was not sure she would have the courage to take herself. Perhaps a part of her had hoped that her sister would ask her to join her on this great adventure, but John had made it clear she was going on her own and Grace was certainly not a part of her plans.

'Promise that you'll write and tell us everything. Ada is hopeless and hardly ever writes any more.'

'Of course I will,' John promised. 'I'm not like her.'

Father kept checking his fob watch as if they were waiting for a tram.

Her parents had objected to John's decision to move, but she had informed them that she had

more than enough in her bank account to purchase her own ticket and was going with or without their permission. She knew Mother found it
very difficult that her youngest daughter was
leaving home to live so far away.

'Don't fret, in two years I will return,' she
promised them.

Mother looked thin and anxious, fiddling with
her gloves as the other passengers began to move.
Father seemed older and smaller as the horn
sounded and John set off towards the wide gang-
plank. Grace supposed it must be hard for them:
Liebert away at sea; Ernest and Cecil living in
America and Canada; Gabriel in London; and
now even Claude and Ethel had become inveterate travellers, moving between Ireland and
Canada. Ethel had some family connections in
that country and her older brother had decided to
set up a legal office there. Ada was settled in New
York, and now John... Poor Mother and Father.
The Giffords were scattering across the world.

Suddenly, in a swirl of perfume and kisses, her
sister was gone, joining the rest of the passengers
as they began to board.

They stood for an age watching until the ship
had left the quays and was moving out of Dublin
Bay and into the Irish Sea, Father and Mother
desperately trying to catch sight of John as the
boat continued to gain momentum and sail away.

The house was quieter without John. Now only
she and Nellie were left at home. When she was
younger Grace used to long for peace and quiet
and wished that she had been part of a smaller

family. Now the house seemed rather lonely, as Nellie spent most of her time in Liberty Hall. So Grace buried herself in work, determined to make her own name. She was printing and selling some of her caricatures and sketches and had recently exhibited in the United Arts Club, which had helped her to get some commissions.

She studied a pen-and-ink drawing she had done for the *Irish Review*. She would let it dry and later post it to the editor, Joe Plunkett, in the hope that it would be printed and she might receive some payment. She regularly sent him work and was getting used to his letters either accepting or rejecting her drawings.

He and MacDonagh were now involved in another new venture together, setting up the Irish Theatre Company. Joe would provide the theatre, an old hall in Hardwicke Street that his mother, Countess Plunkett, had bought that needed renovation. MacDonagh would manage the performances and Edward Martyn, who had fallen out with William Butler Yeats at the Abbey Theatre, would provide the money and write some of the plays. It was all so exciting and Grace was delighted to be asked to design a poster for them. She showed the strange, crooked figure of an old man standing looking in at the new theatre, a figure reminiscent of those who featured in the plays of the other theatres – the theatre of old now, being confronted by a newcomer with a very different programme of plays. Her brother-in-law and Joe Plunkett told her that they planned to produce up to fifty plays a year, which would mean plenty of design work for programmes, posters and stage backdrops. Jack Morrow would most likely get the lion's share, as he regularly worked with Joe and MacDonagh, but Grace would certainly try to get some more work from them.

She was friendly with Jack and his producer brother, Fred, as they were both very involved with the theatre and with staging pageants. Of late she often found herself in the company of their brother Norman, who was also an artist. She would invariably end up talking to him, smoking a few cigarettes with him or sitting beside him at a play or dinner. Norman worked mostly in London but was a regular visitor to Dublin and she found him entertaining company with his stories of the London art world and his work.

'One time I was asked to design the costumes for a big pageant about health and germs that Fred was directing. We had Mr and Mrs Microbe. What do microbes look like? I asked myself.'

'What a task!' Grace grinned.

'I was inspired and made two great big ugly trolls with masks and we had little children running away from them on the stage. I promise you, I had no idea about Lady Aberdeen at the time.'

'You are wicked!' Grace burst out laughing, for Lady Aberdeen had earned the sobriquet 'Lady Microbe' for trying to banish TB from Ireland.

Norman enjoyed dining out and was always good company. As five of his brothers were artists, he seemed to know everyone in the art world. Striding into a room in his rather theatrical style, he would make her smile as he tried to persuade her to move to London to work so that they would be nearer to each other.

241

'Norman, I'm happy here and have some work,' she protested, but she had to admit Dublin seemed always a little quieter while he was away.

Chapter 40

Isabella

Isabella inspected the dining table. The cut glasses and crystal decanter sparkled against the crisp, white linen tablecloth, an arrangement of garden roses at the centre. She had checked that all was in hand with their new housekeeper Julia's preparations in the kitchen. The lamb was roasting, the prawns in aspic were setting on ice in the cold room, the soup was made, the salmon ready to be served. For pudding there were twelve individual lemon possets in their glass serving dishes and a rich cream and apricot layered pastry tart to which Frederick was always partial.

Everything was in good order as Isabella went upstairs to dress before their guests arrived. To-night she would wear the pale lavender-coloured silk dress which was based on a French design; Frederick said it made her look *'très jolie'*. Fixing her hair with a pretty mother-of-pearl comb, she made her way downstairs to wait for their guests.

They had invited three of Frederick's dearest legal friends and their wives, her friend Henrietta and her husband Albert, and their neighbours Jerome and Iris Quinn who lived only a few houses away from them. She greeted each guest warmly as Julia took their wraps and jackets. Iris and Jerome were the last to arrive.

'How is it the closer one lives to one's hosts, the later one always seem to be?' apologized Jerome as they joined everyone in the drawing room.

Isabella smiled to see that the conversation was already in full flow, which she considered a good omen for the rest of the evening. The men all stood together while the ladies sat in a group, laughing gaily. At the signal from Julia, they led their guests into the dining room.

'What beautiful blooms, Isabella dear!' exclaimed Dorothy Pearson.

'The roses are all cut from our garden.'

'You must have green fingers,' put in Dorothy's husband William, who was Isabella's dinner companion.

'Frederick is the one with the green fingers,' she confessed. 'He seems to be able to grow anything. This year we've had the most exquisite camellias and peonies, and he is growing tomatoes and plums for our table.'

Frederick flushed with pride as he accepted compliments, while Julia began to serve the prawns in aspic jelly decorated with cucumber and dill, and the wine was opened. Isabella kept an eye on everything to ensure that it was proceeding as expected. Soon the soup appeared, then the salmon followed and people discussed holiday plans.

'We intend to retreat to a lodge in Kerry where there is good fishing for Robert,' contributed Florence.

'We are back in Wicklow as usual, but now we go only for the month of August,' said Isabella, noting that the lamb was served perfectly pink, with a mint jelly made from their own garden mint. The men all went for second helpings but the ladies politely declined.

As the main course was cleared, Isabella felt she could relax.

'What are the sentiments with regards to this Government of Ireland Bill that the House of Lords has just passed?' asked Edward Whitestone.

'Can you imagine a nationalist-run parliament in Ireland?' responded William testily. 'Ulster at least has been given a chance to vote on whether they wish to participate or not. Carson and his fellow Ulster MPs will never agree to sit with Redmond as leader in a new Irish parliament.'

'It's an intolerable state of affairs,' complained Albert angrily, 'with the nationalists demanding a parliament here in Dublin when we have a perfectly good parliament and representation in Westminster.'

'The Government of Ireland Bill has passed through the House of Lords,' said Frederick, 'so there is not much more that can be done legally. Ulster will have their own vote to decide if they want to come under Dublin's jurisdiction, but if they say no it means a divided Ireland.'

'I'm afraid that Carson and his Ulster Volunteers will never accept Home Rule and not being part of the Union,' said William. 'And by all accounts, after Larne they have large numbers and are very well armed.'

'Thank heaven for that, as we may well have

need of them if this Home Rule nonsense persists,' Henrietta interjected, her face flushed with annoyance.

'Any Irish parliament would still report to the British one,' Robert reminded them as he slowly sipped a glass of red wine. 'But it most definitely is not an ideal situation for us to find ourselves in.'

'It will go through,' Frederick told them calmly. 'It may be delayed but, as we all know, by law it will have to be passed.'

'Why can't the king interfere and put a stop to it?' demanded Henrietta.

'My dear, King George has apparently called a conference in Buckingham Palace to try to get the unionists and the nationalists to come to some sort of agreement on the Bill in the hopes of finding a resolution, but it is a very complex and difficult situation.'

'I don't envy him,' sighed Iris. 'They will never be able to reach agreement.'

'I saw the Irish Volunteers brazenly training in the fields near our house,' said Edward as the pudding was served. 'They have huge numbers joining all across the countryside, prepared to fight for Home Rule and defend themselves from Carson and his forces.'

'How sad – Irish men prepared to fight against other Irish men on the one island,' tutted Iris.

'It was ever so,' nodded William. 'Can anyone imagine an Irish parliament sitting in Dublin with Carson and Redmond at each other's throats? What utter folly that would be!'

Everyone laughed aloud at the notion of it.

'King George has more than enough on his plate given the shooting of Austria's Archduke Franz Ferdinand and his wife in Serbia a few weeks ago and the instability that event has caused in the region,' said Frederick in a worried voice, smoothing his moustache. 'It's like a lit tinder keg ready to blow up.'

'It was a foul deed,' interjected Dorothy to everyone's agreement.

'I fear Frederick is right. Home Rule is not the only issue with which we should be concerning ourselves,' said Robert. 'It's Europe and the situation with Kaiser Wilhelm and his pledge to support Austria against Serbia that we need to worry about.'

'I think it is time the ladies and I retired to the drawing room.' Isabella stood up. To her mind there had been quite enough politicking for one night. The gentlemen got to their feet politely as she led her female guests next door.

'A wonderful meal, dear Isabella,' said Iris.

'You and Frederick are such good hosts.' Dorothy smiled warmly, patting the seat beside her.

Isabella accepted the compliments of their friends. Of late she found they entertained less and less, but she was glad that they had made the effort tonight and that Julia had proved such a good cook.

'Is it true that Sidney has gone to America?' enquired Florence.

'Yes, I'm afraid the house seems quiet without her,' replied Isabella as Julia came in to serve the coffee. 'She sailed only a few weeks ago and is staying with Ada in New York, hoping to write for some of the papers and magazines there.'

'She was always a clever little thing,' said Iris. 'No doubt the American editors will adore her.'

'Three of our six are abroad,' sighed Francesca. 'Married and settled in Kenya and Canada, but it is still a blow when they sail off to the other side of the world.'

'Sometimes I wish our boys were young and back playing cricket in the garden.' Iris stirred her coffee thoughtfully. 'Jerome and I do so awfully, miss them. They are both so far away.'

'In time their regiments will come home,' Dorothy said kindly.

Isabella tried not to think of her own children, especially Sidney taking off to America despite their objections. She worried how her youngest daughter was faring in New York. As for the boys, they rarely bothered to write or reply to her letters.

'Did I tell you that our Jack has finally proposed to Sarah?' interjected Florence excitedly. 'They are planning to wed in September and will travel for three weeks in Italy for their honeymoon. It's so romantic!'

Isabella relaxed as the ladies' talk turned to family matters, which it always did until the men rejoined them. Despite the politics, she considered that the evening had been a great success.

Chapter 41

Muriel

Muriel and MacDonagh walked around the house in Oakley Road in Ranelagh. Muriel instinctively liked it. There was a narrow entrance hall with a tiled floor, a good-sized drawing room and a smaller dining room which were not in any way as grand as her parents' home in Temple Villas, but this was a smaller house that was well suited to a young family. The kitchen had a large range and a narrow window overlooking the garden; there was also a pantry and a scullery with a large Belfast sink. Upstairs there were four bedrooms.

She inspected the small water closet and the tiled green and white bathroom with its big cast-iron bath. It felt like a family home and was situated close to the tram stop, as well as to her parents' and friends' homes.

'What do you think, Muriel?' asked Mac-Donagh, who had been unable to hide his delight on discovering that 29 Oakley Road was for rent.

'I think it will suit us very well,' she said, meeting his eyes.

They walked around with Don, happily exploring the large garden.

'He could have a swing here,' MacDonagh pointed out, standing under a tall chestnut tree.

'Are you sure we can afford the rent?' she

248

asked. They always seemed to struggle financially and she did not want to take on something that they could not possibly afford.

'It is well within our limit,' he assured her.

They moved into Sunnyside a week later.

Muriel loved their new house and only wished that MacDonagh was at home more to enjoy it, but he was often away, talking at Irish Volunteer rallies across the country, from Derry and Kilkenny to Tipperary. More and more people were turning up to hear him speak as he encouraged existing members and new recruits on the importance of drilling, training and being prepared to use arms. He and Roger Casement, a former diplomat, were determined that the Volunteers would become a strong nationalist force ready to protect their territory if necessary.

The Volunteers had raised money both at home and in America to purchase, with Casement's help, a large shipment of arms from Germany which was due to arrive in the seaside village of Howth on Dublin's north side in the *Asgard*, a boat owned by the writer Erskine Childers and his wife, Molly. MacDonagh had organized for the Volunteers to meet the boat and unload the rifles.

'What happens if the police or army discover you?' Muriel fretted.

'We'll see,' was all he answered her.

He left early the next morning and Muriel busied herself by bringing Don to play in the park, trying to distract herself from fears of her husband's arrest.

'We got all our guns safely off the *Asgard* without

249

discovery,' he laughed proudly. 'A troop of Scottish Borderers and a few DMP boys stopped us at Fairview to ask about our guns. It was a bit of a stand-off but we told their major that the guns the men had were all their own and were not even loaded. You should have seen it, Muriel. They could prove nothing against us so they had to let us pass.'

'Oh thank heaven I didn't,' she sighed, relieved.

Later a young lad came knocking at their door with a message for MacDonagh. He left immediately on hearing that the Scottish Borderers had attacked a crowd of people on Bachelor's Walk, deliberately shooting and killing three people and injuring a score or more at least.

'Why would the army do that?' she asked, appalled.

'Apparently the crowd jeered and taunted them about not catching us,' he said, pulling on his jacket. 'They threw fruit, maybe a few stones, at the soldiers. I don't know exactly why and what happened yet, but the lad said the army just opened fire on the civilians.'

He was angry when he returned from town later that night. 'As far as Britain is concerned there is one rule for the unionists and another for us nationalists,' he raged. 'The Ulster Volunteers can import guns and arm themselves in April, but when we try to do the same thing a few months later this is what happens. Innocent people are shot and injured. But their deaths will not go unmarked, for the Volunteers will provide a full guard of honour for their funerals.'

A few days later thousands of Volunteers

carrying rifles formed a massive guard of honour that lined the streets of the city as the victims – an innocent teenage boy, a man and a woman – were taken for burial.

'We are demonstrating our right to bear arms in public as much as the Orangemen in the north,' MacDonagh and Eoin MacNeill insisted as they and their men fell into step, marching together with their rifles.

Muriel joined the large funeral procession with her sisters and friends from Cumann na mBan, Connolly's Citizen Army and Na Fianna. As they slowly followed the three hearses drawn by black horses from Dublin's Pro-Cathedral up towards Sackville Street, she felt a strange shiver of apprehension suddenly grip her. Catching her eye, Grace slipped her hand reassuringly inside hers as the three sisters walked together towards Glasnevin Cemetery.

Chapter 42

Isabella

On 4 August the British prime minister, Herbert Asquith, with a heavy heart, declared war on Germany following its invasion of Belgium. His ultimatum to the Kaiser to withdraw his forces from that country had been ignored and now Britain was at war with Germany.

'How could the assassination of the archduke

possibly lead to this?' Isabella asked.

'I'm afraid this is exactly as I feared, my dear,' sighed Frederick. 'Following his nephew's death the German Kaiser declared war on Serbia, which has forced Tsar Nicholas to react. So now we have the German army declaring war not only on Russia but also on France. The German invasion of Belgium has left the prime minister no other option but to enter the war. It's like a contagion spreading across Europe with no way of halting it.'

'I find all this talk of the Kaiser and the Tsar very complicated,' she confessed as they took tea together, 'but I respect the prime minister and his decision to go to the aid of Belgium. Let us hope this war is as they are saying, just a skirmish, and will be over by Christmas.'

Frederick made no reply as he helped himself to a sandwich.

'You do think it will end quickly?' she pushed.

'Two mighty empires at war with each other...' he said gravely. 'Let's hope that you are right, Isabella – that this war will be short, sharp and over before we know it, for otherwise the danger is that Europe will be torn asunder.'

A huge shadow was cast over the seaside town of Greystones as the implications of war began to sink in. They talked about little else as they promenaded along the seafront, as they picnicked on the beach, at afternoon tea parties and at the nightly concerts in the town.

Army barracks in Dublin city and across the countryside emptied as the Irish regiments were immediately ordered to fight on the Western

Front. Lord Kitchener began an army recruitment campaign and patriotic young men flocked to join up.

'The twins are already talking about joining up,' Frances Heuston told Isabella anxiously as they attended an operetta in Greystones music hall. 'They say all their friends are eager to play their part.'

'The boys only want to do their duty for king and country,' her husband added, 'but they have no idea about the atrocities of war.'

Isabella worried for their own sons too. Liebert was already deployed in the navy, but she was thankful that Cecil and Ernest were both away.

'Perhaps we are needlessly worrying and it will blow over quickly,' murmured Frances hopefully as the band began to play.

But there was no end ... no sense to it...

Isabella could hardly bear to look at the newspapers, for the war quickly escalated. Day after day young Irish men joined the Royal Irish Fusiliers and other regiments. Wives, families and sweethearts waved them off at the Dublin docks as they were sent to fight in Flanders and France, where they faced battle in miles of muddy, rat-infested trenches. There were horrific stories of mounted cavalry units and of horses and riders mowed down by pounding machine guns. Mons, the Marne, Ypres – one battlefield after another where so many brave young English, Scottish, Welsh and Irish men died or were injured. She could see fear and anxiety in the faces of their friends and neighbours as they waited for news of their sons.

'They are fools,' murmured Nellie angrily.

'Nellie, I will not have you saying such things about brave Irish men prepared to do their duty and fight for a small nation like Belgium,' scolded Frederick. 'These young men all deserve your respect and loyalty for fighting in this great war.'

Chapter 43

Muriel

The war was all anyone talked about. Young men full of bravado wanting to go off to fight against the Kaiser to teach Germany a lesson. Muriel's own brothers itched to be a part of it too. Cecil, Ernest and even solid, reliable Claude were all considering enlisting.

'I have some good news!' She laughed as she told MacDonagh that, they were expecting another child. She caught the flicker of apprehension in his eyes, her husband unable to disguise his concern for her health and wellbeing, fearing that she would be so very ill again during and after this pregnancy.

'I am very well,' she assured him. 'I feel different this time – better. Tell me that you are pleased about it?'

'Of course I am,' he promised her, pulling her on to his lap. 'We both know that all little Don wants is to have a brother or sister to play with.'

'Then he will have a playmate next spring.' She

smiled, happy at the thought of their expanding family.

Muriel wrote to John telling her their news. From her sister's letters it was clear that it was proving more difficult to find work as a journalist in New York than she had expected. She had met their old family friend John Yates whose portrait painting was much in demand, but unfortunately work for writers was scarce.

'John should have stayed here – plenty for a journalist to write about with the war,' said Grace sagely.

On his return from a heated meeting held in the Gaelic League in Parnell Square, MacDonagh had confided to his wife that Padraig's suggestion that the Volunteers should concentrate on defending Ireland and securing its ports during the war had met some opposition, for Eamonn and some of their group believed that England's calamity was the perfect opportunity to strike a blow for Ireland.

'What do you believe?' Muriel pressed him in alarm.

'Ah, I'm torn over the whole thing,' he sighed, slipping off his jacket and shoes.

The long-awaited Government of Ireland Bill had finally become law in mid-September, but MacDonagh was disappointed when the prime minister made it very clear that it was not possible to implement Home Rule and the formation of an Irish parliament until after the war.

'While Britain is at war, Ireland is no longer a priority for Westminster,' fretted MacDonagh. 'I fear that Home Rule will be delayed even further.'

'But Asquith and parliament have promised it,' she reasoned with him. 'They will not renege on that.'

To his disbelief, John Redmond, leader of the Irish Parliamentary Party, had assured the prime minister that Ireland and the Volunteers were loyal to Britain and were prepared to fight in the war.

A week later, speaking at a massive Volunteer Rally in Woodenbridge, Redmond had called on their men not to shrink from duty by staying at home protecting Ireland's shores but to enlist and join the field of battle.

'You should have heard him, Muriel,' MacDonagh said angrily. 'He told our men to join the British army and do their duty by fighting because the interests of Ireland are at stake. And the worst of it is, the men listened to him and believed him.'

Her husband and Eoin MacNeill and others issued a statement in the *Irish Review* urging Volunteers not to enlist. MacDonagh, incensed, wrote and published 'Twenty plain facts for Irishmen', which outlined his belief that the role of the Volunteers was to protect Ireland and not to march off to fight under a 'Union Jack flag'. Muriel was proud of her husband's stance.

But it was futile. Words and wisdom were useless, for Redmond controlled much of the committee. There was a massive split in the Volunteers. The vast majority of the 170,000 members made the decision to follow Redmond's leadership and enlist in his new National Volunteers, while only 10,000 men stayed on as Irish Volunteers.

MacDonagh, Eoin MacNeill and Padraig Pearse were broken-hearted. Thousands of men from all across Ireland whom they had trained and drilled had chosen to obey Redmond's 'call to arms' and were now enlisted in the British army.

'The fools, they believe what Redmond says – that the war won't last and that once the war is over, parliament will honour its agreement and introduce Home Rule,' MacDonagh said bitterly. 'They have no idea what they are facing: miles of trenches, with bayonets and rifles against heavy machine guns. Far too many good men have already been lost and maimed, and now our lads will join them...'

'But you still have your core of men in the Volunteers,' said Muriel as she tried to soothe him. 'The ones you can trust and depend on.'

'Yes, we are badly reduced but the men we have now are committed to our cause, to Ireland,' he agreed, but he was unable to hide his crushing disappointment and disillusion from her.

For those remaining Irish Volunteers, training became even more intense. Gun handling and shooting practice in rifle ranges were held a few times a week and war games were organized between Volunteer companies. MacDonagh, appointed director of Training for the whole country, insisted on discipline from all members and even set up a sniping division.

Muriel admired his determination but worried that her husband was doing too much, writing on his typewriter, engrossed in working on the script of a new play, *Pagans,* which he hoped would be staged in the Irish Theatre. He even wrote 'Freedom Hill', a song for the Volunteers, which he would sing for her and Don. It constantly amazed her that the man she loved seemed to have such endless energy and stamina, never tiring and finding everything around him interesting.

'Ask a busy person...' he joked as he set off to give a lecture in the university.

Chapter 44

Nellie

Nellie strolled through Palmerston Park. She could see circles of snowdrops under the trees and the first tips of spring crocuses were beginning to push through the ground. As a child she had always considered this park an escape from home, a place where, undetected, she could climb trees and make secret hideouts and play games away from the watchful gaze of Mother and her nanny.

'That's where we used to play Robin Hood,' a voice interrupted her thoughts. 'And you made a bow and arrow.'

She turned around, recognizing the voice of Harry Johnson, her childhood friend. His parents lived close by and he and his brothers and sisters had always been regular visitors to their home.

'And this was our Sherwood Forest,' she laughed. 'Though it looks a bit small now.'

'Nellie, how are you?' He smiled as he joined her. 'I haven't seen you for an age. I heard you were working down the country.'

'I was, but for the past year I've been back in Dublin, doing some work for the union in Liberty Hall.'

'Larkin's lot!' She caught a look of puzzlement passing over his open, freckled face.

'I teach cookery and, believe it or not, recently I've started to give dance lessons to the union members.'

'I could do with them,' he admitted sheepishly. 'I'm not much of a dancer.'

'What about you?'

'I've just finished working in the old man's insurance company and am shipping out with my regiment on Monday.'

'Oh Harry – don't tell me you've joined up!' Nellie could not hide her dismay.

'I'm with the Dublin Fusiliers along with three pals from my rowing club,' he said proudly. 'We are all in it together.'

'Where are they sending you?'

'Salisbury for training and then on to France, but my friend George thinks it's likely we'll be sent straight to the front line as they are desperately short of men.'

Nellie studied the flowerbeds, not trusting herself to speak.

'Why did you enlist?'

'Duty, I suppose... It seemed the right thing to do,' he answered softly. 'I'm not much good to

259

anyone just sitting at a desk in an office working out quotes and rates. Robert is already out there in Belgium and Father thought it might be a good idea for me to join up too for a few mm-months.'

She noticed his very slight stammer. When he was younger Harry had been plagued with it, teased by his schoolfriends and, worse still, by some of his siblings. She remembered one time Mother had invited him and his sister and brother to a party in the house and one of the other neighbours' boys had started to taunt him as they played out in the garden.

'H-Haarry, Hhh-harry...'

She could still see his face and that sad look in his eyes, and she remembered feeling outrage and turning on the other boy, chasing him and punching him for being mean. Harry had shyly thanked her at the end of the party when he was leaving.

'Harry, promise me that you will take care of yourself over there,' she blurted out.

'Of course I will, Nellie.' He shrugged, embarrassed. 'I'll be like Houdini and get out of anything!'

'I just wish that you weren't going...'

'I'll be home before anyone misses me.' He gave a hollow laugh.

'I'll miss you,' she said, realizing that she meant it. She had always liked him. She found Harry easy to converse with, with his unassuming manner and tall, gangly frame and sandy-coloured hair and freckles. Any time she met him it was as if the years fell away and the friendship between them remained.

'Nellie, would it be all right if I wrote to you sometimes?' he asked shyly. 'All the fellows have someone to write to and I...'

His mother, Georgina, had died of tuberculosis three years ago and his father had always been a rather gruff, distant type of man. 'Of course, and I promise to write back to you with news too.'

'Perhaps we can have tea or go for ddd-dinner when I return?' he suggested, suddenly nervous.

'I'll look forward to it,' she smiled as they shook hands and parted. Harry walked briskly out of the park to the tram stop.

Walking back home, Nellie realized that she was looking forward to sharing a meal with him, rekindling their friendship. She wished that she had not been so stupidly formal and had at least given Harry a hug to wish him well...

Chapter 45

Grace

Grace was meeting Norman Morrow again tonight at an art exhibition that included black-and-white illustration.

He greeted her warmly and she introduced him to her friends as they mingled and chatted, talking about their work. Norman fitted in well with her circle. He was over in Dublin for ten days and they had had dinner last night and were going to the Abbey tomorrow.

As they climbed the stairs of the United Arts Club, Norman gently touched the nape of her neck and told her she was beautiful.

'Behave!' she laughed, though she had to admit she did enjoy his romantic attentions.

They both had a piece on display at the latest exhibition and they stood making complimentary comments about each other's work, which attracted attention. Countess Markievicz joined them and admired his etching, which had also been exhibited in a gallery in London.

'The problem with the war is that no one is buying anything.' He shrugged. 'All the papers want is news journalism and work by war artists.'

Afterwards they slipped away quietly from the crowd to spend time on their own in a nearby café. Grace sat smoking and enjoying a glass of wine as Norman again tried to persuade her to join him in London.

'Grace, it is impossible for someone like me to make a living in Dublin,' he said, running his hands through his thick, curling hair. 'At least in London there is more opportunity for illustrators and political cartoonists like us to work.'

'You were just saying earlier that no one is buying,' she teased.

'Perhaps not as much as usual,' he conceded, 'but war or no war, people will always buy art in London. And there are so many print newspapers and magazines. My brother George has made his fortune working for *Punch* and I am getting some good work from magazines too.'

'I work for the *Review* and the papers and magazines and theatre here too,' she argued.

'But you told me they rarely pay you,' he reminded her.

Grace blushed. 'Art is not just about money,' she retorted hotly.

'I know that,' he apologized, stroking her hand. 'It's just that you are so talented and would definitely get work. Can you imagine us both in London, living and working together in our studio?'

Grace took a slow pull of her cigarette, giving consideration to what he was saying. She was a little in love with him, but Norman had never gone down on his knee or sworn undying love for her; he just talked about them living and working together in some kind of bohemian way. She presumed he meant marriage.

He held her hand and put his arm around her and she tried to imagine sharing her life with him...

'Let's enjoy the next few days,' she said as the pianist began to play 'The Song That Stole My Heart Away' and Norman pulled her into his arms to dance.

When the time came for him to return to London, he promised to write and told her he fully intended to persuade her to join him in the next few months. But Grace was unsure. She could no longer imagine spending the rest of her life in London so far from her family and friends and Ireland...

His letters came regularly, some filled with cartoons and drawings, and she wrote back immediately, adding her own squiggles and sketches. But as the weeks passed she realized that, while she cared deeply for Norman and treasured the time she spent with him, she did not love him enough to move to London to live with him. He in turn did not actually love her enough to make the move to live and work in Dublin.

She wrote to him less and less.

'Are you sad about Norman?' asked Nellie.

'A little – I do miss him sometimes,' she confessed, trying not to dwell too much on their failed romance.

A few months later Norman wrote to tell her that he was going overseas to work as a war artist for one of the newspapers.

Chapter 46

Muriel

MacDonagh was approached about a professorship in English at a university in Switzerland. Eoin MacNeill had recommended him for the position at Fribourg University, which not only offered a good salary but included accommodation for his family.

The idea was certainly tempting, thought Muriel as she read the correspondence on the matter. Switzerland was a neutral country, and they would have a home near the university and perhaps be in a better financial position.

'I would probably have far more time to devote to my writing,' he said, excited by the prospect.

Their baby would be born in only a few weeks, however, and Muriel found it hard to imagine raising their children in Switzerland so far from her family and friends. What would happen if she fell ill again? She knew that he was torn about the offer, but was hugely relieved when he declined it.

'It is far better for the baby and Don to be here in Dublin close to their families,' he explained. 'Besides, I have far too many commitments with the Volunteers to consider moving.'

In March their daughter Barbara was born, petite and quite beautiful. Muriel felt well and strong again almost immediately. MacDonagh had composed a poem for their new, golden-haired baby. He called it simply 'Barbara' and as he read it to her Muriel felt as if her life could and would never be happier.

Minding the baby and Don was often tiring as MacDonagh was so busy and away so much.

'How did Mother do it with twelve of us?' Muriel sighed.

'Your mother had staff – a nanny, a cook and maids,' he reminded her, laughing. 'I'm sure that Isabella rarely bathed, dressed, fed or changed any of you.'

Muriel blushed, realizing the truth of it. Bridget, their nanny, was the one who had raised them and tended to them when they were younger and were practically banished to the upstairs nursery. She remembered that Mother and Father would only dine with one of the children once a week. They had all considered it quite an ordeal sitting at the table with their parents and trying to make conversation. She would never permit such a thing to happen under her roof.

MacDonagh employed a girl from north Dublin to come to help with the children for a few hours three times a week. Mary was friendly, kind and capable, and not only loved the children but helped Muriel with the housekeeping and laundry.

'How can we possibly afford to pay her?' Muriel fretted. 'We will be in debt.'

'Muriel, I don't want you to get ill again,' he insisted. 'I work hard and what I earn is sufficient to provide for Mary's wage.'

Muriel hugged him. He was the kindest, most generous-hearted man and they cared deeply for each other and their children, she thought as she watched him leaning over his desk writing, working on revisions to his new play which was rehearsing the next day and due to open soon.

He passed her a few pages to read. She curled up on the couch, surprised by his ability to capture a woman's thoughts and feelings so well on paper. She began to read the script aloud: two women meeting in a drawing room, a wife and former lover discussing the man they both had loved.

'*Pagans* is a very different play from your others. It is modern and feels real, but it is controversial.'

'Joe felt the same when I gave him the script to read before he went abroad,' he said, lifting his head. 'But that is what our theatre is about, taking risks and putting new work on our stage. Jack thinks it is a grand piece of drama and he makes a great husband.'

'I do wish that I could attend the opening, but I cannot leave the baby yet.'

'Of course not,' he sympathized. 'There will be more plays, and you will be at my side then.'

On the play's first night Muriel waited up at home for MacDonagh's return, anxious to hear of the reaction to *Pagans*. She could tell he was excited and he said his cast had served him well: Una O'Connor was wonderful in the lead role; Elta MacMurrough had played the artist with relish, while his brother was the perfect returning husband. There had been warm applause from the audience, with many of the women telling him that they had been taken aback by the honesty of his writing.

'Countess Plunkett and Grace and Nellie all liked it. Helena teased me about how I learned to think like a woman. I told them I have a wife, a daughter now, and a rake of sisters and sisters-in-law, which helps!'

MacDonagh was invited to speak at a women's anti-war meeting and was surprised when his friend the pacifist Frank Sheehy-Skeffington wrote an open letter to him afterwards urging him to remember his humanity and to stop training the Volunteers to kill.

'Would Frank prefer that they die defending Ireland?' he sighed, showing Muriel the letter.

'You know that he and Hanna will not tolerate violence of any kind,' she reminded him. 'They are both peacemakers opposed to the war and guns, that is all it is.'

In her own mind she agreed with the Sheehy-

Skeffingtons, for peace and an end to this terrible war were desperately needed.

At night their back room was becoming a regular meeting place for MacDonagh and the other leaders of the Volunteers. He was closer than ever to Padraig Pearse, Sean Mac Diarmada and Tom Clarke, the inner group that was at the organization's secret heart. Muriel worried about her husband, for he seemed even more caught up in things than before and lately had taken to wearing a gun.

'Why do you need to wear it?' she had questioned him.

'I am not a violent man, but Tom Clarke says the DMP and the army may well be watching us and could take us or shoot us whenever they want. This pistol is my protection,' he said firmly, hiding it inside his jacket.

Muriel could not help but be afraid, not just for MacDonagh but for herself and the children too.

Chapter 47

Nellie

Nellie and Father were enjoying breakfast together when he put down the morning paper.

'I was in the club last night and I met Arthur Johnson. He was in a bad way, poor chap. Found out only a few days ago that his boy was killed in Flanders – terrible thing.'

Nellie felt a chill run through her.

'Which of the Johnson boys is it?' she demanded of him.

'I'm not sure.' He looked puzzled. 'They've three or four sons.'

'Robert and Harry are the ones serving in the army. Which one is it, Father?'

'He was upset about his boy. He'd had a few whiskeys.' Father looked stricken. 'The awful thing is that he cannot even bring him home to bury him with his poor mother.'

Nellie's mind was in turmoil, gripped by a cold, strange dread.

Father slowly resumed eating breakfast, while she sat feeling sick to her stomach. She sipped her cup of tea and pushed her plate away.

'It's the boy with the stammer,' Father said suddenly, putting down his knife and fork. 'Apparently his regiment of the Dublin Fusiliers had only arrived in Belgium a few days before and came under heavy attack at Ypres. Arthur heard that the British and allied lines were decimated by the Germans using some new sort of poison chlorine gas they have invented. The soldiers had no chance of escape – none at all...'

'That's Harry!' she cried.

'I'm so sorry, my dear, to be the bearer of bad news. I remember you were all friends when you were younger and played together.'

'I met him in the park only a few weeks ago. He told me that he had joined up with some friends from a rowing club.'

'Poor chap! Lord rest him.'

Nellie got up from the table and pushed her

chair away.

She escaped to the park and sat on a bench for hours. The crocuses and snowdrops were gone now and pink and white cherry blossom covered the trees. Golden daffodils grew in clumps along the pathways and a curious squirrel watched her before darting up the branch of a chestnut tree. Alone, she listened to the stillness.

Harry was gone.

She blamed the army generals, parliament and King George. They were the ones responsible for his death and the deaths of thousands of other young men just like him. She abhorred this war.

A week later the postman delivered Harry's only letter to her.

He wrote of the crowded train and transport ship. Of miles of trenches and battle-weary men and the order to move up the line... He told her that he was afraid. Nellie cried her eyes out, then carefully folded the letter and hid it away in the drawer of her bedside table.

Chapter 48

Isabella

Dublin was a city in mourning as hundreds of young Irish soldiers in the Royal Dublin Fusiliers were killed at Ypres and Gallipoli. On the Western Front they were mown down by rapid-action German machine guns or by poisonous gas, dying in rows where they fell.

'I cannot bear it, to hear of so many killed in such a cowardly fashion using gas,' Isabella cried angrily. 'How can the Germans commit such atrocities against their fellow man?'

Frederick read the newspapers almost obsessively as details emerged of the slaughter of the Irish battalion as they landed on V beach in Gallipoli in late April, trying to make it to the shore under heavy Turkish machine-gun fire.

'Those poor young lads stood no chance,' he said, shaking his head. 'Why would Churchill and General Hamilton give such orders?'

The streets of the city and of many Irish towns were now filled with widows dressed in mourning and children wearing black armbands as more and more families were bereaved. They collected the supplementary allowance that the army paid weekly to all widows and their children. Isabella pitied those young wives and stoical mothers dressed in black as they tried to go through the day-to-day motions of their lives.

Isabella had written four letters of condolence over the past two weeks. She and Frederick attended memorial services for the sons of friends and for legal colleagues who would never be able to have their child's body returned to them for a decent burial.

Isabella had just left the haberdashery store in Rathmines one day when her eyes read the newspaper headline:

THE *LUSITANIA* SUNK BY THE GERMANS

She immediately purchased the paper from a cheeky young corner newsboy. 'The Kaiser's gone and done it now, missus,' he said, 'blowing a passenger ship out of the water.'

Appalled, she hurried home.

'Mother, have you heard about the *Lusitania?*' Grace asked, her voice shaking as she joined her in the drawing room.

Isabella was so upset as she read that over a thousand passengers and crew had been killed. A German submarine had deliberately sunk the large passenger liner travelling from New York to Dublin as it neared Ireland. This was no accident like the *Titanic* but a deliberate act of violence by the German empire.

'Ethel and Eric travelled on the *Lusitania* only last year coming from Canada,' she said, shocked.

'How could a submarine sink a ship full of innocent people and leave them to drown?' raged Grace.

'The Kaiser has no decency,' replied Isabella, thinking of Liebert away at sea, worried that the German navy might now plan on sinking ships crossing the Atlantic.

'Hugh Lane was a passenger. He was bringing a valuable new collection of paintings home from New York.'

'Poor man. Art was his life... Remember his big plans for that gallery on the River Liffey,' Isabella remarked, thinking of the controversy when Dublin Corporation had finally refused to contribute to the gallery and Sir Hugh Lane had removed his paintings to London. 'I will write at once to his dear brothers, for they were so good when our Gerald died. It must be a huge shock to the family and to his aunt, Lady Gregory.'

'The Germans have gone too far this time,' Frederick pronounced dourly over dinner. 'The Americans will not take kindly to the killing of their innocent citizens sailing on board a ship across the Atlantic.'

Three weeks later Claude informed them he was doing his duty and had enlisted in the army. He was to be sent to France with the Canadian Expeditionary Force.

Although Isabella and Frederick were very proud of their son's decision and his strong sense of duty and loyalty to the British crown, Isabella felt an icy cold fear grip her heart and soul... All she could do was hope and pray that Claude and his company would somehow stay safe.

Chapter 49

Nellie

Nellie felt a surge of pride every time she crossed the threshold of Liberty Hall, with its anti-war banner proclaiming, 'We serve neither King nor Kaiser but Ireland.' She enjoyed the easy camaraderie and friendships she had made there. She continued to give her cookery classes and she was delighted that her dance classes were also proving popular with the union's members.

'Nellie, you are light on your feet and make it look easy,' teased Rosie Hackett, who had unfortunately lost her job in Jacob's Biscuit Factory again. 'I'm too much of an agitator,' she admitted.

James Connolly had made sure to get Rosie a job, however, and she now worked alongside Helena and Jenny Shanahan running the union's busy Co-operative shop, which was in the building next door to Liberty Hall. It sold workers' shirts, Irish-produced tweeds and garments, as well as the union's newspapers, the *Workers' Republic* and the *Gael*. Nellie enjoyed their company and the bond that existed among them.

Every day as she cycled or took the tram into town, she studied the recruiting posters urging men to join their fellow Irish men and do their duty and fight. It sickened her. Every place you passed, you were accosted with Kitchener's propaganda. So many of the men they had fed in the building during the Lockout had enlisted and now their families were left fatherless and husbandless with no one to provide for them.

'Unfortunately, Nellie, the poor have always been the backbone of the army during a war,' sighed Countess Markievicz.

She helped with passing out leaflets against the war and attended pacifist Frank Sheehy-Skeffington's meetings, but every day more and more Irish men enlisted. From Liberty Hall Nellie watched them in their khaki uniforms with their kitbags, marching along by the riverside to the docks where the transport ships waited to take them overseas. Like Harry, they believed that they were doing their duty, protecting Ireland and

274

helping the smaller nations that were under attack by the massive German army.

As the list of casualties and deaths grew week by week, Nellie knew that many would never return and she became determined to do all in her power to stop any more Irish men enlisting in the British army.

Lord Kitchener had ordered British employers to get rid of all the men who worked in shops and at desk jobs to force them into joining the army, and as the weeks went by young Irish clerks, drapery staff and bank staff began to return to Ireland, many turning up in Liberty Hall looking for work.

'They say parliament plans to introduce conscription in Britain in the New Year because the army are suffering such huge losses,' explained Helena, 'so the situation will certainly get worse.'

'Many Irish men will flee back here, for they will never fight in a British army,' agreed Nellie. 'Perhaps we should think of setting up some sort of office to help them find suitable employment?'

'It could be difficult trying to get them jobs,' Helena warned.

'I'm not afraid of hard work!' Nellie laughed.

It began in a very small fashion. Nellie travelled around various local employers to see if they had staff vacancies, or if they could offer any employment opportunities to young men returning from England. Given the situation, some immediately said yes, but others were most reluctant. Nellie was horrified to discover that a few companies had already made their own Irish employees and apprentices redundant at the request of local army recruiters.

She placed a small notice in Liberty Hall and another in the Irish Volunteers' headquarters offering assistance. Two or three men called to see her in Temple Villas and Nellie interviewed them in the dining room, promising to use all her contacts and even call on old friends in Meath and around the country to try to find work for them. And she succeeded, getting them jobs in warehouses and on farms, down on the docks and in various factories.

The numbers coming to see her continued to grow. Sometimes Julia, their housekeeper, had to leave the men to sit and wait on chairs in the hall.

'Who are all these young men loitering around the place?' Father wanted to know. 'Are they friends of yours, Nellie?'

She explained the situation to him, but her father was not happy to have his home turned into some sort of office. Mother was appalled and warned it could not continue.

'All these male callers – Nellie Gifford, you will get a reputation!'

Nellie described to Madame Markievicz the precarious situation she was in with her small employment agency. The countess sat smoking her cigarette and listened.

'I have some vacant rooms in an upstairs office in Harcourt Street for a few weeks if that is of any use to you, Nellie,' she offered.

Nellie thanked her and, to the relief of her parents, moved her office into town. She talked everything over with her friend Marie Perolz, who had agreed to assist her.

So the Bureau, their small employment office, was set up. As the weeks went on and more men returned from England, jobless and many also needing accommodation, Nellie did her very best to help them.

Chapter 50

Muriel

Muriel was finding motherhood a very different experience this time around as she relaxed in their new home, the baby sleeping in the sunshine in her pram while Don played on the wooden swing that MacDonagh and his brother Jack had made for him.

Hannah had called to tell her that she and two other nurses from Sir Patrick Dun's were going overseas to work in one of the army field hospitals in France.

'Aren't you nervous about going?' Muriel asked, filled with admiration for her nursing friends and their courage.

'They need nurses urgently – the casualty rate is enormous,' Hannah explained gravely. 'And we have plenty of theatre and surgical experience, which is what they require.'

'Promise me that you will take care of yourself.' Muriel hugged her as they said goodbye.

MacDonagh had the summer off from the university, but word had come from America that Jeremiah O'Donovan Rossa, the old Fenian leader, had died and that his body was being returned home for burial. The Volunteers were determined to pay a fitting tribute to the renowned Irish patriot who had spent years in a British prison, beaten and tied until he was eventually granted amnesty and sent to live in exile in America. MacDonagh had been chosen to organize the large funeral, which would be held in Dublin.

'He was a good man and deserves to be remembered for the patriot he was,' he told Muriel as he and Tom Clarke began to make arrangements for the funeral procession through the streets of Dublin to Glasnevin Cemetery. 'We will go away to the seaside afterwards,' he promised her.

Joe Plunkett returned to Dublin, calling immediately to see MacDonagh and congratulating them on the new addition to their family.

'She's a little beauty like her mother,' he said, carefully lifting up their baby daughter.

He looked tired and said little about his travels all over Europe, which she gathered had been very hush-hush. Muriel discreetly disappeared, as she knew the two close friends wanted to be alone to discuss Volunteer business.

O'Donovan Rossa's remains, on their return from America, were placed in a large glass coffin in City Hall for three days. Thousands flocked to see him and pay their respects, just as Tom Clarke had predicted.

The funeral was held on the first day of August.

MacDonagh had worked so hard at all the organizing and arrangements, with Joe's brother, Jack Plunkett, on his motorcycle acting as his messenger. Mary minded the children so that Muriel could join the huge funeral procession alongside Grace, Nellie and their friends. She felt sad for O'Donovan Rossa's wife and daughter, Eileen, as they led the cortège.

Thousands of people took part and bands were playing – it was unlike anything she had seen. They passed a line of DMP policemen standing guard, watching the procession as it made its way towards Glasnevin Cemetery. There was a feeling in the air of unity and resolve to honour a man who all his life had fought for Ireland and its right to freedom. The procession was a massive demonstration of the strength of the Volunteers' numbers and their growing nationalist support.

At the cemetery Padraig Pearse gave the graveside oration. Muriel was moved by the strength of his words as she listened to his voice, loud, clear and strong. He spoke of a new generation carrying on from Fenians like O'Donovan Rossa.

'The defenders of this realm think that they have pacified us ... but the fools, the fools, the fools! They have left us our Fenian dead, and while Ireland holds these graves, Ireland unfree shall never be at peace.'

As she stood there, Muriel was conscious of an overwhelming feeling of national pride among all those listening as Padraig captivated and inspired them with his words. MacDonagh and Tom Clarke, Joe Plunkett and Sean Mac Diarmada, Eamonn Ceannt and Michael O'Rahilly looked serious; the women of Cumann na mBan, many from James Connolly's Citizen Army and Liberty Hall were enraptured. Grace stood tall and perfectly still, her gaze unmoving, as if she were trying to remember it all exactly, like a painting.

Muriel knew that Padraig was a great teacher, but often in company he could appear somewhat shy and aloof, especially in front of girls and women – MacDonagh would tease him about it. But here he stood before an enormous crowd, able to give expression to what they all felt, what they wanted – change; change from British rule to Irish independence.

Coming away on holiday to Greystones a few days later, MacDonagh had made her a promise that for the next few weeks there would be no work, no mention of the Volunteers, just time for the two of them and the children to be together as a family.

They hired a rowing boat and went fishing, took a pony and trap on a picnic up to the big Sugar Loaf Mountain and to the woods near the Glen of the Downs. Among the other holidaymakers new families had replaced the old ones of her parents' generation and she was delighted to see some friends with their small babies and children.

Muriel swam most days, along the shore of the South Beach, feeling the strength and rhythm of each stroke as she pushed through the chilly water. She was a good, strong swimmer and the sea filled her with energy and a joy that had never changed since her childhood days. MacDonagh sat patiently on the stony beach watching her and minding the children, often with camera in hand, taking photographs, as she introduced Barbara to the sea and Don would yell as he splashed and paddled in the water or took a donkey ride.

Don loved the donkeys and every day begged them for a ride, MacDonagh walking along beside him so that he wouldn't be afraid as the little grey donkey plodded slowly along the beach, while Muriel stretched out in the sunshine and the baby played beside her on the rug.

Walking along the seafront one afternoon she spotted one of her mother's friends, sitting on a garden bench in the large front garden of their white gabled home, staring across at the Irish Sea.

'Muriel dear, how lovely to see you again!' Mrs Heuston looked tired, grey shadows under her eyes, as she admired the baby. 'Motherhood agrees with you.'

'Thank you. My husband and I are down for two weeks. I think the sea air must be doing me good, like when I was a child.'

'Those were such wonderful times when you were children.' Mrs Heuston's eyes suddenly welled with tears. 'You and your brothers and sisters, playing with Elizabeth and our twins Frank and Fred. You were all rather wild – a bit of a handful.'

'Is everything all right, Mrs Heuston?' Muriel could not hide her concern.

'Oh my dear, we've had bad news from the War Office two days ago to say that Fred was badly wounded last week. My husband is beside himself with worry. He's sent a telegram back to them asking about the extent of his injuries and if he's been taken to a hospital in Malta or Alexandria, but we are not getting any information,' she explained, upset and agitated. 'He's with the Sixth Battalion of the Fusiliers. He and a few medical-student friends from Trinity joined the big group of "Pals" from the rugby club who signed up. There were hundreds of them. He and a few friends had only just landed in Gallipoli when they were heavily attacked and many mortally wounded.'

'I'm sure the army hospital will look after Fred, and when he is well enough to transport they will send him back home,' Muriel comforted her.

'That's what we are praying for. I always took comfort from the fact that at least Frank junior was safe away from it all in Nova Scotia, but he wrote to tell us last month that he has joined the Canadian Expeditionary Force and is being sent to Salisbury for training.'

'My brother Claude is fighting with them in France,' Muriel said softly. 'Mother thinks that Cecil and Ernest will likely join up too.'

'I don't know if your family heard, but the Duggans got a letter from Lord Kitchener to say that poor George died in Suvla Bay and it seems that his brother Jack may also be missing.'

Muriel gripped the handles of the pram. George was a friend of her brothers', with a wife and small children ... who would now never see him again.

'It's strange to think that perhaps our boys all landed in that awful foreign place together,' Mrs Heuston said sadly as Muriel gently urged her to go back inside to have a rest.

Walking home past Ferney East, the Duggans' large, imposing corner home across from the cove, Muriel could see the curtains were drawn.

The house was in mourning for George.

'It's all right, darling,' soothed MacDonagh as she burst into tears the minute she reached their house.

'I will never let our son fight in such a war,' she said firmly. 'Never...'

As she enjoyed those precious days of summer, Muriel felt they were golden, she and her husband and their children together, paddling on the beach and having fun, capturing special moments on their trusty camera.

Desmond FitzGerald called to see MacDonagh. She knew it was on Volunteer business.

'Don't be cross,' he teased her. 'Poor Desmond has been marooned in Wicklow for months. He ran a Volunteer unit near Dingle, but he and his wife, Mabel, were forced to move by the authorities and are prohibited from living in Dublin. So he's set up a new Volunteer unit close to here, near Bray.'

'But surely he's putting himself in danger?'

'Perhaps, but he wants to stay involved,' Mac-Donagh said, as if risk were of no matter.

She felt sad as the holiday came to an end and she packed up their suitcases ready to return to Dublin.

'I don't want to go home,' Don said, gazing out the train window, wishing he could stay playing on the beach and having rides on Billy the donkey.

'Dadda and I will bring you and Barbara back here to Greystones again next year,' Muriel promised him as the guard blew his whistle and the train began slowly to move out of the station.

Chapter 51

Grace

Grace had called in to the Irish theatre in Hardwicke Street with some sketches she wanted to show MacDonagh for a new production they were mounting. She was surprised to find Joe Plunkett there. He had been abroad for months. She had seen him at the big O'Donovan Rossa funeral, but then he had disappeared again, leaving her brother-in-law and Mr Martyn to run the theatre.

He seemed distracted and her heart sank, for he barely acknowledged her presence.

'I hope you enjoyed your travels,' she said, trying to appear friendly.

'I was kept busy,' he replied, concentrating on a set of figures on a ledger page before him. 'As always, I found it interesting but now it is good to be home.'

'Well, I'm glad you're back.' She couldn't believe that she had said such a thing. She was a professional artist dealing with a potential employer whom she was canvassing for work. What must he think of her?

'Did you miss me, Miss Gifford?'

'Things have been quiet at the theatre in your absence...'

'And now you hope we will give you a commission.'

She stared down at her hands, noticing a broken nail and the tell-tale sign of charcoal under her nail bed. She wished she was a better business-woman, better able to canvass for work and appear insouciant and calm; but she wasn't.

'I have some sketches I promised MacDonagh.'

He gestured for her to show them to him.

'Yes – these would seem to fit the bill. If you leave them with me I will pass them on to Edward and we will be in contact with you in a few days,' he said, barely looking at her.

Grace flushed, gathering up her bag. At times he could be so offhand he was almost rude, so caught up in his work he hardly noticed those around him. She guessed producers and editors were like that, used to firing orders at people.

'Miss Gifford, what do you think of this?'

She just about caught the script he tossed at her.

She sat down again across from him to read it. Perfect – a scathing play about class distinction.

'On stage an extravagant, plush drawing room and a simple box or a table with a candle,' she proposed, 'and for the programme or bill, a sketch of a big, heavy, jowly English man and a thin, hand-some young Irish man.'

'How will we know that he is Irish?'

'Why, he will have a tin whistle,' she teased.

Joe laughed out loud. Grace smiled, unable to disguise her pleasure.

'You should do that more often,' he told her.

She stopped.

'Smile, I mean.'

He was a fine one to talk. Joe Plunkett was always so serious and distant, hunched over his desk or so deep in conversation that you felt you couldn't disturb him.

It was as if he read her mind.

'All work and no play, isn't that what they say? Well, I guess it's time for the latter if you care to join me?'

She was rather thrown by this question and found herself nodding idiotically in agreement.

'Let's get out of this office and do something different.'

'Yes, please,' she said with another smile, intrigued.

He grabbed his tweed jacket and began to lock up.

'Where are we going?' she asked as they fell into step, walking quickly down Hardwicke Street towards the Rotunda.

'You'll see,' he replied, his eyes bright and laughing as he turned into the entrance of the Rotunda roller-skating rink.

Grace looked nervously at the large advertising posters of figures and families skating happily.

'Miss Gifford, have you ever roller-skated?'

'No,' she admitted, giggling. 'Never.'

'Then this will be the first time,' he said happily, paying for two tickets.

'My brothers Cecil and Ernest had skates, but Mother wouldn't let my sisters and me ever use them as she said skating was unladylike,' she confided as a plump lady in the kiosk enquired about her shoe size and passed her a pair of metal roller skates; she handed Joe a much fancier-looking pair.

'Well, I am betting you will enjoy it.' He beckoned for her to sit down as he fitted and fastened the skates to her shoes. 'Does that feel all right?'

'Yes.' She tried to stand up and almost slipped, Joe grabbing her and making her sit back down while he pulled on his own pair of skates.

'Try to walk on your toes to the rink,' he advised as she clunked and stumbled along beside him towards the entrance. Music played and girls, boys, men and women all skated around at speed, lost in a haze of colour, noise and laughter.

Panic overwhelmed Grace. She could hardly stand let alone move in the heavy, awkward metal skates with their rolling wheels. She felt so unstable and unsure.

'I will hold you and help you,' Joe reassured her, 'but I promise you will soon get the hang of things.'

She felt like a small child trying to learn to walk, the wheels of her skates going in all directions, making her slip and slide and wobble alarmingly.

'Push one foot and skate forward and then the other,' Joe instructed her gently, keeping a firm hold of her arm.

'I'm going to fall!' she wailed, grabbing hold of his sleeve.

'I won't let you,' he promised, and he held her securely as they began to skate around the edge of the rink.

She was so slow and so rigid, more terrified than she had ever been. She was also frantically trying to maintain her decorum and wished she had worn a better skirt as she tried to keep her balance and not fall. Slide, roll, slide ... somehow she was getting round the rink.

The other skaters, sensing her nervousness, were giving her a wide berth as they flew around her.

Laughing, Joe caught her as she almost lost her footing and fell. 'It happens to everyone,' he soothed her.

She could not believe his patience and kindness as he skated gently, almost supporting her, round and round.

Gradually she was beginning to get a sense of how her feet and wheels worked, and was managing to stay a little more upright as she achieved a very slight rhythm. Young boys and girls skated briskly past her, but she grimly continued, determined to get the feel of it.

'Grace, you are doing very well for a beginner,' Joe praised her, his dark eyes darting in his long thin face.

'I don't know,' she sighed.

'I am a qualified skating teacher,' he told her adamantly, 'and, Miss Gifford, you are proving to be a very good pupil.'

'Thank you, Mr Plunkett,' she laughed, almost going down and grabbing frantically at his jacket to save herself, suddenly conscious of his long, strong arms gripping her fast and holding her.

Over the next hour he brought her back and forward, further into the centre of the rink away from the rails. He encouraged her to skate a little on her own. He even got her to increase her speed.

'I have to have a rest,' she begged. 'Please!'

She sat near the edge, watching as he skated off on his own, conscious of his speed, height and sureness on the roller rink as he sped around, then did a number of jumps and fancy manoeuvres which brought gasps from fellow skaters. Joe Plunkett, a skater! She would never have believed that the serious editor, writer and poet would have the slightest interest in such a pastime. But it was clear from the greetings of some of the other skaters that he was a regular here. As he skated, he looked younger, more relaxed, enjoying the speed as his thin frame stretched and hurtled in all directions.

Ten minutes later he was back, encouraging her to join him again.

'Where did you learn to skate like this?' she asked as he got her back out on the rink.

'I was never built to play rugby or some of those other sports, but being all arms and legs seems to work with skating. It is fast and requires dexterity, and is pretty good exercise, don't you think?'

This time she really concentrated, keeping close to him and using her own long, thin frame the way he did. Grace was relieved as she managed to skate and keep her balance. She was finally beginning to somewhat enjoy it.

They had tea and cake afterwards in a nearby café and she wondered if he would ask her to come skating with him again. But he said nothing. Instead, he politely escorted her to the tram stop, telling her that he had business in town and needed to call to his friend Tom Clarke's tobacconist's shop.

Chapter 52

Grace

Grace met Joe again a few days later at Muriel's. She was just about to leave to go home when he stopped her at the front door.

'I was wondering if I could perhaps call on you on Saturday,' he said, his eyes scanning hers. 'I could take you out for a walk or a meal?'

'Take me out?'

'I mean as work colleagues, as friends,' he said awkwardly.

She could feel his gaze was fixed on her.

'Yes, that would be nice, Mr Plunkett.'

'Then it is all arranged. I will collect you at three.'

She was about to give him her address.

'Temple Villas, isn't it?'

Grace nodded, realizing that they had been in postal correspondence with each other for a number of years.

Saturday was fine and she decided to wear her new green skirt and her favourite white blouse. Long after three o'clock there was still no sign of him, so she was about to go upstairs and change again when she heard the loud noise of an engine outside on the road and peeped out the window. It was a big black motorcycle and side-car stopping just at their gateway. Joe Plunkett dismounted and walked up to the house.

'Grace, there is a gentleman here to see you,' Father called loudly as she hurried to greet him.

Joe stood in their drawing room holding a helmet and goggles, looking around politely as she introduced them.

'Father, this is Mr Joseph Plunkett. He's involved in the Irish Theatre with MacDonagh.'

'Of course, we have heard mention of you,' Father said, shaking his hand. 'Is that your motorcycle outside?'

'Yes, sir,' he said proudly. 'It is a fine machine and a joy to ride once you get the hang of it.'

Joe had surprised her again. She would never have imagined him riding, let alone owning, a motorcycle. He had always seemed so serious and intent and bookish.

'I promise to take good care of Miss Gifford, sir. She will ride in the side-car, which is very safe. My mother and sisters have all been passengers.'

Grace had to stifle a laugh at the idea of the bulky figure of the renowned Countess Plunkett even venturing into such a contraption.

'Well, I shall rely on you to do that,' replied Father rather sternly.

'Grace, I suggest you bring a warm coat or wrap and a scarf, as it can get rather blowy,' Joe advised as they prepared to leave.

She ran upstairs, meeting Mother on the landing.

'Who is that caller with that motorcycle? Is it someone your father or brothers know?'

'Mother, it is a friend of mine, Mr Plunkett, and we are going for a ride on it.'

291

'You are going on a motorcycle? It is hardly very ladylike or safe,' Mother reminded her.

'Mother, I promise that I will be fine,' she smiled, putting on her coat and wrapping her scarf around her.

'Who is this Mr Plunkett?' Mother pestered.

'He is very respectable,' Grace explained. 'You must know his parents, Count and Countess Plunkett.'

'Those people – the Plunketts. I'm not sure that the family are at all suitable.'

'Mother!' she exclaimed, exasperated. 'Mr Plunkett and I often work together. He is a good friend of MacDonagh and Muriel's and is a highly regarded writer, poet and editor.'

'I still believe a lady should not be seen riding a motorcycle.'

'Oh Mother!' Grace pushed past her and headed towards the door where Joe was waiting. 'You are so old-fashioned.'

She was conscious of her parents watching her as Joe helped her into the side-car. It was small and low, and she felt nervous as she stepped into it. He closed her door, making sure she was comfortable before climbing on to the motorcycle and starting up the engine, which seemed to roar loudly in her ear as they took off and began to move along the leafy road.

'Are you all right?' he asked, peering down at her as the houses, gardens and trees sped by.

She could see people stop to look as he turned the bike and headed on the road out of town. Although she was meant to be protected, she was glad of the scarf as her hair blew across her face and the wind caught her eyes, taking her breath away. It was exhilarating and strange but she liked it.

'I thought we might drive out by Enniskerry. There is a nice tearoom in the village where we can stop.'

'Sounds lovely,' she shouted above the noise.

The side-car seemed to be almost flying, barely touching the road as they roared along. Sometimes when they slowed she was aware of the bumpiness of the road surface beneath the wheels and the strange rattle coming from the walls that enclosed her.

They passed Dundrum and continued up along winding country roads, passing green woods and fields. Finally they came to a stop in the village with its stone houses, pretty church and square. When Joe opened the door of the side-car to let her out her legs felt like jelly and he had to catch her to stop her from collapsing on the ground as she tried to regain her composure.

'Grace, are you all right?' He sounded concerned.

'I'm fine and dandy, but a little shaken.'

'It is a bit of a bone-rattler,' he admitted with a grin as they made their way through the village. She needed to stretch her long legs a bit, so they walked for three quarters of an hour before sitting down at a table in the tea-room.

As he put his helmet and goggles down, it struck Grace that Joe was different from any of the men she had known. He was excited, explaining to her about engines and telling her that he was building a wireless radio.

'You must come up to Larkfield and see it sometime.'

'I always presumed that you were only interested in poetry and plays, and words and politics,' she mused as the waitress brought them a pot of tea. 'But you are like my brother Ernest, good with machines and mechanical things.'

'The world is changing faster than we know, with all kinds of new inventions. It's exciting, don't you think?'

'Yes.' Grace hadn't given it much thought, but his enthusiasm was infectious.

'It seems strange talking about such things when there is the war which is bloody and awful and they invent new weapons, new gases capable of such carnage. For some, this unfortunately is what science has come to.'

'My brother is with the expeditionary forces in France,' she said quietly.

'One of my good friends, Frank O'Carroll, was killed in August,' he said, struggling to control his emotions. 'He was only twenty-one. We also lost George, one of my relations, at Gallipoli.'

'Oh Joe, I'm sorry. It must be hard on you.'

'The war is hard on everyone,' he said, passing her a slice of rich, treacly ginger cake, Grace, noticing that he had five or six rings on his fingers while she had none.

'This ring I bought at a market in Algeria. It is a special stone and is said to bring luck and protection,' he said, deliberately lightening the conversation. 'This gold one used to be my grandfather's,' he said, turning his hand. 'This one is said to date back two hundred years and is a family heirloom. This one is for my poetry book *The Circle and the Sword,* and this last one I got on my birthday. It has two beautiful sapphires.'

He looked at her bare hands, touching her fingers.

'With painting and drawing I have a tendency to lose things,' she explained.

'Some day you will wear fine rings and gold and diamonds on those pretty fingers,' he said solemnly.

'I'm not sure that I ever will,' she sighed.

They sat for an hour or two, talking about everything. Grace told Joe about her large family, her passion for art and about attending the Slade art school in London. He told her of his childhood, how he had been sent away to warmer climes because of illness and had gone to schools in France, Ireland and England.

His mother had often been away, leaving him and his brothers and sisters to fend for themselves in their large country house with hardly any food or money, his father often too caught up in his work to notice.

'Poor you – it all sounds very different from my mother, who always wants to know everything we do and keeps tight control of our household. She even used to design and make our dresses and hats when we were younger.'

'Ma would be far too busy for that and would never worry about such details as new clothes that would actually fit us, or about food or money.' He shrugged. 'My sisters and brothers and I were often left to our own devices, so we had to find our own way.'

'What parents we had!'

'They meant well,' he said. 'Besides, they encouraged us to be independent.'

They talked about religion, which surprised her, for he was deeply spiritual. Because his health had been bad, he had travelled a great deal, visiting Africa, America and most of Europe, and he had the ability to speak many languages.

'That's how I met MacDonagh,' he laughed. 'I wanted to learn my own native tongue, Gaelic.'

Joe Plunkett might seem showy and dramatic, and cosseted by his upbringing and family background, but it was very clear that he cared deeply for his country and longed for it to be free of British rule.

'The time is coming for change,' he said fervently.

'You mean Home Rule when the war is over? My parents and brothers are all opposed to any break from the crown and Britain.'

'I am not sure such promises to Redmond will ever be kept by a British parliament, so perhaps Irish men will have no choice but to take what is rightfully theirs.'

His eyes were serious, and she could see a vein throb in his neck. He might be tall and lanky and thin, but there was a huge gravity and strength to him that few possessed. He was the type of person who said exactly what he meant.

The waitress hovered about them, clearing away their tea things.

'We must go,' he said abruptly, standing up and going over to pay the bill.

He touched her hand as she climbed into the side-car and she felt as if a spark of that new electricity was running through her. His eyes met hers, both startled.

At home, he helped her out of the side-car, holding her as she steadied herself. He thanked her for coming. She hesitated, not wanting to go inside.

'I do hope you will agree to come for a ride with me again?'

She moistened her upper lip.

'When?' she blurted out.

He looked momentarily surprised, fiddling with his glasses.

'Next week, if that suits you, Grace?'

'Yes,' she smiled. 'It most definitely would.'

'Perhaps if the weather is clement we might take a picnic...'

Stepping inside the house, she watched as Joe Plunkett rode off on his noisy motorcycle. It was strange: they had known each other for years and yet only now was she discovering that he was the most interesting, exciting and complex man she had ever met.

Chapter 53

Grace

Joe brought her out on his motorcycle again. This time they went to Killiney, where they sat on a rug and shared some sandwiches overlooking the sweeping seascape of Dublin Bay. He kissed her and she enjoyed it, so he kissed her again and again. His eagerness and passion surprised her, and on her own part she returned them. She soon found herself counting the hours and days between seeing him.

They went to the theatre and to ceili dances together, and to dinner. Joe wrote her letter after letter and poems too. She sat curled up on the window seat reading them. She had never been wooed in such a fashion and to her surprise she found she liked it. When she wrote back she often attached silly drawings to her words.

'I see the poor postman is being kept busy again,' teased Nellie as another letter from Joe arrived.

'I do hope that you are not getting yourself too involved with that young Plunkett man, Grace. It is clear he has a poor constitution and I hear rumours that he was in a sanatorium a few years ago,' warned Mother.

'That was when he was much younger. He is well again now,' she replied hotly, wishing that her mother would stop interfering in her life.

'No young woman wants to bind herself to an invalid,' Isabella warned dramatically.

As the weather became colder Joe collected her in his motor car, which she had to admit was far more comfortable. He took her on romantic drives up around Stepaside and Dublin's pine forest.

'Grace, I'll teach you to drive,' he laughed one day, stopping suddenly on a quiet country road.

'I'm afraid, Joe,' she protested in alarm. 'I don't know how to work a mechanical engine.'

Joe slipped out of the car and made her slide across into the driver's seat and take the wheel, while he sat beside her on the passenger side. Terrified, she felt the car shudder and start, then it began to move. He made her drive for about two miles, one moment the car going slow and the next thing speeding up alarmingly as Grace tried to concentrate on keeping hold of the wheel and steering, which was much harder than it looked... But suddenly she began to get the hang of it and Joe insisted that she keep driving for another few miles until they came to a fork in the road. Laughing and nervous, Grace felt exhilarated, realizing that her life with Joe would never be boring or dull. He was a risk-taker and would always be at the centre of things, ready for something new.

'Now I think it's best I do the rest of the driving,' he teased as she moved back into the passenger seat and they motored on towards a little place in Kilmacanogue where they would have lunch.

They would sit for hours and talk – talk about poetry. Grace was moved by many of his poems. Her particular favourite was 'I See His Blood

Upon the Rose', and he would explain it to her, along with its spiritual significance. Books were another passion, and they discussed the sad realism of James Joyce's *Dubliners*. They enjoyed arguing about art, both classical and modern, or talking about theatre and cinema, or discussing life and death, spirituality, religion and the existence of an afterlife. Joe was a passionate, highly intelligent man and when they were together Grace was never bored. He made her think.

When he took her hand as he looked into her eyes, Grace knew without any doubt that already she was beginning to fall in love with Joe Plunkett – and somehow it scared her a little to realize how important he had become in her life and how much she was growing to care for him.

Coming out of Clerys, having delivered the finished design work for advertising a new soap and cologne, Grace found herself suddenly drawn to go to visit the church that Joe always talked about, St Mary's, the Pro-Cathedral. It was situated right in the heart of the city, just off Sackville Street and close to the Abbey Theatre and Liberty Hall. She often passed it but had never even considered going into the Catholic church, which looked like a tall Grecian temple situated on a narrow Dublin street.

Joe's religion was deeply important to him, and Grace was curious to see if the cathedral lived up to his fulsome praise. As she went through the heavy doors she suddenly became conscious of the absolute quiet and stillness inside. It was almost empty except for two or three people praying.

Grace sat down and looked around her. It was a beautiful old building, ornate compared to their church, with a high marble pulpit and statues and carvings. It had a Roman feel to it; she knew that the main high altar with its angels had been carved by Peter Turnerelli, a Dublin-based sculptor with Italian parents.

Sunlight filtered through the tall stained-glass windows depicting Mary and the Irish saints Kevin and Laurence O'Toole. The high dome and windows ensured the church was bright. She instantly liked it. After only a few minutes she forgot that Sackville Street with its trams, hotels and shops was so close by. She felt strangely cloistered here. It truly was a place of prayer and she knelt down in silence. Joe was right – it was a very special church.

She watched as an old beggar man shuffled down from one of the front pews, her nose wrinkling at the sour smell as he passed. He would not even have been let into her church, let alone allowed to sit up at the front. A young mother with small children slipped into a pew a few rows ahead of her, lost in momentary prayer, her baby in her arms. So this was the house of God, the house of prayer. Bowing her head, Grace prayed too.

As she was leaving the church the young mother was also going.

'Excuse me, but a friend told me that the choir sings here sometimes,' said Grace.

'The Palestrina choir sings at mass here on a Sunday,' the sharp-faced young woman confirmed. ''Tis like listening to the angels. You should come along, miss, though the church gets very crowded at times.'

Grace vowed to return.

Chapter 54

Grace

Grace's relationship with Joe was changing and becoming more serious.

Over dinner in Sibley's one night Grace was excited, chatting and laughing as she made plans for next year, wondering where it would bring them, when she realized that Joe seemed cool, detached and uninterested.

'What about your programme for the theatre next year?' she pressed, trying to lighten his mood.

'Who knows?' he shrugged.

Perhaps he was already bored by it ... bored by her... Joe seemed suddenly non-committal. Hurt, she drew back.

Later, sitting in her bedroom reading his letters and poems, Grace felt strangely bereft. Perhaps he had just come into her life like some kind of storm and would now disappear out of it again. Maybe Mother was right – she and someone like Joe Plunkett were not destined to be together.

The next day, however, she received a letter from Joe declaring that he loved her and wanted to marry her. Overcome, she read it again – then her heart sang as she read it over and over again.

Joe loved her and wanted to marry her. It was a proposal of marriage!

Grace scoured every single word of his letter, her heart and mind racing. She laughed at his postscript declaring himself a beggar with no income or earnings and implying there were other reasons no one should marry him. He could be such an idiot sometimes!

A few hours later another letter came, this time apologizing for behaving like a fool, telling her that he loved only her. 'I love you a million million times...'

Grabbing her pen, Grace immediately wrote back: 'Yes, yes, yes...'

She didn't care about what objections her parents or his parents might make to their marriage. She was going to marry the man she loved – Joseph Plunkett.

The Plunkett family were somewhat shocked by the unexpected announcement of their engagement. Count and Countess Plunkett and Joe's sisters and brothers were surprised that Grace was suddenly going to become his wife and part of their well-known family. Joe, however, assured her that his mother, who was away in America, was delighted with the news.

His sister Geraldine, to whom he was very close, had recently become engaged to Tommy Dillon.

'Maybe we should make it a double ceremony,' suggested Joe happily. 'A Plunkett family double celebration!'

Grace smiled, but she could tell from the slight coolness in Geraldine's demeanour that her future sister-in-law was not too keen on the proposal.

'Congratulations,' Joe's younger brothers George and Jack echoed each other warmly.

Grace felt like pinching herself – it was all moving so fast. In a few months' time she and Joe would be married, a proper couple with a home of their own. She dreaded telling her own parents, suspecting that Mother would certainly not approve.

'We'll tell them soon,' she promised him.

Her sisters were delighted for her; they had a high regard for Joe.

'I am so pleased for you both!' cried Muriel, hugging her, when Grace told her the news and showed her the ring Joe had given her. 'MacDonagh and I are so fond of him and soon he will be my brother-in-law!'

'I intend telling Mother and Father soon,' she said to Kate, 'but you know what she will be like...'

'Pick the right moment,' Kate advised sagely. 'Mother's disapproval is horrendous...'

'That's what I fear,' said Grace nervously.

'Her bark is far worse than her bite,' said Nellie reassuringly. 'Mother has accepted MacDonagh and Walter as sons-in-law, and she will accept Joe too.'

Grace hoped that her sister was right.

'I never thought that I would actually fall properly in love and get married,' she admitted. 'I thought that I would end up the old spinster artist aunt working up in some attic with my paints and covered in ink and charcoal.'

'That was never going to happen!' chorused her sisters.

Joe too was happier than she had ever seen him, writing her love letters and proudly telling his close friends about their plans to wed in a few months' time.

They attended the big Anti-Conscription Meeting that Frank Sheehy-Skeffington had organized in the Mansion House; it drew thousands of people. Joe linked his fingers discreetly through hers as they listened to both Padraig Pearse and James Connolly give impassioned speeches. Grace realized how proud she was of the fact that Joe would always beat the heart of things, always ready to stand up and fight for what he believed in... She could see people looking at them together, wondering, for they were an unlikely couple... But fate had somehow brought them together and decreed that she would marry such a man.

Chapter 55

Isabella

Isabella sat alone eating her usual breakfast. The morning newspaper, which had just been delivered, lay beside Frederick's place at the breakfast table. She finished her porridge and was helping herself to a slice of soda bread and marmalade, trying not to be irked by his tardiness. She had left him dressing in their bedroom and preceded him downstairs. Their daily routine usually involved her husband's reading aloud of the newspaper's headlines and a discussion of such over a pot of tea. She was tempted to open the paper herself, but knew how much Frederick enjoyed reading it before he left for the office. Likely there would be an obituary for Dr Francis Heuston. She had attended the respected surgeon's funeral only last week. His poor wife was insistent that he had died of a broken heart following the death of one of their twin sons, Fred, at Gallipoli. Isabella and Frederick both understood such grief.

'Madam, will I hold the breakfast for the Governor?' asked Julia.

Concerned, Isabella left the table and went upstairs.

As she entered their large bedroom she immediately saw him slumped near the side of the bed.

'Frederick, what is it?' She rushed over, leaning down beside him. He seemed to be having a problem speaking and there was a strange twist to his mouth. She managed to lay him against the pillows and bring his feet up on to the bed before calling for help from Julia and her daughters.

Nellie quickly came in and took charge.

'Father, can you hear us? Are you in pain? What is it?'

Frederick tried to say something, but despite his efforts could not get the words out properly. He closed his eyes as if he had not the energy to respond.

'I'll run and see if Dr Mitchell is still at home,' offered Grace.

'Go quickly!' urged Isabella, trying to suppress her mounting sense of panic.

Fortunately Grace was in time and the doctor came immediately to Temple Villas.

'Isabella, you were lucky to catch me before I left for the hospital,' James Mitchell said as he approached Frederick, who seemed barely able to speak or respond.

'Well, Frederick old fellow, what seems to be the matter? Bit of a turn, I believe.'

She watched as the doctor tested his arms and hands, took his blood pressure and listened to his heart. She could see concern written on their neighbour's face.

'Frederick, to my mind you have had a stroke. Your speech and swallow and movement down one side have, I'm afraid, been affected. I know it is alarming for you, but you must rest so we can see how things develop.'

Fear flooded Frederick's now twisted, distorted face, with one drooping eye from which a tear escaped. Isabella felt dizzy and weak herself with the shock of it all.

'Lie back, Frederick, while I have a word with your good wife,' Dr Mitchell said reassuringly as he led her out of the bedroom to the landing.

'Will he die?' she burst out tearfully.

'It is a possibility, for strokes are difficult to treat, and they can recur. We cannot tell if there will be another worse event in the brain which Frederick would not be able to survive,' he replied frankly. 'He may have problems with his breathing and I suspect will not be able to manage to drink or eat properly without risk of choking – that is a common occurrence.'

'What am I to do? Should he go to hospital?'

'Moving Frederick may make the situation worse. My advice is to arrange full nursing care for your husband here at home and I will visit him regularly. But I think you should inform the family and perhaps arrange for them to visit their father.'

Isabella reached for her handkerchief, trying not to cry.

She sent Julia with a message for Muriel and Grace sent a telegram to Kate, informing both of them of their father's illness. This evening she'd write to Ada and Sidney in America and to all of the boys to tell them about Frederick's condition.

A sturdily built young woman appeared. She was an experienced nurse from Sir Patrick Dun's and she took charge at once, settling Frederick in bed in a position that was more comfortable for him and made it easier to breathe.

Muriel arrived immediately, having left Mary to mind the children.

'What has happened to Father?' she asked tearfully as she raced upstairs.

Kate was there two hours later and was in a state as she sat by his bed.

Frederick seemed to be sleeping heavily, saliva running from one side of his twisted mouth which the nurse wiped away.

MacDonagh came and Isabella could see her son-in-law was upset. He and Frederick enjoyed a close friendship and he went in and sat beside the bed to talk to him.

'Has Frederick had the last rites?' he asked her.

'I will ask our rector to come to see Frederick.'

'I mean the priest,' MacDonagh persisted. 'Has

he had the priest to anoint him?'

'No,' she replied tersely.

'Frederick would want the priest,' he said firmly. 'The priest from the church he attends in Rathmines.'

'Mother, if Father could talk I'm sure he would want his own priest, not the rector,' agreed Grace. 'He is Catholic, after all.'

Isabella could feel a strange tightness and tension in her head.

'I will not have a priest under my roof,' she insisted fiercely.

'This is Father's roof too,' Kate reminded her gently. 'It is his faith.'

'Grace is right,' continued MacDonagh. 'Frederick should have the priest come to the house to give him the rites. The man is entitled to that.'

'I forbid it!' she found herself shouting. 'I will not have it.'

She could see MacDonagh flush with annoyance and a look of disappointment in her daughters' faces. A few minutes afterwards her son-in-law said his goodbyes to Frederick and left the house angrily.

An hour later a priest came to the door enquiring for Frederick and Julia showed him upstairs. Isabella was about to despatch him back to his parish church, but on seeing Frederick the priest immediately greeted him warmly and stepped over near the bed. Grace and Kate were clearly daring her to interfere as the priest began his prayers in Latin and Frederick opened his eyes in recognition.

She could not bear to watch and went downstairs. Nellie brought her a soothing cup of tea in the drawing room from where she refused to budge until she saw the priest leave her house. Muriel went home and a night nurse arrived to take over from her colleague.

Frederick appeared calmer, more relaxed.

'He's holding his own,' the nurse informed her.

The following two weeks were exhausting, but Frederick clung tenaciously to life. Every time he took a small sip of water or tried to swallow a spoon of clear broth Isabella was sure it would be his end.

MacDonagh had not returned to Temple Villas and she hated the coolness that now existed between her and Muriel. Christmas would soon be here. She wanted her daughters and her grandchildren around: this might be the last Christmas they would all share together.

Burying her pride, Isabella took out her pen and wrote to MacDonagh, asking for his forgiveness and inviting him, Muriel and the children to join them at Temple Villas for Christmas dinner.

Chapter 56

Grace

Grace listened to the Palestrina choir singing some Handel as she sat in the crowded wooden pew. Their voices were pure and beautiful, the music so stirring that tears pricked her eyes. The long mass in Latin seemed no hindrance, as the voices of the choir filled the roof and dome of the great cathedral.

The boys and young men of the Palestrina well deserved their reputation; it was the finest choir she had ever heard. They were like a host of angels singing and it moved her deeply. Joe had told her that the world-famous tenor John McCormack, when he was younger, had trained and sung here, his first audience the poor from the nearby tenements who were able to listen to such a voice sing at their masses.

This church was so very different from their church in Rathmines, for here no well-to-do Dublin families were given pride of place and positioned in the front pews. St Mary's was a church of the people. Some of the families she recognized from Liberty Hall and from serving school dinners with Maud Gonne and her sisters – factory and dockworkers kneeling to pray alongside shop-keepers, students and bankers. Mother would have hated it.

Grace's faith had always been assumed, marching to Sunday school and service with her family. Now she was an adult and she wanted to make a choice about it. To Joe his spirituality and faith meant so much. Father, despite Mother's disapproval, had kept his faith, praying in his own church. It had seemed weak when she was young, but now she realized the hidden strength that Father possessed.

Kneeling down, she put her head in her hands and prayed.

She thought of her father. Getting up to leave,

she stopped in front of the brass candlestand with its little flames flickering in front of a large statue. She reached into her purse and dropped a few pennies into the stand, taking a small candle and lighting it.

'Lord, this is for my father. Look after him, please.'

Mother was sitting quietly reading in the drawing room when she returned home. The nurse was upstairs minding Father. Mother looked tired. Father's illness had taken its toll on her too.

'Mother, I want to talk to you about something important.'

Her mother put down her novel and looked up.

'Are you all right, dear?'

'Yes ... Mother, I'm engaged to be married – to Joe Plunkett.'

For a second Mother looked confused.

'The Plunkett boy with the car and the motorcycle? You intend marrying him?'

'Yes,' she said, keeping her voice level. 'We love each other.'

'How can you even consider such a marriage?' snapped Mother. 'The Plunketts may be wealthy property owners, but I have heard of creditors and unpaid bills. They say the countess is a law unto herself and does what she pleases.'

'Mother, I am not marrying the count or countess, I am marrying Joe. Joe Plunkett is the man I love. I will not let religion be a barrier.'

'Why am I so afflicted with such daughters?' Mother sighed dramatically. 'There are also rumours that that Plunkett boy is consumptive and has to travel abroad for his health.'

'He has had pleurisy but is much better now,' Grace returned angrily.

'But what if his tubercular illness returns? You could be left a widow.'

'Mother, with the war thousands of wives will be left widows. I can't think of such a thing. Why would you even say it?'

'I am only thinking of your good.' Mother's eyes flashed.

'Can't you be happy for me, that I have found someone to love and be loved by? I am twenty-seven years old, nearly twenty-eight – do you not want to see me married like my sisters?'

'Grace, I want only what is best for you.'

'Then be happy for me, for marrying Joe Plunkett is my happiness.'

Mother said nothing more and picked up her novel.

'I wanted to tell you, as Joe and I intend officially announcing our engagement as is the custom.'

She went upstairs and sat beside her father. He had lost weight and could not stand, walk or talk. One side of his body was still weak. She reached for his hand and his eyes opened.

She told him about Joe.

'I am happy, Father – very happy.'

He tried to talk and she knew that he approved of their engagement. Grace kissed his cheek and sat with him awhile.

1916

Chapter 57

Nellie

January brought cold weather and the British prime minister's announcement of the Military Service Act introducing conscription for all single men between eighteen and forty-one years of age in Great Britain.

'Thank heaven that Ireland is not included,' sighed Nellie, who suspected that her employment bureau would be inundated with Irish men returning from England. She was greatly relieved that her artist brother, Gabriel, had made the wise decision a few weeks ago to escape the war by leaving London and sailing to America.

Unfortunately, she and Marie could no longer use the upstairs room in Countess Markievicz's building, but MacDonagh, hearing of their plight, arranged for them to have space for a small office in the Volunteers' headquarters in Dawson Street. Nellie was filled with gratitude for her brother-in-law's kindness.

Asquith's announcement of conscription triggered an immediate exodus from Britain of young Irish men returning home, many coming to the Bureau for assistance. They urgently needed to find both employment and accommodation. A few were already members of the Volunteers and many others were now prepared to join.

The bureau was busy but she and Marie dealt with each man's situation discreetly, James Connolly helping as much as he could to find jobs for them on the docks or in warehouses or factories. Joe and the Plunkett family had generously offered to help too and had agreed that some of the men could stay in Larkfield, their home in Kimmage. The Volunteers already used the place for training. Set in acres of land, with outhouses, large barn, bakery and mill, it was ideal and provided much-needed accommodation for those anxious to avoid conscription.

Joe called into Nellie's office.

'Joe, we are very grateful to you and your family for helping the men,' Nellie thanked him. 'It's a relief to know that we have somewhere for those coming from Liverpool and London to stay if they need it.'

'The men are welcome,' he nodded modestly. 'Some of them have started our own unit of the Volunteers.'

'No finer fellows,' she smiled.

'Nellie, if by any chance you come across a chap looking for work who is a bookkeeper and well able for accounts, I could do with him,' he sighed, cleaning his glasses. 'The accounts are in a state. Mother has gone off travelling and I'm stuck with all her ledgers and figures and trying to keep track of things, while Geraldine is at the end of her tether with so much to do, so we need to find someone.'

Nellie knew that the Plunketts owned property and collected rent all over Dublin; they were rumoured to have built many of the finest houses in Rathgar, Rathmines and Donnybrook.

'I have some important business of my own I must attend to and don't have the time for it,' he went on. 'If we could find someone to help out a few days a week it would be ideal.'

'I'll see what I can do,' she promised.

A few days later she was interviewing a young man from west Cork named Michael Collins. He had just crossed from London, where he had been a very active member of No. 1 Company of the Irish Volunteers. Both his parents were dead and he told her that he was keen to find work. He was twenty-six, with an excellent head for figures. On moving to London he had worked in the Post Office Savings Bank in Kensington, then for a stockbroker and for the Board of Trade; lately he'd been employed in the Guaranty Trust Company of New York's London office. He'd done his civil service exams and was well used to double-entry systems and balance sheets.

In her opinion, the young man from Clonakilty seemed extremely bright and capable, a likely bookkeeper for the Plunkett family. Nellie contacted Joe immediately. He returned to the Bureau where Nellie introduced them and the two men seemed to get on very well. They were soon deep in conversation, ranging from the Gaelic League and the influence of Arthur Griffith to plays Collins had attended on the London stage. Nellie smiled as she watched them walk out to Joe's car together.

The interview was successful as Michael Collins was employed by Count and Countess Plunkett and Joe to work a few days a week at

Larkfield managing their financial affairs, while the rest of the time he spent working in the nearby offices of an accountancy firm.

Nellie was pleased that her employment bureau had managed to find him work and Grace soon told her that Mick Collins was proving invaluable to Joe, and also that he had become immediately involved with helping to run Larkfield's local Volunteer group.

Chapter 58

Grace

Grace pulled on her sturdy boots, warm coat, hat and gloves as she set off to visit Larkfield. Joe was ill, laid up there with a bad throat and a chest infection. Even though he wrote, she missed him terribly and longed to see him.

She took a tram to Kimmage and briskly walked the rest of the way along the muddy road and avenue to Larkfield. It was an imposing mansion surrounded by fields, cottages and outbuildings. Approaching the house she noticed a large group of men standing near the barn, while others were kicking a football around.

Inside, the old house was rather ramshackle, with a fine staircase on either side of the large hallway with a balcony overlooking it.

Joe looked pale and drawn, his eyes huge in his long face, and he seemed even thinner than usual, his dark hair standing up in greasy tufts.

'Oh Joe, what is the matter with you?' Grace gasped, unable to hide her alarm at seeing the large swelling on his throat.

'Don't worry Grace, I am fine,' he reassured her. 'The old glands always give me trouble when I am low, but I'm on the mend and feeling better for seeing you.'

A fire blazed in the grate, warming the room which had maps and diagrams of the city scattered over the floor. On a table in the drawing room lay a wireless radio with pieces of wire and metal which he was tinkering with. He fiddled with some of the dials and buttons, causing the machine to buzz alarmingly. Grace was startled.

'It won't bite or burn or hurt you, I promise.'

Dubious, she tested the equipment, as he demonstrated to her how to use it to transmit signals and Morse code. He also showed her another, smaller wireless he was working on.

'The aim is for this one to be easily portable,' he explained.

'Who will use it?'

'The men use it to send messages and to keep in contact with each other and other Volunteer units.'

Despite being ill it was clear that Joe was involved in planning some kind of large mission with the Volunteers, judging by the equipment and charts that were scattered around the place.

'Are all the men outside Volunteers?' she enquired, watching them from the window; a group of them seemed to be drilling.

'Yes, some of them have only recently arrived

from Liverpool to avoid conscription.'

'Poor Nellie is rather swamped trying to help them.'

'My parents have agreed that they can stay here. It's out of the way and they are safe and have shelter. It's good to see them training.'

'It's like an army,' she laughed.

'Have you ever thought of joining Cumann na mBan?' he asked lightly. 'Or the Citizen Army?'

'Joe, can you imagine me in tweeds and boots, marching and learning how to clean and store guns and use bandages?' she joked, running her fingers through her hair. 'You know I'm not at all like Nellie or your sisters.'

They had tea together – Grace made him tasty Welsh rarebit from some cheese, bread and Worcestershire sauce.

'Joe, I want to tell you something,' she said firmly as they sat by the fire.

She could see a look of concern fill his dark eyes.

'I have decided that I want to become a Roman Catholic.'

'Grace, there is no need for you to convert on my behalf,' he said quietly, taking her hand in his. 'My love, it will make no difference to us marrying.'

'I know that, Joe, but I have been considering it for a long time. Attending masses in the Pro-Cathedral has renewed my faith and given me great spiritual comfort. I've talked to your friend Father Sherwin in the University Church and he has very kindly agreed to instruct me and baptize me formally. I want to convert before our marriage so that you and I will share the same faith and can have a Catholic wedding ceremony.'

'Grace, you know how happy this will make me,' he admitted, 'but what of your family?'

'Mother will be livid and disapproving. That is why I want it to be our secret.'

'Very well, we will keep it quiet if that is what you want,' he agreed.

Geraldine and their brother George appeared then, so, as it was starting to get dark, Grace walked back up the avenue to catch the tram home. She hated leaving Joe and couldn't help but worry about him; he looked so unwell despite his assurance that all was bully as they hugged goodbye.

Chapter 59

Nellie

'I do think you girls should consider joining the VAD,' urged Mother enthusiastically as they sat having tea. 'As part of the war effort, the Royal College of Science has set up a sphagnum moss depot which sends moss to the army field hospitals.'

'Sphagnum moss – it sounds disgusting!' Grace said with disdain. 'I'm far too busy to spend my time sorting heaps of some dirty old moss.'

'Dorothy says it is a miracle plant. Far better for healing wounds than ordinary bandages and dressings, and they are using it in all the hospitals,' said Mother defensively. 'Her daughter and daughter-in-law both find the work in the depot very rewarding.'

Nellie had heard of the great success army surgeons on the front had, using moss with the badly injured, but she was stretched already with her work in the Bureau and at Liberty Hall.

'Nellie, you could volunteer to help out, surely? They are urgently trying to recruit some more ladies.'

'Mother, I am already working hard for the war effort,' she protested. 'I am trying to stop young Irish men being conscripted into the army so that they will never fight or have need of moss dressings to treat their battle wounds!'

Mother looked disappointed. She was already involved with the church committee, sending parcels of knitted socks, scarves and gloves, along with cigarettes and sweets to the regiments on the Western Front.

Nellie sighed, for nothing she ever did seemed to please her mother. Grace was different because Mother could see her work and boast to her friends that Grace had a sketch in the paper, or had designed the theatre programme for a play they attended. Nellie, on the other hand, was involved in all the type of things that Mother despised.

'I was just thinking about your brothers and that it would be good to see the women of the family involved in the war effort too,' Mother continued doggedly.

'The boys shouldn't take any part in it,' Nellie blurted out. 'This war is not their fight.'

'This family has always been loyal to the crown and the empire,' Mother reprimanded her. 'Your brothers all know their duty and will decide what to do for themselves.'

'Even if it is the wrong decision.'

Mother flushed and Nellie felt immediately contrite. Her mother was bound to be worried about her brothers: she spent much of her time attending memorial services or calling to give her condolences to friends who had lost a son in the war.

'I'm sorry, Mother, but I cannot get involved,' she apologized.

'Nor me,' added Grace.

'I would offer my own services if I hadn't your father ill at home to contend with,' Mother said pointedly before taking her leave of them.

'Moss – did you ever? I have all kinds of arrangements of my own to make for the wedding,' Grace confided when she was sure Mother was well out of hearing.

'When are you going to tell Mother about it?'

'As late as possible, for if she had her way Joe and I would never marry.'

'Is everything all right?' Nellie probed, for of late Grace was rarely at home and had become somewhat secretive.

'Fine,' she replied, giving little away. 'Joe and I are just busy planning things.'

Nellie could not help but feel a little envious, wishing that she was married like Kate or Muriel, or even engaged like Grace. Sometimes it seemed that love was passing her by. Every day she was surrounded by men and yet she had never been in love, never had a man write her a love letter or tell her that he loved and cared deeply for her.

'Love will find you, Nellie,' kind-hearted Kate reassured her. 'You just have to be patient.'

Chapter 60

Grace

Joe wrote to her every day, letter after letter, some days including a few lines of his poetry. When Grace read the words of 'New Love', a poem he had written about her and their love for each other, she felt exhilarated and giddy with happiness, for she knew that Joe truly loved her.

Their engagement had been published in *Irish Life* magazine a few days before Valentine's Day, so now the whole world knew that she and Joe were to be wed. Furious, Mother refused to speak to her, she was so angry and annoyed with her. So Grace divided her time between visiting Joe at Larkfield and staying at Muriel's.

Joe was still unwell and Grace worried that Mother's suspicions that he had TB might be true, but he stated resolutely that the doctor had said that it was *not* consumption and that soon he would be his old self again.

Joe was always busy, searching for books or writing. She could not help but see that the dining table at Larkfield was covered with maps and plans of the city and of train and tram lines; there were also scrawled lists of numbers and names. He was clearly involved in some kind of planning or strategy for the Volunteers.

Nellie had certainly found the perfect man to assist Joe not only with the Plunkett financial affairs but with the Volunteers: Mick Collins was at his side constantly, totting up and working out figures too. He and Joe had already established an easy, close friendship and Mick helped with training the 'Liverpool Lambs', as the growing number of men staying at Larkfield were known. Sometimes Grace watched from the window as he took a few men out to the shooting range for target practice.

One day when she arrived, Mick Collins got up from his pile of bills and ledgers and offered her some tea from the pot in the kitchen. Sturdily built and handsome, Grace suspected that many young women would lose their hearts to him.

'You are proving a great help to Joe,' she said gratefully.

'I'm glad to be useful to Joe and the family,' he replied, his blue eyes sincere as he passed her the milk jug before discreetly disappearing off to another room with his ledgers to let them have time on their own.

Joe's health rallied and they went to a concert. Another night they went to dinner in Jammet's restaurant, where they were given a warm welcome by the head waiter, who led them to one of the romantic corner tables in the restaurant.

Over the meal they discussed their wedding plans and the future. Joe was keen for them to get married around Easter time, as they hated being apart from each other and longed to be together. He felt a wedding during Lent would be best.

'We cannot marry then,' Grace protested. 'Lent is not the proper time to hold a church ceremony. Why don't we marry at Easter instead? I've always liked Easter.'

'We may be running a revolution then,' he answered cryptically, his dark eyes serious as he watched for her reaction. 'But if we are married, we can go into it together.'

Grace did not know what to say... A revolution. She thought immediately of the maps and diagrams scattered about his room and all over the dining table at Larkfield.

Joe refused to be drawn any further and Grace tried to push her fears aside, for she had no idea of military matters. Besides, it might never happen.

'Joe, all I want is for us to be married,' she said quietly, meeting his gaze.

'Then as you say, my love, we will arrange to marry at Easter,' he agreed. 'It will be a double family wedding with my sister and Tommy Dillon.'

'That sounds absolutely wonderful,' she sighed, relieved, folding her fingers in his.

'That way if your family do not attend at least there will be plenty of us Plunketts,' he teased.

Although Joe and his sister were very close, Grace felt Geraldine would certainly not be pleased with the idea of such a wedding. She looked down on Grace because she was not academic and considered talk of science and political matters tedious. Grace's passion was reserved for the colourful world of art and theatre and writing.

She knew that people often considered her aloof and rather arrogant – too independent and carefree – but with Joe it was different ... *she* was different. For Joe Plunkett knew her heart and soul with no pretences. Neither of them was perfect, but they loved each other dearly and were committed to one another ... and in only a few short weeks she would be his wife.

Chapter 61

Muriel

The tall man was standing across the road from their house; Muriel could see him clearly. He was wearing a long coat and smoking a cigarette, pretending to lean against the wall waiting for someone to arrive.

'I can see him again,' she informed MacDonagh. 'He's watching us and he has a notebook. I saw him writing down when Mary called to bring Barbara for a walk and when Grace dropped over to see me this morning. Why is he watching and spying on us? Why is he allowed to stand gawping at us and our home? He is some kind of spy. Surely that must be unlawful?'

'He's a DMP man and is just following orders and doing what he is told.' Her husband shrugged nonchalantly. 'Sometimes he has another policeman with him.'

'Do you mean that bald man with the glasses?'

'The very same. They are a right pair of detect-ives.'

'I don't like it,' she whispered. 'It's making me nervous having them spying on us. What are they looking for? Someday I am going to walk up to one of them and ask him.'

'Muriel, don't get upset. They won't do any-thing, I promise. They are just trying to discover who I see and where I go. Tom Clarke warned us that the Castle is watching us all and to be care-ful.'

Over the past two months MacDonagh had changed. He was distracted and clearly involved in something, but would say little to her. When he campaigned for Home Rule he had been full of it, full of rhetoric and plans, and the same when he had spoken out for women's suffrage and even when he had tried to help negotiate between employers and the union during the Lockout. He had made speech after speech railing against the Volunteers' involvement in the war. But now he was quiet and secretive – something she was not used to.

A large quantity of rifles had been delivered to their house one night, stashed away in cupboards and wardrobes and hidden under floorboards. Over a number of days the guns had been collec-ted by members of the Volunteers. Muriel was terrified that the DMP men might stop and search the visitors to their home.

'It will be all right,' MacDonagh said sooth-ingly. 'Nobody knows about them.'

MacDonagh constantly met with Padraig, Joe, Eamonn Ceannt, Sean Mac Diarmada, Tom

Clarke and James Connolly. Sometimes they came to Oakley Road.

'Is it Volunteer business again?' Muriel probed, but he said little.

They had always shared things, so now when he said nothing to her she could not help but worry.

That spring, Volunteer marches, parades and drills were held in the city and a massive rally took place on St Patrick's Day at which Eoin MacNeill, their leader, took the salute. MacDonagh was proud of such a large demonstration of well-trained men.

They'd celebrated Barbara's first birthday a few days later, Muriel making a special cake and inviting some family and friends to join them.

It didn't matter what her husband said, Muriel couldn't help but be anxious about whatever he was now embroiled in. He and Tom Clarke, Sean, Joe and Padraig were always in a huddle talking together. He had confided to her that he was now a member of the Irish Republican Brotherhood and there seemed to be endless meetings. From snatches of overheard conversation, she guessed that they were organizing something and she suspected that it might be not only risky but dangerous.

Poor Desmond FitzGerald, who had come to meet MacDonagh during the summer, had been arrested under Dublin Castle's Defence of the Realm Act and was imprisoned in Mountjoy. Muriel worried about what would happen if MacDonagh were arrested too. She couldn't bear it.

Chapter 62

Nellie

Nellie had just finished interviewing John Hennessey, an insurance agent who had crossed over from Liverpool, and she was walking him out to the door to Dawson Street when Michael Mallin, chief of staff of the Irish Citizen Army, arrived.

'More recruits?' he gestured.

'Yes, I'm afraid that I'm going to have to ask Mr Connolly again for some help placing the men.'

'I'll be heading back down to Liberty Hall later. I'll bring a message to him,' he offered.

'Will you have a cup of tea?' she invited him. 'I'm just going to make one.'

'Yes,' he smiled, perusing the *Volunteer* and the *Workers' Republic* newspapers, which lay on her desk, as she boiled the water and filled the teapot.

She liked and respected Michael Mallin, for he was the one who trained and drilled Nellie and the other women in the Citizen Army, teaching them how to load and unload a gun and how to use their weapons. He insisted on target practice for everyone, male and female. The first few times Nellie had used a heavy rifle her shoulder had ached and her shots had gone wildly off target. She was hopeless, but Commandant Mallin, with great patience, had insisted she keep on trying until she had a good aim and could hit the target area.

'Have you read the article about training?' he asked with a heavy sigh.

'I did,' she said, pouring him some tea. 'It annoyed me, that part all about the Volunteers parading and parading till all their glory faded.'

'Well, the time for only parading is almost gone,' he confided. 'It is all fixed now.'

'Fixed?'

'The rebellion is fixed for a few weeks' time, for Easter Sunday,' he said slowly as he took a sip of his tea. 'And it will be far more than a parade when the Volunteers and the Citizen Army all go out together...'

Nellie caught his eyes. She could see he was serious and also that he trusted her with this information, valued her as a member of the Citizen Army. She felt strangely nervous and excited, aware that finally the talk of rebellion was over and in only a month their long hours of marches, training and target practice would be put into action.

She kept silent about the rebellion. When Grace chatted about her plans for an Easter wedding, she held her tongue. When Muriel worried why Mac-Donagh was so frequently away at so many meetings and rarely at home, she said nothing. Even when Mother asked her about treating herself to a new Easter hat, Nellie encouraged her to arrange an appointment with her favourite milliner.

A few days later she called into Tom Clarke's tobacconist shop to get a newspaper and met Michael Mallin again. He and Tom, James Connolly, William Partridge of the Citizen Army and Sean Mac Diarmada were deep in conversation at the counter with a pretty young lady.

The group greeted her as Mr Clarke got her paper and enquired pleasantly about the Bureau.

'Miss Nellie Gifford, let me introduce you to Miss Margaret Skinnider,' said William, smiling and stepping forward politely. 'She's over visiting from Scotland.'

Nellie shook the other woman's hand.

'Margaret is an old friend of mine,' continued James Connolly. 'She's been staying at Surrey House with the countess for a few days but returns home tomorrow.'

'But I'll be back in Dublin in a few weeks,' she reminded them. 'Back for Easter.'

The word hung in the air. Michael caught her gaze, Nellie aware suddenly that this conversation was serious, a meeting between the Citizen Army leaders and Tom Clarke and Sean Mac Diarmada of the Volunteers.

'Nellie, Miss Skinnider will be back in Dublin before Easter. Would you be able to meet with her and show her around certain parts of the city?' Michael asked.

'Of course,' she agreed.

'Then I look forward very much to us meeting again,' smiled the young Scottish woman as Nellie took her leave of them.

Walking back up Sackville Street, Nellie's heart pounded as she realized that plans and strategy for a rebellion were moving forward and that soon she would be part of it all.

Chapter 63

Grace

Grace was torn between nervousness and excitement as she set off for town, for today she would be baptized into the Catholic Church.

Father Sherwin welcomed her to the church on St Stephen's Green. Joe's younger sister, Fiona Plunkett, was her sponsor, standing smiling near her side as Father Sherwin took her gently through the ceremony and baptism rite. As the priest anointed her with holy oils and washed her forehead with water, Grace felt a strange sense of elation, as if she had finally come home. She dearly wished that Joe could be there with her, but he was too ill. He had written the most beautiful poem to mark the occasion of her baptism and her eyes had filled with tears as she read and re-read it. Their love was not just a physical one but also one of the spirit.

She wanted to shout about her new faith, her love of Joe and their planned marriage on Easter Sunday, but she knew that she must keep it secret a bit longer. She would tell Father, for he was the only one who could fully understand and approve of her decision.

To Grace's dismay, Joe's old health troubles had come back; it was clear that he was very ill with a severe infection. He was admitted to Mrs Quinn's Nursing Home on Mountjoy Square to have surgery to remove the enlarged gland in his neck. It was a big operation and Grace was beside herself with worry.

When she came to see him after his operation she could not disguise her shock at his appearance, for Joe looked ghastly, lying in the bed battered, bruised and exhausted with a huge dressing on his neck. The nurses came in regularly to check on him.

Dr MacAuley, his surgeon, came into the room and Grace sat listening as he told Joe in no uncertain terms that there was no question of him getting up or discharging himself he was far too ill for that. Joe looked down at the bedclothes as the doctor tried to lay down the law to him.

'Miss Gifford, I hope you can use some of your powers of persuasion on your fiancé as he is proving a hopeless patient and refuses to rest.'

'I'll try,' she promised.

But it was useless. Every time she came to see Joe over the next few days there were groups of people around the bed – Mick Collins, MacDonagh and Sean Mac Diarmada – and they seemed to be discussing some big plan for the Volunteers for Easter.

'But we are to be married at Easter,' she reminded him gently when the others had left.

One day a document was delivered to the nursing home. Joe became agitated, poring over it and scribbling notes, then, despite his doctor's orders, he insisted on dressing and returning to Larkfield.

Alarmed, Grace rushed to visit him there.

'I'll make you a hot drink, some tea or cocoa?' she offered, wishing that he would sit down quietly and rest like his doctor had ordered.

'No, thank you,' he replied. 'I need help with this document, Grace.'

His bed was covered with sheets of paper with letters crossed out.

'This all has to be deciphered,' he said in a sombre voice.

'Do you want me to go and find someone – Mick or George?'

'No, Grace, I need you to help me. Get a pen and some paper and write down exactly the letters I tell you in the precise order,' he explained, getting out his notebook. 'If I make a mistake, cross it out and then put in the one I say, or if you are unsure, ask me to repeat it.'

'Yes,' she agreed, worried because he needed to rest. But, grabbing a fountain pen and slipping off her jacket, she sat down at his bedside.

He began to read a few words, a sentence. Grace tried to concentrate and make some sense of it.

'Replace C with an A,' he instructed. 'Replace U with a T. I'm not sure if that is a B or D – try D.'

She jotted the words down as quickly as she could, trying to keep the order and follow what he was saying. It was some kind of shorthand or code, but she could already clearly read that the members of Sinn Fein and the executive and heads of the Volunteers were all to be arrested.

A chill ran over her as she continued to write, for

the document detailed plans to arrest the members of the organizations of which so many of their family and friends were part. It also outlined plans to confine members of the DMP and even the RIC to their barracks while British military authorities took over Liberty Hall, Larkfield, Countess Markievicz's home Surrey House, the Volunteers' headquarters, St Enda's school, Eoin MacNeill's home and the O'Rahillys' house in Herbert Park.

'Joe, where did you get this?' she demanded as she finished and began to read over what she had written down.

'It's a document from the Dublin Castle authorities which we received through a friend of a friend,' he said, pushing his bony fingers through his hair, distracted. 'They obviously plan to arrest us all, even though we haven't done a thing yet. What irony!'

Grace swallowed hard. She knew they were planning something, but he had chosen not to confide in her and now it would be to no avail.

'We will all be arrested and deported, the organization decimated, and all for nothing.' He was utterly crestfallen.

'I'm sorry, Joe.' Grace put down her pen.

'They can't get away with this,' he went on angrily. 'We need to get copies of this to everyone. Let them know what they are planning.'

Grace was filled with trepidation that Joe would be arrested. Armed DMP men and soldiers had surrounded Larkfield only a few weeks earlier and then mysteriously disappeared.

'Joe, you are not well. It is too dangerous for you to stay here,' she pleaded. 'The military may come and arrest you.'

'Go and find George,' he begged. 'Tell him we need to print this with our own press and send copies of it to warn people of what lies ahead. Call their bluff and print it in the newspapers.'

Later that evening an exhausted Joe finally agreed to return to the nursing home.

The papers refused to print the document Grace had helped decode; Dublin Castle took immediate steps to ensure that its publication was suppressed. But Frank Sheehy-Skeffington had a copy and soon word of the Castle's plans to move against the Volunteers and Sinn Fein spread.

Even though it was clear that he and his friends were now all in danger of arrest, Joe continued to study his maps, charts and plans despite Grace's objections.

'Joe you need to rest, to get well,' she implored him.

As she kissed him good night she was filled with a sense of foreboding that something terrible was going to happen to the man she loved.

Chapter 64

Nellie

As Easter drew near, Liberty Hall became a hive of activity: preparations for the rebellion were in hand. Beneath the ground floor of the union building, men worked secretly, making bullets, grenades and bombs, stockpiling a large arsenal of weapons. Only a few weeks earlier the DMP had raided the union's shop, where Rosie and Helena worked, and everyone had been terrified they would find the hidden arms supply.

'They'll be back,' warned Helena ominously.

James Connolly and Michael Mallin had called all members of the Irish Citizen Army together, asking them 'Are you prepared to fight for Ireland's freedom?' and 'Are you prepared to fight alongside the Irish Volunteers?'

'Yes!' answered Nellie proudly, aware that she was pledging her commitment to fight in the rebellion that would soon begin.

William Partridge had often suggested to James Connolly that they fly the green flag of the Irish Republic over Liberty Hall.

'Wouldn't it be a grand thing to have the green flag flying there proudly for the entire world to see?'

Now Connolly finally agreed that the time had come for the flag, the symbol of Irish freedom, to fly over the union building and the date was set for Palm Sunday, the Sunday before Easter. Notice of the event was printed in the *Workers' Republic*.

When the day came, Nellie joined the thousands of people gathered in the April sunshine. Beresford Square was packed, as were Butt Bridge and O'Connell Bridge. Tara Street and all the roads around were blocked, with huge crowds of people lining up along the quays and the river, everyone craning to witness the momentous occasion of a green Irish flag without the crown being flown over such a public building.

The Citizen Army stood in formation on three sides of the square outside Liberty Hall, Nellie joining her friends in the women's section. The Boy Scouts and the Fintan Lalor Pipe Band stood all together in the warm open air. James Connolly, in his Citizen Army uniform, smiled as he, Commandant Mallin and Countess Markievicz took in the huge crowds that had come to witness the event despite rumours that the army might intervene to prevent such a display of nationalism.

Great care had been taken in choosing the colour-bearer who would have the honour of raising the flag and Connolly had finally picked sixteen-year-old Molly O'Reilly, a member of the Women Workers' Union and the Citizen Army. Molly, who lived on Gardiner Street, had helped Nellie in the soup kitchens during the Lockout and Nellie believed that the choice of such a bright young woman demonstrated James Connolly's and the union's regard for both women and the working class.

Molly was escorted by a colour guard-of-honour. Everyone fell hushed as she stepped forward and James Connolly officially handed her the green flag while the guards presented arms and the buglers sounded the salute. Captain Kit Poole and a guard of sixteen men then escorted her as she carried the flag into Liberty Hall.

Nellie held her breath, the crowds silent, until a few minutes later a radiant Molly appeared up on the roof. Everyone watched as the flag was hoisted and began to unfurl, catching the wind and blowing proudly in the clear blue Dublin sky, the

341

green flag of Ireland with its golden harp flying there for everyone to see.

A huge roar erupted, the crowds bursting into tumultuous applause and cheering, hats flung in the air. Nellie herself was overcome with emotion, tears filling her eyes. Looking around, she could see that the men beside her were equally affected, as were many others in the crowd.

The pipe band began to play joyfully as the cheering and celebrations continued. Connolly ordered the Citizen Army battalion to present arms as the bugles sounded again, then he asked all those present to be prepared to give their lives if necessary to keep the Irish flag flying.

Looking up, Nellie thought of the regiments of young Irish soldiers that passed by Liberty Hall on their way to being shipped out to fight in the war. For many, this fluttering green flag might be one of the last sights they had of the country they loved.

That night Connolly called them together to tell them that the 'Rising' would happen next week. He instructed them in ways to occupy and burrow through buildings, and to fight from the rooftops.

'The odds are a thousand to one against us,' he explained gravely.

Looking into his brown eyes and seeing the sincerity, courage and integrity there, Nellie knew that she, like everyone else, was ready to follow James Connolly and fight.

Chapter 65

Isabella

Liebert had surprised them by returning home to Dublin after years away at sea. Isabella warmly welcomed her dearly loved son, who had a few weeks' leave from his ship. Life in the navy suited him: he was tanned, fit and more muscular, but had also become more confident and mature. She had missed him terribly, for with his easy way and good humour he had always been a particular favourite of hers. His return to Temple Villas brought great joy and Frederick's eyes welled with tears when he saw their son.

'Your father is in good spirits despite everything, and your visit home has cheered him up immensely.'

'I'm so sorry, Mother,' he apologized, shocked to see how infirm his father was. 'I should have come sooner. I cannot believe that Father has become such a frail old man.'

She watched as he tried to make his amends for such a long absence from home.

They still employed a nurse to assist with her husband's care and had purchased a wheelchair, as Frederick was barely able to walk or stand unaided and his balance was very poor. With infinite patience, Liebert helped his father downstairs and into the wheelchair, bringing him for walks in the park and down to Rathmines, and even wheeling him out to the garden if there was any sunshine.

'The prodigal has returned,' teased Nellie and Grace, though Isabella knew that her daughters were delighted to have their brother finally home in Temple Villas.

He regaled them with stories of the navy and shipboard life, as well as of the exotic places he had visited around the world – Africa, Egypt, South America and Hong Kong. He also described the unseen danger of German U-boat attacks that now filled the sea. He would sit with Frederick in the bedroom telling him of his voyages and sea crossings, of the huge blue whales that lived in the deep oceans and of schools of jumping dolphins and coloured flying fish.

Liebert scooped Muriel's children up in his arms and declared them two little rascals, and he enjoyed meeting MacDonagh, whom he declared a fine brother-in-law even if they did disagree politically.

Isabella had heard only a week before his arrival that young Frank Heuston, the second of the Heuston twins, had died at Ypres. She was overwhelmed with sadness when she thought of the kind young man, who only months ago had been let home on leave to attend his father's funeral. Now he was dead, just like his twin brother. She made the decision not to tell Frederick: it would upset him far too much.

'You cannot distress Father with such news,' agreed Muriel, who had accompanied her to the Heustons' home on St Stephen's Green to pay their respects.

Liebert read the papers aloud every morning for Frederick and Isabella begged him not to mention the casualties of the war but to concentrate on good news, if there was any...

Her son spent much of his time catching up with many of his old friends, some now married with families of their own. He brought her out to lunches and to a show in The Gaiety. Her daughters all seemed so caught up in their own lives now and were rarely at home, so it was a joy to have her son to escort her.

She confided her worries about Grace's engagement to Joe Plunkett.

'Grace will pay absolutely no heed to my concerns or wishes in this regard,' she complained. 'She and your sisters all have minds of their own and refuse to give any credence to anything I say or advise.'

'From what I remember they were always like that,' he joked, 'so I see that nothing has changed.'

'Liebert, I do wish that you could stay in Ireland,' she ventured nervously. 'It would be wonderful for your father to have you back living here, at home or close by – whatever would suit. Frederick does miss you boys so much.'

'Mother, I return to my ship in a few weeks,' he answered patiently. 'I enjoy being at sea – I could not imagine anything else. I have no plans to return to live here.'

'Of course,' she replied, trying to hide her crushing disappointment.

'Let us enjoy the time I have left in Dublin,' he

345

said. 'What about a trip to the Botanic Gardens or to Kingstown for a stroll down the pier and some afternoon tea?'

'The gardens would be nice,' she agreed, smiling. 'Your father used to like to bring me there.'

'Very well,' he said, 'Glasnevin it is next week then.'

Liebert went off to visit a friend and Isabella sat for a while in the drawing room alone, listening to the tick of the clock, the house silent, chiding herself for her foolishness in being upset at his response.

Chapter 66

Muriel

Muriel was beside herself with worry, for Mac-Donagh was rarely at home. He had taken to staying overnight in safe houses with various supporters and friends scattered throughout the city, often returning only in the morning to Oakley Road to see Muriel and the children.

'Why can't you sleep here in your own bed?' she begged him. 'I miss you so much.'

'I do not want to put you or the children at risk,' he explained, holding her hand and stroking her palm and fingers gently.

At night she lay awake, filled with trepidation. Their home was under constant watch and she could not help but worry: she feared for her husband's safety. Joe Plunkett had come through his big operation and she knew MacDonagh spent much of his time visiting him in the nursing home.

'You know what Joe is like! His spirit is strong and he is determined to make a good recovery,' he told her.

'What about his marriage to Grace?'

'He is set on it.'

Grace often stayed with her at night to keep her company. Her sister could not wait to be married, but the situation with Joe's illness worried her. She also confided in Muriel about the Castle document she had helped Joe decode.

'I saw it myself. Muriel, they intend arresting Joe and Padraig and MacDonagh and all of them and deporting them,' Grace said, her face pale.

Muriel was barely able to hide her utter dismay at the thought of such a thing happening and the next morning she accosted MacDonagh on his return, asking him about the truth of it.

'Yes, we all know about it,' he admitted. 'Joe says they'll swoop down on us when we least expect it, but we are prepared. If I am to be arrested I will not go without a fight, I promise you.'

Muriel worried about what would happen to her and the children if he were arrested. 'I couldn't bear it if something were to happen to you!' she cried, unable to hide her upset and fear.

'Nothing will happen to me,' he reassured her, pulling her into his arms.

He went upstairs to collect some papers and clean clothes; he was getting ready to leave again.

'Can't you stay a bit longer?' she requested. 'Please?'

'I'm sorry, my love, but I have to go,' he replied, buttoning up his jacket.

'Will you at least be home here for Easter with us?'

'I have issued an order in our newsletter for manoeuvres to be held on Easter Sunday in every part of Ireland,' he said, kissing her and the children before he left. 'So don't go making any family plans for me that day.'

'Your regular manoeuvres?'

MacDonagh deliberately didn't answer her, but quickly took up his overcoat and left.

Muriel's heart was beating so fast inside her chest that she felt almost dizzy. Now she was certain that he was keeping something from her. She was not stupid and realized that whatever he and his friends were planning must be highly dangerous. Why else would he hide it from her? She suspected that, in his usual gallant fashion, her kind husband was desperately trying to protect her.

Chapter 67

Nellie

The weather was overcast when Nellie cycled into town on Easter Saturday to meet Margaret Skinnider, the young Scottish teacher, at Liberty Hall. Margaret had borrowed a bicycle from Nora Connolly, James's daughter, and Michael Mallin had given Nellie a map with the area around St

Stephen's Green park and Leeson Street all marked out. Nellie wondered what was special about this area as the two of them set off, cycling through the city.

Margaret kept asking her questions all along the way, taking special note of side streets and laneways, walking up and down them, recording vacant premises, the rooflines and heights of buildings on the streets that they passed. They strolled around St Stephen's Green itself, no one paying the slightest heed to them.

Nellie discovered that, even though Margaret was from Glasgow, both her parents were Irish and she always considered herself Irish.

'I'm a member of the Glasgow branch of Cumann na mBan, which Countess Markievicz set up,' Margaret told her proudly as they wheeled their bicycles along. 'She's a remarkable woman, an inspiration.'

'Indeed she is!' agreed Nellie. 'She's a stalwart of the Citizen Army and is one of the kindest women I know. She helped me with the Bureau. She is not at all what people expect, but is always set on fighting for justice and doing what she believes is right, no matter what people think of her.'

'She brought me to Ash Street the last time I was over as I wanted to see the other side of Dublin. Glasgow is no perfect city, I admit, but, Nellie, I was appalled by the poverty and deprivation that I saw.'

'That's the great shame of Dublin,' Nellie said angrily.

'How do the authorities permit so many children and parents to live here in those terrible run-

349

down tenement buildings, crowded together in one room with no sanitation?'

'No one cares, but it has to change,' Nellie nodded. 'That's what Jim Larkin and the union fought for, and what Mr Connolly and the countess and all of us believe and want – an Irish nation governed by its own people.'

'That would be a fine thing.'

Nellie pointed out Harcourt Street station and the canal.

'I joined a rifle club in Glasgow for good Scottish women who wanted to play their part in the defence of the British Empire.' Margaret laughed. 'I kept going to it because the gun training was excellent. The other ladies didn't care much for guns and shooting, but by the time it closed down I'd become a good markswoman, a sure shot.'

'I've been trained to use a gun with the Citizen Army,' said Nellie ruefully, 'but I'm most definitely not a sure shot.'

'The countess is a very fine markswoman,' Margaret confided. 'When she advised me of plans for a rebellion, I knew that the opportunity might come for me to be of assistance in the fight for nationalism.'

Nellie studied the earnest young mathematics teacher, her gentle and scholarly demeanour hiding her independent, feisty spirit and determination.

'So every time I cross over here to Ireland I bring something special. I hid a few detonators under my hat the last time I came.'

'Detonators!' gasped Nellie. 'Were you not terrified?'

'I admit I was a bit afraid that something might spark if I was sitting in a cabin,' she giggled, 'so I sat out on the open deck in case I ignited or worse still, blew up!'

'Are you nervous about tomorrow?' Nellie asked as they cycled back together in tandem to Liberty Hall.

'A wee bit, but I volunteered to come over to Dublin because I want to be part of it all.' She shrugged as they passed along the quays.

Liberty Hall was in a state of high excitement and preparation as Nellie and Margaret arrived back there. Men were busy polishing and oiling their guns, while the women were organizing food rations, with joints of meat being prepared, batches of scones and loaves of bread baked. Medical supplies and equipment were also being checked and packed for tomorrow.

James Connolly gave them last-minute orders to parade at 3.30 p.m. on Easter Sunday in full uniform at Liberty Hall, where they would join with the Volunteers.

People were in and out of the building and the air of expectation for the next day and what it would bring was palpable. Many of the men agreed to stay overnight while Nellie, like most of the women, headed home, excited about what tomorrow would bring.

Chapter 68

Grace

It was almost mid-morning when, to grace's surprise, Mick Collins called at Temple Villas.

'Is it Joe?' she asked, fearing bad news. 'Is he worse? Am I to go to the nursing home?'

'Ah Grace, it's nothing like that,' he told her kindly. 'He sent me to give you these.'

He passed her a package. Perhaps it was a message about their wedding tomorrow, but it felt strangely heavy and she immediately opened it. It was a revolver and also there was £20 in notes wrapped up beside it.

She suddenly felt terribly afraid.

'Mick, why do I need a gun?'

'Joe wants you to have it if you need to defend yourself. The money is in case you have to bribe some of the military. He's afraid you may be captured, Grace, or might be arrested because of him.'

'Arrested?' Grace gasped out loud.

'Ssshhh,' Collins warned, stepping forward and taking her arm.

'Mick, do you think they will come here?'

'Who can say what they will do or what they might be planning, but Joe just wants you safe. He's checked out of the nursing home.'

'But he's far too sick! The doctor told him he

had to stay – why would he do such a silly thing?'

'You know what he's like when he wants some-thing, Grace, how determined and set about things Joe can be.'

She nodded dumbly.

'He's got a room at the Metropole Hotel and he asks you to come in to see him this evening.'

'Tell him I'll be there,' she promised, watching as the tall figure of Michael Collins, message delivered, disappeared back outside.

She felt the heaviness of the gun and touched the trigger. She had never even held a gun in her life and could not imagine herself ever using one. Aiming at another human being and killing or injuring them – it was something she could not personally contemplate, even if Joe did want her to have it for self-defence.

Running upstairs, she hid the revolver and the money in her bag, hoping that she would never have to use either.

'Who was that man that called to see you?' asked her brother Liebert curiously.

'Just a friend giving me a message,' she said lightly.

Grace took a tram into Sackville Street, arriving at the Metropole Hotel around six to see Joe. She was surprised to see him suddenly appear down the hotel stairs. He looked terrible: his hair was shaved tight to his skull, he had lost weight and now even in his new uniform and hat he looked positively skeletal. She ran to greet him and they embraced. Tomorrow morning they'd be wed.

'I was about to give you up as a bad job,' he

said, touching her face. 'Why didn't you come earlier? I waited in all the afternoon for you.'

'But I was told to come only now,' she said, trying not to get upset.

'No matter about the muddle, you are here,' he said tenderly. 'But I am afraid I will have to leave in a few minutes.'

They found a quiet spot and sat down beside each other.

'Joe, why did you leave Mrs Quinn's? You should be in bed resting.'

'Grace, I promise this is no time for rest. There is far too much for me to do, but I needed to talk to you about tomorrow,' he said quietly, holding her hand. 'I'm so sorry, my love, but there will be no wedding in the morning in Rathmines. We have to postpone it.'

'Why?' she demanded loudly.

'Ah Grace, there was some awful mix-up with the priest about our banns and they haven't been read, which means that we cannot get married tomorrow with Geraldine and Tommy like we planned.'

Utter disappointment overwhelmed her, but Grace was a lady and would not create a scene or cry in such a public place. With all Joe's talk of rebellion and the slow recovery from his operation, the possibility of their marriage on Easter Sunday had become more remote over the past few days. She had already quietly steeled herself for such news, but she was still deeply hurt and upset.

'But I promise you with all my heart, once the banns are read and we have permission from the

354

Church, we will be wed immediately. I want you to be my wife,' he pledged. 'Somehow in the next few days in some nearby church we will take our vows, be husband and wife, and all that is mine will be yours. Just be ready, Grace, when I send you word.'

'I will,' she promised.

'Grace, I wish that I could stay here with you, but I have to take a cab to an urgent meeting on important Volunteer matters. Come with me.'

She sat with him in the back of the cab, her hands in his, fearful suddenly that she would never see him again. Joe kissed her gently before getting out at the bridge near Gardiner Street, which was only a few minutes away, and saying goodbye. He seemed relaxed and fearless as he waved to her.

Grace resisted the temptation to run after him...

She could not bear the thought of returning home to Temple Villas and instead ordered the cab driver to take her to Muriel's house on Oakley Road.

Chapter 69

Muriel

Muriel found it hard to disguise her mounting disquiet as all day a stream of visitors called at their home on Oakley Road, seeking directions and orders and information about where to go for tomorrow's Easter Sunday Volunteer manoeuvres. She was acutely conscious of the DMP men watching the goings-on and taking notes to report to their superiors. Visitors were given the information they needed and sent immediately on their way.

MacDonagh had still said nothing to her and was constantly away at meetings of some sort or another.

Grace arrived at the house, overwrought and upset after meeting Joe in town. 'The wedding is postponed,' she said tearfully.

'I'm so sorry,' Muriel said, hugging her sister and making her sit down.

'I should have gone to the Metropole Hotel earlier,' Grace reproached herself. 'I barely had time to see Joe or talk to him.'

'Grace, I'm sure that once the banns are read you and Joe will get married in a few days,' Muriel consoled her. 'You just have to be patient and wait.'

'I don't want to wait,' her sister insisted, sounding strangely frantic. 'We have to get married now, as soon as we can.'

MacDonagh returned home and Grace joined them for tea. Sitting at the table he refused to be drawn on the large-scale event that they were planning in Dublin and around the country for the next day.

'It's a bit of a stir to celebrate the anniversary of the Battle of Clontarf,' was all he would say.

Muriel suspected that it was far more than that.

Later Grace went off in a car with MacDonagh and his brother John to a meeting being held in

Seamus O'Kelly's house in the hope of meeting Joe there, but she returned disappointed.

When MacDonagh came home he was in a state. He had seen Eoin MacNeill and Arthur Griffith at the meeting and it was clear there had been some terrible disagreement or falling-out between them.

'After all our planning and organizing, Eoin wants to call tomorrow's events off,' he said angrily, banging the table. 'There are admittedly problems – we've lost a shipment of arms down in Kerry, but I don't believe that means that we should cancel the arrangements for tomorrow.'

Muriel tried to look sympathetic but she hoped that his old friend Eoin's voice would hold sway. They barely got a chance to speak of it, however, as MacDonagh quickly packed a suitcase, took his Volunteer uniform and a few days' rations then disappeared off into the night once again.

'Every night it's the same. The children and I miss him terribly, for he's hardly ever at home these past weeks,' she told Grace. 'And I'm so worried for him.'

'Joe's the same. Tomorrow should be our wedding day, but instead of making our vows in the church, he is caught up in these plans with the Volunteers. It's madness – he's not fit for manoeuvres and should still be in hospital.'

They stayed up for hours, talking late into the night like they used to when they were younger, sharing their fears and worries. It was so strange, both of them in love with men who were such close friends and who were so deeply dedicated to the cause of Irish nationalism.

'Perhaps we should have been good daughters and married stalwart, sensible Protestant solicitors and doctors like Mother wanted us to do,' Grace mused.

'Too late,' laughed Muriel wryly. 'We followed our hearts...'

Chapter 70

Nellie

Nellie slept badly, tossing and turning, anxious about the rebellion. Next morning she attended the Easter Sunday church service with Mother and her brother, praying silently that she and the other members of the Citizen Army were doing the right thing and that they would have the courage and resolve to begin the fight for Ireland's independence.

She excused herself from Easter lunch, guiltily hugging Mother goodbye as she left for town. By the time she arrived at a crowded Liberty Hall she was filled with anticipation and excitement.

Groups of men in full uniform stood outside talking as the place began to fill.

However, as Nellie entered she discovered that an air of utter gloom and despondency hung over the place.

'What has happened?' she asked, stunned. 'Have our plans been discovered?'

'Everything has been cancelled,' Rosie said

angrily. 'It's all been called off because of the Volunteers.'

'Cancelled? Why would they do such a thing?'

'Eoin MacNeill, the head of the Volunteers, gave the orders last night to cancel the rebellion. He sent messengers across the country to all the branches, and wrote a notice to be printed in all the newspapers this morning, telling the Volunteers that there would be no manoeuvres for any of their members today. He's gone and banjaxed the lot of us,' she hissed.

Nellie could clearly see that large groups of Volunteers had still turned up and that they were equally baffled by their new orders.

'They must not have seen the notices.' Rosie shrugged as she handed Nellie the newspaper and pointed out the notice that Eoin MacNeill had placed in it cancelling all Volunteer manoeuvres planned for Easter Sunday.

'Ina and I came down from Belfast to tell Father that the Volunteers up north had received the order too and were obeying it,' Nora Connolly added dejectedly.

'But why would MacNeill do this?' Nellie asked as she read in the *Sunday Independent* that all orders given to the Irish Volunteers were rescinded and that no parades, marches or movements of Irish Volunteers would take place, with every Volunteer strictly ordered to obey.

'A shipment of guns from Germany that the Volunteers were expecting was intercepted by the British down in Kerry,' explained Helena Molony, who had come over to join them. 'They've arrested Roger Casement on suspicion of organizing it, and to top it all two Volunteers sent to work the radio signals were killed in a motor-vehicle accident somewhere nearby.'

Nellie's heart sank at hearing how many things had gone wrong. Calamity after calamity. It was a disaster.

'MacNeill feared that it was far too risky to go ahead, as the British could well be aware of their plans,' Helena continued under her breath, 'but the countess and Tom Clarke and most of the others are furious and still want to go ahead with the Rising.'

Everyone stood around upset and confused, not knowing what was happening. The crowd was growing both inside and outside Liberty Hall, all prepared to join in the planned rebellion. What were they meant to do – return home?

Michael Mallin, William Partridge and the countess were in a huddle talking together, the countess loudly threatening to shoot Eoin Mac-Neill if she got her hands on him. Meanwhile all the members of the Irish Republican Brotherhood's Military Council were upstairs in Room 7. It was clear from the raised voices that some kind of meeting was going on between the heads of the Citizen Army and the Volunteers in a desperate effort to try to resolve the situation. James Connolly, Padraig Pearse, Tom Clarke, Eamonn Ceannt, MacDonagh, Joe and Sean Mac Diarmada looked deadly serious when they finally emerged and went to talk to their captains and commandants. Everyone was on tenterhooks, anxiously watching and awaiting their decision.

Most could not hide their disappointment when

they were told that the rebellion was postponed until tomorrow at midday, when everyone would assemble here again. They all knew in their hearts that now their numbers could be seriously depleted, and that they ran the risk of the Castle arresting them if they delved into why such a notice had appeared in the papers.

Michael Mallin's wife, Agnes, came with her four children to see her husband briefly before he left. She was a pretty woman and was naturally anxious: she clearly knew what was happening today and wanted to spend a few precious minutes with her husband. Nellie, suspecting that Agnes was in the family way again, made sure to get her a chair and the two of them talked together quietly.

A few hours later James Connolly assembled a large group of them. It was clear that he was absolutely furious about the change of orders.

'The Citizen Army does not have to obey Mr MacNeill's order,' he told them angrily, 'so get ready to move out on a route march.'

He and Commandant Mallin led them off, marching across Butt Bridge, along College Green, up Grafton Street and around by the park where Nellie had brought Margaret yesterday. Eighteen-year-old bugler William Oman was instructed to sound his bugle in front of certain key places on the route as they headed along York Street and down George's Street to Dame Street and Sackville Street, the very centre of Dublin city. Nellie found herself taking particular notice of where they went. The crowds around ignored them.

Returning to Liberty Hall, they prepared tea for everyone. Usually on Sundays a very popular concert was held here and it was decided to carry on with it as normal so as not to arouse suspicions. As Nellie listened to the singing and piano playing it seemed so strange that tomorrow they would all go out together. Michael Mallin played his flute, his music touching the audience as he gazed around the crowded hall.

The men of the Citizen Army had been ordered to sleep the night there, but the women had been told they were not to stay, so Nellie, yawning, slipped out of the union building and went home.

Chapter 71

Grace

The sun was shining in her window, dappling the bedclothes, as Grace stretched out. All her fears and worries about Easter Sunday had been for nothing. There had been no rebellion, no demonstrations and no arrests. Joe must be safe, for the day had passed quietly. The Volunteers, it seemed, and their grand plans were in disarray after Eoin MacNeill had somehow got wind of everything and cancelled all Volunteer drilling and meetings, putting notices in all the newspapers and sending messengers around the country to all the organization's branches.

She had met MacDonagh briefly yesterday

night at Muriel's and it was the first time she had ever seen her usually calm brother-in-law so upset and angry. Padraig and Willie Pearse had also called, grim-faced. The three of them were in heated discussion in the living room when she said her discreet goodbyes and came home.

All day yesterday she'd felt a sense of despondency and gloom, as it should have been their wedding day. Geraldine, Tommy Dillon and the Plunkett family had celebrated at a wedding breakfast in Geraldine's home in Belgrave Square and the newly wed couple had stayed in the Imperial Hotel, the place where she and Joe had also booked to stay for a night or two. It made her sad and lonesome to think about it.

But no more dawdling and lazing in bed, she chided herself, and she washed and dressed quickly and went downstairs to breakfast.

Mother had decided to breakfast in Father's room. He still had such difficulty eating and swallowing that even a simple bowl of porridge could near choke him. Mother felt it was her duty to keep him company, talking to him about the day and trying to keep his spirits up. The nurse would arrive a little later to wash, change and shave him and give him his medicines.

Liebert planned to go to the Easter Monday races in Fairyhouse with a few old friends and Grace could hear him singing in the bathroom as he got ready.

A letter had just been delivered for her and she eagerly read it. Joe had written it yesterday, telling her he intended returning to the nursing home last night to rest. He said everything was bully, and despite his own illness he was worrying about her. Relief washed over her that he was safe. She would go into town to see him. Perhaps he might even have news of the plans for their wedding. She sat at the table; she would have a little scrambled egg and perhaps one slice of bacon and some of Julia's brown soda bread, which was good for the digestion.'

Nellie came in to join her, immediately taking a large plate and heaping it with eggs, several slices of bacon and two sausages.

Adding a few slices of bread, she came and sat beside her.

'You must be hungry,' Grace teased, passing her more bread.

'How's Joe?' Nellie asked.

'He looks awful,' she blurted out. 'We met at the Metropole on Saturday because he went and checked himself out of Mrs Quinn's even though it's clear that he's still very unwell. But, thank heaven, I just got a letter from him to say he decided to go back there again last night to rest.'

'Did you visit Muriel?'

'Yes, I stayed with her on Saturday night. You know how nervous she gets being on her own, but thank heaven MacDonagh came home yesterday, which was a great relief. Little Don was delighted to see him. Apparently all the big plans for the Volunteers for Easter Sunday were cancelled. He's upset and angry with Eoin MacNeill, but Muriel is very relieved.'

Nellie buttered her slice of bread thoughtfully.

'All I will say, Grace, is don't believe all you hear.'

'What do you mean?' asked Grace, perplexed.

'Just what I said.' Nellie smiled cryptically, getting up and taking another helping of egg.

'Have you got drilling and manoeuvres today, is that it?' Nellie kept eating, refusing to answer.

'Muriel said that all Volunteer movements were cancelled.'

'Perhaps,' said Nellie as Julia came into the room with some fresh tea and proceeded to take their plates away.

Sometimes Nellie drove her mad with her stupid loyalty to Countess Markievicz and James Connolly and the Liberty Hall crew. She spent more time with them than she did with the family.

'I plan to visit Joe today, cheer him up,' Grace remarked.

'I have to go,' said Nellie with a smile, getting up from the table. 'I'll run upstairs to say good morning to Father before I leave.'

Something made Grace sit there waiting until twenty minutes later she saw the small figure of her older sister, dressed in her green jacket, a pretty white linen shirt, her tweed skirt, heavy walking boots and green hat, putting a flask of water into the leather kitbag hanging across her body. Nellie checked herself in the mirror as she began to go towards the front door.

'Idiot!' Grace told herself. It was today. Nothing had been cancelled. Could she not see by her sister's attire and attitude that, whatever everyone said or thought, the orders for the Volunteers and the Citizen Army had simply been changed, events postponed from yesterday until today.

'Wait, Nellie, please!' she begged, racing past

her and up to the bedroom. She grabbed her bag and almost ran back down to where her sister stood, puzzled, at the open front door.

Grace reached inside her bag, took out the small revolver and pushed it into her sister's hands.

'Grace – where did you get this?' Nellie asked, shocked, as she cradled the gun in her hands.

'Joe gave it to me, but Nellie I want you to have it.'

'I can't take it,' protested her sister, trying to hand it back to her. 'Joe wanted you to have it.'

'Nellie, you are to take it!' she insisted. 'You may have far more need for it than I ever will.'

Wordlessly, Nellie nodded and slipped the revolver carefully into her own leather bag.

'Take care of yourself!' Grace said, impulsively hugging her tight.

Nellie refused to admit or say anything and Grace watched as she turned right, walking briskly towards the tram stop for the city.

Grace dressed quickly. The Volunteers were bound to be involved in whatever was going on. She had a terrible feeling of dread that, despite still getting over his operation, Joe would want to play his part. He was that kind of man. Would he leave Mrs Quinn's to join them? She had to try to waylay him somehow and persuade him to stay out of whatever was being planned.

She was just ready to leave when her brother appeared, dressed jauntily in a smart suit and boater hat.

'You look very handsome,' she teased.

'I'm off to Fairyhouse races with a few of the

pals. You are welcome to join us, Grace, if you want,' he offered politely.

'No thanks, Liebert, I have no intention of cramping your style. But we can take the tram together into town if you like.'

The tram was already busy, with passengers waiting at every stop – off-duty soldiers enjoying the Bank Holiday Monday, likely going to meet their sweethearts; families with children and picnic baskets headed to the Phoenix Park. A few Volunteers in their uniform sat quietly talking together down the back. Pinpricks of alarm ran through Grace as she saw more groups of Volunteers awaiting the next tram and a group of youths in the uniform of Countess Markievicz's Fianna gathering near the canal.

'Busy today,' murmured Liebert, unconcerned, as she sat there worrying, suspecting why the Volunteers were all converging on the city today.

They both got off at Sackville Street and said goodbye. Grace watched yet another group of Volunteers cross the street and casually stroll in the direction of Liberty Hall.

She went straight to Mrs Quinn's in Mountjoy Square, hoping that she would find Joe there. To her dismay, she discovered that, despite the protests and pleas of his doctor and nurses, he had discharged himself from the nursing home.

'He was very weak, but he left with that big Cork fellow and another man,' one of the nurses told her.

Grace's heart sank. She had no idea what to do. She called at the Metropole Hotel, where the lobby was full of British soldiers, many off duty and heading for the races. The desk clerk informed her quietly that Mr Plunkett had already checked out of his room and had taken a cab from the hotel door.

Back outside, Grace crossed over the busy street, unsure of what to do. She saw another group of Volunteers walking towards her.

'Are you going to Liberty Hall?' she asked them.

'Why?' replied one.

They looked suddenly shifty, wary of answering her. Reaching into her bag, Grace took out her small drawing pad and scribbled a brief note for Joe to tell him that she was nearby. She would go to the Imperial Hotel and wait for him there.

'Do you know Mr Plunkett, Joseph Plunkett?' she said, trying to keep the note of hysteria she felt from her voice. 'I would be very grateful if you could give him this note.'

There was no one offering.

'I am his fiancée,' she explained, trying to smile.

One of the men stepped forward.

'I know him, miss. I'll try to give it to him if I see him,' he promised.

'If you by chance don't see him, can you give the message to Mr Michael Collins?' she added. 'I believe he is with Mr Plunkett.' She could see the fellow was embarrassed, presuming it was some kind of love note. 'I am very grateful to you,' she said, passing him the folded paper.

She watched as they went off down the street, hoping that somehow Joe would get her message.

Chapter 72

Nellie

Nellie hastened her pace, the Easter Monday trams already busy. She had not expected to encounter her sister Grace this morning of all mornings. Her sister may be engaged to Joe Plunkett, but Nellie found it hard to ascertain how much she knew of the planned Rising. Grace had always had a way of hiding what she was thinking or what she knew, which Nellie found exasperating. Grace got away with everything when she was a child as she always appeared uninvolved, able somehow to disguise her emotions, while the rest of them often got into trouble with Mother or their nanny.

How much had Joe actually told her? Yet Grace had given her the gun Joe had sent her, so she must have a definite sense that something was happening today. Perhaps Joe, whom Nellie knew was a member of the IRB's Military Council and was deeply involved with planning the Rising, had deliberately kept things from Grace so that if she was arrested and questioned she would not be able to give much information to the DMP or the army.

At Liberty Hall, a number of men stood outside in the sunshine guarding the building and she could smell breakfast being cooked for those who had stayed overnight. She doubted they had got much sleep, so she went to work serving tea and bread, and helping make sandwiches. Tom Clarke, Padraig Pearse, Sean Mac Diarmada and James Connolly were talking together, grim-faced, as small groups of men willing to fight began to appear. MacDonagh and his brother Jack were there too.

Nellie watched as members of the Volunteers, the Citizen Army and the Cumann na mBan women gradually began to assemble. James Connolly looked serious as he moved among them; he had his fifteen-year-old son, Roddy, with him. His daughters Nora and Ina had been despatched to the north with messages for the garrisons there, telling them to rise up. Commandant Mallin had stayed overnight with most of the Citizen Army men and now went around talking and encouraging them as they began to get organized. Nellie set about helping as they cut bread on a slicing machine and issued rations of bread and meat to all the men and women. She checked the remaining food – sandwiches, scones, tea, crackers and other provisions were all ready for transport to the different garrisons.

Today it's for real, she thought as she felt the gun heavy against her hip.

Dr Kathleen Lynn was busy supervising all the first aid supplies and with a few helpers was issuing everyone with a personal first aid kit. Rosie Hackett had been assigned to work with Madeleine ffrench-Mullen and was given a long white coat with a red cross.

'It's a bit big!' she laughed, for she was small and it came down to her heels; she quickly had to set about shortening it.

Nellie's mouth felt strangely dry as she checked all the last-minute supplies, so she sipped a cup of water. Margaret Skinnider came over to have a chat.

'Today's the day,' she said quietly, her gun and ammunition at the ready.

Suddenly Nellie saw Joe arriving with Mick Collins and another man, both of them helping him walk. Connolly and Pearse went over and greeted him warmly. She could not disguise her surprise: she had thought Joe was still in hospital. He looked wretched and had some sort of scarf or bandage wrapped around his throat. He was carrying what looked like a Japanese sword.

She went over to see him and he told her that, although he was still recovering from his operation, he was determined to play his part. He introduced her to Captain William Brennan-Whitmore, a former army man who had come up from Wexford. She was relieved to see that he had Mick Collins by his side too, keeping a protective watch over him. Joe disappeared upstairs to Connolly's room with no one, not even Countess Markievicz, allowed to disturb them.

Later there was a flurry in the middle of the hall as Joe's two younger brothers appeared.

'We came by tram – I paid for tickets for everyone,' George Plunkett laughed, followed into the hall by a group of about forty Volunteers who lived and trained at Larkfield. 'But Jack's come on the motorbike and a few lads cycled.'

'The day we all have waited for and trained for is finally here!' Bill Partridge said solemnly as he

371

surveyed the group.

Liberty Hall was filling up, but it was very clear even to Nellie that far fewer people than yesterday had turned up prepared to fight. James Connolly and Padraig Pearse appeared, standing together to address the group, and announced that today the members of the Irish Volunteers and the Citizen Army would fight together as one force, one army – the Irish Republican Army.

MacDonagh nodded over to say goodbye as he and his brother left for where the 2nd Battalion was to mobilize. As the various companies began to assemble outside Liberty Hall, Nellie's head was filled with thoughts of what lay ahead and the impossible odds they were facing with such reduced numbers, but like everyone else she was prepared to fight, to play her part in taking the city.

James Connolly, as his eyes roved over the gathering, confided to one of his men that he feared they would be slaughtered. By twenty to twelve it was clear that the full quota of those willing to participate in the Rising were present, perhaps about four hundred or so, and they could wait no longer. Glancing around, Tom Clarke was clearly worried by the numbers too.

'We should have gone yesterday,' he said, shaking his head in disappointment. 'We've lost the advantage of numbers.'

Nellie was relieved to see so many stalwarts of the Citizen Army ready to do their part. Margaret Skinnider, who was on a bicycle, was sent on ahead of them to scout their route. Captain Kit Poole ordered bugler Bill Oman to sound the command to fall in and Michael Mallin ordered them into formation, ready to move out.

She observed as the other garrisons left. Captain Richard McCormick's small troop went first – they had been ordered to Harcourt Street station; then Sean Connolly and his men, who were headed for Dublin Castle. Everyone was strangely silent: there was no waving to comrades or calls of goodbye or good luck, and it gave Nellie a sense of the gravity of their mission. James Connolly, Padraig Pearse, Joe and Captain Brennan-Whitmore led the next garrison off. She watched as Mick Collins, Connolly's young son, the Plunkett brothers and their large contingent left Liberty Hall for Sackville Street, with Tom Clarke and Sean Mac Diarmada, who had a bad limp, driven there by motor vehicle.

Then it was their turn. Commandant Michael Mallin gave the signal and Nellie and her garrison left Liberty Hall and began to march proudly from Beresford Place up along the quays.

Chapter 73

Grace

Grace enquired at the imperial hotel's reception desk and did not know whether to be relieved or upset that a room was still booked there in the name of Plunkett.

'It is one of the bigger ones that overlooks Sackville Street,' explained the young porter as he showed her into the very room where she and Joe should have spent their wedding night. She had left a message for Joe at the desk to say where she was and that she was waiting for him.

Hoping that she would not encounter Joe's sister and her new husband, who were also booked to stay there, she fled through the heavy mahogany door of the luxurious bedroom with its grand view of the street and the crowds milling around below. She kicked off her shoes and stretched out on top of the bed for a few minutes, but did not dare nap in case Joe arrived. She prayed that he would get her message and come soon. Once everything was in order they would immediately go ahead with their marriage plans. Father Sherwin would surely agree to officiate, or perhaps the priest at the Pro-Cathedral, where they both liked to worship.

Getting up, Grace gazed out over Sackville Street. Many of the shops and businesses were closed for Easter Monday, but the large General Post Office across the street from the hotel was still open to sell stamps and for people to post letters and parcels or collect their army pensions or the Supplementary Welfare payments they received while their husbands and sons were away fighting. She watched the constant flow of these 'supplementary women' entering and leaving the building. Some were widows, their pension earned by the death of their husband in some muddy trench on an unknown battlefield.

Young ladies in their spring finery, with fashionable new dresses and Easter bonnets, paraded

374

along Sackville Street with their beaus and husbands.

Suddenly, coming from the corner with Abbey Street, Grace espied a large group of men marching into Dublin's broad main thoroughfare.

It looked like the Volunteers and Connolly's Citizen Army! What were they doing?

She pressed her face to the glass as they drew nearer, immediately recognizing Padraig Pearse and James Connolly at their head, with Joe and another man. Joe looked pale and gaunt, but despite that he was wearing his uniform, breeches, boots and a hat, a silk scarf around his neck to hide his recent surgery, marching steadily with them and brandishing the shining sabre he kept at Larkfield. Mick Collins, ramrod straight and tall, was marching behind him. Women from Cumann na mBan, heads held high, and boys from the Fianna marched with them. A number held rifles with bayonets and shotguns, others had only pikes and an assortment of other weapons.

Grace searched for sight of her sister or MacDonagh, but couldn't see them. She recognized Michael O'Rahilly's car and could see George Plunkett leading a group of the Larkfield Volunteers, marching along in good spirits while his younger brother, Jack, was on the motorcycle up near the front. Two horse-drawn carts filled with weapons and supplies followed as part of the strange parade. Passers-by glanced at them briefly, but continued with their own business.

Grace was tempted to run outside on to the street to call Joe, beg him to come and join her, forget whatever they had all planned. She held her breath as the group came to a stop outside the large classical building that dominated the street – the General Post Office. James Connolly seemed to say something, give an order, and suddenly they all charged at the building, swarming in through the main entrance, gaining entry and overrunning it in only a few minutes.

Shocked, Grace stood watching as terrified customers fled the Post Office and the doors were locked to prevent others entering. A group of supplementary women gathered at the door of the GPO, shouting and howling abuse at Padraig, James, Joe and the rebels for locking them out and preventing them from collecting their weekly money, which was all they had.

Grace held her breath as snipers in Volunteer uniform appeared up on the high roof of the GPO. Suddenly two flags were hoisted up into the air, unfurling as the breeze caught them: the green Sinn Fein flag and the green, white and gold Irish flag, blowing high across the city for all to see.

The windows of the building were smashed and knocked out, glass covering the street. Quickly they were sandbagged and protected with papers and books.

What were they doing, Grace asked herself – did they intend holding the mighty GPO for a few hours or even overnight to teach the British a lesson?

There seemed little movement, from what she could see, except for shadows behind the remaining windows and more glass being broken. A few pieces of furniture were moved outside to make barricades. There was no sign of the Dublin

Metropolitan Police or the army appearing to eject the rebels.

Grace stood transfixed at the window, worried for Joe. A small crowd had gathered around the building. Suddenly Padraig Pearse came out on to the street, flanked by Tom Clarke, James Connolly and Sean MacDermott, and began to read loudly from a large sheet of paper. Unfortunately she could not hear what he said, but while some people listened to the words of a great orator, others simply ignored him, turned their heads and left. A few minutes later Padraig and the group went back inside the GPO, but a young Volunteer headed towards Nelson's Pillar with printed pages and left them there for people to read.

The street was unusually quiet for what seemed an age. The trams had stopped. Suddenly Grace became aware of a commotion coming from the top end of the street, up near the Rotunda. It was a brigade of the Royal Irish Lancers on horseback, riding along slowly at first down the centre of the street, then suddenly building up speed, urging their horses on faster.

She could barely see, but the Volunteers seemed ready for them and were putting up a fight near the Parnell Statue. She could hear shooting as the Lancers tried to charge down Sackville Street to attack the rebels. Most were held back, but a few broke through and she could see about twenty horses and their riders nearing the front of the GPO.

There was a huge burst of rifle fire and two or three horses were shot, falling down on the ground with their riders, the others wheeling around, trying to turn back up the street to escape from the rebels' attack. A few of the Lancers were clearly badly injured. Grace was shocked by the gunfire and blood. She watched the huge horses whinnying pitifully and one lay dying on the street. It was terrible to watch the terrified animal, yet she felt immense relief that Joe and the rebels were safe for the moment.

There would be a new onslaught, a new attack, of that there could be no doubt. The military were now aware of the rebels' position and possible numbers, and they would regroup and return.

She was afraid for Joe, afraid for all of them. Was Nellie with them? How could they possibly expect to defeat the large numbers of the British army garrisoned in barracks all across the city? They would be wiped out. She stayed watching from the window, frozen with dread at what might happen once the army launched a proper attack on them.

Fifteen minutes later there was a knock on the door of her room. She ran to it, hoping that it was Joe. Instead a young Larkfield Volunteer nervously handed her a message.

It was from Joe, telling her that she must leave *immediately* as it was too unsafe for her to stay in Sackville Street. He had signed it with all my love forever, Joe.

Suddenly afraid, Grace went downstairs as quickly as she could and left the hotel.

Chapter 74

Nellie

The sun shimmered on the river Liffey as they marched up towards College Green past Trinity College, heads held high, singing as they turned up Grafton Street, the bells of Clarendon Street church ringing out midday.

People paid little heed to them, assuming they were on yet another route march or manoeuvre.

'Isn't it a grand day for you to be out playing soldiers?' jeered a policeman.

Minutes later they had reached St Stephen's Green. Nellie had always loved the city-centre park, which was only a few minutes from her father's legal office and close to the Volunteers' headquarters. Peter Jackson had the keys to the main gate and they quickly entered through the tall Fusiliers' Arch. The smaller gates were open, the park already busy with families, children running around with bats and balls and toys, nannies pushing perambulators, young couples walking hand in hand, older couples sitting enjoying the beautiful warm Easter sunshine.

They streamed into the park, telling people to 'Move' as they began to surround it.

MacDonagh and his 2nd Battalion had assembled over on the west side of the park. He immediately sought out Michael Mallin, asking if any more men were coming.

'Unfortunately it's just us,' the commandant replied tersely.

'We should have had thousands of men here,' MacDonagh said, unable to hide his deep disappointment. Obviously, like Connolly, he had expected that a much larger contingent of Volunteers would amass at the park, but unfortunately MacNeill's counter-order had been rigidly obeyed.

Nellie watched as her brother-in-law and his garrison took their leave and began to march away.

'St Stephen's Green is under the control of the Irish Republican Army and you must leave immediately,' they ordered the public loudly as they set about clearing the twenty-acre park and gardens. Frightened, most families gathered their young children quickly and fled, though some argued and refused to budge.

'This is a public park and we are entitled to remain here.'

Nellie, with some of the other women, went about trying to calm the situation, urging people to leave for their own safety; nobody wanted to see a baby or child or anyone else injured.

The head park keeper stubbornly refused to leave, saying it was his duty to protect the plants, the waterfowl and the facility. An elderly priest who had been visiting the park gave absolution to some of the Citizen Army men before he left. There were a few off-duty soldiers relaxing in the park and Nellie felt pity for them as they were immediately arrested and held in the glasshouse.

Laurence Kettle, chief of the city's electrical department, was spotted and held at gunpoint too, by order of Commandant Mallin, in case he could be useful if the city authorities tried to take action against them. His brother Tom was a friend of MacDonagh's and Nellie remembered how he had tried to broker a peace between the unions and the employers during the Lockout. Laurence told her proudly that Tom was now serving overseas in the British army.

Eventually they had cleared the park, then locked and barricaded the gates, using benches, wheelbarrows and tools to keep the civilians out. The men from their company were set to digging trenches for gunpits all around the edge of the park, while Madeleine ffrench-Mullen set up a Red Cross area in the bandstand, a Red Cross flag hoisted over it. Nellie joined Mary Hyland and Kathleen Cleary organizing a kitchen in the summerhouse.

Countess Markievicz arrived in her car – dressed in full uniform. She was a sight to see, wearing a man's pair of trousers and sporting a green hat with a jaunty white feather, her gun on a belt around her body. She was inspecting the garrisons, but Mallin told her that she was urgently needed in the Green with them as he was short of people who could use a gun. He appointed her his Vice-Commandant and they all gave a cheer as she agreed to join them.

The countess set off to patrol the park and soon got involved in a loud, heated argument with a DMP man on duty across from the far entrance who refused to abandon his post and ordered them to leave the Green. In the end the countess took out her gun and aimed a shot at him.

Although Nellie greatly admired the countess, she felt shocked. The men of the Dublin Metropolitan Police Force were unarmed, so the man could not retaliate or defend himself. The shooting of another human being was not something she could bring herself to do unless confronted with no other choice.

A gunpit was set up at the edge of the Green opposite Dawson Street, across from the Shelbourne Hotel, by James O'Shea and young Jim Fox. The hotel was busy with soldiers and visitors and soon shooting began as the rebels aimed at soldiers driving by in their cars. Nellie's heart was in her mouth as she listened to the shots ringing out in the still air.

She and her group were sent to commandeer extra food supplies, stopping cars, delivery vans and carts that passed along by the Green. Mary Hyland held up a milk cart. Young Lily Kempson bravely jumped out brandishing a gun at a poor bread man, who was terrified.

'Give us all your loaves and soda breads and brown breads,' she demanded fiercely. Nellie helped her carry it all back to their makeshift kitchen.

Some of the men were building roadblocks and barricades in the streets around the Green and Nellie watched as a man adamantly refused to let them have his cart.

'You boyos are not taking my cart! It's got costumes and props to deliver to the D'Oyly Carte Opera at the Gaiety Theatre,' he argued, pulling his cart back. 'I'm not one of your rebel army – I'm a decent working man.'

Despite his protests the cart, complete with its contents, was fixed into the tall barricade. As the rebels moved away the man returned and, red-faced, climbed over and pulled it out again, but three of their men pushed it firmly back into place. Next thing, to Nellie's horror, the man was shot as he tried to remove it again. He lay on the ground bleeding profusely from his head, a woman passer-by screaming loudly as onlookers rushed to carry him to the nearby hospital.

Groups from their garrison had been despatched to take the station and also Portobello and Leeson Street Bridges; and they could hear the distant gunfire. Margaret was sent on her bicycle to the GPO to inform the leaders there that all was well and that they held the Green.

Later that Monday evening, as Nellie was bringing bread and milk to some of the men, they noticed a drunken British soldier standing up close to the park railings, staring at their gunpit.

'You should be fighting for your king and country,' he slurred, goading them.

'Go away home,' James O'Shea told him, ignoring him.

The soldier began to curse and Nellie and Kathleen blushed as he started to say terrible things about them and use bad language. 'Prostitutes,' he taunted them. 'That's what you girls are, agreeing to fight with these fellows.'

Young Jim Fox blushed, embarrassed by his swearing.

'You shouldn't talk like that in front of these ladies. I'll give you one last chance to get away,' said James slowly, but the soldier refused to budge.

'He's not drunk,' James murmured. A second later he had shot the man.

'He's a spy,' he told them. 'Not a whiff of drink on him. He's been trying to assess our defences here.'

Nellie felt shaky as men came to take their soldier friend to the hospital.

As it began to get darker it got colder and colder, then it began to rain. There were very few places to shelter in the park, so she and the other women all huddled together to sleep in the band-stand near to where the wounded lay. They certainly had not prepared for this.

'We should have taken the Shelbourne Hotel or one of the big clubs overlooking the Green,' Nellie yawned. 'Then we would have had a roof over us and beds and food at least.'

'That was part of the plan,' admitted Madeleine ruefully as she wound up some rolls of bandages, 'to block all the roads around here and to take over the hospital and the hotel, but we hadn't the numbers.'

Near dawn they were woken by the sound of rapid machine-gun fire from the Shelbourne Hotel.

There was utter panic and pandemonium as bullets rained down everywhere. They were under heavy gunfire. Screams and shouts filled the early-morning air as men ran or crawled among the bushes and shrubs for some form of cover from the relentless attack. They were like ducks on a pond, with nowhere to hide, for while they slept the British army had crept in and stealthily taken over the hotel and the nearby United Services

Club. Their soldiers were firing a barrage at them from the front windows of the hotel, where a Vickers machine gun and rifles were positioned. Bullets whizzed loudly all around, banging and exploding everywhere. Poor James Corcoran from Wexford was shot dead immediately.

It was hopeless. They couldn't stay here or they would all be killed, they were such an easy target. They had to try to find cover and escape. Another machine gun from the United Services Club also began to fire at them. Some of the men took their positions and started to fire back, but this only seemed to help the British gunners take aim at them. They were pinned down by machine-gun and rifle fire.

Nellie watched in horror as sixteen-year-old Jim Fox, to whom she had been talking the night before, desperately tried to get away and find cover. He was caught in a hail of bullets, screaming in pain as he tried to crawl away, but he was shot at again and again. Tears filled her eyes as she was forced to stand uselessly by and watch him die.

Commandant Mallin, under heavy fire himself, carried the badly shot Philip Clarke to safety but, unfortunately, he died of his wounds.

The Red Cross flag flying over the bandstand provided no protection and the women too were soon under fire as they tried to tend to the wounded, risking their own lives. As the bandstand came under increasingly heavy attack, Madeleine urged them to make for the gate keeper's lodge. Nellie felt certain they'd all be shot unless they found some way to escape, get out of this park.

Michael Mallin had sent out some scouts earlier to search for a place of safety and soon the order came. He blew his whistle, the sound thinly penetrating the gunfire.

'Evacuate the Green! Evacuate!'

They were all to leave carefully by the west side, where the statue of Arthur Guinness, Lord Ardilaun stood. In units of fours and fives they were to try to make it safely across to the College of Surgeons on the opposite side of the street which Countess Markievicz and a few of their men had managed to take.

'Don't stop! Don't hesitate even for a second!' ordered Captain Poole. 'Ignore the shooting and go as fast as you can.'

Nellie's heart was in her mouth as she watched the groups try to reach the safety of the tall, grey-granite medical school building with its three striking statues of Athena, Asclepius and Hygeia, the gods of wisdom and war, medicine and health, looking down on them while the British snipers and machine guns kept firing. They were forced to leave most of their precious food and first aid supplies behind, and the bodies of their dead lay abandoned on the ground in the early-morning rain.

The enemy now centred their attack on the College of Surgeons, bombarding the short open route they had to cross. Christine Caffrey hunkered down in front of their group.

'Wait till they have to change their magazines of ammunition,' Captain Poole ordered, getting ready to signal them when to move. 'You have only a few seconds.'

Suddenly he gave the signal and Chris began to duck and dive and run.

Nellie took a deep, shuddering breath and said a silent prayer as she followed, running as fast as she could through a hail of bullets, the sound ringing in her ears, her breath catching as she kept going towards the sanctuary of the college and its York Street entrance.

To their shock, a crowd of angry women from the tenement buildings beside the college, whose husbands were away fighting in the war, tried to block them entering their street. Chris pulled her gun on them and they let them pass. Terrified, Nellie reached the door and felt arms reaching to pull her safely inside.

Chapter 75

Nellie

They all held their breaths, waiting near the narrow side entrance for the rest of their comrades to make it safely across into the College of Surgeons. Some of their own snipers went up to the roof to try to provide some cover for them.

Nellie worried how Michael Mallin, James O'Shea and a few others would get across when the enemy were concentrating all their fire on the building. As the bullets hit the granite they had to shut the door. Outside, the mob of supplementary women were still set on preventing them gaining entry to the college.

'The army will have you.'

'Traitors!'

Suddenly Commandant Mallin and the last of his men banged at the side door, Captain Mc-Cormick with blood flowing from his head as they managed to drag him inside. Madeleine and Rosie rushed forward straight away to help him.

'All men up on the roof,' ordered Mallin, barely looking around. He was convinced the enemy would now mount a full-scale attack on the medical college.

Nellie was struck by an awful smell that permeated the area as they pushed into the nearby anatomy room. The long, bright room, with its tall windows and high ceiling, was laid out with table after table for the medical students. Nellie's stomach lurched at the strange, sickly-sweet smell. Around them jars filled with thick fluid containing various parts of the human body filled her with disgust, and there were large, detailed, coloured-wax figures of the human anatomy minus skin, which were terrifying.

'The smell is formaldehyde,' explained Madeleine. 'They use it for preserving bodies.'

'Ugh!' grimaced Nellie, Rosie and the other women, feeling nauseous.

'And don't go near the end of the room, for I think there is a cadaver stored on ice that the students use to practise their skills.'

Passing through the large entrance hall of the college, the towering statue of William Dease, the founder of the college and its first professor of surgery, stared down at them, and other busts of famous medical men looked on benignly as the college was transformed into a garrison for the Irish Republican Army. The heavy front of the building was now locked and heavily barricaded. Countess Markievicz and Frank Robbins had managed to gain access when the porter, Mr Duncan, who had already locked up the building against them, opened the door a fraction to warn an elderly professor that the college was shut. She and two scouts had seized the opportunity, managing to force their way into the building by threatening to shoot the porter.

They swiftly blocked up the windows of the entrance hall with piles of heavy books and medical tomes before moving upstairs and quickly searching through the building. Some of the men crouched down on their knees, their rifles at the ready, in front of the tall windows of the big council room, which stretched across the front of the building. It gave them a clear view not only of the park but of the Shelbourne Hotel, the position of their enemy.

Off this room was the college hall, which was used for lectures and classes. Commandant Mallin declared that it would serve as the men's quarters, as it was a spacious, high-ceilinged room with circular glass skylights but not as exposed as some others. A canvas screen used by the tutors hung near the back of the hall, dividing the room, and Madeleine chose the far side of it as a makeshift first aid hospital area. All the windows around them were barricaded, using desks, books, wooden benches and shelves.

Searching down in the basement they discovered only a small kitchen, the larder shelves almost bare, for the college and its students were on holidays. Nellie explored further, finding a large classroom with an open grate which could be used for cooking.

The porter, his wife and child had been imprisoned in a bedroom in their living quarters, the rest of the porter's accommodation commandeered for use as the women's sleeping quarters. Nellie found sugar, a little flour, tea, a big drum of porridge oats and a few large tins of cocoa powder – provisions that she suspected were for the college porter or staff.

'There's no food here. What will we do?' Lily asked, dismayed.

'We have some bread from yesterday and most people still have some rations left. Let's fill these big kettles with water and set them to boil. At least we can make some tea and cocoa for everyone and use these two big pots to make some porridge.'

'We'll need to get food supplies somewhere tomorrow,' said Kathleen, sounding worried.

The constant noise of gunfire and shelling went on and on without any reprieves or lull as the Vickers heavy machine gun and the one on the roof of the United Services Club rapidly spat out hundreds of rounds of ammunition. The sound filled their heads and unnerved them. Up on the roof their snipers, armed with only simple rifles, were busy returning fire all through the day. Margaret had gone up on the roof with them, hiding in a hole and taking careful aim as she calmly targeted the army snipers; she took a few of them out. The din was horrendous as bullets rained down and across at them. One of their men, Mick, was badly hit in the face and had to be lifted gingerly down from the roof, which was very dangerous. Bill Partridge too was injured and they bandaged up his head. Then one of their guns accidentally went off and shot one of their men in the eye. Madeleine, afraid that he would die, insisted he be taken to the nearby hospital.

Everyone was worn out, but there was no chance to rest or take a break. Nellie knew that they would have to be fed, so she and Mary set about making up two huge pots of porridge, cooking them over the grate in the classroom as she and the other women prepared to feed their hungry garrison.

'We're parched up there on the roof, with the heat of the guns,' reported one of their snipers who'd come down to the kitchen to get water as all their own water bottles were empty. Nellie helped him to refill them while he told her about how intense the fighting and din and smoke were up on the narrow roof.

At last, as it got darker, the enemy firing eased off, both sides exhausted.

'They're servicing the machine guns, getting ready for tomorrow's attack,' Commandant Mallin stated, ordering most of his own men to take a rest.

In the hall Nellie and the other women served bowls of piping-hot porridge laced with sugar, along with mugs of hot cocoa and tea to the men, making them sit and rest for a while.

'That's the best porridge I've ever had,' declared

391

a pale-faced young man, his eyes red-rimmed with lack of sleep as he licked his bowl clean.

'Well, you deserve it,' Nellie told him with a smile, wishing that she'd had a little milk or cream to add to it.

Commandant Mallin, a true soldier, had in his usual organized army fashion set up duty rosters, insisting that some of the men rest before going back on duty in the middle of the night.

'Falling asleep with a rifle up on the roof is not an option,' he warned. His army training meant that he always kept discipline, making it clear to all of them that he would not tolerate sloppiness or disorder in his garrison.

Nellie's eyes were feeling heavy, and once they had collected and washed up all the bowls and cups she was determined tonight to try to get a little sleep herself.

Chapter 76

Isabella

Isabella adjusted her hat as she got ready to leave the house on Tuesday. She was meeting Dorothy for lunch but had a few things she must do first. She needed skeins of embroidery thread and ribbon, new stockings, a bottle of syrup of figs and some corn plasters from the pharmacy.

Liebert had just arrived downstairs and was asking Julia to cook him some bacon and kidney.

'I won't be home for lunch,' she reminded her, 'as I am going into town.'

'Mother, I'm not sure you should venture into town today. There was terrible trouble yesterday,' Liebert warned her. 'The Sinn Feiners have taken over parts of the city – the GPO, City Hall, perhaps even Dublin Castle itself. There were no trams or carriages last night. The army had tried to attack and take the rebels on Sackville Street but had come under heavy fire and had to retreat.'

'Mam, I heard they were fighting on the street,' added Julia dramatically. 'Shooting at each other.'

'Who would do such a thing?'

'The soldiers say it is the Volunteers and the Citizen Army – that lot from Liberty Hall where Nellie works that are behind this,' her son explained.

'Why would they do this while we are at war?' Isabella asked, perturbed.

'Because the war provides the perfect opportunity for the rebels to strike against Britain,' he said bitterly. 'They have declared an Irish Republic.'

'What nonsense!'

Isabella could not believe that such a thing could happen in Dublin, the second city of the empire. She was sure that her son and maid were exaggerating. Annoyed that her plans for the day were now in disarray, she returned to the hallway and took off her coat.

'They say Padraig Pearse and James Connolly, the union man, are behind it,' Liebert continued slowly, 'but I suspect Muriel's husband may be involved too. He's a friend of Mr Pearse's, isn't he?'

'MacDonagh would not do such a thing! You

must be mistaken, Liebert.'

'Perhaps...'

She tried to persuade herself that her son's information must be wrong. Her son-in-law was a respected university lecturer and surely would not involve himself in such an endeavour.

'What will happen to these rebels?'

'The army will regroup and I'm sure send fresh reinforcements from Britain today or tomorrow. The Sinn Feiners will not be able to hold out for long against such a force. I promise you they will all be captured and taken.'

'Your father must not hear one word of this,' she declared. 'I will not have him distressed.'

Liebert agreed before sauntering into the drawing room.

Isabella went upstairs immediately to ask her daughters about all this – to find out exactly what they knew of this so-called rebellion.

To her dismay, Grace's room was empty, and when she went to Nellie's bedroom it was clear she had not returned to sleep there last night.

Isabella sat on Nellie's empty bed, torn between anger and a deep fear at the idea that any of her family might be involved in such an act of treason against His Majesty and his forces. She would not tolerate such a thing. What if her daughters were part of this Sinn Fein rebellion?

Chapter 77

Muriel

Muriel had barely slept, for MacDonagh had not returned home on Monday and she had had no word of his whereabouts.

Grace had told her how she had seen Joe, Padraig and James Connolly with the Volunteers and the Citizen Army taking over the GPO and setting up barricades around Sackville Street. Surely MacDonagh must be there too, somewhere in the Post Office, fighting with his men. It was rumoured that they had also taken St Stephen's Green and other parts of the city, but the British had them under heavy fire. Min Ryan had called to the house and told her that she'd been in the GPO to try to talk to her boyfriend Sean Mac Diarmada but hadn't seen him and intended returning.

Martial law had been declared and there were no trams. A strange confusion about events hung across the city, with people avoiding going out.

Don wanted her to play with him but she had no mind or heart for it as she worried about her husband. She had to see him, try to talk to him. She must go into town herself to try to find out what was happening. Mary could mind the children. If she let Grace know where she was going, she suspected that her sister would insist on coming too. But Muriel needed to go alone and talk to him.

The baby had gone down for a nap and Mary was busy playing with her small son and his box of coloured wooden blocks as Muriel grabbed her light coat and a hat and slipped outside. It was a bright, warm spring day and the DMP man was still standing across from their house on Oakley Road, watching it as usual. She was tempted to wave at him defiantly, but today she wanted no trouble. She had her shopping basket on her arm as if she were just going to get some food for her family. Head down, she kept walking purposefully towards Ranelagh and the local shops, hoping that no one was trailing her.

Passing Mount Pleasant, she just kept walking, crossing the canal, going along Charlemont Street and up Camden Street. She would take the back streets, avoiding the crowds, as she hastened her pace. Around Dublin Castle and City Hall could be dangerous – perhaps the Volunteers held them too? She would take another shortcut which would bring her out across Dame Street and from there make her way through the winding cobbled streets which ran towards the Liffey, then across the river and up by Liffey Street towards the back of the General Post Office.

As Muriel got nearer, she could see that the streets were covered in broken glass from the shop windows that had been smashed or riddled with bullets. Shop doors were gaping open, their stock gone, taken by the looting crowds that roamed the streets. Men, women and children, all laden down with their booty of clothes, bed linen, shoes and luxuries. The children carried bats, kites and balls from Lawrence's toy shop, which now lay empty. She passed women flaunting their finery in silk dresses, sporting expensive coloured shawls, wraps and furs, all purloined from the city centre's shops.

'What are you looking at, missus?' growled a drunken old woman wearing a pretty pink hat with a feather in it and carrying a big white lace tablecloth and a silver teapot. 'These are all mine.'

'I'm sorry, I'm just trying to find some food for my family,' she said, praying that the woman wouldn't turn on her and block her path.

The woman hesitated.

'I've two small children and my husband is away,' Muriel pleaded, lifting her basket. 'I have to find something for them to eat.'

'Good luck to ye. Take what you need from the shops is what we say.' The woman stepped aside, her two friends nodding in agreement.

As she got nearer Muriel could hear gunfire, the noise loud and shocking. One person would shoot, then another. Then there came a barrage of shots. She could hear shouting. As she approached the magnificent General Post Office building she could see that many of its windows were broken. Then she saw the barricades across different streets to block British soldiers from approaching the GPO. One was made of bicycles and wire, another of heavy clocks stacked one on another. A dead horse lay on the ground further up, its legs stiff, its congealed blood spattered on the street. Poor animal, it was awful – would no one take it away? Muriel kept her head down, conscious that there must be snipers high up in most of the buildings on both sides of the wide expanse of Sackville Street, with no telling which building was held by the Volunteers and which by the British. The large, heavy front door of the Post Office was locked firmly, so she darted around the side of the building hoping to find some other entrance. Perhaps she could get admittance through the rear.

She walked around slowly and soon found a smaller door. She rapped and tapped on it, then rapped again. There was no answer for ages, but eventually a boy of about fifteen or sixteen opened the door partially and stared suspiciously at her.

'The Post Office is shut, missus, and there are no pensions for anyone,' he said, starting to close it again. 'So there is no point you waiting for it.'

'I'm looking for my husband,' she insisted, trying to prevent him closing the door. 'Mr Thomas MacDonagh. He's a leader of the Volunteers and should be inside here with Mr Pearse and Mr Connolly. Please check and bring me to them. I'm Mrs MacDonagh.'

'I know who Mr MacDonagh is,' the young lad said, now holding the door ajar. 'He talked to our class in St Enda's last year.'

'Then please let me in,' she begged, conscious of a group of young women approaching her carrying armfuls of leather boots and shoes purloined from a nearby shop.

Seconds later Muriel had gained admittance and was walking through the huge building, crossing the big sorting room where enormous baskets and boxes of letters lay piled up. The cubby holes with names of parts of the city and country written on them stood empty. There would be no letters or financial payments for people this week, no news from soldiers fighting in France and Belgium delivered to their worried parents, wives and sweethearts.

'I don't know where Mr MacDonagh is,' admitted the boy, scratching his short hair, 'but I'll bring you to see Mr Pearse.'

'Thank you.'

Muriel passed groups of men stockpiling weapons and arms in some kind of storage area. They barely glanced at her. She was taken to a large central hall where Padraig was sitting at a table writing notes. Most of the fine glass windows were broken, men standing at them fully armed with rifles. Some doorways were blocked with huge reams of paper, furniture and heavy mail sacks to stop entry. There were men in army uniform with guns and other weapons all around them. Hardly any women – just one in a nurse's uniform rolling up bandages and another who seemed to be typing letters. She saw many of her husband's friends from St Enda's. Michael O'Rahilly and Sean Mac Diarmada, deep in conversation, paid her no attention as she searched for sight of her husband.

'Muriel, MacDonagh is not here,' Padraig said, standing up. 'He and his men have taken Jacob's Biscuit Factory in the name of the Republic.'

'Then I must go to see him there.'

'Muriel, it would be most unwise and MacDonagh would be very angry with me if I let you do such a thing. You must return to the safety of your home and to the children.'

'But I need to see him. What if something should happen to him? I trained as a nurse and—'

'Your place is with your children,' Padraig insisted. Sheets of paper covered his desk and it was clear she had interrupted him. 'Please go home, Muriel.'

A young man in uniform hovered beside them, waiting to speak to him. Looking around, Muriel could see James Connolly, who seemed to be in charge. He was talking to a group of ten men, directing them to take up positions in another part of the building. Recognizing her, he nodded over. He might seem to have a brusque manner but Muriel knew him as a man full of kindness and courage who would always somehow or other be involved in the fight for justice. Tom Clarke was instructing two men to go up on the roof with their rifles. He might be older than the others, but she could tell he was very much in control of what was happening around them. She could see his surprise at her presence.

'Is Joe here?' Muriel asked. 'Grace said that she saw him with you yesterday.'

Padraig stopped what he was doing momentarily and directed her to the far side of the room, where Joe Plunkett lay on some kind of pallet bed. He looked bad. His face was pale and even from a distance she could see blood oozing from the bandage around his throat.

'Muriel, what are you doing here?' he said, struggling politely to get up. 'MacDonagh isn't here. He's leading the Jacob's garrison. His brother is with him.'

'I know,' she replied, unable to hide her concern at Joe's poor physical condition.

'You shouldn't be here, Muriel – it's far too dangerous.'

'Neither should you, Joe. You have had an operation and are only just out of hospital. Grace is out of her mind worrying about you. I didn't dare tell her I was coming here.'

'I'm grand,' he insisted, his dark eyes glowing. 'I wasn't going to miss taking my part in this after all we've planned and worked for.'

'Joe, that dressing on your neck needs to be changed,' she advised.

'I'll get Julia to check it later. Muriel, promise me that you will go home!' He hesitated, his face serious as he lowered his voice. 'But may I ask you to do something for me? Will you tell Grace that I love her and that somehow or other we will be wed, no matter what happens, I promise her that.'

'I'll tell her,' she promised, leaning forward and giving him a brief hug. Joe seemed thinner and sicker than ever.

As she turned to leave the GPO, passing men stacking ammunition, she noticed a piece of paper stuck on to one of the granite columns. It was a printed Proclamation:

The Provisional Government of The Irish Republic to the People of Ireland

IRISHMEN AND IRISH WOMEN: In the name of God and of the dead generations from which she receives her old tradition of nationhood, Ireland, through us, summons her children to her flag and strikes for her freedom...

We declare the right of the people of Ireland to the ownership of Ireland ... we hereby proclaim the Irish Republic as a Sovereign Independent State, and we pledge our lives and the lives of our comrades in arms to the cause of its freedom, of its welfare, and of its exaltation among the nations.

Muriel read it line by line, some of it already familiar to her from pages she had seen her husband writing and scribbling.

The Republic guarantees religious and civil liberty, equal rights and equal opportunities to all its citizens ... cherishing all of the children of the nation equally...

As Muriel read the words of the Proclamation, her heart leapt when she saw MacDonagh's name printed on the bottom alongside those of his friends. She felt suddenly achingly proud of her husband and these men, his friends, who had stood up beside him for this new Irish Republic.

All the secrecy, the meetings and planning – this is what it was all about: her husband's long-cherished dream of an Irish Republic.

Taking a last glance around the inside of the General Post Office, Muriel wondered how Padraig, Joe and the men and women stationed here could possibly withstand a major onslaught from the mighty British army. She felt afraid for them and what the end of it all might be.

As she made her way through the corridors to the back of the building, ready to go home, Muriel felt heartsore, but she was determined that she too would play her part. Her two small children needed her and her duty was to stay with them, to protect them no matter what happened to MacDonagh and his friends.

Chapter 78

Nellie

The college of surgeons was bombarded so constantly over the next few days that Nellie was amazed the building could withstand such an unrelenting attack. Their men remained up on the roof, guns in hand, skin burned raw and red, defending their position while the British forces seemed to amass and gather strength around them.

Michael Mallin was a disciplined leader, as were Captain Poole and Captain McCormick, all of them properly trained army men used to combat and battle. The commandant insisted that proper army-fashion beds were neatly made and order was strictly kept by their garrison. One of the men had deliberately damaged a portrait of Queen Victoria hanging in the council room and the commandant had threatened to shoot the culprit if he found him.

Mallin despatched a search party to look around the building, for he knew that there was an Officer Training Corps in the college and he suspected that they would hold a stock of rifles for shooting practice. They hunted up and down and all over the warren of corridors and rooms but to no avail, for the weapons could not be found.

He sent parties of their men to cross, unseen, on a high, narrow plank from the roof of the college over to the roof of another building. Still hidden, they were digging and boring through the neighbouring buildings, with orders to try and get nearer to the enemy's gun position.

Margaret volunteered to cycle by the Shelbourne Hotel and throw bombs into it.

'Their snipers and gunners have us pinned down. It's the only way we could ever hope to take them out. No one is going to suspect a lady on a bicycle,' she insisted stoutly. 'I'm sure I can get close enough to throw the bombs.'

But the commandant and the countess had both declared it a mad act of folly which would surely cost her her life, so her plan was overruled.

The only lull in the constant din and pressure of fighting was an agreed truce, morning and evening, to let the park keeper feed and check on the ducks and swans on the lake in St Stephen's Green. There were strict orders that at these times no one was to dare fire a single shot, and both sides obeyed the order. Nellie was relieved that the birds would be protected from the mayhem around them.

'I tell you, they care more for those ducks than they care for us,' joked Bill Partridge, who had a way of cheering everybody up.

The porter and his family were moved down to the basement, as he had been caught sending a message for help and for food and water, lowering it down on a rope from his bedroom window.

Nellie felt guilty, as poor Mr Duncan had been forgotten about in all the action, and now he and his wife and child would have to try to survive on the same meagre rations as the rest of them.

The porridge they served was now reduced to a thinner gruel-like consistency and they had to ration it.

'What are we going to do?' Kathleen fretted, staring at their almost vanished supplies. 'Without food the men will not be able to last out.'

The men never complained, but it was clear that they were hungry.

Then Hanna Sheehy-Skeffington surprised them by arriving with some food for the garrison, knocking quietly at the side door with packets of tea, crackers and bread, and swiftly passing it inside before disappearing again.

Good old Skeffy! thought Nellie. She was very fond of Hanna, the women's right-to-vote campaigner, who had such a kind heart and was such a practical woman.

In the early hours of the morning they were woken by the arrival of two female messengers from the GPO carrying urgent despatches for Michael Mallin. Much to their delight, Elizabeth O'Farrell and Julia Grennan also carried sacks of much-needed bread.

'We didn't think we'd get through,' admitted Julia. 'The supplementary women are still watching the streets, but with our sacks on our back they presumed that we were looters like them.'

'Looters?' Nellie was puzzled.

'You should see Sackville Street and some of the other streets. The locals have picked the shops clean. They are looting and stealing everything they can lay their hands on!'

'There isn't a cup or plate or teapot, or even a seat, left in the DBC café,' added Elizabeth. 'They've carried them off to use in their homes.'

'We were lucky we met Mr Sheehy-Skeffington on the way here.'

Nellie was surprised to hear that Hanna's husband, the well-known pacifist, was about so late.

'He was trying to stop the looting. He got some lads to assist us carry the sacks part of the way.'

'James Connolly told us that your garrison needed food supplies urgently as you were under heavy fire, so we brought as much bread for you as we could manage,' Julia explained with a smile.

'We've been under fire and attack in the GPO too, but so far we are well defended,' Elizabeth told them. 'Captain Brennan-Whitmore has taken the corner of Earl Street and we have a garrison in the Metropole Hotel too. We get our food supplies from the hotels on the street – and thankfully they were very well stocked for Easter.'

Nellie could not help but be envious and cursed the fact that their garrison had not had the foresight to take a hotel instead of where they were.

'We'll tell Connolly you need more supplies urgently and try to get them to you,' the two women promised as they set off back to the GPO.

Nellie began to count the loaves. At least the men would have bread in the morning with their mug of tea. They all knew the odds were stacked against them and that every day they managed to hold their position here against the enemy was a victory.

Chapter 79

Nellie

Nellie was regularly despatched to the abandoned houses and buildings they now controlled, running between Grafton Street towards Cuffe Street, hunkering down as she clambered through holes and dust and rubble with her messages, and also with rations for some of the men, who had nothing to eat.

Across Dublin city there were food shortages, with no bread, milk, meat or grocery deliveries. Business was at a standstill. Martial law had been declared by Lord Wimborne, the lord lieutenant. A British gunship had sailed up the River Liffey and, according to the despatches they received, was inflicting massive damage on Sackville Street, bombarding the area all around the GPO and Liberty Hall.

They cheered when reports came in that on Mount Street the Volunteers had attacked the Sherwood Foresters, a large contingent of British soldiers recently landed in Kingstown, as they marched along the route into the city, killing and wounding many. Despite this, more and more British troops were flooding into the city.

Low in food and ammunition, near midnight Michael Mallin and the countess sent Nellie and Chris Caffrey to Jacob's Biscuit Factory garrison where MacDonagh was the leader.

'The British are servicing their machine guns, so you may be able to get to Jacob's,' Mallin said.

Chris had dressed up in a black shawl and black veil, for all the world looking like a widowed allowance woman with a badge and corsage.

'I found it in the bedroom of one of the houses and it's a godsend for moving around the streets unnoticed,' she explained. 'Here, you put this on, Nellie.'

She passed Nellie a widow's black felt hat and scarf

Nellie tucked her hair up under the hat and wrapped the itchy woollen scarf around her shoulders and chest.

The college was in darkness as they left, as they could use barely any candlelight in case it attracted enemy attention or sniper fire. As they neared Jacob's they spied a group of women hanging around on nearby Aungier Street, but fortunately the women ignored them. The factory was heavily barricaded, but walking around the back Chris gave the signal and code. A voice told them to get around to the north side, where a window was opened and strong arms reached down to pull them safely up into the factory.

Nellie was surprised to find that Maud Gonne's former husband, Major John MacBride, was part of the garrison.

The biscuit factory was huge, spread out over a number of floors, the giant machinery silent. They were led to meet MacDonagh.

'I see you've been under constant fire and attack from their heavy machine-gunners up on the roof.

No wonder you need ammunition and more men and supplies,' her brother-in-law sympathized as he read the despatch. 'Ammunition we can help you with. Commandant Mallin wants me to release any Citizen Army men here to his garrison, which I will consider. Food-wise, I believe there are still some cakes and sacks of flour, but I'm not sure what use they are to you.'

Nellie indicated that she would be grateful to be shown and suddenly Maire Nic Shiubhlaigh, an actress friend of hers, appeared.

'Nellie, we've some enormous sacks of flour and salt and baking powder, and some oats on the next floor,' she explained as they walked around the factory. 'But eggs, and most of the butter and a bit of milk that was left, are gone.'

Nellie noticed some dried fruit, desiccated coconut and chopped nuts.

'We still have a few fruit cakes, but I warn you they seem to play havoc with the men's stomachs. Most of the men prefer the plainer biscuits and crackers, but to tell the truth we are all getting mighty sick of them,' Maire admitted. 'Too much of a good thing.'

'We'll take anything you can spare,' Nellie said, grateful for any nourishment she could bring back for their garrison.

As she returned to the main floor, Jack Mac-Donagh appeared, enquiring about the situation in the College of Surgeons as he led her back to his brother.

'It is far too dangerous for you ladies to be out on the streets,' MacDonagh said, trying to persuade them to stay with his garrison. 'Muriel

409

would kill me if I let anything happen to you, Nellie. I promise that I will send men with supplies to your garrison, but you two must stay with us here.'

'We are expected back,' replied Chris curtly, 'with some ammunition and some food.'

'MacDonagh, I know you are only thinking of our safety, but we have our orders from Commandant Mallin to return to the college,' said Nellie. 'We are needed there.'

As they prepared to leave, Major MacBride issued them with a supply of ammunition which they hid about their persons while Maire gave them some flour, dried fruits, tins of biscuits and cakes.

'What have we here?' jeered the supplementary women, appearing out of nowhere in the darkness of the street outside as they began to walk back to the college.

'Brazen hussies!' yelled a stout woman, her face red with anger.

'We are decent widow women like yourselves, with hungry children,' retorted Chris, standing her ground.

Before they knew it, two of their biscuit tins were given up to the women, who then grudgingly agreed to let them pass. But as they approached York Street Nellie became aware of footsteps following them again.

'I told you – they're Sinn Feiners,' a voice shouted accusingly, as the supplementary women came chasing after them. Nellie and Chris ran as fast as they could. Reaching the side door of the college, they hammered frantically to be let in. A voice demanded the password before they were safe in its sanctuary.

True to his word, a few hours later MacDonagh sent a group of about fifteen of his men to their garrison with supplies of ammunition, heavy sacks of flour and cakes. Bill Oman, the young bugler who had sent them off only a few days earlier, was among them, following orders to stay and fight with Michael Mallin.

Exhausted, Nellie slept, but she was woken in the early hours by an absolute barrage of gunfire. They were under a massive attack. In the darkness their enemy had positioned another machine gun on the roof of the nearby University Church and had placed more snipers in position around them while they slept. They now had three heavy machine guns trained on them. Slowly and stealthily they were being surrounded. Nellie took her turn on duty a few hours later with some of the other women, all with their guns at the ready in front of the tall windows of the council room as the men were ordered to rest and, if possible, sleep.

Disaster struck when Margaret Skinnider, Bill Partridge and a small team were despatched to try to destroy the new enemy gun position by approaching from the Russell Hotel. They were spotted and young Fred Ryan was shot dead. Margaret was badly wounded too. Bleeding heavily, Bill and the other men somehow managed to carry her back to the college despite coming under intensive fire.

Nellie could see her friend had been seriously wounded by four bullets and was barely breathing. Madeleine ordered them to lay the young Scots woman gently on a bed in the Red Cross area as she examined her wounds. Commandant Mallin wanted to transfer her to one of the hospitals, but Margaret managed to indicate she did not want to go. The countess paced up and down, smoking and anxious, as the Red Cross women treated her. A huge closeness had grown between all the women of the garrison and none of them could bear to contemplate anything happening to their friend.

Rosie and the other women in the Red Cross area were rushed off their feet tending to the large number of casualties they had suffered. Margaret now lay among them, her face ashen, her body shivering and shaking with shock and blood loss.

Nellie brought a cup of hot tea to a shocked Bill, secretly wondering how much longer they would possibly be able to remain here, for, even though they had finally found the college's hidden arsenal of sixty rifles, the situation in the garrison was worsening day by day.

Chapter 80

Nellie

The sky was red. It was eerie, the streets quiet and deserted, and above them the sky an intense, burning, reddish-orange glow, while a thick, black, smoke-like cloud covered the centre of

Dublin. Nellie had never seen anything like it before. Maybe the British army had decided to burn them out and had set the GPO and Sackville Street ablaze. The air was heavy and humid, and she had a strange sensation of ash in her mouth and lungs. How could anyone survive such an inferno? The sound of heavy artillery and machine-gun fire seemed to be coming from all across the city on both sides of the river.

Up on the roof of the College of Surgeons they were under heavy fire too, Nellie moving among the exhausted men with cold water for them to drink and some of the remaining cake and broken biscuits. It was like being in hell up on the narrow parapet and she tried not to feel giddy as she looked down into the street and park. Sniper fire and machine-gun fire peppered the air around her.

'Hold my gun,' begged one of the young lads as he slumped against the roof and thirstily drank some water she offered him, closing his eyes. She could see his hands were raw and scorched from the heat of the gun, which had given her a fright when she touched it. He was close to collapse.

'Soldier, you are relieved,' barked one of the older army men beside her. 'Tell the countess to send a man up to replace you and get some salve on those hands.'

The past twenty-four hours had been desperate, many of their men collapsing with tiredness, hunger and lack of sleep. The commandant was trying to rotate and relieve them, and everyone had to take a turn up on the roof while others were sent down to try to rest.

Nellie kept hold of the young man's gun as he scrambled past her on the narrow ledge, grateful to be sent down to the college hall to rest.

'Will you stay on watch until his relief comes?' asked the captain.

Nellie nodded and settled down into position.

'There's a sniper over there,' called out the captain. 'But don't engage him.'

Bullets ricocheted all around her until her ears rang with the sound. Suddenly there was an explosion and the roof tiles and granite around her disintegrated in dust as she ducked her head.

'On the right – have you got him, lads? Can you see him?'

With all the dust and smoke Nellie found it hard to see anything.

'We've got him!' they yelled as they began to fire.

Despite the barrage of shots the sniper seemed to dive and disappear, leaving only the tip of his rifle visible.

'He's on the lower part of the roof, hiding beside the gutter.'

The captain and two men took immediate aim. Then came a cry of 'We've got him! Hold fire!'

A few minutes later they could see the injured sniper scuttling from the roof towards safety. Nellie was relieved that he was alive but no longer a threat to them.

Time passed. Nellie didn't know how the men stuck it up here for hours on end, unable to rest or move away, so surrounded did the enemy have them.

Dublin was burning, fires across the city getting worse, the fighting concentrated on the other side of the Liffey as the army gunship kept up its unending bombardment.

They were in a hopeless situation, but all were determined to fight on for as long as they could possibly last out. She thought of MacDonagh and his men, and of Joe Plunkett, James Connolly and all the people she cared about who were caught up in this desperate battle for freedom. Muriel and Grace must be worried out of their minds. She preferred to be up here in the heat and sweat of the roof, serving with her garrison, than at home imagining what was happening. No doubt Mother would be horrified to know that she was so deeply involved in the rebellion.

The bullet-marked tricolour flag still flew high overhead, flapping lazily in the breeze, somehow surviving the constant hail of bullets. Nellie felt tired and overwrought herself, needing to sleep. Her eyes were sore but she dared not shut them: she had to remain alert and on watch.

A few hours later she was happy to pass the gun to one of the former Jacob's men and resume her duty bringing water to their sentries. They all looked so tired and she urged them to eat a bit to try to keep their energy up.

'But I don't eat raisins,' one grumbled as she managed to cajole him into swallowing a few.

Looking around her, she had absolutely no idea how much longer they could last under such conditions. They, had lost a few good men and a number of their company had been badly injured, but so too had many innocent citizens, children too, shot crossing the street or getting caught in gunfire. It grieved Nellie deeply to think of them.

The fire was getting worse, the sky black with smoke, ashes blowing in the air throughout the next twenty-four hours. It seemed the whole city was burning, building after building destroyed. At night the garrison joined together to say the rosary, the countess joining in the litany and repetition of prayers. Some sat in silence, writing letters for their families. The countess quietly asked Michael Mallin to witness a letter she wrote. Nellie suspected it might be her will, for she was certainly a wealthy woman compared to the rest of them. Nellie had a huge regard for her and her enthusiasm, utter loyalty and bravery, and was very proud to have served as her aide-de-camp over the past few days.

They were all aware that it was only a matter of time until they faced certain bombardment and an all-out attack by their British enemy, who now had them totally surrounded.

Chapter 81

Nellie

An air of desperation hung darkly over their garrison on Sunday morning as their isolated situation became clearer. Heavy military cordons and barricades were now set up across most of the city, and they were hopelessly outnumbered by the

British military. From the flames and smoke they suspected that the headquarters at the GPO and much of Sackville Street were most likely destroyed. They had no communication or despatches about the safety of their leaders, James Connolly, Tom Clarke and Padraig Pearse.

Yesterday they had managed to get some food, including flour, sugar and eggs from a pastry shop, and a large piece of bacon which they had served to their hungry and exhausted fighters. As they eked out the last of their provisions Nellie suspected they might be starved out of their garrison.

A knock on the York Street door was answered to Nurse Elizabeth O'Farrell. This time, instead of bearing bread, Elizabeth was grim-faced. She was waving a white flag of surrender and carrying orders from General Lowe, commander of the British forces, for Michael Mallin.

She was led inside and told that the commandant was sleeping, but that Countess Markievicz was next in command. When the countess was handed the typewritten order by Nurse O'Farrell it was clear that she was shocked. She went off immediately to discuss it with Commandant Mallin.

Nellie watched anxiously, presuming that the order from the British general demanded some kind of offer of a truce or surrender.

Elizabeth was upset as she told them that the GPO and much of Sackville Street had been destroyed by fire. James Connolly had been shot and badly wounded, but, most of the main garrison had escaped safely through the lanes to Moore Street. However, surrounded by the army and with many innocent men, women and children being caught up in the fighting, on Saturday afternoon Padraig Pearse had ordered surrender.

The commandant appeared, his face drained of colour as he told Nurse O'Farrell that he had read the general's order but that he could not give her his immediate answer to bring to Major de Courcy-Wheeler as he needed to consult with the countess and his officers. Elizabeth returned to the major with this response.

Nellie could see despair and disbelief in the eyes of those around her as the news spread that Padraig Pearse, James Connolly and general headquarters had surrendered and had now ordered that all the other garrisons surrender too in order to avoid further slaughter of innocent people and to save the lives of their men.

Countess Markievicz sat with her head in her hands, devastated by the news of the surrender of the other garrisons. Everyone was heartbroken at the prospect of accepting defeat and surrendering themselves to a British major. Some of the women began crying.

Messengers were sent to all the outposts, ordering their men to return to the college for a meeting. The hall was silent as their commandant stood up.

'Commandants James Connolly and Padraig Pearse have ordered us to lay down our arms and surrender to the British,' Michael Mallin told them. 'We will now obey this order by James Connolly to surrender.'

All around Nellie men shook their heads angrily. Some eyes filled with tears.

'We should not surrender.'

'We should fight on.'

Many begged the commandant to be allowed to continue the fight, no matter how hopeless it appeared; others objected, refusing to accept surrender. The countess and Bill Partridge talked to them quietly, telling them that they must obey Connolly's orders.

Bill Partridge stood shoulder to shoulder with Michael Mallin, his arm around his commandant, as he broke the news, reading the order again to the men returning from the outposts, unable to hide the fact that he too was deeply upset.

'We have fought the good fight, but now the fight is over and all garrisons are to obey orders from the command to surrender,' he said firmly.

Madeleine explained the situation to the wounded and made the decision that Margaret, who was still desperately ill, must be evacuated to hospital before the British forces came for them.

Michael Mallin ordered men to go up on the roof and take down the tricolour flag of Ireland, which had flown there so proudly over the college. They all stood silent and sombre, looking at the flag when it was brought down, but Commandant Mallin was determined that the British would not get their hands on it.

He and the countess came over to Margaret and, with Madeleine's help, carefully wrapped the Irish flag and hid it inside the injured woman's long coat. Determined still to help, Margaret was again carrying another precious secret cargo for them. Nellie squeezed her hand as they said goodbye and a group of men lifted Margaret gently on to a stretcher, carrying her down the stairs and out of the building to a waiting ambulance which took her to the nearby hospital.

The commandant urged them to return home, encouraging some of the men to dress in civilian clothes taken from the houses they had occupied and so hide their identity. A few men talked of escaping to the Dublin Mountains, where at least they could continue their fight for freedom.

'If any of the good ladies present wishes to flee to safety, now is the time,' Mallin advised.

Nellie could see that, after all they had been through, the women were not prepared to be separated from the rest of their garrison. They were as much a part of the rebellion as the group of over a hundred men and they had no intention of changing their loyalties now. She had never imagined such a scene of calamity, regret and sadness.

They surrendered at midday. Commandant Michael Mallin ordered them to put down all weapons and assemble. A white flag was raised over the roof of the College of Surgeons to signal the surrender of their garrison.

Michael Mallin shook everyone by the hand, his face pale and haggard as he thanked them for their loyalty and service. He told the captains and officers to join the rest of the ranks so that they could not be singled out for punishment when the British arrived.

He and Countess Markievicz agreed to surrender when Major de Courcy-Wheeler and another officer entered the building. Mallin called the garrison to attention as he presented his own sword to the major. Countess Markievicz defiantly kissed her gun before handing it over. The major admitted his surprise at how few men and women had served in the garrison: he had expected to find at least another hundred.

Soldiers surrounded them as they left the building with a blanket each and began to march in formation. Nellie's eyes brimmed with tears as she looked back and caught sight of the white flag now flying from the roof of the College of Surgeons.

A huge crowd had gathered outside to witness their surrender, most people booing, hissing and cursing as soon as they caught sight of them.

'Hold your heads erect,' William Partridge told them as they stepped outside and were immediately surrounded by the hostile crowd. The countess, dressed in her Citizen Army tunic, riding breeches and flamboyant hat with its ostrich feather, attracted huge attention.

Onlookers flung rubbish, pelting them with rotting vegetables and potato skins. Only a few wished them well, saying they would pray for them. They marched on, Nellie hurt and shamefaced by the reaction of their fellow Dubliners to their valiant attempt to gain Irish Freedom.

As they walked down Grafton Street the crowds got bigger, the supplementary women baying at them like a pack of hounds ready for blood.

'They should be shot.'

'They've destroyed the city.'

'Bayonet the traitors!'

Nellie refused to cry and give in to their intimidation as they shoved and jostled to try to get at them. The army soldiers, arms at the ready, were now actually protecting them from the massing hostile groups who threatened them.

On Dame Street they met a cohort of the Dublin Fusiliers, just returned from fighting in the war, who jeered and taunted them as they arrived at Dublin Castle.

There they were ordered to Richmond Barracks to join the rest of the rebels.

Nellie, Mary Hyland and Rosie Hackett worried about what lay ahead. Rosie suspected that the leaders of the rebellion might possibly be hanged or transported to some far-flung British colony.

Nellie's heart sank as she saw Michael Mallin, their stalwart commandant, being separated from his group of men and led off somewhere on his own. The countess was also singled out, a flicker of fear flitting across her thin face as she too was marched away.

'Those two are for it now!' one of the soldiers laughed loudly.

Chapter 82

Nellie

Richmond barracks was overcrowded, everyone stacked and crammed together like sardines. Separated from the men, the women tried to get some rest, but many of the soldiers were taunting and jeering at them. Like all her comrades, Nellie was famished and glad of the bully beef and biscuits they were given.

British justice did not tarry, and she watched as men from their garrison and others were gathered to be marched to the north wall, from where they would be transported to jails in England or Wales.

'You ladies are to be moved to Kilmainham Jail,' they were brusquely told by a burly sergeant.

They marched at dusk to Dublin's infamous prison. Over the previous hundred years or more Kilmainham had held not only criminals and murderers, but the renowned Irish rebel leaders Robert Emmet and Charles Stewart Parnell.

'They are sending us to the right place!' joked fair-haired Madeleine ffrench-Mullen defiantly. There was a large group of women from the Citizen Army and Cumann na mBan, all of whom had played their part in the rebellion.

Nellie's sense of bravado disappeared as they crossed the cobblestones and entered the stone archway at the entrance to Kilmainham, a tall, austere, grey-brick building. Despite its being spring, she shivered at the cold and damp in the old west wing of the jail. During the rebellion the Volunteers had cut the gas supply, so they had only candlelight to direct them to their cells. She was led into a cell where she was ordered to undress and take off her boots and stockings as two female warders searched her for hidden weapons.

Nellie was handed a blanket and moved to another cell to put her clothes back on. She was sharing with Julia Grennan and Winifred Carney, both of whom had served in the GPO. All their blankets were infested with fleas and Nellie and her companions were soon covered in bites which

423

became a scourge as she itched at them constantly.

'Try not to scratch them or you will only make it worse,' Dr Lynn advised them all as they exercised in one of the prison yards.

The food was terrible, their dinner an awful stew that was more like a greasy soup served with biscuits.

'It's disgusting!' complained Julia as she nibbled at the hard prison biscuits.

There was little comfort in the cramped cells and Nellie wondered how she would survive weeks or months, or even years, in such a place. But she was determined not to get downhearted. She wondered if her sisters or parents were even aware that she had been imprisoned and if they would be allowed to visit her. She supposed she and the other women might also be sent to prisons in England.

They told each other stories of their garrisons. Winnie was proud to have served as James Connolly's secretary.

'He's the bravest man I know, for he was badly shot in the leg and hardly complained. I heard that he was taken to Dublin Castle, where hopefully the doctors will attend to his wounds and blood loss.'

'He's far too ill to be imprisoned here,' asserted Julia, who had helped to nurse him.

Nellie had a huge regard for Connolly, who had been so kind to her every time she set foot in Liberty Hall and she prayed that he would recover from his injuries.

All the women were allowed to exercise in the yard together which gave them the opportunity to try to discover what was going on not only within the prison walls but also outside. They heard that the city, much of it destroyed, was under heavy military rule, the army suspicious of everyone, with a curfew still in operation and cordons and barricades in most parts of the city.

Countess Markievicz was also in Kilmainham but was kept isolated in a cell away from the rest of them and not allowed to exercise with them.

'They say she will stand trial with the other leaders,' whispered Rosie.

'What will happen to them?' Nellie asked, thinking of MacDonagh and Joe and their own commandant.

'One of the wardens told me that he heard that the military governor, General Maxwell, has ordered that all the rebellion leaders are to be tried and sentenced to death for treason.'

'They would never do that!' Julia cried vehemently.

Nellie felt sick. Surely the British general and his men would never carry out such a sentence and instead would exile and transport them to a prison in some godforsaken colony. How would Muriel and the children ever survive without MacDonagh?

A rumour spread that Padraig and Willie Pearse and some of the other leaders were in cells on the landing on the other side of the prison. She tried to cajole a warder into giving her some information about her brother-in-law, MacDonagh, and Grace's fiancé, Joe Plunkett, but the dour heavy-set woman was unforthcoming.

Chapter 83

Muriel

Fear and anxiety overwhelmed Muriel when she heard that the rebels had surrendered, Jacob's garrison one of the last to capitulate to General Lowe. MacDonagh and his men had been marched to Richmond Barracks, where they were still being held.

During the Rising MacDonagh had sent her messages from Jacob's and she in turn had managed to send him notes, but now she was frantic to see and talk to her husband.

Over the past week her Ranelagh home had been filled with the wives, sweethearts, families and friends of the Volunteers, everyone calling, desperate for news. Padraig's mother and sister; Min Ryan and her sister; Michael O'Rahilly's American wife, Nancy; and Aine Ceannt, who, for safety reasons, had fled her home with her son to stay with Caitlin Brugha. Muriel made pot after pot of tea and told them about the GPO as they compared the messages and information that they had received. They had all presumed that, at most, the Volunteers and the Citizen Army would hold out against the army for only a day or two, and as the week had gone on they could not believe that they were somehow managing to fight and hold their positions despite

426

coming under such heavy attack from the British forces that were pouring into the city. No one had expected it, but the women all shared the same concern and fear of how it would all end.

Now that the rebellion was over, all Muriel wanted was to see her husband, to talk to him, to allay her fears that he had been wounded or injured. Dublin was full of rumours, with talk of trials, courts martial and arrangements for the rebels to be deported to a prison overseas. She had to discover what would happen to Mac-Donagh. Would he be sent to prison? She was determined to see him.

Then there was Nellie. They had word that her sister had been arrested along with Countess Markievicz and the other women from the Citizen Army who had been fighting in the College of Surgeons.

'They won't hurt the women,' Grace assured her. 'It would cause such uproar. I'm sure Nellie and the rest of the women will all be released and sent home.'

'You know Mother won't have her home,' Muriel said angrily. 'She considers Nellie and the rest of us traitors, disloyal not only to "the Crown" but to the family name. Nellie will have to come and stay here.'

'What do you think they will do to MacDonagh and Joe?'

'I fear that it will not go easy for them, that General Lowe will make an example of them.'

'Some say the leaders will all be tried and executed,' Grace cried, distraught. 'That General Maxwell has been sent over to crush the rebellion and intends executing everyone involved.'

'The British government and the Irish Parliamentary Party would never allow such a thing,' Muriel said, trying to convince herself as well as her sister that the king and the Westminster parliament would not consider such drastic action when they were so deeply embroiled in the war in Europe. 'The likelihood is that Joe and MacDonagh will be deported, imprisoned – I don't know where or for how long. Perhaps they may even be sentenced to life in prison.'

Muriel could not imagine such a thing: being parted from her husband, not being near him when they loved each other so much. It was unbearable.

'If MacDonagh is imprisoned I don't know how the children and I will survive without him.'

'Joe and I should have been married by now,' Grace sobbed. 'What if I never get to see him or speak to him again?'

'That won't happen,' Muriel consoled her sister, hugging her. 'We must both try to be patient and wait for news of the two of them.'

But Muriel herself was frantic and tried to talk to the Dublin Metropolitan Police to ascertain what was happening to Thomas MacDonagh.

'If he is a prisoner I should be let visit him,' she pleaded. 'I am his wife.'

'No visitors are permitted,' they told her.

From the group of soldiers camped near their home she discovered that many of the prisoners were being sent immediately to Wales and England – perhaps her husband was one of them.

Her mind was in turmoil and the children were lonely and upset, missing their father, while she could not hide from them the tension she was under as they awaited news.

Grace was also trying to ascertain what had happened to Joe. She had gone to Belgrave Road to talk to his sister Geraldine.

'Geraldine told me that Joe's parents have been arrested for their involvement with the rebels and she thinks they are being held in Richmond Barracks with George and Jack. The countess put up a bit of a fight, apparently, when the soldiers came to their house.'

'What does Geraldine think will happen to them?'

'A friend of Count Plunkett's informed them of the possibility that the leaders of the Rising may be tried for treason and sentenced to death.'

Muriel felt dizzy, a desperate clanging in her ears.

'Oh Muriel, I'm sorry to upset you,' apologized Grace, making her sit down. 'Perhaps they are wrong and MacDonagh will not stand trial.'

Muriel doubted that, for MacDonagh was not only a leader of the Volunteers but, along with Padraig, Joe, Tom Clarke and Sean Mac Diarmada, was part of the small circle of the Irish Republican Brotherhood who were deeply involved in planning every aspect of the rebellion. Why, he had even signed the Proclamation of the new Irish Republic – she had seen it herself.

Heavy-hearted, Muriel read the next day that by order of the Crown the leaders of the rebellion would all be tried. Thomas MacDonagh, her beloved husband, she suspected would be found guilty.

The hours went so slowly, and no matter whom she talked to Muriel could get no information about what was happening. If only Father had been well he could have used his Castle contacts, but she doubted her poor father even realized that there had been a rebellion, much less that Nellie and his son-in-law and Grace's fiancé had all been involved.

A soldier came and knocked on their front door. Three-year-old Don ran ahead of her as she went to open it.

'Where is my dada?' he demanded, seeing the man's army uniform.

'Your father is to be shot,' the man said coldly and her little boy, scared and hysterical, ran back into her arms.

Muriel began to shake.

'Mrs Muriel MacDonagh, it has been ordered that Mr Thomas MacDonagh, who is convicted of treason, is to be executed at Kilmainham Jail tomorrow. The prisoner has requested that you visit him. You are hereby granted permission by General Lowe to visit the prisoner prior to his execution,' the soldier said, his gaze unflinching, not even meeting hers.

Execution ... execution... The very words made her feel weak and she tried to steady herself.

But this was no time for weakness. She had to see MacDonagh. Grace had gone out earlier searching for information, so she was all alone with the children, the baby already asleep, but she

430

would ask Mary to come over and mind them.

'I will come as soon as I can,' she replied calmly. 'Please inform Mr Thomas MacDonagh and General Lowe that I will be there immediately to see him.'

Less than half an hour later she was on her way. Her mind was spinning, but she tried to concentrate on the fact that she was going to see Mac-Donagh and would be able to talk to him. There must be some mistake, some legal loophole they could find to commute his sentence. She would talk to her husband. She would not think of him being executed.

The city was still under martial law, a war zone, full of barricades and damaged buildings, so much destruction and debris everywhere. The acrid smell of smoke still clung to the air. The curfew was still in operation and Muriel had to stop at a checkpoint manned by some soldiers with their bayonets.

'You should not be out, missus,' they warned. 'Return to your home.'

'A member of your army came to my home in Oakley Road to inform me that I was requested to visit my husband, Mr Thomas MacDonagh, who is imprisoned in Kilmainham Jail tonight,' she said quietly.

'Show me your permit please,' demanded an older soldier.

'I don't have one. The soldier who came never gave me a permit or note from General Lowe,' she replied, realizing that she had absolutely nothing to prove her case.

'He would have given you a written permit to break the curfew and cross the city,' the man said knowledgeably.

'I promise you, he gave me nothing. He just told me that he had been sent to inform me that my husband is to be executed and that I have permission to visit him in Kilmainham.' Muriel's voice was breaking.

'We have no knowledge of it,' the army man said testily, 'and have strict instruction to enforce the curfew as some of the rebels are still at large.'

'Please!' she begged. 'Let me through. My husband is to be executed tomorrow. I have to see him ... please.'

She could see three of the soldiers talking behind the older man.

'Must be one of the traitor leaders!' one called. She flinched.

'Please. My husband, Mr Thomas MacDonagh, was a commandant in the Irish Volunteers. He is in Kilmainham Jail and the governor and General Lowe himself have granted me permission to visit him. Don't stop me doing what any wife would want to do when she hears such terrible news.'

'We cannot let you pass,' he repeated stubbornly. 'You get a permit, missus, and return and we will let you through.'

'Where can I get such a permit at this late hour?' she pleaded. 'Tell me...'

He shrugged his shoulders and simply turned away from her. She could hear them all laughing.

'Come back in the morning, after curfew,' called another younger soldier.

Muriel ran back to Oakley Road, to the home of

432

neighbours who possessed a new telephone machine and begged them to let her use it to phone Kilmainham or someone in authority to get the necessary pass, but realizing that her husband was one of the rebels her neighbours, despite her pleas, shut the door on her.

Over the next few hours Muriel frantically attempted twice more to get through barricades and checkpoints, but all to no avail. It was long past midnight when, tearful and exhausted, she returned home, determined that tomorrow morning at first light she would go immediately to Kilmainham to see MacDonagh.

Still dressed, she curled up in their bed and tried to imagine that he was close beside her, telling her never fear, my love, all would be well and soon they would be together again...

Chapter 84

Nellie

As dawn was breaking Nellie and her cellmates were woken by sudden gunfire, a whole volley of shots and then utter silence. It sounded close within the prison. The three women sat up in their cell, then got to their feet.

Nellie stood on the stool on tiptoe, peering out over the narrow window ledge, hoping to see anything outside in the prison yard other than the high stone walls and the grey-streaked dawn.

It sounded as if a few soldiers were shooting together. The women's senses were on alert as they wrapped their blankets around them.

After what seemed only about fifteen or twenty minutes there was another loud volley of shots, then silence and stillness; and fifteen minutes later a repeat of loud simultaneous gunfire again.

She and Winnie and Julia all looked at each other, unwilling to say the words but each of the same mind.

The soldiers were shooting the prisoners one after another...

Chapter 85

Grace

It had been an awful night, Grace filled with a deep sense of unease about Joe, poor Muriel in a terrible state, waiting for the sun to rise and the curfew to end so that she could visit MacDonagh.

Grace had a strange premonition that she must go to Joe immediately. Ever since she was a child she had had a sense of telepathy about things and she knew that she must act on it. Fate had brought her Joe's letter, written in Richmond Barracks and delivered by a soldier to her parents' home yesterday; Liebert had brought it over to her at Muriel's.

Joe wrote telling her that the only thing he cared about was that he was not with her. He had heard that he would be sent to England, but said it might be possible for them to be wed by proxy and that she should go and talk to Father Sherwin about their marriage. Grace sensed that she should not delay.

Muriel was just getting ready to leave the house to go to Kilmainham to see MacDonagh when an early-morning bread-delivery van stopped outside. A priest got out of it and knocked on the door, asking to see her sister.

Grace's heart sank. Had he word of Mac-Donagh?

Father Aloysius came inside and took Muriel by the hand. Gently, he told her that her husband, Thomas MacDonagh, had been executed by firing squad earlier that morning in Kilmainham Jail.

Muriel gave a strange piercing inhuman cry, her skin like alabaster, listening to his words, then she quietly asked the priest to repeat them, over and over again...

Father Aloysius had been with MacDonagh before he was shot and had given him the last rites. He told her how much her husband loved and cared for her and his two children – his last thoughts were of them – and that he died with no rancour or bitterness in his heart.

Grace felt as though her own heart would break with the sadness of it. She made tea and fetched a warm blanket, then held Muriel and tried to comfort her.

Father Aloysius told her that Padraig Pearse and Tom Clarke had also been executed that morning and that unfortunately, more executions of the rebel leaders were planned over the coming days.

Fearing that Joe, instead of being deported, would surely meet the same fate as his best friend MacDonagh, Grace knew she could not delay any longer.

Mary arrived and promised she would look after her distraught sister, who had finally begun to cry and weep for the loss of her beloved husband. Their brother Liebert, having heard the news of Thomas MacDonagh's execution, also came to the house to see if he could do anything to help, promising Grace that he would stay with their sister.

Grace set off immediately to town to meet Father Sherwin, determined to try to get the necessary licence for Joe and her to wed. Father Sherwin advised her to talk to the priest in the same parish as Kilmainham – perhaps he was the one who could help organize a marriage in the prison. He gave her a note for Father Eugene MacCarthy, who was the prison chaplain, as he might be able to get permission from the governor of Kilmainham, Major Lennon, to perform the ceremony.

'I have to get married to Joe,' she confided to the priest tearfully as he promised to help them.

It was getting late and some of the shops on Grafton Street had begun to shut. Grace was keenly aware of the staff putting up shutters and winding back canopies, getting ready to lock doors as the final customers in their shops left. The large jewellery shop was still open and she glanced quickly at the tray of rings on display in their window before pushing the door open.

A man stood behind the counter covering the

trays of expensive jewellery in heavy velvet cloths, ready to store them in the shop's safe.

'I'm sorry, but we are getting ready to close, miss,' he said, barely looking up at her.

'Please, I need to see your wedding rings,' she said, trying to keep control of her voice.

'I'm afraid I have put some of them away already.'

'I saw some in the window – please may I see them?'

Reluctantly stopping what he was doing, he walked over to the window, leaned in and took out the velvet-lined tray, carrying it over to the dark mahogany counter and placing it in front of her.

'Gold bands, rounded, and a few straight. Some young ladies like a traditional narrow band and others prefer it wider,' he recited.

Grace touched the curving bands with her fingers.

'May I try one or two of these rings on?'

The jeweller looked pointedly at the clock.

'A marriage band is for life, the fitting and choice and purchase of which is not something usually to be rushed,' he advised.

Grace blushed and swallowed hard, standing resolutely at his counter.

'Please, I wish to try this one.' She indicated a simple, narrow gold circle from the centre of the tray and he took it out and passed it to her. She put it on her finger, but it was far too big.

'Try this one,' he offered, handing her another ring.

It was still too big.

'We usually size the ring to fit your finger exactly,' he explained kindly. 'I promise that it will only take us a few days to make one to fit you perfectly.'

Grace felt like crying and pointed urgently to two more rings.

One was tiny and only fitted her little finger; the other was a curving design which she did not like.

'Please – you must have more,' she begged, trying to keep the hysteria out of her voice. 'I need to buy a wedding ring today that fits me. I have to find one.'

The jeweller stopped and considered for a few seconds before putting the tray aside. She was clearly a lady of quality, so he went down to the far end of the shop and returned about a minute later with another cloth-covered tray which he set in front of her.

'Have a look at these, miss. This one here is very popular with our brides. It is eighteen-carat gold and what we call a classic design.'

Grace went to slip it on her finger but it stopped at her knuckle. Disappointment threatened to overwhelm her.

'Never mind, miss, I'm sure I have another that will fit,' he offered, leaning over and studying the tray. 'Try this.' He pulled out a slim gold band.

Grace held out her hand and he slid the wedding ring smoothly on to her finger. He tried to move it back and forward. It wasn't too tight and sat perfectly on her long, narrow finger.

Grace studied her hand with the gold band – her wedding band. It was just what she needed. As she looked at her finger she could feel tears welling up in her eyes and was filled with such a deep sadness at the absolute unfairness of it all and what might befall Joe. She began to shudder and cry.

'I'll take this ring,' she sobbed, her voice breaking, aware of the man's concern as he stared at her.

'Weddings are a beautiful time but emotional for everyone. Why don't I put this ring aside for your young man to come in and pay for it later in the week?' he suggested. 'Wrap it up all nice for him.'

'Please, I have to buy the ring now,' she insisted tearfully, slipping the band off her finger and giving it back to him. 'He cannot come in, so I will pay for it.'

'Very well, I will wrap it for you,' he agreed slowly.

'Please, I don't need a fancy box – just something simple to carry it in,' she said, shaking.

'Are you all right, miss?' he asked, worried, reaching under the counter for a small wine-coloured box. 'Are you in trouble?'

She guessed that brides in such a state of upset and tears in his shop were a very rare occurrence.

'Please do not cry, miss. I'm sure your wedding will be a fine, happy occasion. When is it to take place?'

'I am to be wed tonight,' she whispered.

'Tonight?' he repeated, puzzled.

'My fiancé is Mr Plunkett. He is one of the rebels being held in Kilmainham,' she explained slowly, awaiting his hostile reaction as she reached into her purse. 'We are to be married there tonight, for I fear that he is to be executed.'

She gripped at the counter to steady herself as dizziness swamped her.

'Oh my dear – I am so very sorry. The whole city is full of what happened to some of the leaders there this morning...' He trailed off. His sheer kindness threatened to undo Grace as she found the notes and passed them to him.

As he wrote her a receipt in his book, Grace dabbed at her nose with her handkerchief, fighting to compose herself. He held the door open for her as she left.

'Good luck, miss,' he said gently as she turned her attention to getting to the prison to see Joe.

Chapter 86

Grace

Grace steeled herself as she approached Kilmainham jail, notorious in the past as the place where thieves and murderers met their end, many hanging from a high noose swinging outside the prison entrance. She shivered as she thought of Joe and his friends now held captive there. It was after six o'clock when she walked across the cobblestones and knocked on the door for admittance.

A soldier questioned her roughly and for a moment she felt like running away, but she stated her name and address and her reason for being there, and showed him the official piece of paper that the priest had given her. He went off to check something, then came back a few minutes later and led her to the office of Major Lennon, the governor of Kilmainham. Grace tried to control her fear and trepidation as she was ushered inside.

'Marriage in prison is an unusual request,' Major Lennon said gruffly, barely looking at her.

'I have all the necessary church documents and permission here,' she said, pushing them on to his desk.

'It would be one of the prison chaplains from St James's parish that would perform such a ceremony if it is authorized,' he said, reading them.

'I have spoken with Father MacCarthy already,' she explained.

Grace said nothing more. It was clear this decision now rested in his hands; Major Lennon would be the one who would decide her fate.

'You do know Mr Joseph Plunkett has been tried and found guilty of all charges, and by order of General Maxwell is due to be executed with the rest of the leaders of the Sinn Fein rebellion?'

Grace swallowed hard, shaking her head. She did not want to believe the dreadful words he had spoken.

'Mr Plunkett and I had planned our marriage before this,' she said firmly, trying to control the desperation in her voice. 'It was our intention to have been married at Easter, but events delayed it. We both love each other very much and it is Joe's last wish that we are wed.'

He nodded understandingly.

'I have to wed,' she continued, unable to hide the panic she felt. 'Joe and I have to be wed. Do not deny us this, Major Lennon, for it is all both of us want.'

Silence hung between them.

She considered telling him that her brother Claude was away fighting in France, that Liebert was in the navy and that her twin brother, Cecil, was about to enlist, and begging him to help her, but perhaps he would consider that she had shamed her family enough.

She watched as he studied the documents in front of him.

'Miss Gifford, everything seems to be in order,' Major Lennon agreed. 'You and Mr Plunkett have permission to marry today.' Relief washed over her as she was escorted outside by a soldier to a small waiting area. She and Joe were going to be wed.

'When will I see Mr Plunkett?' she asked.

'Relatives are to wait here,' the soldier explained curtly, disappearing as she sat on a small wooden chair in the damp, chilly room. Hopefully it would not be too long till she and Joe were reunited and would have their wedding, be officially married as they had planned, and that something good would come out of this terrible situation. Of course she had never imagined being wed in a place like this with a prison priest, but then she had never imagined that she and Joe would be caught up in such a tragedy.

Grace waited and waited. Eventually she called out, asking to be allowed to see Joe, but there was no response. Precious time was ticking by and she was filled with a desperate anxiety that perhaps they were playing some kind of trick on her.

She could hear distant footsteps, men shouting,

442

men calling out.

Did Joe even know that she was here? Rumour had it that her sister Nellie was also being held in Kilmainham. How she longed to see her and talk to her.

She thought of MacDonagh, shot by a firing squad only a few hours ago. She would always remember his kindness, his generosity and good humour, and his deep, abiding love for her sister. His death was unbearable. He and Joe were always the best of friends, and now the two friends would meet the same fate.

It felt as if the room was closing in on her, so she slipped out to a small enclosed yard with towering stone walls. It was hard to believe that she was in the city, as all she could see from here was the sky and a few birds flying high above her. She could hear cabs and horses and the hooting horn of a distant car, but otherwise this place entombed her as she walked and walked around the yard, trying to calm herself so that mounting panic didn't overwhelm her.

She had decided to wear her pretty new pink and white gingham-edged dress and a simple head-piece with a slight veil. She wanted to look well for Joe, but as night began to fall she could not help but feel the coldness wrap around her and she wished that she had chosen something more practical and warmer. She shivered and moved inside. It was getting late, the hour mocking her.

Grace sat for a while again, hoping that perhaps fate would intervene and that Joe would not be shot but sent away to prison like his brothers. In time they could have a life together, living abroad. He would write and she would draw and they would have a small family of their own and be happy. The thought of it warmed her. Joe was always full of plans for the future and for their life together.

The night sky darkened and the prison fell silent. It was about eleven thirty when a soldier from the Royal Irish Regiment finally came and led her to the prison chapel, where the priest waited.

Grace could barely see, as there was no gas-light, just two soldiers holding flickering candles to provide light. She swallowed hard, saying a silent prayer as she walked towards the altar. She had sworn to herself that she would do her very best to remain composed: Joe did not need to see her distraught and hysterical.

A few seconds later Joe was led in. He looked desperate, hardly able to walk or stand, a ragged, bloody bandage around his neck. His gaunt face was pale, already like a ghost in the flickering light. He tried to smile at her and she longed to hug him, touch him, kiss him, but the soldier kept them apart. Father MacCarthy gestured to the soldier and he undid Joe's handcuffs. Joe, holding his scrawny, bruised wrists, rubbed at them as they gazed at each other.

'We will celebrate the holy sacrament of marriage in this chapel,' began the priest. 'It is agreed that these two soldiers here will be your witnesses.'

Grace was tempted to beg them to search the prison and bring her sister or any of the Plunkett family to the chapel, but it was made clear that this ceremony would be as brief as possible and that they were not permitted even to speak.

She and Joe stood beside each other and she could hear each of their breaths as the priest began to lead them through the words of their marriage vows. She passed the ring to Joe and he took her shaking hand as he slid the bright gold band on to her ring finger and they repeated their vows 'To love each other until death do us part'.

Grace's voice caught and she felt emotion would make her break down, but Joe squeezed her hand tight, his dark eyes locking on hers, giving her a strange strength and courage as the ceremony ended. With the priest's guidance, they and the soldiers signed the marriage register and Joe was immediately re-cuffed.

She prayed for a little kindness, compassion for them to be given a few minutes alone with each other as a newly married couple, husband and wife, but instead Joe was taken immediately from the chapel and led back to his cell, Grace left standing like a marble statue in front of the holy altar, unable to move or even to say a word.

Chapter 87

Grace

Her heart was heavy as she left the prison. It was dark, and instead of a bride's happiness and joy, here she was alone, afraid, and overcome with an immense sadness that she could not dispel.

Father MacCarthy joined her. 'Mrs Plunkett, I

fear that you will not be able to get back across the city with the curfew,' he said, worried. 'I will see if I can find you a safe place to stay for the night.'

She nodded dumbly, trying not to give in to the tears that threatened.

They walked along James Street to a nearby convent, but the nuns were all asleep in their beds and offered no assistance.

'The bellringer, Mr Byrne, lives nearby,' the priest sighed. 'Perhaps he can help us.'

The bellringer was surprised to be disturbed at such a late hour, but the priest explained Grace's situation, that she was the wife of one of the rebels due to be executed. Mr Byrne, nodding in sympathy, kindly welcomed her inside his small, simple home. She had a cup of tea and a slice of soda bread that he insisted she eat before he led her up the narrow stairs to a small, dingy room overlooking the back yard.

Exhausted, she lay on the brass bed with its musty horsehair mattress and pulled the rough blanket over her. She prayed silently for Joe, that God would somehow intervene and that miraculously he would be pardoned, his death sentence commuted, even if he were deported to some far-off prison in the British colonies. Rolling on her side, she longed for sleep as she cried and struggled to contain her grief.

Suddenly she was woken by Mr Byrne standing at the end of the bed, telling her she must get up immediately as a motor vehicle had been sent from the prison to collect her and bring her to see Mr Plunkett. In a moment she was dressed and slipping her shoes back on, then quickly using the outside lavatory, brushing her hair and dabbing some cologne on her wrists and neck as she thanked Mr Byrne for his hospitality to her.

The driver, a policeman, refused to be drawn about the reason for her visit as they passed through the empty streets and once again Grace found herself inside Kilmainham's high walls.

It was the middle of the night, two o'clock, and it was hushed and quiet, the prisoners sleeping in their cells. She wondered if her sister slept too, unaware of her presence and her marriage to Joe.

She was brought again to the governor's office, where one of the guards informed her that, as Mr Plunkett's next-of-kin, his wife, she was permitted to visit him in his cell prior to his execution. Major Lennon had given permission for her to say goodbye to her husband.

She stood there not trusting herself to speak, her eyes drawn to a letter left lying on the governor's desk addressed to Mrs Pearse from Padraig. Grace was briefly tempted to steal it to give to his poor mother.

'This way,' said the soldier, leading her through the cold, damp prison corridors.

Nervous, she shivered and touched her new wedding band as she followed him. The light was poor and she had to concentrate so that she did not trip or stumble.

Eventually they stopped and the door to a small, narrow, dark cell was opened. In the gloom she could see Joe, sitting with a blanket around him on a plank of wood which served as a bed on the floor, with only a bench, a bowl and a cup. He looked up, surprised, and in that instant she could see the love for her in his eyes. She longed to fling herself into his arms and caress and hold him, but the cell was crowded as soldiers crammed in behind her. Some carried bayonets and one pointedly held a watch.

'Ten minutes,' he said firmly.

Grace's heart pounded alarmingly and she could feel the trembling in her leg and foot. Her hands began to shake too as fear of what lay ahead for Joe almost engulfed her.

He stood up. He looked pale and the bandage around his neck was filthy, but his eyes reassured her as he reached for her hands and stilled the tremors. He was so calm and even in these last minutes she knew that Joe cared deeply for her, never thinking about himself but worried for her, wanting still to protect and love her for as long as he lived. She knew if she spoke she would break down, perhaps even turn to attack the soldiers around her like a wildcat, so she sat down beside him, trying to gather her thoughts and emotions.

'Darling Grace, you must be brave,' coaxed Joe, unselfish as ever. 'You are my wife now and I promise that you will be cared for always.'

A heavy tear slid down her face.

She listened as he spoke quietly of his friends and his belief in a new republic, a new Ireland. Their fight for freedom, the Rising, was only the beginning.

Joe had his faith and told her that he wasn't afraid to die.

'I am happy, dying for the glory of God and the honour of Ireland.'

She squeezed his hand, feeling the familiar pressure of his thumb caressing and circling her palm. There was so much she wanted to say, to tell him, but she knew if she even began to speak, a torrent of words and tears would pour from her, like a river bursting through a dam, and that she would not be able to control it or hold it back.

'Your ten minutes are up,' declared the sergeant.

Grace could not believe that ten minutes had passed and they had barely said anything to each other. They needed more time, needed privacy. But there was none. Joe nodded at her quietly and they held each other's gaze for those last few seconds as the sergeant ordered her to leave.

A moment or two later Grace was being escorted from the cell and back out through the prison. The memory of Joe's eyes, the touch of his hands, his words and his immense courage were seared in her heart.

Somewhere a prisoner screamed, like a child having a nightmare. Voices shouted, telling him gruffly to go back to sleep.

Grace stopped, feeling weak, barely able to breathe or move. A young soldier offered to get her some water. She leaned against the wall and sipped at it slowly, thinking of Joe alone in his cell.

The soldier confided to her that, along with Joe, three other prisoners were to be executed before dawn. One of them, she discovered, was Willie Pearse, and she let out a gasp at the mention of his name. She thought of Willie, with his art and sculpture and devotion to his older brother. When she was only seventeen he'd twirled her around the dance floor at college socials.

It was still dark when she walked out through the heavy prison door. Flecks of light peeped through the darkness and she could hear bird-song in the early hours of that still May morning.

She could not return home and it was unfair to go back to Mr Byrne's home and waken him once more. Father MacCarthy hoped to organize somewhere else for her to stay, or a motor vehicle to drive her to her sister Kate's home.

Grace stood waiting near the prison wall, a shiver running through her, for she felt such a strange coldness surrounding her. She wanted to stay: she still harboured a forlorn hope that perhaps there would be some last-minute reprieve, a change of mind about Joe's sentence. Grace still had hope.

Suddenly in the creeping morning light she heard rapid gunshots. Was it a firing squad? Fear gripped her. Once again there came the sound of gunfire. Shot after shot in the silence. Then more yet again.

Was it Joe?

She breathed slowly, then the stillness was broken by another booming volley, so loud and clear, breaking the calm of that early morn. A few seconds later, a single shot.

Grace's mind was filled with the image of Joe and the firing squad, and she knew instantly in her heart that this time it was him. She doubled over in pain at the realization that she would never see or speak or touch Joe again in this lifetime.

She stood there transfixed. It was over. Finally over. Joe was dead – shot like his friends Mac-

Donagh, and Padraig and Willie and brave Tom Clarke. The rebellion crushed. His life taken from him because he had dared to dream, dared to fight for a new republic, an independent, free Ireland.

Mother had said they were fools, traitors, disloyal to the crown. A strange weariness came over Grace. How could she ever return to her childhood home again? She had nowhere to go now that Joe was dead. He had told her to be brave, but she was not like him...

The sky was getting lighter, brighter, the dawn with its first faint streaks of sunlight breaking the darkness. She looked upwards, thinking of Joe on the other side of the high wall only a few seconds ago.

Then she saw it – a bird, flapping its wings, its long neck and head and beak stretched forwards, rising upwards and upwards across the new morning sky. She watched it, looking up at the sky, dizzy, the bird flying free above her, soaring high over the city.

It wasn't over. Joe was right. It wasn't over at all.

This was just the beginning...

Afterword

Following the surrender and arrest of all those involved in the rising, General Sir John Greenfell Maxwell, the newly appointed military governor of Ireland, was determined to quell any further

451

chance of rebellion. He immediately ordered that hundreds of prisoners be transported by ship to prison camps in England, Scotland and Wales. He ordered the trial by court martial and then the execution of all those suspected of organizing the Rising.

Fourteen leaders of the rebellion were shot by firing squad in Kilmainham Jail: Padraig Pearse, Thomas MacDonagh, Thomas Clarke, Joseph Plunkett, Willie Pearse, Michael Mallin, Edward Daly, Sean Mac Diarmada, Eamonn Ceannt, Con Colbert, John MacBride, James Connolly, Michael O'Hanrahan and Sean Heuston. In addition, Thomas Kent was executed in Cork and Roger Casement was tried for treason and executed by hanging in Pentonville Prison in London.

Dubliners, who had developed a grudging respect for the amateur army, were shocked by the executions, especially that of the badly injured James Connolly who, unable to stand, was shot sitting in a chair. Public opinion began to change.

Memorial cards of the dead leaders of the Rising were circulated throughout the city. General Maxwell and the British soon realized they had somehow made martyrs of the men and halted the executions, but it was too late. The Rising and its leaders' belief in a new Republic of Ireland had caught hold. The insurgents once considered traitors or fools for their actions were now becoming heroes.

The fight for Irish freedom continued, led by Michael Collins and Eamon de Valera on their release from prison. Sinn Fein won seventy-three seats in the 1918 elections and set up an Irish parliament, Dail Eireann, on 21 January 1919. The War of Independence followed, with the IRA carrying out new, guerrilla-type attacks against the British forces in Ireland.

In December 1921 Michael Collins, Arthur Griffith and Britain's prime minister, Lloyd George, signed the Anglo-Irish Treaty, ending the war and recognizing the formation of an Irish Free State. However, 'the Treaty' kept Ireland within the British empire and excluded the six counties in the north. This caused a huge split among republicans, which led to a violent civil war. Michael Collins was shot dead before his country finally gained its freedom from Britain and became an independent nation. Ireland became a republic in 1949.

Nellie Gifford Donnelly

Nellie was imprisoned in Kilmainham Jail until June 1916. On her return to Temple Villas her mother refused to let her cross the threshold. Nellie begged to see her father, but sadly she was only allowed to see him briefly before she moved to America where her sisters Ada and Sidney were both living. She toured around parts of the US recounting her experiences of the Rising, fundraising for the widows of the Volunteers and organizing talks promoting the republican movement. She married publisher Joseph Donnelly in New York and had one daughter, Maeve. In 1920 she returned to Ireland and, following the break-up of her marriage, became a successful writer and broadcaster, writing stories and plays for the new Irish radio station 2RN and for newspapers.

Fearing that people would forget the Easter Rising of 1916, Nellie was determined to gather together a collection of items related to the rebellion. In 1932 she persuaded the National Museum to exhibit her collection at the time of the Eucharistic Congress and Tailteann Games in Dublin. Among the 250 exhibits were Countess Markievicz's green jacket, pamphlets, guns and valuable personal items belonging to family members and friends. At the end of the popular exhibition it was clear to Nellie that a permanent home for the collection was needed. Much of it now forms the basis of Ireland's important historic 1916 Collection housed in the National Museum in Dublin. In the 1960s Nellie became a founder member of the Kilmainham Jail Restoration Society. The prison is now one of Ireland's most popular visitor sites.

After a long life filled with many interests, Nellie Gifford Donnelly died in 1971.

Muriel Gifford MacDonagh

Muriel was devastated by the execution of her husband, Thomas MacDonagh. With his death she could no longer afford to continue renting their home in Oakley Road. Her mother, Isabella, called to see her, but instead of giving support, spoke out against Muriel's husband and his role in the rebellion. Countess Plunkett, who had always had a huge regard for Thomas MacDonagh and was fond of Muriel, offered her one of the Plunkett houses in Ranelagh in which to live.

Dressed in her widow's clothes Muriel was striking and beautiful, and the British authorities feared that her appearance at rallies and events would incite even more resentment of their actions.

In July 1917 a seaside holiday was organized for 'the Widows of 1916' and their children in Skerries, and Grace and Muriel decided to join all the other women. One day Muriel went out swimming as her two-year-old daughter Barbara sat playing with shells on the beach. Tragically, Muriel, although a good swimmer, got into difficulty and drowned. It was suspected she had suffered heart failure. In Dublin huge crowds gathered for her funeral, watching silently as black-plumed horses drew her coffin towards Glasnevin Cemetery.

Grace Gifford Plunkett

The tragic story of Grace Gifford's wedding to Joe Plunkett appeared not only in Irish newspapers but also across the globe, with Grace finding herself thrown into the spotlight. Unable to return to her parents' house, she went to stay in Larkfield, the Plunkett family home.

Grace's appearance at republican rallies drew huge support. She designed anti-British posters and leaflets for election campaigns and she herself was elected to the Sinn Fein executive. Like most of the wives of the leaders of the Rising, Grace was firmly opposed to the Treaty. She wrote to the press and created a series of anti-Treaty cartoons. In 1923 she and her sister Kate, who had also become a republican, were arrested and imprisoned in Kilmainham Jail for seven months. There Grace drew a mural of 'The Madonna and Child' on her cell wall.

Following the end of the Civil War in 1923, Grace continued to work as an artist and she also published a number of books of cartoons of the Abbey Theatre's actors. She often struggled financially. She had little contact with the Plunkett family and in 1934 took legal action against them as they had failed to follow the terms of Joe's will, which asked for her to be given everything he possessed. Countess Plunkett refused to honour it and eventually the matter was settled out of court, with Grace receiving a one-off payment from the family.

Grace died in 1955 and was buried with full military honours in the Plunkett plot in Glasnevin Cemetery. Grace Gifford Plunkett is considered to be one of Ireland's leading female artists. A ballad about her and Joe's wedding became very popular and all those who visit Kilmainham Jail in Dublin hear of the tragic love story of Grace Gifford and Joseph Plunkett.

Isabella Gifford

Isabella blamed Countess Markievicz for influencing her daughters. Frederick Gifford died in September 1917, after which she sold the large house in Temple Villas and made her home in nearby Ranelagh. In time she was reconciled with her daughters and saw her grandchildren. Isabella died in 1932.

ACKNOWLEDGEMENTS

I owe huge thanks to my daughter Fiona Conlon-McKenna for your belief, enthusiasm and help in researching this book.

And thanks also to my husband James for your unstinting support through all my years of writing, and to my amazing family, Mandy, Laura, Fiona and James, my sons-in-law Michael Hearty, Mike Fahy and James Hodgins, and my pets Holly, Sam, Ben and Max.

I would like to express my grateful thanks to the following people and organizations who so generously helped me with the research for this book:

Muriel McAuley, for sharing some of your Gifford/MacDonagh family memories with me, and also her daughter, Michelle Drysdale.

Meadhbh Murphy, Archivist at the Royal College of Surgeons Ireland, 23 St Stephen's Green, Dublin 2. Thanks for all your help, for giving me the tour and also for sharing information and stories of the 1916 College of Surgeons' garrison.

Attracta Maher (née Brennan-Whitmore) and her daughter Ann, for talking to me about William Brennan-Whitmore, father and grandfather, who served as Commandant in the Earl Street garrison and for giving me a copy of his wonderful memoir *Dublin Burning.*

Nancy Gallagher-Scanlon, for your kindness and help with researching the Gifford family.

Ann Clare, for your years of dedication and research in compiling and writing your marvellous biography of the Giffords, *Unlikely Rebels,* and for kindly agreeing to talk to me.

Sandra Galligan, for telling me about your grandfather Paul Galligan's trip to Dublin on Easter Monday 1916.

The National Library of Ireland, Kildare Street, Dublin: heartfelt thanks to all the curators and librarians who so kindly assisted me during the research for this book and were endlessly patient.

Kilmainham Jail, Dublin: special thanks to its staff and the wonderful guides and curators.

The Slade School of Fine Art, University College, London: a wonderful place to visit and my special thanks go to Robert Winckworth for your assistance.

The Pearse Museum, Saint Enda's, Rathfarnham, County Dublin.

The National College of Art and Design, Thomas Street, Dublin.

The Bureau of Military History, Dublin: thanks to Hugh Beckett and Noelle Grothier for your assistance.

The Royal College of Physicians of Ireland, Kildare Street, Dublin: thanks to Harriet Wheelock.

The Church of Ireland, Representative Church Body Library, Churchtown, Dublin: thanks to Mary Furlong.

The National Museum of Ireland, Collins Barracks, Dublin.

The National Gallery, Trafalgar Square, London.

And a special mention for my local Libraries in Stillorgan and Deansgrange for all their help and assistance in sourcing books.

Thanks as always to Caroline Sheldon, my wonderful agent, for your loyalty, encouragement and belief in my work, and to Felicity Trew. Also thanks to Rosie Buckman, my foreign rights agent.

For my editor, Linda Evans: after years working together I will miss your good humour, friendship and encouragement. Thank you so much for everything.

Thanks to my new editors at Transworld, Harriet Bourton and Francesca Best, for your enthusiasm and for not being overwhelmed when faced with this big Irish book.

Huge thanks to my wonderful copy-editor Brenda Updegraff, production editor Vivien Thompson, Natasha Barsby and designer Sarah Whittaker. Thanks to everyone at Transworld UK for your support and hard work on yet another book.

And my special thanks to Eoin McHugh of Transworld Ireland for your support.

Thank you to all the team at Gill Hess in Dublin – Gill and Simon Hess, Declan Heaney and the wonderful Helen Gleed O'Connor – for all the years of looking after me and my books.

Thanks to Michael McLoughlin of Penguin Random House Ireland. It's nice to work together again. Also thanks to publicity manager Patricia McVeigh for all your hard work.

Sarah Conroy, for your endless patience and help with my website.

Sarah Webb and Martina Devlin for your friendship, wisdom and encouragement.

Thanks to all my fellow writers for the endless book chats and to all my lovely friends.

And a big thank you to all the wonderful booksellers and bookshops that bring us writers and readers together.

For all my readers both at home in Ireland and overseas: thank you for being part of the journey and for reading my books.

The publishers hope that this book has given you enjoyable reading. Large Print Books are especially designed to be as easy to see and hold as possible. If you wish a complete list of our books please ask at your local library or write directly to:

Magna Large Print Books
Magna House, Long Preston,
Skipton, North Yorkshire.
BD23 4ND

This Large Print Book for the partially sighted, who cannot read normal print, is published under the auspices of

THE ULVERSCROFT FOUNDATION